PUFFIN BOOKS

# YOUNG SAMURAI

## THE RING OF WIND

Praise for the Young Samurai series:

'A fantastic adventure that floors the reader on page one and keeps them there until the end. The pace is furious and the martial arts detail authentic' – Eoin Colfer, author of the bestselling Artemis Fowl series

'Fierce fiction . . . captivating for young readers' – *Daily Telegraph*

'Addictive' – *Evening Standard*

'More and more absorbing . . . vivid and enjoyable' – *The Times*

'Bradford comes out swinging in this fast-paced adventure . . . and produces an adventure novel to rank among the genre's best. This book earns the literary equivalent of a black belt' – *Publishers Weekly*

'The most exciting fight sequences imaginable on paper!' – *Booklist*

Winner of Northern Ireland Book Award 2011
Shortlisted for Red House Children's Book Award 2009
School Library Association's Riveting Read 2009

Chris Bradford likes to fly through the air. He has thrown himself over Victoria Falls on a bungee cord, out of an aeroplane in New Zealand and off a French mountain on a paraglider, but he has always managed to land safely – something he learnt from his martial arts . . .

Chris joined a judo club aged seven where his love of throwing people over his shoulder, punching the air and bowing lots started. Since those early years, he has trained in karate, kickboxing, samurai swordsmanship and has earned his black belt in *taijutsu*, the secret fighting art of the ninja.

Before writing the Young Samurai series, Chris was a professional musician and songwriter. He's even performed to HRH Queen Elizabeth II (but he suspects she found his band a bit noisy).

Chris lives in a village on the South Downs with his wife, Sarah, his son, Zach, and two cats called Tigger and Rhubarb.

To discover more about Chris go to *www.youngsamurai.com*

*Books by Chris Bradford:*

*The Young Samurai series (in reading order)*
THE WAY OF THE WARRIOR
THE WAY OF THE SWORD
THE WAY OF THE DRAGON
THE RING OF EARTH
THE RING OF WATER
THE RING OF FIRE
THE RING OF WIND

*(available as ebook only)*
THE WAY OF FIRE

# YOUNG SAMURAI

## THE RING OF WIND

# CHRIS BRADFORD

**PUFFIN**

PUFFIN BOOKS

Published by the Penguin Group
Penguin Books Ltd, 80 Strand, London WC2R ORL, England
Penguin Group (USA) Inc., 375 Hudson Street, New York, New York 10014, USA
Penguin Group (Canada), 90 Eglinton Avenue East, Suite 700, Toronto, Ontario, Canada M4P 2Y3
(a division of Pearson Penguin Canada Inc.)
Penguin Ireland, 25 St Stephen's Green, Dublin 2, Ireland (a division of Penguin Books Ltd)
Penguin Group (Australia), 250 Camberwell Road, Camberwell, Victoria 3124, Australia
(a division of Pearson Australia Group Pty Ltd)
Penguin Books India Pvt Ltd, 11 Community Centre, Panchsheel Park, New Delhi – 110 017, India
Penguin Group (NZ), 67 Apollo Drive, Rosedale, Auckland 0632, New Zealand
(a division of Pearson New Zealand Ltd)
Penguin Books (South Africa) (Pty) Ltd, 24 Sturdee Avenue, Rosebank, Johannesburg 2196, South Africa

Penguin Books Ltd, Registered Offices: 80 Strand, London WC2R ORL, England

puffinbooks.com

First published 2012
001 – 10 9 8 7 6 5 4 3 2 1

Text copyright © Chris Bradford, 2012
Cover illustration copyright © Paul Young, 2012
Map copyright © Robert Nelmes, 2008
All rights reserved

The moral right of the author and illustrators has been asserted

Set in Bembo by Palimpsest Book Production Limited, Falkirk, Stirlingshire
Made and printed in England by Clays Ltd, St Ives plc

Except in the United States of America, this book is sold subject to the condition that it shall not, by way of trade or otherwise, be lent, resold, hired out, or otherwise circulated without the publisher's prior consent in any form of binding or cover other than that in which it is published and without a similar condition including this condition being imposed on the subsequent purchaser

British Library Cataloguing in Publication Data
A CIP catalogue record for this book is available from the British Library

ISBN: 978-0141-33971-9

www.greenpenguin.co.uk

MIX
Paper from
responsible sources
FSC
www.fsc.org  FSC™ C018179

Penguin Books is committed to a sustainable future for our business, our readers and our planet. This book is made from Forest Stewardship Council™ certified paper.

ALWAYS LEARNING                    **PEARSON**

*For the Moles,*
*Sue, Simon, Steve, Sam and all the cousins!*

# CONTENTS

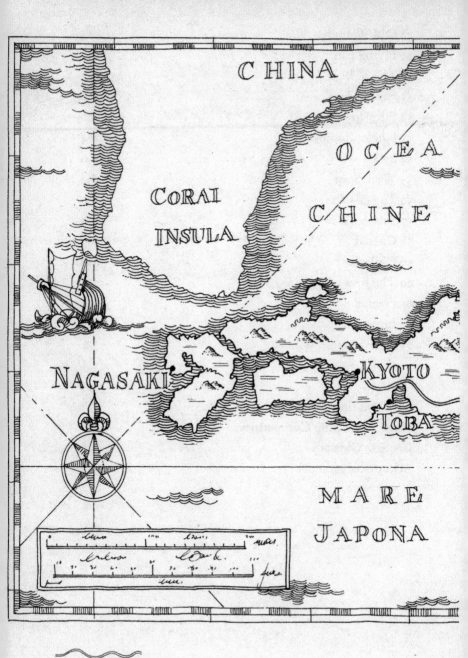

CHINA

OCEA
CHINE

CORAI
INSULA

NAGASAKI

KYOTO
TOBA

MARE
JAPONA

TOKAIDO ROAD

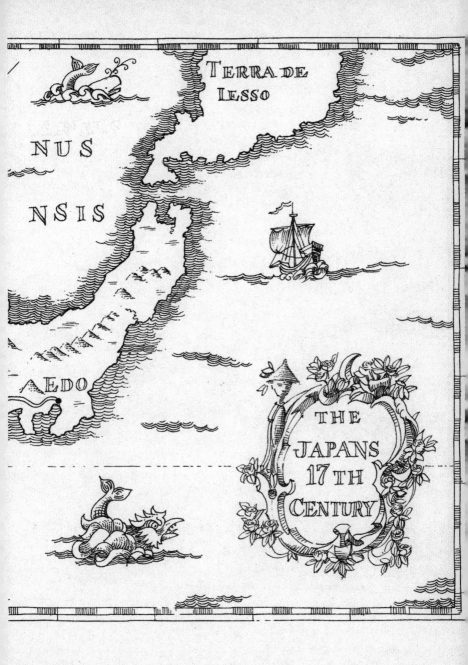

# THE LETTER

*Japan, 1614*

*My dearest Jess,*

*I hope this letter reaches you one day. You must believe I've been lost at sea all these years. But you'll be glad to know that I am alive and in good health.*

*Father and I reached the Japans in August 1611, but I am sad to tell you he was killed in an attack upon our ship, the Alexandria. I alone survived.*

*For these past three years, I've been living in the care of a Japanese warrior, Masamoto Takeshi, at his samurai school in Kyoto. He has been very kind to me, but life has not been easy.*

*An assassin, a ninja known as Dragon Eye, was hired to steal our father's rutter (you no doubt remember how important this navigational logbook was to our father?). The ninja* was successful in his mission. However, with the help of my samurai friends, I've managed to get it back.

This same ninja was the one who murdered our father. And while it may not bring you much comfort, I can assure you the assassin is now dead. Justice has been delivered. But the ninja's death doesn't bring back our father — I miss him so much and could do with his guidance and protection at this time.

Japan has been split by civil war and foreigners like myself are no longer welcome. I am a fugitive. On the run for my life. I now journey south through this strange and exotic land to the port of Nagasaki in the hope that I may find a ship bound for England.

The Tokaido Road upon which I travel, however, is fraught with danger and I have many enemies on my trail. But do not fear for my safety. Masamoto has trained me as a samurai warrior and I will fight to return home to you.

One day I do hope I can tell you about my adventures in person . . .

Until then, dear sister, may God keep you safe.


Your brother, Jack

P.S. Since first writing this letter at the end of spring, I've been kidnapped by ninja. But I discovered that they were not the enemy I thought they were. In fact, they saved my life and taught me about the Five Rings: the five great elements of the universe – Earth, Water, Fire, Wind and Sky. I now know ninjutsu skills that go beyond anything I learnt as a samurai. But, because of the circumstances of our father's death, I still struggle to fully embrace the Way of the Ninja . . .

# 1

# AMBUSH

**Japan, spring 1615**

Miyuki held a finger to her lips in warning. Jack, Saburo and Yori fell silent, glancing with unease round the forest clearing. It was barely dawn and, although the four friends hadn't encountered anyone in days, they remained on their guard.

The Shogun's samurai were proving relentless in their hunt for Jack. As a foreigner, a *gaijin*, Jack had been banished from Japan. But he was *also* a samurai warrior. Having fought against the Shogun in the Battle of Osaka Castle, he'd been accused of treason. It didn't matter that he was a mere boy of fifteen. There was a price on his head and, as a *gaijin* samurai, he was wanted dead or alive.

The dirt track ahead looked deserted. There was no movement among the bushes, nor any sounds to betray a hidden enemy. But Jack trusted Miyuki's instincts. Being a ninja, her senses were highly attuned to danger.

'Ten or so men passed through here,' Miyuki whispered, studying a patch of downtrodden grass. 'Less than an hour ago.'

'Which way were they headed?' asked Jack, not wishing to cross their path.

'That's the problem,' she replied, her dark eyes narrowing. 'They went in *all* directions.'

At once, Jack understood what she was implying. An ominous feeling like the tightening of a noose seized him. His awareness heightened by the potential threat, he scanned the undergrowth a second time. Having trained in the Art of the Ninja himself, he knew what signs to look for. Almost at once, he spotted several broken stems among the bushes as well as debris disturbed underfoot. He then realized the forest was too quiet and the birds had stopped their singing.

'We have to get out of here!' said Jack, shouldering his pack to run.

But it was already too late.

A flutter, like the wings of a startled sparrow, heralded the ambush. Ducking at the very last second, Jack dodged the steel-tipped arrow targeted for his head. It clipped his straw hat before embedding itself in a nearby tree trunk. A moment later, a troop of fully armed samurai burst from the bushes on all sides and charged towards them.

Instinctively, Miyuki, Saburo and Yori formed a protective circle round Jack.

'We won't let them take you,' Yori promised, holding his *shakujō* in both hands. The wooden staff with its pointed iron tip and six metal rings was the symbol of a Buddhist monk. But it was also a formidable weapon. The rings jingled as the fearful yet valiant Yori braced himself for the fight.

'And I won't let them harm you,' said Jack, knowing that Yori as a monk preferred to avoid confrontation.

He drew both his *katana* and *wakizashi*. A parting gift from his closest friend Akiko, their perfectly balanced razor-sharp blades glinted in the early morning light as he raised them into a Two Heavens guard. Likewise, Saburo unsheathed his *katana* in preparation to do battle. Although he'd trained at the *Niten Ichi Ryū* with Jack, he hadn't been taught the legendary double-sword technique.

'At least the odds are better than last time,' Saburo quipped, referring to the forty bandits they'd confronted in Tamagashi village the month before.

Sounding a battle cry and brandishing their weapons, the samurai soldiers closed in for the kill. Miyuki turned to face the first of their attackers. Before he was within striking distance, she flicked a *shuriken* from her hand. The deadly throwing star flashed through the air and struck the soldier in the neck. He choked and stumbled. Miyuki leapt into the air, executing a flying side-kick that sent the samurai sprawling to the ground. As she landed, the next samurai swung his sword to cut off her head. Pulling a straight-bladed *ninjatō* from the scabbard upon her back, Miyuki blocked the attack and engaged in a vicious sword fight with the man.

Weapons clashed as Jack, Saburo and Yori fought the other samurai warriors. Jack was confronted by three at once and had to use all his skill to keep them at bay. His swords whirled above his head as he deflected each of their strikes. At the same time, Yori was thrusting the iron tip of his *shakujō* at any samurai who dared to get close. He winded one in the stomach and was driving another back when Jack caught a movement in the bushes. The samurai archer was taking aim.

'Yori, watch out!' cried Jack.

But, with no cover nearby, Yori was an easy target.

Using a lightning-fast Autumn Leaf strike, Jack disarmed his nearest assailant, then kicked him hard in Yori's direction. The defeated samurai staggered backwards into the line of fire just as the archer released his arrow. The arrow hit him square in the chest and, groaning with pain, he crumpled to the earth. But the precious seconds Jack took to save Yori's life now put his own into harm's way. One of the other samurai lunged with his sword. The steel tip was set to impale Jack when a second blade came out of nowhere and deflected it aside.

'Saved your life . . . yet again,' Saburo gasped, jumping between Jack and his assailant. With a furious shout of *kiai*, Saburo charged forward and forced the warrior to retreat.

Grateful as he was, Jack had no chance to thank his friend as the next samurai advanced on him. Jack also realized the archer now had him in his sights. Almost at full draw, the man was ready to release his deadly arrow. While the samurai was proving no match for his sword skill, Jack couldn't hope to stop the archer.

Then Jack recalled a ninja technique from the Ring of Fire.

Fending off his samurai attacker with his *katana*, Jack held his *wakizashi* aloft and angled its polished blade to catch the early morning sun. The sudden blaze of light dazzled the man. He lost his aim and the arrow shot wide.

But Jack knew this was just a short reprieve. The archer would kill them one by one if they remained in the open much longer. He shouted to his friends, 'Into the forest!'

Miyuki was still battling her samurai. The man was strong and threatened to overpower her. Just as her defeat seemed inevitable, she reached inside her jacket and threw *metsubishi* powder into her attacker's face. Blinded by the mix of sand and ash, the samurai was powerless to stop Miyuki side-stamping his knee and crippling him.

'This way!' cried Miyuki as the samurai collapsed in agony.

Without a moment to lose, the four friends sprinted from the clearing into the dense undergrowth. Behind them, they heard roars of rage as the surviving samurai soldiers crashed through the bushes in hot pursuit.

# 2

# TRAPPED LIKE CRABS

'Do you think we've lost them?' panted Saburo, his chest heaving.

Hidden behind a tree, Jack and the others peered back through the forest. Being young had been an advantage in their escape, since their larger, less agile pursuers were slowed by the dense thicket. Gradually, the shouts of the samurai had grown more distant until they'd faded altogether.

Braving another look, Saburo ventured further from the cover of the tree.

*Thunk!*

An arrow implanted itself in the trunk just short of his nose.

'I think that answers your question!' said Miyuki, dragging the startled Saburo away.

The four friends shot off again. They fled through the forest, paying no heed to direction. Branches whipped at their faces and tore at their clothes. Jack felt the air burn in his lungs as they vaulted fallen logs and weaved through clumps of trees.

To Jack, it seemed as if he'd been running forever.

Before his friends had joined him, he'd been chased by samurai, ninja, *dōshin* officers, *metsuke* spies and, most relentless of all, his old school rival Kazuki and his Scorpion Gang. And since departing Tamagashi village, every day had been a perilous tightrope of evasion, concealment and constant flight. Cautious to avoid major settlements and the busy coastal road, the four fugitives had been forced to negotiate tangled forests and treacherous mountain paths. They couldn't risk staying for more than a night in a single place, fearful of being spotted and reported to a local samurai lord. Yet despite this urgency, their progress had been slow upon their journey southwest towards Nagasaki, the port from where Jack hoped to find a ship bound for England.

The one good thing was that the further south they travelled, the better the weather became. Signs of spring were emerging and the snow of winter had all but melted away, only clinging to the mountain peaks. With this came a bountiful supply of food as the forests around them sprang to life. Blessed with a ninja's knowledge of fieldcraft, Jack and Miyuki knew how to live off the land. This meant they weren't so reliant upon local farmers for provisions.

Yet they couldn't avoid contact all the time. Early in their journey their route passed through the riverport of Kurashiki. For a few days they sheltered in the village of Kasaoka while Yori recovered from a fever, until rumours of their presence were leaked to a passing samurai patrol. And on several occasions they had to stop and buy more rice. But their greatest concern had been the castle town of Fukuyama. The settlement was swarming with samurai. Unfortunately, it was the sole crossing point for the Ashida River. There were no bridges along this broad fast-flowing watercourse, only a ferry service within the town itself. Having no other option, the four of them took to Fukuyama's backstreets. With Jack keeping his head down – his foreign face, blue eyes and blond hair concealed beneath a wide straw hat – they made the ferry crossing unnoticed. Or so they had thought . . .

'This way!' cried a furious samurai, hacking a path through the undergrowth.

Jack and the others increased their pace, Miyuki leading the way up a ridge. The ground underfoot became rocky, then began to slope downwards. All of a sudden, they broke into a clearing of hard-packed gravel. Miyuki skidded to a halt beside a small wooden temple. Inside, a statue of the Buddha sat facing east towards a view of such breathtaking beauty that it caused them all to pause.

A glassy blue sea like a mirror to the sky stretched towards the horizon, from where the rising sun shone bright as gold. Myriad islands shimmered like emerging clouds, each one melting into the next. At the foot of the hillside, the gentle sweep of a horseshoe harbour cradled a small fishing port. Grey and blue tiled roofs rippled down the slopes to the water's edge, where a flotilla of boats bobbed quietly beside the jetty.

'The Seto Sea,' Yori breathed in awe.

Jack also gazed in wonder at the sight. This was the first time he'd laid eyes upon any sea since leaving Akiko in Toba the year before. The vision brought a lump to his throat as a wave of memories and hopes for the future washed over him. Prior to his samurai training, he'd been a rigging monkey on-board the *Alexandria*. His father had been the ship's pilot and they'd set sail round the world to make their fortune. It was upon this voyage that Jack had learnt his father's skills and been introduced to the *rutter* – an invaluable navigational logbook that was the only means of ensuring safe passage across the world's oceans. His father had taught him its secrets and the logbook had become their bond. Jack could feel the *rutter*'s reassuring weight in his pack now and, combined with the sight of the sea, an unexpected smile lit up his face as he recalled happier times in his life. The ocean was beckoning to him. Home felt closer already.

Miyuki was less impressed by the view. 'This is a headland. We've got nowhere left to run!'

An arrow whizzed past, sounding a heavy beat as it struck a wooden pillar of the temple.

'We've no choice but to keep going,' urged Jack, the pursuing samurai almost on their heels. 'Perhaps we can lose them in the port, then double back.'

Leaving the shrine, the four of them raced down the gravel path and entered the port's narrow twisting streets. They flew past bleary-eyed fishermen, weaved between the wooden shuttered shops and homes, and ducked down alleyways. Behind, they heard the outraged calls of the soldiers as they lost sight of their quarry. Cutting down a narrow alley, they passed a line of white plastered warehouses before coming to a dead end.

'Back the other way!' said Miyuki in alarm.

They retraced their steps to the previous street, but heard the pounding of urgent footsteps headed their way. With nowhere to go, the four of them dived behind a wooden water butt and pressed themselves flat against the alley wall.

A moment later, two samurai appeared. But they only gave a cursory glance down the alley before running on.

Breathing a sigh of relief, Jack whispered, 'They've split up. We need to keep an eye out for the others.'

He led his friends across the street and down an opposite passageway. This time they found themselves at the water-washed steps of the harbour, where a majestic stone lantern, the height of a small tree, stood as the port's lighthouse. There was a salty whiff of seaweed and drying fish, further reminding Jack of his seafaring days. Alongside the dock, he noticed the first catch of the day was already laid out for sale – baskets of prawns; racks of bream, mackerel, sweet fish and other seafood; as well as large pots of squirming crabs, all trying to escape their fate.

At the opposite end of the harbour, a second group of samurai charged out of an alleyway. Before they had a chance to spot the four fugitives, Miyuki slid open a door to a ware-house and ushered everyone inside. They entered the cool interior of a *saké* brewery. Round casks of rice wine were piled ten high in readiness for shipment.

'Now we're really trapped!' Saburo exclaimed, finding no other exit from the darkened warehouse.

*Just like those crabs*, thought Jack.

# 3
# PILGRIMS

'It's only a matter of time before they find us,' said Yori, peeking through the gap in the door.

The samurai were scouring the streets and checking each of the buildings in turn. But, with the sun up, the harbour was coming to life and the soldiers' task was hampered as clusters of people gathered along the harbour side.

'We have to make a stand,' said Miyuki, reaching for her sword.

Jack shook his head, realizing the futility of their situation. 'If I hand myself over, at least there's a chance you can all escape.'

'Jack, we didn't come this far to give up now,' countered Saburo.

'I can't let you sacrifice yourselves like this –'

Yori interrupted him. 'Remember what Sensei Yamada once said: *A samurai alone is like a single arrow. Deadly but capable of being broken. Only by binding together as a single force will we remain strong and unconquerable.*'

He went and stood beside Saburo and Miyuki.

'*Forever bound to one another*. Isn't that what Akiko vowed to you, Jack? Well, we are too.'

Jack looked at his friends. Their unwavering loyalty astounded him. He knew this was what it meant to be samurai – and ninja, for that matter.

'I'm honoured to have such friends,' he said, humbled, and bowed his respect. 'We had better make a plan then.'

Miyuki patted one of the *saké* casks upon which an oil lamp sat. 'We can set fire to the place as a diversion.'

Jack shook his head. 'Too many innocent people could be hurt.'

'What about hiding among the crowd?' Saburo suggested. 'It's getting busy out there.'

Jack and the others peered through the doorway. Aside from the fishermen and dockhands, there were several groups of men and women queuing to join boats lined along the jetty. Many of these were dressed identically in white breeches, white jackets, straw hats and sandals. A white bag was slung across each of their shoulders, and round their necks hung a dark-blue stole – the rectangular cloth being the only item not coloured white. In one hand, each held a set of rosary beads; in the other, a wooden staff with a small bell attached to the handle.

'It's like a gathering of winter ninja,' remarked Jack, throwing a wry grin in Miyuki's direction. When she'd come looking for him, she'd been wearing an all-white *shinobi shozoku*, the customary ninja garb for missions in snow. Miyuki had since reversed her clothes to the black side, concealing them beneath a plain brown kimono.

'They're pilgrims,' explained Yori.

'We could ask them to pray for our escape!' Saburo quipped, his nerves evident in his strained attempt at humour.

Jack saw the samurai working their way down the harbour, getting closer with every step. 'I think we'll need more than prayers.'

Yori turned to him. 'This fishing port must be Tomo Harbour. Followers of Kobo Daishi, the Great Saint, pass through here to get to Shikoku Island, where they embark upon a pilgrimage of eighty-eight temples in his honour.'

'But why are they all dressed in white?' Jack asked.

'In Buddhism, white is the colour of purity and death. It symbolizes a pilgrim's readiness to die as they set off on their pilgrimage. And the risk is real. They have to cross high mountains, deep valleys and rugged coastline to reach all the temples. The journey takes at least two months and the pilgrims depend upon charity for all their needs.'

'That's very admirable,' replied Jack, 'but it means we'll be easily spotted by the samurai in the crowd.'

'Not if we're pilgrims too,' said Miyuki, with a cunning gleam in her eyes. 'Have you forgotten everything you learnt as a ninja, Jack?' She gave him a teasing smile. '*Shichi Hō De* – "the seven ways of going".'

Jack remembered how he'd once dressed as a *komusō* monk to avoid detection on a mission. 'Of course! A ninja must be a master of disguise and impersonation.'

'But where will we get matching outfits?' asked Saburo.

'From other pilgrims,' replied Miyuki, as if the answer was obvious.

Yori pursed his lips, uncomfortable at the suggestion. 'It's against my vows to steal.'

'We'll just be *borrowing* them,' she explained kindly. 'I presume these pilgrims accept *o-settai*?'

Yori nodded. 'Custom dictates they can't refuse any gift.'

'Excellent,' said Miyuki, snatching up a ceramic jug that sat beside the lamp and hurriedly filling four cups with *saké*. 'A long pilgrimage must be thirsty work.'

# 4

# O-SETTAI

The tinkling of bells alerted them to the arrival of more pilgrims.

'We're in luck,' said Jack, spotting four walking down the alleyway next to their warehouse.

'You should hide,' instructed Miyuki.

Jack positioned himself behind a stack of casks in the corner.

Checking there were no samurai in sight, Miyuki slid open the door. 'Now remember what I told you, Yori.'

Yori nodded somewhat reluctantly. He didn't agree with the methods of Miyuki's plan but realized there was little other option. He scampered out of the brewery and into the pilgrims' path. Bowing low, he announced, 'Our master wishes to offer you *o-settai*. A cup of his finest *saké* in return for your blessings upon his brewery.'

Unable to refuse yet equally happy to accept, the four pilgrims followed Yori to the open door, where Saburo greeted them and beckoned them inside. The first two were weather-beaten old men who appeared to be brothers, the third was a middle-aged woman and the fourth a young man, tall and bony as a bamboo stem.

Jack watched as Miyuki presented each pilgrim with a full cup. They gratefully received the offering and drank the contents. The brothers downed their *saké* in one go and smacked their lips with satisfaction. According to tradition, the four pilgrims then put their hands together in prayer and began to chant the mantra, '*Namu Daishi Henjo Kongo . . .*'

Yori had told Jack that the pilgrims would repeat this phrase three times before handing over an *osame-fuda*, a paper name-slip that would confer their blessings upon the brewery.

But they never got that far.

The woman was the first to pass out, her cup falling from her hands and clattering upon the wooden floor. Saburo immediately stepped forward and eased her to the ground. The two brothers were next, collapsing like puppets whose strings had been cut. The fourth, blinking in shock at the fate of his companions, swayed unsteadily. Then he bolted for the door, screaming for help.

Miyuki leapt on him in an instant and drove her thumb into a pressure point at the base of his neck. The cry died in the man's throat as he fell limp, dropping lifeless at her feet.

'You promised you wouldn't hurt anyone!' Yori exclaimed.

'Don't worry,' said Miyuki, giving him a reassuring smile. 'He'll just have a nasty headache when he comes round.'

'What about the others?' asked Jack, emerging from his hiding place and inspecting the unconscious woman and two inert brothers.

'I only put enough *doku* powder in the *saké* to knock them out for a few hours,' explained Miyuki. 'Any more than a few grains and it *would* have killed them.'

'Good work, Miyuki,' said Jack, satisfied their victims were still breathing.

The four of them quickly removed the pilgrims' clothes and began to dress themselves. Being small of stature, Yori was swamped by his outfit and had to roll up the legs and sleeves. Jack anticipated the opposite problem – as a foreigner he was tall by comparison to the Japanese – but he was fortunate the younger pilgrim was so gangly.

Yori helped Jack adjust his blue stole. 'This is a *wagesa*. It's a cloth symbolizing a monk's robe and is meant to show your devotion to the Buddha.' Yori handed him the rosary beads. 'These are *nenju*. The number of beads equal the one hundred and eight *bonnō*.'

'What are *bonnō*?' asked Jack, fingering the wooden beads as he absorbed Yori's information. It was vital to know such facts if he was to pass himself off as a real pilgrim.

'They're the misleading Karmas that bind people in *Samsara*, the world of suffering. You must carry both the *wagesa* and *nenju* to be considered a true worshipper.'

Jack picked up the pilgrim's staff. 'What's the bell on the end for?'

'The bell acts as an *omamori*, like the amulet Sensei Yamada gave you,' explained Yori, pointing to the small red silk bag attached to Jack's pack. 'It protects the traveller upon the road.'

'Well, it didn't work for them,' Saburo chortled, glancing down at the comatose pilgrims as he wriggled his generous belly into a pair of the brothers' breeches.

Yori rolled his eyes at his friend's irreverence, then continued. 'Treat the staff with respect. It represents the body of Kobo Daishi, who spiritually accompanies all pilgrims on their path.'

Nodding, Jack studied the staff in more detail. There were five characters etched into the handle. Thanks to Akiko, he not only spoke fluent Japanese but had a basic understanding of *kanji*, its written form. Yet, even without this knowledge, these characters were instantly familiar to him:

| 地 | 水 | 火 | 風 | 空 |
|---|---|---|---|---|
| *Earth* | *Water* | *Fire* | *Wind* | *Sky* |

'The Five Rings,' breathed Jack, turning to Miyuki who'd already finished dressing and was dragging the bodies out of sight.

'The Buddhist monks apply them for spiritual purposes,' she replied quickly, giving Jack a meaningful look to keep secret their ninja arts, even among friends.

Jack held his tongue. He'd been taught about the Five Rings from the Grandmaster. These five great elements of the universe formed the basis of a ninja's approach to life. They used the Rings' power and influence within their fighting techniques and survival tactics. This is what gave the ninja their strength and made them so deadly and feared.

Placing the staff to one side, Jack turned his attention to the pilgrim's white bag. Inside he found incense, candles, a *sūtra* book, coins, a set of bells for chanting, a small notebook and a supply of paper nameslips. He removed the notebook to make room for his own belongings.

'I'd keep that,' said Yori. 'The *nōkyōchō* is for collecting visitor stamps from the temples. More importantly, it's a travel permit. You'll need it for passage to Shikoku Island.'

Heeding Yori's advice, Jack returned it to the bag and took

out the bells instead. There was just enough room to stow the most precious item he carried – his father's *rutter*. The logbook wasn't only of sentimental value to him; it was his means of getting home and also highly sought after by those who knew of its power. With the *rutter*, the trade routes between nations could be controlled. And Jack had promised his father never to let it fall into the wrong hands. That's why he had safeguarded it with his life and he wasn't going to leave it behind now.

His only other item of value, apart from his swords, was the black pearl Akiko had given him the day he departed for Nagasaki. It had a golden hairpin attached on account of a thieving merchant, but this proved useful for securing inside the lapel of his kimono. That left his four remaining *shuriken* stars, a gourd of water and the food supplies in his pack. While Jack contemplated where to stow these, Yori emptied the coins from his pilgrim bag and put them in a small pile, along with some rice from his own provisions.

'We're going to need that food,' said Saburo.

'We're not thieves,' chided Yori. 'We should at least leave the pilgrims a gift for their involuntary kindness.'

Feeling a touch guilty, Jack took out his pilgrim's coins and left a couple of his *mochi*. Saburo, unwilling to part with his supply of rice cakes, threw down a samurai helmet with a round dent in the peak.

'They can sell that if they want.'

'But that's the proof to your father you're a hero,' exclaimed Jack, recalling the moment Saburo had taken a bullet in the battle against the bandits.

'It's too bulky. Besides, if we don't escape, it won't matter whether I'm a hero or not!'

'Hurry up, everyone,' Miyuki urged, tossing a rice cake on to the pile. 'The samurai are closing in.'

'What should we do about the weapons?' asked Saburo, holding up his swords. 'They're not exactly typical of a pilgrim.'

'I've an idea,' said Jack, pulling out a canvas bag from behind the stack of casks where he'd hidden earlier. 'Put them in this. They'll simply look like goods for shipment.'

Stashing their weapons, packs and remaining supplies in the bag, they donned their straw conical hats. Pulling the brim low over his face, Jack peered out of the door. A unit of samurai was entering the warehouse opposite.

'Quick, let's go!' said Jack.

With Saburo carrying the canvas bag, they joined the other pilgrims. The urge to run for the boat was overwhelming.

'Slow down,' whispered Miyuki as they approached the jetty.

'But two samurai are headed this way!' Yori breathed in terror.

'Whatever you do, don't stop,' she instructed through gritted teeth.

The soldiers drew ever nearer. Fortunately, their attention was focused on the alleyways and buildings. Yori and Miyuki passed unnoticed. But, with the samurai so intent upon their search and Jack keeping his head down, one of the soldiers accidentally collided into him.

The samurai turned on Jack and glared.

'*Sumimasen*,' apologized Jack, bowing low and keeping his eyes to the ground in respect.

Miyuki and the others slowed their pace, Saburo reaching inside the canvas bag for his *katana*, Miyuki palming a hidden *shuriken*.

The samurai stepped up to Jack, his hand moving towards the swords on his *obi*. Jack held his breath and prepared to run.

'My apologies, pilgrim,' said the samurai, pulling a coin from the pouch on his belt. 'I have no wish for bad luck. Please accept my *o-settai*.'

Stunned, Jack took the money and was about to walk away when he remembered the ritual. Putting his hands together and keeping his head bowed, he chanted '*Namu Daishi Henjo Kongo*' three times. Then he handed the samurai a nameslip. The soldier appeared satisfied and resumed his search for the fugitives, oblivious to how close they really were.

# TURNING OF THE TIDES

'We made it!' Yori sighed, showing their travel permits and climbing on-board the boat bound for Shikoku Island.

'All thanks to Miyuki and your pilgrim knowledge,' agreed Jack.

They found a spot near the bow to stow the canvas bag and sat down. While the other passengers were finding their own places for the voyage, Jack took the opportunity to glance up and give the vessel a quick inspection. It was quite different in design from the mighty three-masted ocean trader he'd sailed upon to Japan. This wooden ship had a single mast with a square canvas sail, a flat keel and a wide, open deck. It was perhaps a third of the size of the *Alexandria*, with room for fifty passengers. Its cargo of rice bales and lamp oil was piled high on the deck and in the hold. The gunwales were raised with a diamond-shaped latticework of bamboo guardrails and the stern's upper deck was given over to a large rudder and extra-long tiller. To Jack's eye, it was more a coastal vessel than an ocean-going ship, but it looked seaworthy enough. He relaxed, knowing they would soon be under way.

'It's not over yet,' warned Miyuki, looking back down the harbour.

A samurai patrol had just entered the brewery.

'Why aren't we setting sail?' Saburo demanded, becoming nervous.

The boat was full but the captain seemed in no urgency to depart.

'Perhaps there isn't enough wind?' suggested Miyuki.

Jack shook his head. 'There's more than enough.'

Yori turned to a kindly-looking man sitting nearby, who was contemplating the sea and mumbling to himself. 'Excuse me,' asked Yori, 'what's the delay?'

Blinking as if disturbed from a trance, the man offered a cordial smile, then in a soft voice replied:

'Horseshoe harbour
Where the great tides turn
my life flows in and out.'

His cryptic answer made Jack wonder if the man was in his right mind.

The smile on the man's lips faltered as he looked expectantly at Yori. 'So . . . what do you think?'

Yori appeared pensive before replying. 'Like the sea, your *haiku* is deep and moving.'

The man beamed upon hearing such gracious praise. 'You're a poet too!' he exclaimed.

Yori bowed his head in humble acknowledgement.

'I'd be honoured if you'd share a *haiku* of yours with me,' requested the poet, excited at the prospect.

'Of course,' replied Yori, trying to keep his calm under the mounting pressure of the samurai. 'But first we were wondering why the boat hasn't sailed yet?'

The poet seemed surprised at such a question and replied matter-of-factly, 'We must wait for the tides to turn.'

'And *when* will that happen?' pressed Saburo as Jack glanced again towards the warehouse. The samurai had yet to emerge, but they had surely discovered the bodies by now.

'When the time is right,' declared the poet. 'Upon rising, the great tidal streams flow in from both east and west and meet just offshore from Tomo. When falling, they recede again in both directions – taking us and every soul upon this boat along with them. Tomo Harbour isn't merely a stop-off upon a journey, it's a place to wait for the "tide of life" to turn.'

At that moment, the samurai burst out of the brewery. They began to accost any pilgrim wandering along the harbour. Some soldiers backtracked into the village, while others worked their way towards the jetty. Not wanting to draw attention to themselves, Jack and his friends could only sit and watch as the samurai advanced. Jack realized this was a turning point in his life. He and his friends would either escape or die, their fate seemingly dependent upon the pull of the moon.

Two of the samurai had already boarded the first boat in line, when the captain of the pilgrims' ship gave the order to unfurl the sail and cast off. Jack felt the sweat on his brow as he prayed their captain wouldn't notice the disturbance further down the dock.

The samurai were now running along the jetty to stop any more vessels leaving. On-board their ship, Jack exchanged a worried look with Miyuki. At this rate, they had no hope of escaping. The soldiers were halfway down the jetty when the boat eased away from the harbourside, the breeze filling the sail.

But its progress seemed excruciatingly slow to Jack and his three anxious companions. Shouting to the captain, the samurai were sprinting headlong to draw level. Luckily, the wind buffeting the sail muffled their cries and the captain remained focused on navigating through the narrow mouth of the harbour. All of a sudden, their boat picked up speed. Caught by the ebbing tide, Jack and his friends were carried out with the current and into the haven of the Seto Sea.

For the first time in over a year, Jack truly felt at ease. They'd escaped the samurai and he was back at sea. Saburo was fast asleep, snoring, his face shaded from the bright spring sunshine by his pilgrim hat. Yori was exchanging *haiku* with the poet, while Miyuki, vigilant as ever, was keeping a watchful eye in case a boat followed them from Tomo. But their vessel was making such headway that Jack knew it would be impossible for the samurai to catch up now.

Jack sat upon the prow as their boat cut through the waves. Every so often he risked a glance up, relishing the breeze upon his face, and breathed in a deep lungful of sea air. The boat's constant pitch and roll was as comforting as a mother's arms. And the rushing lap of water against the hull sent a familiar thrill through him. He was back in his element.

He hadn't realized how much he'd missed the ocean life – the feel of the rough wooden deck beneath his feet; the snap of the canvas sail beating with the wind. Almost four years had passed since he'd sailed aboard the *Alexandria*, and it seemed like a lifetime ago. With all his training at the *Niten Ichi Ryū*, he was now more samurai than seaman. But his seafaring instincts were too deeply ingrained to be lost. His late father had seen to that. With a quick glance, Jack could tell the captain wasn't sailing the ship on its optimum tack. The sail could be trimmed to get at least another knot of speed out of her. His eye remained sharp for navigational signs: the light blue hue of the water indicated where the seabed was relatively shallow and he could tell by the position of the sun they were headed in a southwesterly direction, following the coastline.

As he made these observations, his body gently swayed, unconsciously counterbalancing the rise and fall of the ship's prow.

*You can take the sailor from the sea, but you can never take the sea from the sailor.*

His father had often jested with his mother about that every time he'd returned from a voyage. And it was never long before his father got the urge to set sail again. That very same impulse had drawn Jack to the ocean and his father's trade as a ship's pilot. The two years spent sailing from England to the Japans as a rigging monkey had been some of the happiest in his life. During the voyage, his father had taught him how to navigate by the stars, gauge the weather, plot a course and, most importantly, decipher the cryptic notes and observations in the *rutter* – the logbook having been encoded to prevent prying eyes from discovering its valuable secrets.

Gazing across the Seto Sea with its countless islands glimmering like jewels, Jack could almost sense the spirit of his father by his side. With a wistful sigh, he surrendered himself to the memories.

Many of the other passengers – a surprising mix of pilgrims, merchants, a couple of court nobles, a monk and several travellers – were also enjoying the view, each wrapped in their own thoughts.

A man got unsteadily to his feet and approached the bow. Jack caught sight of him out of the corner of his eye. Glimpsing the hilt of a samurai sword on his hip, he momentarily panicked. But the man was a little green with seasickness and had no interest in him. Unkempt, with a stubbly face and wayward hair, he was thickset and had battle scars across his arms. He wore a shabby brown kimono with no visible *mon*, the crest that would indicate his allegiance to a particular samurai lord. Without it, Jack guessed he was a *ronin*, a masterless samurai.

The ship suddenly pitched over a wave and the *ronin* stumbled. As he tried to regain his balance, he accidentally kicked the canvas bag. One of Jack's swords tumbled out, its blade sliding from its *saya*. The razor-sharp steel gleamed in the sunlight, the name *Shizu* clearly etched upon its surface.

The *ronin* stared in disbelief at the samurai blade, then turned to Jack.

'What sort of pilgrim travels with Shizu swords?'

# 6

# SCHOOL OF NO SWORD

'Answer me, pilgrim!' demanded the *ronin*. 'Or perhaps you're not a pilgrim at all . . .'

Jack daren't look up and reveal his true identity. Yet he didn't know what to say either. Nor did Saburo — startled from his sleep, he could only gawp at the exposed weapon. With their lives at risk, Miyuki was about to snatch up the *katana* when Yori stepped between Jack and the *ronin*.

'They're gifts,' he explained in an innocent tone, leaving Miyuki to repack the sword before it attracted anyone else's attention.

'Gifts?' spat the *ronin*, unconvinced. 'A Shizu sword seems an *incredible* gift.'

Every samurai knew Shizu-san was one of the greatest swordsmiths to have lived, and his blades were revered for both their quality and benevolent spirit. With only a few true ones in existence, their value was inestimable.

Yori nodded sincerely. 'They're offerings for the gods at Oyamazumi Shrine on Omishima Island. We're donating them on behalf of our *sensei*.'

The *ronin* squinted at Yori. 'But this boat isn't headed for Omishima Island.'

'We're . . . going there after the pilgrimage,' stated Yori, but his hesitation made the reply sound hollow and the *ronin* remained sceptical.

'What sword school do you belong to?' he demanded.

Yori paused before answering, 'The School of No Sword.'

Since the *Niten Ichi Ryū* had been closed by order of the Shogun, Jack knew it was wise of his friend to give another school's name. But even Jack was surprised by such a preposterous-sounding one.

The *ronin* snorted in disdain. 'What sort of ridiculous sword style is *that*?'

Yori swallowed nervously. 'Would you like a demonstration?'

Grinning with malicious delight, the *ronin* grunted, 'A duel! Most definitely.'

As the *ronin* began to clear the deck of passengers, Jack grabbed Yori's arm. 'What do you think you're doing?'

'We have to get rid of this *ronin*,' Yori insisted. 'Otherwise he'll discover who you are.'

'But did you *have* to challenge him to a duel?' Jack knew Yori wasn't a fighter at heart and he feared for his friend's life. The *ronin* may be suffering seasickness, but judging by the scars on his arms he was a battle-hardened and dangerous foe. 'Let me take your place,' suggested Jack.

'Trust me,' Yori replied, with only a slight tremble to his voice. 'I can handle him.'

'What's going on here?' The captain, a burly man with a face weathered as old leather, strode down the steps from the stern's upper deck.

'A duel!' cried one of the merchants excitedly.

'I won't have fighting on-board this ship,' ruled the captain.

Unwilling to lose face, the *ronin* stepped forward. 'The challenge has been set. My honour is at stake. We *must* duel.'

'My ship, my rules,' said the captain firmly.

'I'm a samurai,' said the *ronin*. 'Do what I say.'

'I'm the captain,' he shot back, unfazed by the *ronin*'s belligerent attitude. 'At sea, you do what I say.'

A tense stand-off occurred between the two men and the ship fell silent.

Coughing for their attention, Yori bowed to the captain. 'Perhaps you would be kind enough to lend us the rowing boat? Then we can duel on that island over there without injuring any of your passengers.'

Yori pointed to an uninhabited outcrop of rock, crowned with trees and ringed by a small beach. The captain regarded Yori thoughtfully, his curiosity roused at the prospect of a fight between a samurai and a pilgrim.

'That's acceptable,' agreed the captain, giving the order to drop anchor.

A couple of his crew lowered the rowing boat over the side. The *ronin* climbed down the rope ladder and waited impatiently for Yori to join him.

'Let me come with you,' suggested Saburo.

'It's best that I go alone,' Yori replied, taking a grip of the swaying ladder.

'Don't you want to carry a knife at least?' asked Miyuki, offering him her hidden *tantō*.

Yori shook his head and descended into the rowing boat. The *ronin* took the oars and began to paddle. Powerless to

33

prevent the duel now, Jack, Saburo and Miyuki stood by the guardrail, watching their friend bob across the water towards the island.

'That *ronin* will cut him into eight pieces,' sighed Saburo mournfully.

By now, all the passengers and crew were gathered along the gunwale, eagerly awaiting the start of this unusual match. Jack noticed the merchants and court nobles were placing bets on the outcome of the duel – and the odds weren't favourable for Yori.

As the rowing boat approached the little beach, the *ronin* shipped the oars and leapt on to the sand. Within the blink of an eye, he'd drawn a bloodstained sword and assumed a battle stance.

'Time to prove yourself, pilgrim!' he snarled.

Jack's heart was in his mouth as he saw Yori stand up to follow his opponent ashore. All of a sudden Yori snatched up an oar and pushed the rowing boat back out to sea. The *ronin* stared in outrage and utter bewilderment as his adversary left him stranded.

Rowing calmly away, Yori cried out, 'There's your demonstration in defeating the enemy . . . with no sword!'

# 7

# SEASICKNESS

Yori reboarded the boat to the sound of applause. In awe of his peaceful resolution, the pilgrims clustered round him asking for his blessing. Meanwhile, the merchants and court nobles were arguing over their bets – some believing Yori to be the clear victor, others protesting that an *actual* duel had never occurred.

'What about the *ronin*?' a deckhand asked the captain.

The samurai was stamping up and down on the beach, waving his arms furiously at them.

'He'll be picked up by another boat . . .' replied the captain, '. . . eventually!'

With a booming laugh, he gave the orders to weigh anchor and they resumed their journey towards Shikoku Island.

'Did you see the look on the *ronin*'s face?' Saburo chortled, when Yori finally managed to rejoin his friends. 'It was as if he'd swallowed a fish whole.'

Jack laid a hand upon Yori's shoulder. 'You *really* had me worried for a moment.'

Yori smiled ruefully. 'Sorry, but it was the only way I could think of to get the *ronin* off the boat without a fight.'

'That is *ninja* cunning!' Miyuki remarked. 'Still, you should've taken a weapon, just in case.'

'I did,' replied Yori, tapping a forefinger to his temple. 'The mind is the greatest weapon.'

Jack grinned at his friend. Every day Yori was becoming more and more like their old Zen master, Sensei Yamada – not only in manner but in wisdom too.

The boat sailed on and the passengers settled down again, dozing in the sun or gazing across the glistening waters of the Seto Sea. Returning to their position at the bow, Jack and the others ensured the canvas bag was kept securely between them. But they needn't have worried. The other travellers now maintained a respectful distance from Yori and his companions, his honourable act having enhanced his status on-board the boat.

Jack looked towards the distant horizon. Shikoku Island was not yet in sight. Surveying the huge expanse of water before him, he suddenly experienced a deep ache in his heart. England lay two years' voyage on the other side of the world, divided by vast oceans and fierce storms. Yet being at sea, he felt closer to home than ever before. He yearned to set foot on English shores once again – to find his sister, Jess, and to finally stop running. Jack had no doubt that she still prayed for his and his father's safe return, even after all these years. But he was worried about what had become of Jess without a family to protect and care for her.

'I feel awful,' groaned Saburo, holding his head in his hands.

Jack took one look at his friend's pale face. 'You're seasick. Stand up and keep your eye on the horizon.'

Getting shakily to his feet, Saburo leant against the guardrail. Jack fished out a gourd from the bag and offered it to him. 'You need to sip lots of water.'

Saburo took a swig. Wiping the back of his hand across his mouth, he moaned, 'Oh, I wish this deck would stop moving.'

'This is nothing!' laughed Jack. 'Wait until we hit a storm. The deck heaves so much, the sky becomes the sea and you don't know which way is up!'

Saburo now appeared even more queasy. 'How did you bear this for *two whole years*?'

'Don't worry,' said Jack, patting his friend gently on the back. 'After three days, your body adjusts to the motion and you stop being seasick.'

Saburo's eyes widened in dismay. 'Three days! There must be *something* that can be done before then?'

The boat crested a wave and he vomited.

'There is,' replied Jack, stepping back a pace as it splattered the rail. 'Point your head downwind!'

Leaving Saburo to wrestle with his sickness, Jack returned to sit beside Yori and Miyuki.

'Will he be all right?' asked Yori.

Jack nodded. 'Yes, he's finding his sea legs, that's all.'

Miyuki was staring thoughtfully around the boat. Then she leant close to Jack's ear. 'Yori and I have been talking. Rather than making our way to Nagasaki on foot, why don't we sail there instead? We'd avoid all the samurai patrols, the checkpoints on the roads and hopefully any more trouble.'

Jack considered this. It seemed so obvious now. Alone, such a voyage was impossible. No captain in his right mind would willingly carry a foreigner, for fear of incurring the wrath of the Shogun. But with his friends to hide and protect him . . . 'Do we have enough money to sail that far?'

'I don't know,' admitted Yori. 'Perhaps we could work our passage.'

'Or else *borrow* a boat,' suggested Miyuki, a sly grin on her lips. 'Jack, you know how to sail and could teach us. With a ship like this, we could even sail to England!'

Jack laughed out loud, then shook his head regretfully. 'This boat sits too low in the water. She'd be swamped in the open ocean. We'd need a ship at least three times the size just to cope with the storms.'

'Maybe we can find a bigger one at the next port,' insisted Miyuki, unwilling to be put off so easily.

Jack grinned at her determination and zeal. 'It's not that simple, I'm afraid. The distances between landfall are vast. We'd need food for several months. Not just for us, but a whole crew as well, since we couldn't sail a ship that size without help. The *Alexandria* carried a hundred souls on-board and well over a thousand tons of supplies. To have any hope of making such a voyage alive, we require a galleon – and with the Shogun banishing all foreigners, the only place we might find one is in Nagasaki.'

Miyuki appeared a little deflated and Jack felt bad at having crushed her idea so thoroughly. But those were the hard facts of attempting to sail around the world.

'It doesn't stop us getting a boat to Nagasaki, though,' encouraged Jack. 'All we need to know is the route and what bearings we'd have to take.'

At that moment, a deckhand approached them.

'With compliments of the captain,' he said, putting down a large plate. Cut into thin strips were a freshly caught bream and a couple of mackerel, along with some pickled ginger and soy sauce for taste.

'Thank you,' said Yori, bowing his head in appreciation. As the deckhand went to depart, Yori asked, 'What's the best way to reach Nagasaki by boat?'

The deckhand thought for a moment. 'If you cut short your pilgrimage, you could stop at Yawatahama in the south and cross the Bungo Channel to Sagaseki. But then you'd have the long trek across Kyushu.'

'Isn't there a more direct route by sea?'

The deckhand whistled through his teeth. 'That's the entire length of the Seto Sea and more. It's risky. But if the winds and tides are with you it could be far quicker.'

He looked to the horizon where the distant shimmer of Shikoku Island was now visible. 'Once we dock at Imabari, take a boat due west along the Seto Sea and through the Kanmon Straits to the Sea of Japan. Then bear south-west along the coast to Nagasaki itself.'

'Is this ship going that way?' asked Jack hopefully, keeping his face hidden beneath the rim of his hat.

The deckhand laughed. 'Not likely! There are more pirates in that area of the Seto Sea than mosquitoes.' He pointed to a small red-and-white striped flag that fluttered from the boat's stern. 'See that? The captain pays the pirates along this route not to attack him. The flag guarantees safe passage – but only between Tomo Harbour and Shikoku Island. You'll have to find another boat in Imabari.'

Leaning close to Yori, the deckhand whispered, 'A word of warning – you take your life into your own hands sailing that route. I've heard tales of man-eating sea dragons!'

Walking away, he left them all with horrified expressions on their faces.

'Perhaps we *should* stick to the road,' said Yori, swallowing fearfully.

'He's just trying to scare us,' said Miyuki. But she appeared equally unsettled by the idea, and turned to Jack for reassurance. 'There aren't sea dragons, are there?'

Having encountered many strange creatures in the ocean, Jack could understand why people might believe in dragons. But he'd never seen one for himself. 'Our real concern should be pirates. We need to find a ship with a flag.'

'And a fast one, just in case we meet a dragon,' added Yori.

Attempting to change the subject away from dragons, Jack offered the plate of fish to Saburo. 'Would you like some food?'

Usually the first in line to eat, Saburo shook his head feebly.

'Ginger is good for settling the stomach,' insisted Jack, but his friend just heaved and hung his head over the side.

# 8

# PIRATE WAR

As their boat made its final tack towards the port of Imabari, a castle loomed into view. Surrounded by sheer stone walls, the imposing structure rose directly out of the water. The central keep – a stark white tower with slate-grey curving roofs – soared five storeys high to command unbroken views across the Seto Sea. Like an armoured sentinel, it stood guard at the entrance to the port.

'That's *Mizujiro*,' explained the poet, noticing how awestruck Yori and his friends appeared at the sight. '*Daimyo* Mori's infamous Castle in the Sea, built to keep watch over the Kurushima Straits.'

Jack felt a hard knot of dread form in the pit of his stomach. Where such a fortress existed, so did numerous samurai patrols – and they were sailing straight into the midst of them.

'Look! Part of the castle's floating away,' exclaimed Miyuki in astonishment.

Glancing up, Jack saw a wooden section of wall on the eastern flank detach itself from the main complex. But, as their boat drew closer, it became apparent the floating wall was something else entirely.

'That's an *atake-bune*,' the poet said grimly. 'One of *daimyo* Mori's warships.'

Jack couldn't blame Miyuki for her mistaken observation. The immense vessel was built just like a battlement. On all four sides, solid wooden walls towered upwards to form an impregnable box-like shell. Along its length were two rows of diamond-shaped loopholes from which cannon, guns and bows could be fired. And an enclosed cabin on the upper deck completed the illusion of a fortified rampart.

In fact, the only clues to it being a ship were a tall mast and the forest of oars that projected from a hidden lower deck. The oarsmen themselves were shielded behind a protective skirt of bamboo screens, just above the waterline.

As the *atake-bune* pulled away from the castle, a large square sail was raised aloft. Emblazoned at its centre was the *mon* of a golden shell. Across the waters, Jack could hear the rhythmic *thud-thud-thud* of a drum, like the beat of a monster's heart. With each strike, the oars dipped into the water to be followed by the grunts and groans of eighty oarsmen as they strained to move the great beast across the sea.

The captain of their own vessel kept well clear of the warship's path. Built for battle, the *atake-bune* was heavy and had limited steerage, but once it had picked up speed, it would stop for no one.

Several smaller boats followed in its wake. Three were of a similar design to the *atake-bune*. These *seki-bune* possessed equally strong defences, but were half the size and had pointed prows, each tasselled with a coiled rope. Upon the open deck, Jack saw thirty samurai warriors stationed along the gunwales, armed with bows, muskets and half a dozen cannon. The four

42

remaining vessels were the smallest yet fastest of the fleet. Powered by twenty oarsmen and carrying ten samurai, these *kobaya* cut through the water. But, being little more than glorified rowing boats, there was no wooden planking for side protection. With the deck completely exposed, the crew would have to rely on speed and fighting skill to survive in a sea battle.

'You'd think there was a war still going on,' remarked Miyuki.

'There is,' replied the poet, the *atake-bune* dwarfing them as it surged past.

'But the Shogun won,' said Yori.

'*Daimyo* Mori isn't fighting the Shogun. He's waging a pirate war,' the poet explained. 'That's just one of many Sea Samurai patrols. The *daimyo* has built an entire navy for the sole purpose of wiping the pirate clans out.'

'Are there *that* many pirates?' asked Jack.

'Who knows their number? The Seto Sea is vast and has thousands of islands and hidden coves. But the *daimyo*'s campaign is personal. His son was killed by a pirate.'

'And that justifies a full-blown war?' questioned Yori as their boat entered the harbour.

'You clearly don't know *daimyo* Mori,' the poet sighed heavily. 'On news of his son's death, he rounded up the first fifty pirates he could find, whether guilty or not of the crime. He crucified them all, nailing them to the seawall as a warning to other pirates. Then he commanded his torturer to pierce each of their bodies with spears. The pirates suffered a long and excruciating death. It was said the pirate leader had *sixteen* spears inserted without puncturing a single vital organ. It took him five whole days to die.'

With a sorry shake of his head, the poet stood up in readiness to disembark.

'Believe me, you don't want to get on the wrong side of *daimyo* Mori.'

Jack, Yori and Miyuki exchanged an anxious look as the poet wished them luck on their pilgrimage and, bowing his respects, departed. Stepping ashore themselves, they helped Saburo off the boat and over to the shade of a cedar tree. The dockside was bustling with fishermen, pilgrims and a disturbing number of samurai. Fortunately, with so many white-clad travellers, no one paid them any attention.

'Am I glad to be back on dry land!' sighed Saburo, slumping against the tree.

'Don't get too used to it,' said Jack. 'We need to find another boat as soon as possible.'

Saburo was crestfallen.

Miyuki handed Jack the canvas bag. 'With so many samurai, you should stay here with Saburo,' she suggested. 'Yori and I will see what we can find.'

Jack nodded his agreement and settled down beside his friend. He watched as Miyuki and Yori worked their way along the dock. Wooden vessels of all types and sizes were moored to the jetty – from tiny dinghies, to fishing boats, to large cargo ships.

'Is there any food left?' asked Saburo.

'You're clearly feeling better,' smiled Jack, fishing out a *mochi* from the bag.

While Saburo chewed slowly on the rice cake, Jack risked another glance round the port. Compared to the quiet fishing village of Tomo Harbour, Imabari was a noisy centre for trade and shipping. Dockhands were loading and unloading goods of all kinds: rice, *saké*, lacquerware, porcelain, wood, silk, spices and – given the heavy presence of samurai guards – presumably copper, silver and gold too.

He noticed the majority of pilgrims were making their way out of the harbour and taking the road south to begin their epic journey. As they cleared the port, he and Saburo became more and more conspicuous. Jack silently urged Miyuki and Yori to hasten their search for a suitable boat.

Footsteps from behind alerted him to someone's approach. But without turning round he could tell by the clink of armour they didn't belong to a pilgrim.

'We're in trouble,' Jack whispered to Saburo.

A samurai guard strode purposefully up to them. 'Travel permits,' he demanded.

Jack kept his head bowed while Saburo pulled out their *nōkyōchō* books.

'What's wrong with him?' said the samurai, giving the permits a cursory glance as he scrutinized Jack's hunched form.

'Seasickness,' explained Saburo, with an apologetic grin.

The samurai snorted, 'Soft-stomached pilgrims!'

He handed back the *nōkyōchō* and walked on.

Jack breathed a sigh of relief. 'Quick thinking, Saburo.'

'Thanks, but that guard's bound to get suspicious if we stay here much longer.'

The tension grew with each passing moment, Jack imagining more and more samurai eyes turning towards him. He spotted the same guard pacing along the dock, heading back their way.

'I think we should go –'

'No, I see Miyuki,' said Saburo, pointing to a pilgrim hurrying towards them as fast as she dared.

'What took you so long?' asked Jack. 'And where's Yori?'

'He's at the boat.'

'You found one!' exclaimed Jack, trying to imagine what sort of vessel she'd acquired.

Miyuki nodded. 'There were too many patrols to steal a boat. But we did find one ship sailing all the way to Nagasaki,' she revealed, although her expression didn't look particularly jubilant. 'We must be quick; it's leaving now.'

Jack and Saburo picked up the canvas bag and followed Miyuki along the dock.

'Most captains weren't going that far south or were too afraid of pirates to try,' continued Miyuki. 'But, judging by how much this captain is charging, he's as mercenary as any pirate!'

She slowed before a magnificent cargo ship loaded with barrels of *saké*. Propelled by a single large sail, it had a reinforced hull to bear the weight of the heavy barrels.

'This looks ideal,' said Jack, impressed. 'Even in a storm, she should fare well.'

'Not that ship,' said Miyuki regretfully. 'It's the next one.'

Jack redirected his gaze and his heart sank. Yori stood beside a single-masted boat similar to the one they'd arrived on, but this vessel was in a sorry state. The square canvas sail was patched up, the rigging frayed, and the hull showed signs of several repair jobs. On top of that, the decks were dangerously overloaded with cargo and she sat worryingly low in the water.

Yet what choice did they have? They were on borrowed time. News of their escape from Tomo Harbour would soon reach the ears of Imabari's samurai. A patrol was working its way along the jetty at this very moment. Yori waved them urgently on-board, the captain giving the order to cast off. As Jack ran up the gangplank, he glanced towards the stern. There was no protection flag.

# 9

# OMISHIMA ISLAND

The boat slipped out of Imabari port, its warped deck creaking and its sail flapping like a broken wing. Waves occasionally breached the gunwales, soaking crew and cargo alike. In a vain attempt to keep dry, Jack and his friends perched among the crates of pottery and bundles of bamboo. They were the only passengers on-board and Jack could understand why. Not only did the ship appear unseaworthy but the captain and his deckhands were a surly bunch. None of them smiled and, surprisingly for Japanese people, they were unkempt and unwashed.

The captain, a stout man with rough skin, a ragged beard and bald head, stood at the stern, leaning upon the tiller. His listless crew of four went barefoot and wore only the simplest of kimono or just a plain white loincloth.

'The captain wants payment upfront,' said Yori.

'That's *all* our money,' Saburo complained, handing over the pilgrims' coins and his own funds. 'We won't have any for food.' Then, at the very thought of eating, he lay down and closed his eyes in a vain attempt to fend off the seasickness.

'But it takes us *all* the way,' reminded Miyuki.

'Tell the captain he can have half now and the rest upon arrival, if we make it that far,' said Jack, eyeing the old sea dog mistrustfully.

Yori clambered over the crates and up a wooden ladder to the stern. The captain grunted his dissatisfaction at the half payment, protesting it was a smear upon his honourable character. Nonetheless, he quickly pocketed the money. They conversed a little longer before Yori fought his way back across the listing deck to sit beside Jack. The captain had informed him the entire voyage could take up to a month, depending upon the tides, winds and weather conditions. He'd also be making a number of stops en route at various islands to deliver and collect goods. Much to Yori's delight, their first port of call was Omishima Island. They would reach its shores by dusk.

Having been on the run for so long, exhaustion finally took its toll. Stowing the canvas bag out of sight from the crew's prying eyes, Miyuki and Yori succumbed to the gentle roll of the ship and joined Saburo in sleep. Not far from sleep himself, Jack took one last look in the direction of Imabari. The port was slowly retreating into the distance as their boat sailed north-west through the Kurushima Straits. But the white tower of *Mizujiro* remained on the horizon like an all-seeing eye. Until that disappeared, Jack wouldn't believe they had truly escaped.

Sensing a shift in course, Jack roused himself from his slumber. The boat was now bearing directly north. Sitting up, he spied the haze of a mountain peak and presumed this was Omishima Island. But he decided against waking the others, since landfall was still some distance off.

Needing to stretch his legs, Jack made his way to the stern's upper deck, the only spot on the ship that wasn't crammed with cargo. Lifting the brim of his hat, he scanned the horizon and was glad to discover *Mizujiro*'s keep was no longer in sight. Nor could he see any vessels following a similar course to them.

This time they *had* made it.

With the mountain and several smaller islands surrounding them, it was relatively easy for Jack to judge the boat's progress. Compared to the vast emptiness of the open ocean, the Seto Sea was blessed with numerous navigational markers. If the southwesterly breeze held, they were little more than an hour's sail from their first destination.

But Jack knew the presence of land brought its own set of problems. For the inexperienced pilot, a ship could run aground on a hidden sandbank or strike an underwater reef. Sudden changes in wind direction caused by a nearby land mass could capsize a boat. And he was already aware of the major influence that tidal currents played in this region. Jack wished he had a pen and ink, so he could note down his observations in the *rutter*. This seafaring knowledge could prove invaluable with time. He remembered his father always jotting down notes in the logbook wherever they sailed. It was second nature to him. *Observe, write, remember*, he would always say. Jack felt compelled to follow his father's lead and tried to commit his observations to memory.

'Bit of a seaman, are you?' grunted the captain, noting the ease with which Jack rode the pitch and roll of the deck.

'I . . . sailed with my father,' replied Jack, hastily adjusting his hat to shield his face.

'A fisherman, eh?'

'No. A navigator.'

'Hmm,' said the captain, reassessing the pilgrim before him. 'What's our current bearing?'

'North,' replied Jack. 'And before that, north-west.'

The captain smiled for the first time. 'Take the tiller,' he ordered.

Before Jack could protest, the captain let go and strode over to the guardrail. 'Hold her steady!' growled the captain as he relieved himself over the side.

Jack leant his weight against the long arm of the rudder. He could feel the rush of the sea vibrate up the wood and the power of the wind as it thrust the boat through the waves.

Turning back, the captain caught a glimpse of the wide grin on Jack's face.

'The *Golden Tiger* may not be much to look at, but she fair flies with the wind, eh?' he said with pride.

Jack nodded, although he feared the ship would disintegrate in anything more than a strong breeze.

'Why doesn't the *Golden Tiger* carry a flag?' Jack asked.

'Pirate tolls are costly,' replied the captain indignantly. 'Besides, her looks make her an unappealing prize.'

Considering the sheer amount of cargo on-board, Jack wondered if the boat's poor condition wasn't more of an *incentive* to a pirate. But he sensed that the captain was more interested in profit than protection. Fortunately, there were no pirate ships in the vicinity. The forested slopes of Omishima's mountain drew ever closer. Surveying its rocky shore, Jack couldn't see any obvious harbour.

'Bear north-west,' ordered the captain, pointing to a gap

between the headland and a nearby islet. 'Beware that outcrop, though. There's a vicious current that'll drag you across if you're not careful.'

Jack leant on the tiller until the *Golden Tiger*'s prow was aimed dead centre of the gap. The lead edge of the sail started to flap in the wind.

'Shouldn't your crew trim the sail?' Jack suggested, knowing that a new tack required an adjustment to take best advantage of the wind.

'My crew are a useless bunch,' snorted the captain. 'They wouldn't know the wind's direction even if it farted in their faces!'

He shouted at them to tighten the sheets. Wearily, the deckhands did their duty. The sail stopped flapping and the *Golden Tiger* picked up speed.

'Why hire them if they can't sail?' asked Jack in amazement.

'They're cheaper than real sailors!' laughed the captain, taking over the tiller as the boat rounded the headland.

A sheltered cove came into view. The wind dropped and the *Golden Tiger* coasted towards a long wooden pier that jutted out from the beach. Bizarrely, the pier was covered by an ornate green-tiled curving roof with bright red pillars. Jack was surprised that a humble fishing port would have such a grand jetty.

Then he heard Yori gasp in rapture.

Upon the headland, overlooking the bay, was a magnificent red and gold temple.

# 10

# WARRIOR SPIRIT

'Aren't you going to pay your respects at the shrine?' enquired the captain, wondering why his passengers hadn't disembarked. 'We may be some time unloading.'

Reluctant as they were to leave the ship, Jack and his friends had no choice but to follow custom. They couldn't appear anything less than devout worshippers, otherwise they would arouse suspicion. In spite of their misgivings, Saburo welcomed a return to dry land and Yori was delighted at the opportunity to visit such a renowned temple.

'Oyamazumi is one of the oldest Shinto shrines in Japan. Some monks call it "the seat of the gods",' he recounted excitedly as they left the pier and passed through the first *torii* gateway. 'Sensei Yamada insisted that I visit here at least once in my lifetime.'

Climbing the stone steps up the mountainside, Jack was equally awed by the shrine. Tucked into the forested side of the headland, the temple sat like an ancient god within the throne of the cove. The walls – painted bright red and studded with large iron bolts – resembled the armoured breastplate of a warrior. Its gilded eaves glistened in the late evening light.

And crowning the main Hall of Worship was a green gabled roof with golden *shachihoko* adorning each corner – these gargoyles had the body of a carp and the head of a dragon.

The four false pilgrims wound their way up the wide path towards the shrine's courtyard. At its heart was an immense camphor tree, its ancient trunk twisting skyward to where a lush green canopy revealed a mass of white flowers emerging for spring. As they passed beneath its branches, Yori whispered in a reverential tone, 'This tree was planted by Jimmu Tennō himself – the first Emperor of Japan!'

Jack began to appreciate the shrine's significance for his friend. The Emperor was viewed as a living god and such a gesture would have bestowed great spiritual wealth on the temple.

Yori led them over to a fountain housed within a small covered pavilion. Fresh water spouted from an ornate dragon's head into a stone basin. Setting aside his pilgrim's staff, Yori picked up a wooden ladle and washed both his hands then mouth in a purification ritual. Saburo, Miyuki and Jack observed the same rite before entering the Hall of Worship.

Within its cool darkened interior, they were greeted by calming wafts of jasmine incense and the soft murmur of prayer. Several monks in white robes and black cloth hats knelt in a line, hands clasped in worship. Behind them were a group of pilgrims, some local fishermen and three samurai bearing arms. Although their heads were bowed in devotion, Jack kept his distance from the warriors. He knelt to Yori's far side as the four of them paid their respects.

'The shrine is dedicated to Oyamazumi, the protector of sailors and samurai,' whispered Yori. 'He's the brother of Amaterasu, the sun goddess –'

The monks' incantation stopped and the head priest rose to his feet. He walked over to the three samurai, who prostrated themselves and held their swords outstretched.

'Many samurai make such offerings in the hope of success in battle, or as thanks for victory,' Yori continued under his breath. 'Sensei Yamada told me *daimyo* Kamakura came here after he won the Battle of Osaka Castle.'

Jack felt his heart harden at the mention of the name of the Shogun. He was the man responsible not only for the civil war and the exile of all foreigners but for the banishment of Jack's guardian, Masamoto. If it wasn't for *daimyo* Kamakura, Jack wouldn't be on the run with a price on his head.

Accepting the samurai's weapons, the priest walked over to a large set of double doors. As he approached, they opened to reveal an adjoining chamber.

'That's the Hall of Offerings,' explained Yori, seeing Jack's eyes widen in amazement. 'It houses every gift donated in honour of Oyamazumi.'

The chamber was overflowing with ceremonial swords and armour. Blades hung like silver scales from every wall, tall racks of spears and bows lined the sides, and taking pride of place in the centre of the room was a gleaming suit of silver-white armour.

'That belonged to Minamoto Yoritomo, the first Shogun. Such gifts are the reason why the temple possesses so much divine power. Many believe the spirits of the great warriors live on through this shrine. At night, monks have even heard battles in the Hall of Offerings.'

The priest returned, closing the doors behind him. The

monks' incantation resumed as the priest presented each of the samurai with an *omamori* talisman.

'I wish I hadn't left my helmet in Tomo,' Saburo whispered. 'We could have made an offering ourselves – for good luck on the voyage.'

'We can still pray for such fortune,' said Yori, closing his eyes and putting his palms together.

The four of them fell into silent worship. Jack took the moment to pray to his own Christian God, letting his mind drift with the monks' chant. But he was soon distracted by a ray of light playing upon his face. Opening his eyes, he discovered the setting sun was streaming in through one of the latticed windows. It overlooked a path that led to a cliff. An elderly man was perched upon a rock near the edge, directly in line with the sun. His movement causing the beam of sunlight to flicker.

All of a sudden, the man toppled forward and disappeared.

Jack blinked, unsure if he'd really seen him at all. No one else in the temple apparently had. His friends remained deep in prayer and, not wishing to disturb them, Jack hurried out to discover if the man was alive or not . . . or if he'd even existed.

The courtyard was deserted as he ran along the path to the cliff edge. Bracing himself for the worst, Jack looked over to see a dizzying drop. The cliff plummeted straight down into the sea. Waves churned at the bottom and offered no prospect of survival. Then a head bobbed to the surface. The man swam for the shore, but another wave rolled in and he disappeared once more.

Jack spied a rock-strewn animal track leading to a ledge at

the cliff base. Without a thought for his own safety, or the fact that he'd reveal his identity, he scrambled down in a wild attempt to save the drowning man. Jack was almost halfway when he burst back to the surface. But yet another wave engulfed him. Breathless, Jack bounded over the last few steps and hurried to the water's edge. He searched the turbulent sea for any sign of the man. But the churning white mass offered little hope.

A huge wave rolled in and broke against the cliff. Jack jumped back to avoid getting dragged in himself. As it retreated, he was stunned to see an elderly man sitting casually upon the ledge, wringing the salt water from his beard.

'Are you hurt?' asked Jack, offering a hand to help him up.

The man stood on his own. 'Why should I be?'

'How could anyone survive in there?' said Jack, pointing to the deadly confusion of rocks and white water.

'It's easy,' replied the man, his slate-grey eyes taking in Jack but showing no concern for his foreign appearance. 'I follow the way of the water and do nothing to oppose it – its nature becomes my nature.'

The man started up the track, pausing briefly as an invitation for Jack to follow. Jack was surprised by the nimbleness and speed with which the old man scaled the steep face.

'The fall alone should have killed you,' Jack insisted, unable to believe the man was unharmed.

Reaching the top, the elderly man picked up a bird's feather and held it before Jack's nose.

'Watch this,' he instructed, and let it go. The sea breeze caught the feather and it fluttered across the bay, floating towards the beach. 'You see, the feather doesn't resist. It simply goes where the wind blows.'

Jack immediately understood. The old man was talking about the Ring of Wind. The Grandmaster had used the exact same words. This element of the Five Rings embodied the spirit of *ninjutsu* – evasion, open-mindedness, the ability to respond to any situation, be ready for any attack as it occurs. *To go where the wind blows.*

The man pointed to a tree beside the temple, the bough broken and the trunk split. 'That oak tried to resist the wind. Strong as it is, the tree lost the fight.' He looked Jack directly in the eye. 'Bear this in mind, young samurai, for when an old enemy returns anew.'

A shiver ran down Jack's spine, as if someone had walked across his grave. *How could this old man know such things?*

He was about to ask when he heard a shout from behind.

'Jack!' cried Miyuki, waving frantically from the courtyard. 'The boat's leaving without us!'

# 11

# WIND DEMONS

They raced along the beach, shouting for the captain to stop. But the ship had raised its sail and the crew were casting off. Either the captain didn't hear them, or he chose not to.

Their feet pounded on to the wooden pier. Miyuki was the fastest, flying down its length and leaping catlike to land upon the ship's deck. A crewmember stumbled back in shock.

Still the boat pulled away.

Jack and Saburo tossed the canvas bag with all their might and Miyuki caught it. Springing mid-step, Jack flew through the air to land deftly on the gunwale. He dropped on to the deck before turning to help the others. Saburo, his cheeks red and wheezing like a pair of bellows, began to flag. With each step, the gap between the pier and the boat grew ever wider.

'Jump *now*!' shouted Jack.

Ditching his pilgrim's staff, Saburo threw himself across the water. Arms extended, he crashed painfully into the guard-rail and clung on for dear life. Jack and Miyuki dragged him on-board. Only Yori remained. Lagging behind because of his smaller stride, he was still halfway along the pier. Yet the boat was almost at the end and heading out into open water.

'Stop the ship!' cried Miyuki.

The captain held up his hands apologetically. 'I can't. The tides have turned.'

'Come on, Yori!' urged Jack, running to the stern.

Yori sprinted after them, his short legs pumping furiously.

'JUMP! I'll catch you,' shouted Jack, leaning over the rail.

The boat cleared the pier. Yori made a leap of faith. Legs and arms flailing, he launched himself towards Jack's outstretched arms.

'He's not going to make it,' said Saburo. Seizing Jack's waist, he and Miyuki shoved Jack further over the side. Jack, fingers splayed, stretched for all he was worth. Yori tumbled towards him. Jack missed the left hand and Yori fell away before his eyes. But the extra reach allowed him to snatch at Yori's pilgrim staff. He clamped down hard, gritting his teeth as the wood slipped through his fingers.

Yori cried out, desperately clinging on. He swung helpless above the water and Jack thought he was about to lose his friend, when the staff juddered to a halt. The Five Rings characters etched into the handle gave him just enough grip to halt Yori's fall. With muscles straining, Saburo and Miyuki pulled them both to safety. They all collapsed on the deck, breathing heavily.

'You left us on purpose!' accused Miyuki, glaring at the captain.

'I forgot we had passengers,' the captain replied with unconvincing innocence.

Miyuki rose to confront him. 'If you ever forget us again, you'll live to regret it.'

'What are you going to do?' snorted the captain. 'Throw your prayer book at me?'

Miyuki started forward, but Jack took her by the arm.

'He's our only passage to Nagasaki,' Jack reminded her quietly.

Fuming, Miyuki stormed down the steps to the main deck.

'She's lucky you stopped her,' remarked the captain, puffing out his chest.

*No,* you're *lucky I stopped her*, thought Jack, wondering how the captain would have steered with a broken arm.

Jack joined the others amid the chaos of the cargo. As the boat sailed round the headland, Jack realized he'd never said goodbye to the old man on the cliff. Looking up, he could make out his silhouette against the dying light of the day. The old man was sitting upon the rock again, staring out to sea. Jack waved farewell to him.

'Who are you waving to?' asked Saburo.

'The old man up there.'

Yori and Saburo both glanced up.

'That isn't a man,' said Yori with an amused smile. 'That's Taira Rock.'

'What?' said Jack, eyeing the figure more carefully.

'It's named after Taira Masamori, the Great Pirate Queller,' explained Yori. 'Five hundred years ago, as *daimyo* of Aki Province, it was his responsibility to stop their raids. Every time he defeated a pirate clan, he honoured the gods at this shrine. Then one night pirates attacked Omishima Island and captured Masamori. They threw him off that cliff top. Somehow he survived, climbed back up and killed them all. But during the fight he suffered fatal wounds and died upon that spot. Legend says, when his body was found, it had turned to stone.'

'But I *talked* with him,' insisted Jack.

'Jack's speaking with warrior spirits now!' chuckled Saburo, tucking into a piece of dried fish in an effort to eat before he became seasick again.

But Jack didn't laugh. He swore he hadn't imagined the encounter. Yet, as their boat pulled away from the cove, the figure revealed itself to be nothing more than a large rock.

Jack stood upon the bow, deep in contemplation. The sun had set and the Seto Sea now reflected a starlit night sky. A gibbous moon hung in the heavens, casting a silvery sheen across the crest of the waves.

*An old enemy returns anew.*

The phrase haunted his thoughts. He remained convinced that his experience at Taira Rock had been genuine. The bottoms of his white breeches were still damp from where the wave had broken over the ledge. Yet Miyuki didn't remember seeing anyone when she'd called to him from the shrine.

Jack sighed. Daydream or not, he realized it was likely that Kazuki and his Scorpion Gang had picked up their trail. His old school rival could easily have got word of their escape from Tomo Harbour. Tenacious and resourceful, Kazuki would deduce they'd gone to sea and wouldn't rest until he'd captured Jack. At least his enemy's continued pursuit meant Akiko was safe, since he couldn't fulfil his vow to punish her for crippling his right hand.

Holding a palm to his chest, Jack felt the press of Akiko's pearl against his heart. It still lay securely pinned to the lapel of his jacket and its reassuring touch calmed him. Jack looked to the sky, searching out Spica, one of the brightest stars in the heavens. He'd shown Akiko its position one night when they'd been alone together in the Southern Zen Garden. Smiling at the memory, Jack hoped that she gazed up at it sometimes, just as he did.

'Still communicating with spirits?' asked Miyuki with a mischievous grin.

Jack was startled out of his dreaming. Miyuki possessed a ninja's unsettling habit of moving with absolute silence. The sea breeze stiffened and Miyuki drew closer to him. Her eyes, black as midnight, held his gaze. Knowing the affection she held for him, Jack wondered what she was about to do next . . .

'Isn't it dangerous to sail at night?'

'No . . . not if you know the waters,' replied Jack, regaining his composure. 'Of course, there's always a risk. But I suppose the captain's trying to avoid pirates.'

'Possibly, or . . .' Miyuki lowered her voice, glancing round to check none of the crew was nearby, '. . . because he's an illegal trader.'

'What makes you say that?' asked Jack.

'In the hold, hidden beneath the crates of pottery, I discovered bundles of the finest silk cloth. He must be trying to avoid paying port taxes. And *that* might cause us problems.'

Jack considered this. 'Why? Isn't the fact that he's avoiding the authorities good for us?'

'Perhaps,' Miyuki conceded. 'On the other hand, his criminal activities could attract the sort of interest we don't want.'

Jack nodded in agreement. 'Let's discuss this with the others in the morning –'

All of a sudden, there was a shriek. One of the crew was pointing port side with a trembling hand.

'*Fuma!*' he cried, his face drawn back in horror. '*Wind Demons!*'

# CLOSE-HAULED

Out of the darkness materialized a white sail upon which a huge black spider had been painted. The ship, twice their size and with a second foresail for speed, was cutting through the waves towards them. The crew began to panic, cowering beneath the cargo in a futile attempt to hide. As the apparition bore down on their boat, the captain stood rooted to the deck, gawping with a combination of fear and disbelief.

Jack grabbed the nearest crewmember. 'What are Wind Demons?'

'N-n-ninja pirates,' spluttered the man, his face pale as a ghost's in the moonlight. 'Wind Demons capture and eat their victims alive!'

Ignoring the man's ravings, Jack turned back to Miyuki. 'If they're ninja, we've nothing to worry about. We just need to show them the Dragon Seal.'

Jack formed the secret hand sign the Grandmaster had taught him, the one that ensured a bond of friendship between any true ninja.

Miyuki gravely shook her head. 'Not with the *Fuma* clan. They're more pirate than ninja.' She stared darkly at the approaching vessel. 'After the samurai, the *Fuma* are a ninja's worst enemy.'

The pirate ship was gaining on them fast. If the captain didn't take evasive action soon, they would be rammed and boarded.

'What are we going to do?' asked Yori, joining them at the guardrail with a sickly Saburo.

'We have to outrun them,' replied Jack.

'In this piece of junk?' groaned Saburo. 'We haven't got a chance!'

'Handled right, she'll go faster than the wind,' said Jack. *If her battered hull and wrecked rigging can hold out long enough*, he thought. But he didn't admit this to his friends. 'The three of you start throwing crates and the bamboo overboard. We need to lighten the load.'

'NO!' cried the captain. 'Those are my goods.'

'They'll be no good to you if you're dead,' Jack shouted back, before darting up to the stern's deck and wrestling the tiller from the inept captain.

'This is *my* ship!' he protested, shocked by the apparent mutiny.

'Then let me save it for you,' replied Jack, revealing his face to the captain for the first time.

'Y-y-you're a *gaijin*!'

'I'm also a sailor and a pilot,' said Jack, leaning hard on the tiller and steering the *Golden Tiger* on a westerly course.

'What are you doing?' cried the captain in alarm. 'We should be running before the wind, not heading into it!'

'The Wind Demons have two sails,' stated Jack. 'They'd catch up with us in no time. Our only hope is to outsail them.

We need to be close-hauled. Now get your men to trim the mainsail.'

The captain looked thoroughly unconvinced by Jack's plan of action. Nonetheless, still in shock at his foreign appearance and with the pirate ship surging towards them, he ordered his crew to pull in the sheets. The canvas stopped flapping, no longer spilling precious wind power, and the *Golden Tiger* immediately picked up speed.

Jack realized he was taking a great risk. Close-hauled was the most challenging point of sail and the hardest in which to get the best out of a boat, especially one as battered as the *Golden Tiger*. The difficulty lay in how close to the wind he could get. Jack had to aim the *Golden Tiger*'s bow as high as possible, while maintaining the fastest attainable speed. He'd be sailing on a knife's edge. The brisk breeze meant a sudden gust could capsize them at any moment. If he steered too much into the wind, the *Golden Tiger* would enter the no-go zone and stop dead in the water. If he angled further away from the wind, the boat would increase speed but have to cover a lot more ground – and this would allow the faster pirate ship to gain on them.

Jack's sole hope relied upon their enemy being less manoeuvrable and unable to take such an acute angle to the wind. This would force the ninja pirates to tack more often, slowing their progress every time they had to beat a new course.

Miyuki, Yori and Saburo continued to dump cargo into the sea. Whimpers of pain and loss sounded from the captain with each crate thrown overboard. But the *Golden Tiger* benefited from the reduction in weight and began to fly through the water.

'They're still going to hit us!' wailed one of the crew.

Jack glanced back. The fearsome pirate ship, its black spider sail seeming to swallow the stars behind, crested a wave like a breaching whale. Its exposed hull revealed timbers reinforced for ramming. As its bow came crashing back to the sea, plumes of white spray spurted into the air.

'Change tack!' insisted the captain to Jack. 'They're headed straight for our port side.'

'No,' replied Jack, steadfastly keeping his bearing. The *Golden Tiger* was virtually nose to the wind, the telltale feathering of the canvas warning Jack of just how close they were to disaster.

'*CHANGE COURSE!*' screamed the captain, throwing his arms over his head and bracing himself for the impact.

The pirate ship drove towards their port quarter . . . and missed. It sailed past like a great black ghost, its menacing crew glaring over the side at their escaping quarry.

Unable to sail Jack's line, the pirate ship was forced to tack several more times in order to make another run at them.

'Pin that sail in tight!' Jack shouted to the crew, seeing the canvas begin to flap again. Waves lapped over the leeside gunwale as he fought to keep the boat on its extreme bearing. The wind whipped past, sending chill sea spray into Jack's face. The *Golden Tiger* groaned under the strain, its rigging threatening to snap.

'She won't take much more of this,' warned the captain.

'We don't have any other choice,' replied Jack, gritting his teeth as he held firm to the tiller.

The *Golden Tiger* was now maintaining its lead, but wasn't pulling away. Jack needed to get even more from the boat. *But at what cost?* This single square-sailed rig wasn't built for such demanding sailing.

Miyuki clambered over the heeling deck to join Jack at the stern. 'That's every bit of loose cargo we can shift.'

Jack considered their options. The pirate ship was relentlessly pursuing them, picking up speed for a second collision course. He *had* to squeeze another knot of speed from the *Golden Tiger*.

'Get everyone aft and on the windward side,' ordered Jack.

Miyuki ran off to collect Yori, Saburo and the crew. They gathered on the stern deck beside the port quarter.

'Now sit on the guardrail and lean out,' instructed Jack.

'Are you crazy?' said Saburo, glancing fearfully with Yori at the rushing sea beneath them.

'We need to counterbalance the wind and keep an even keel,' explained Jack. 'The heeling of the ship is slowing us down.'

Without needing to be told twice, Miyuki jumped on the rail and, grabbing hold of a rope, hung herself over the side. The four crew slipped their feet through the gaps in the bamboo latticework and leant back as far as they could. With great reluctance, Saburo took hold of two ropes and did the same. Drawing in a deep breath, Yori perched on the guardrail and, closing his eyes, suspended himself above the open sea.

'And you, Captain!' ordered Jack.

As everyone threw their weight to port, little by little the *Golden Tiger* righted itself.

'Please tell me, we're going faster?' Yori begged, unwilling to open his eyes.

'Yes! Yes! We're losing the Wind Demons!' shouted a crewmember in delight.

Gradually, the distance between the *Golden Tiger* and the pirate ship began to increase. Jack reckoned if they could maintain their speed, the black spider sail would be no more than a dot on the horizon by dawn.

Jumping on deck, the captain slapped Jack on the back. 'Fine sailing, *gaijin*! Get us to Hiroshima in one piece and I'll forget about the cargo you ditched . . . and the fact that you're a foreigner.'

Jack's gamble had paid off. The crew smiled with relief at their narrow escape and gazed in wonder at the *gaijin* sailor who'd saved them.

Suddenly a rigging line snapped, the sail slackened and the *Golden Tiger* lost speed. Behind, the Wind Demons closed in again for the kill.

# 13

# SEA DRAGON

'Head for that island,' said the captain urgently, pointing to a dark outline off their starboard bow. 'There's a sea cave on the far side of the bluff. I've used it once before to hide from these cursed *wako*.'

Jack adjusted course. If they could make it round the headland, they might have a chance. The darkness of night would help conceal their movements and, with any luck, the pirate ship would pass them by.

'The Wind Demons are catching up,' warned Miyuki.

'I know,' said Jack as he continued to spill wind from the sail. But he daren't risk putting any more pressure on the damaged rigging.

The *Golden Tiger* limped on towards the fortress of rock that thrust up from the sea, its peak capped by a mantle of windswept trees. The shoreline was craggy and treacherous, and Jack had to precisely follow the captain's instruction to avoid running into submerged rocks – even more so, when a cloud slipped across the moon, muting its pale light.

The pirate ship disappeared from view as they rounded the bluff.

'There's the cave!' said the captain, pointing to a black crevice at the base of a huge cliff. It was hard to make out in the gloom, but that made it an ideal refuge.

Wind bleeding from the sail, Jack allowed the *Golden Tiger* to drift towards the opening. Their progress seemed excruciatingly slow. At any moment the pirate ship would clear the headland and the *Golden Tiger* would be in plain sight.

They all silently willed the boat to go faster.

'We're almost there,' breathed Yori, his knuckles having gone white from gripping the guardrail so hard.

Jack stared dead ahead, his focus entirely upon the cave entrance. He wiped a forearm across his eyes. *Was that a glimmer of movement inside?*

Suddenly a ball of flame burst forth, followed by an almighty roar. In the blinding flash, Jack and the others confronted a terrifying vision — a ferocious dragon with an armoured spine of spikes, a devil-horned head and razor teeth like scythes spat fire at them. A split second later, the *Golden Tiger*'s mast exploded.

'*Sea dragon!*' screamed one of the crew, his eyes wide as the moon with sheer horror.

Unable to believe his eyes, Jack yanked hard on the tiller, desperately attempting to alter their course. The *Golden Tiger* veered away and was blessed with enough momentum to head back into open water. But there was little hope of escape. The mainsail was ablaze with hellfire and the *Golden Tiger* was crippled.

'Cut the rigging!' ordered Jack, relinquishing the tiller to the captain. 'The whole ship will go up in flames.'

Miyuki raced along the deck to where their canvas bag was

hidden. She pulled it clear and began to hand out weapons to Saburo, Yori and Jack. The captain was in too much of a panic to wonder why his pilgrim passengers carried samurai and ninja swords. He was furiously waggling the rudder in a fraught attempt to propel the *Golden Tiger* away from the sea dragon's lair.

On deck it was raining fire. Jack unsheathed his *katana* and in one clean sweep sliced through the first of the halyards tethering the burning sail. Miyuki hacked with her *ninjatō* along the other side.

'Clear the deck!' warned Jack as he severed the last of the rigging.

Like a dying phoenix, the mainsail tumbled from the sky. Sparks flew like fireflies and there was a great crackle and splutter as the canvas extinguished in the sea . . .

But half still lay across the deck, burning fiercely.

Yori thrust at the blazing canvas with his *shakujō*, trying to push it over the side. Rushing to his aid, Saburo and two of the crew grabbed the last remaining lengths of bamboo and shoved with all their might. The sail slipped over the guardrail and the roar of flames died. Darkness engulfed them once again and an eerie silence descended – all that could be heard was the lapping of the waves against the hull.

'Where's the sea dragon?' asked Saburo, breathless, staring into the black recesses of the cave.

Their eyes adjusting to the night, Jack and Miyuki scanned the waters surrounding them. Off their port bow, a great shadow loomed.

In the chaos and confusion, the Wind Demons had caught up.

Their vessel drew alongside the *Golden Tiger*, its deck towering over them. Without warning, several sections of the gunwales fell away and smashed on top of the *Golden Tiger*'s guardrail. Great iron spikes bit into the deck, holding the *Golden Tiger* fast. An instant later, black shadows swarmed across the bridges to board the crippled cargo ship.

A crewmember screamed as the steel tip of a blade burst through his chest. Blood spewing from his mouth, he collapsed to the deck, dead. Behind, a ninja crouched, his sword slick with the man's entrails.

Jack stood frozen with fear. He was reliving the nightmare of that fateful night four years ago, when ninja pirates had attacked the *Alexandria* and slaughtered the entire crew. The heart-rending moment when his father had been brutally murdered by Dragon Eye. Once again Jack felt like the powerless boy he'd been – the one who'd been unable to prevent his father's death. Then he reminded himself that he was no longer that defenceless boy. He was a trained samurai *and* a ninja. Breaking his paralysis, he launched himself at the enemy, swords raised, and cried, 'REPEL BOARDERS!'

The Wind Demons, dressed head-to-foot in black, were impossible to see – just the moon-silver glint of their blades visible. Jack jumped aside as a sword scythed for his neck. He deflected the attack with his *wakizashi*, simultaneously thrusting with his *katana*. But the ninja pirate effortlessly evaded it as if he were no more than a leaf in the breeze. His blade circled round for another killing strike on Jack.

Yori leapt to Jack's rescue. He drove the iron tip of his *shakujō* into the ninja pirate's back. The force of the blow stunned the invader, sending his slash wide. At the same time,

Jack side-kicked his attacker with all his strength. The ninja pirate slammed into the guardrail. With another shove from Yori's *shakujō*, he toppled over the side into the watery depths below.

But more Wind Demons instantly replaced their fallen comrade.

Saburo, still with bamboo pole in hand, wielded it like a massive *bō* staff. He swept the deck in front of him, keeping the Wind Demons at bay. Meanwhile, Miyuki was perched upon the starboard rail, fending off two vicious ninja pirates. She injured one with her *ninjatō*, then kicked the second Wind Demon in the face. But she was fighting a losing battle as other pirates joined the attack.

Too far away to help, Jack spotted one of the severed pieces of rigging lying across the deck. It was still fixed to its cleat at the other end. Sheathing his *wakizashi*, he snatched up the rope and yanked hard. As the line pulled taut, it snagged the legs of the Wind Demons, toppling them like skittles.

In a deft leap along the guardrail, Miyuki joined Jack by his side.

'Thanks for that,' she breathed, flicking blood from her blade.

'Don't thank me yet,' replied Jack as more ninja pirates stormed the *Golden Tiger*.

The remaining crewmember on the main deck fled for the stern. Out of the darkness, a hooked knife on a chain flashed through the air and struck him in the back. A second later, he was jerked off his feet and dragged screaming across the deck into the seething mass of Wind Demons. His agonized cries were cut short as a sword severed his head from his neck.

'Fall back!' ordered Jack to his friends.

Keeping a protective line, they retreated to the stern's upper deck. Behind them, the captain and his two surviving crew cowered beside the tiller. Their expressions were a combination of terror at the Wind Demons and awe at the battling pilgrims. The four young warriors valiantly held off the invaders. Jack disarmed one ninja pirate, knocked another unconscious and threw a third over the side. But the sheer weight of numbers was overwhelming. An evil hiss emanated from the Wind Demons' masked mouths as they closed in for the kill.

Realizing this would be their last stand, Jack and his friends formed a tight circle and prepared to defend each other to the bitter end. But the Wind Demons halted a sword's length away.

'Having second thoughts, are you?' growled Saburo, discarding his pole and unsheathing his *katana* in a final display of samurai courage.

On the upper deck of the pirate ship a Wind Demon appeared. Unmasked, he wore a dragon-horned helmet bearing the emblem of a black spider.

In a voice as deep as the ocean, the pirate captain ordered, 'Take them . . . alive!'

# 14

# SHARK BAIT

The watery light of dawn coloured a cloudless sky as the pirate ship sailed south. Jack and his friends were imprisoned on its main deck, held like animals in a bamboo cage with nine other unfortunate captives. The captain of the *Golden Tiger* crouched alone in the corner, looking dejected and grief-stricken. His ship, deemed unworthy for salvage by the pirate captain, had been ransacked of its cargo, then set adrift.

The other prisoners were a mix of Japanese sailors and Korean slaves. Emaciated and with haunted expressions, they regarded the new arrivals warily. All stared at the strange blond-haired, blue-eyed boy in the pilgrim's outfit and whispered words of a 'white demon' and a '*gaijin* devil'.

Jack ignored them, preferring instead to concentrate on devising an escape plan. The previous night's stand-off with the Wind Demons had ended when a large net had been thrown over them. Entangled by the webbing, Jack and his friends had quickly been subdued and disarmed. There was shock at discovering Jack's foreign identity, but the pirate captain had issued orders to cage them all, announcing that he would deal with the rebellious young pilgrims and unexpected *gaijin* in the morning. But, with the sun rising, they were fast running out of time and still no closer to escape. The cage was solidly built, with a pirate guard posted at the locked gate. All their weapons and belongings, even Miyuki's hidden ninja utility belt, had been confiscated and they'd had no food, water or sleep for the entire night.

'Even if we got out of this cage,' whispered Miyuki, her fingers blistered from where she'd tried and failed to loosen the bars' bindings, 'there must be at least seventy ninja pirates on-board. Without our weapons, we'd be cut to ribbons.'

'We only need to reach the side,' replied Jack under his breath.

'What then?' asked Yori, his face exhausted and drawn. 'We're in the *middle* of the Seto Sea.'

'We time our escape as the ship passes an island . . . and swim for it.'

'Jack, we don't have the luxury of waiting for an island,' said Miyuki. 'The Wind Demons intend to kill us.'

'Or else make us slaves,' added Yori, glancing round at the haggard and hollow-eyed men in dirty loincloths.

Jack realized his friends were right. And jumping ship was a death sentence in itself. They wouldn't survive long in open water – dying either from hypothermia, drowning, or a shark attack.

'There is *some* good news,' said Saburo.

Jack and the others turned to him expectantly.

Saburo forced a smile. 'I don't feel seasick any more!'

Jack shook his head in disbelief. The old Saburo was back! But they weren't likely to enjoy each other's company much longer. A group of ninja pirates were heading across the main deck to the cage.

In the light of day the Wind Demons were even more terrifying to behold. Their black *shinobi shozoku* had been exchanged for a motley array of coarsely woven jackets, tied in at the waist with belts. A gruesome range of swords, knives and battleaxes hung from their hips. Some wore random pieces of samurai armour, spoils of war donned as badges of honour. A few paraded silk shawls, apparently having plundered the *Golden Tiger*'s hidden stock of fine silks. Most of the pirates went hatless or else tied a bandanna around their dishevelled manes of black hair. And all the men boasted an unkempt beard or drooping moustache.

But their most distinctive feature was the profusion of tattoos that decorated their bodies. One brawny pirate had a tiger emblazoned across his chest. Another had a pair of swords in the shape of a crucifix on his back. Down the leg of a tall skinny man was a two-headed red snake. Along with their own personal designs, every ninja pirate was branded with a black spider tattoo upon his neck. The man fronting this grisly gang was the most monstrous of the lot. He wore a gold earring, had blackened teeth and a deathly skull tattooed over his entire face.

'*They're going to eat us for breakfast!*' whimpered one of the *Golden Tiger*'s crew, sniffling as he wiped a hand across his nose.

The ninja pirate with the skull face leered in through the bars.

'Any of you fishermen?' he asked.

No one answered. Jack noted the slaves and Japanese sailors kept their eyes firmly fixed on the deck and their mouths shut.

'You see, we need to catch a shark,' explained Skullface. 'Help us and we'll let you go.'

At this promise of freedom, the terrified crewmember of the *Golden Tiger* proclaimed, 'I'm a fisherman! I'll help!'

The ninja pirate grinned, his mouth a gaping black hole in his skull tattoo. 'Excellent.'

He indicated to the guard to open the gate. Jack realized this might be their only chance of escape. If he leapt on the guard, the others could make a break for it. But Miyuki laid a hand on Jack's arm and silently shook her head. The ninja pirates were diligent, two of them held barbed spears pointed at the gate's entrance. Anyone who attempted to get out would be skewered like a suckling pig.

The crewman eagerly climbed from the cage and followed the pirates over to the starboard side, where a block and tackle had been rigged. The man gazed at it in bewilderment.

'The sharks in these waters are really BIG!' explained Skull-face.

Desperate to prove useful, the crewman replied, 'Then you'll need squid or . . . a whole mullet fish to catch one.'

Skullface pulled thoughtfully at his gold earring as he considered the suggestion. Behind him, his gang had begun to snigger.

'We don't have a mullet, but . . .'

Without warning, Skullface struck the crewman across the jaw. The man went sprawling to the deck. Three ninja pirates pinned his arms and legs, while the tiger-tattooed pirate bound the end of a rope to his ankle. A second later they'd hoisted their prisoner into the air. Dazed and confused, the crewman flailed his arms in an attempt to right himself.

'. . . we do have you.'

'He's a frisky one!' grunted the pirate with the sword cruci- fix tattoo.

Skullface pulled out a knife from his belt and slashed its blade across the crewman's forearm. Blood dripped from the wound on to the deck. 'That'll get a feeding frenzy started.'

As the tiger-tattooed pirate swung their live bait over the side, the crewman started begging for his life. 'PLEASE! I've a wife and child at home! DON'T DO IT!'

His shouts drew the attention of the other pirates on deck and they stopped what they were doing to watch. Skullface turned to the tiger-tattooed pirate, apparently having a change of heart. 'All right . . . let him go.'

For a brief second, the crewman hung there, breathing out a huge sigh of relief. Then the tiger-tattooed pirate released the rope and the crewman disappeared. There was a splash and all the ninja pirates rushed to the gunwale.

'I can see a fin already!' cried the two-headed snake pirate.

For a minute or so, there was intense silence as they followed the progress of the shark through the water. Jack and the other prisoners couldn't see the grim show – nor did they want to. There was a cry of disappointment as the shark apparently missed the bait. Then came a cheer, followed by a spluttering scream of agony.

'He's caught it,' yelled the crucifix pirate with glee. 'Tiger, pull him up!'

The tiger-tattooed pirate hauled in the rope. After several strong pulls, the crewman swung before them. His face was pale and his mouth fixed into a howl of pain. His right arm was missing, bitten off at the elbow.

'You let it go!' exclaimed the two-headed snake pirate in disappointment.

The ninja pirates laughed heartily at the joke. Jack felt sickened to the pit of his stomach.

'Try again,' ordered Skullface. 'This time ensure a shark takes a good hold.'

The bleeding crewman was dumped back into the sea. The water churned and the ninja pirates whooped and hollered in delight as several other sharks appeared. A bloodcurdling scream rent the air. Then all went quiet.

Tiger tugged on the line. This time it came up easily. At the end of the rope dangled a single ragged leg.

Skullface cuffed Tiger round the head. 'Idiot! You lost the bait!'

# 15

# CAPTAIN KUROGUMO

'*That's* why the *Fuma* are more pirate than ninja,' said Miyuki darkly, as Skullface and his gang left the disembodied leg swinging in the wind, just beyond the reach of the snapping sharks. 'They lack any spirit of *ninniku*.'

Jack understood. *Ninniku* was the ninja's equivalent of the samurai code of *bushido*. As part of their training, a ninja strived to cultivate a pure and compassionate heart, one that didn't harbour grudges and always sought peace and harmony. In Jack's eyes, these Wind Demons didn't even possess a heart.

'But that's not the only reason why the ninja and *Fuma* are enemies,' continued Miyuki, talking to divert their attention away from the grim reminder of their own potential fate. 'Twenty years ago, the *Fuma* clashed with the ninja. Grand-master Soke told me the whole story . . .'

Jack, Saburo and Yori gathered closer to listen – anything but think about the crewman's horrific death.

'The ninja Grandmaster Hattori and his clan were hired by the *daimyo* of Suo Province to wipe out the Wind Demons, who'd been raiding villages up and down the Seto coastline. Hattori set sail with a fleet of warships. He found the *Fuma* hiding in Beppu Bay. There was a great battle. Hattori destroyed almost all the Wind Demons' boats. It seemed victory was assured. But the *Fuma* sent a fireship into the midst of Hattori's fleet. Knowing that it could explode at any moment, Hattori gave the command to withdraw. What he didn't know was that the *Fuma* had swum beneath their ships and disabled their rudders. With no way to avoid a collision, Hattori ordered his men to jump ship, but to their horror they discovered the whole bay was covered in a slick of oil. Before any of them could swim to safety, the *Fuma* ignited the trap and the whole clan, including Hattori himself, perished in the flames.'

'That's a cheery bedtime story,' said Saburo.

'It's meant as a warning,' replied Miyuki. 'The *Fuma* are merciless *and* cunning. That makes them very dangerous. Soke cautioned me to steer clear of them at all costs.' She gave a resigned sigh. 'I was never any good at following Soke's advice.'

'We're doomed then!' cried the last crewmember of the *Golden Tiger*.

'Hey, we did survive the sea dragon at least!' said Saburo, half-heartedly attempting to lift the man's spirits. But the reminder of that fearsome beast just turned the crewman into a quivering wreck.

'That's true . . .' said Jack, still doubting his own eyes as to what he *actually* saw. 'If that was a dragon, why didn't it attack the Wind Demons? We might have stood a chance if they'd had to battle a monster too.'

A lice-ridden slave coughed and shuffled over. His eyes had a crazed look and his bare back showed the scars of numerous whippings.

'The *Fuma* control the dragon,' he croaked.

Jack and his friends regarded the Korean man dubiously.

'No man has such power over wild beasts,' said Yori.

The slave cackled. 'The Wind Demons aren't men. They're gods of the Seto Sea! And we're no more than fish food . . .'

He trailed off, a terrified expression on his face as he retreated towards the back of the cage.

'I trust my crew are treating you well?' enquired a gruff voice.

Jack and his friends looked up into the intimidating face of the pirate captain. His eyes were snake-like gleams of jet-black, his high cheekbones were sharp and his chin pointed with a long tuft of beard. He still wore the dragon-horned helmet and was robed in a green and black suit of body armour; the breastplate and square shoulder guards were constructed from hundreds of tiny leather scales that gave it the appearance of dragon skin. The pirate captain's right arm was tattooed with a large spider's web that stretched all the way from his wrist to his neck, where a black widow spider nestled, the tattoo unsettlingly real.

Despite the man's fearsome demeanour, Miyuki was outraged by the question. '*Treating us well?* They just fed one of us to the sharks!'

'Sharks are hungry animals,' the pirate captain stated matter-of-factly, grinning to reveal a set of teeth filed into razor-sharp points.

Yori, who was closest, recoiled in horror. The captain laughed at his reaction.

'Captain Kurogumo at your service. Welcome aboard the *Black Spider*,' he said, bowing contemptuously. His shark-like grin vanished. 'Now! Who are you?'

'We're . . . just pilgrims returning from Shikoku Island,' replied Yori, quickly regaining his composure.

'And I'm the Emperor,' he mocked. 'It's evident from your weapons and swords skills that you're far from pilgrims.'

'We're samurai,' said Saburo with pride.

Captain Kurogumo regarded Saburo for a moment. 'You may be. But *she* certainly isn't.'

He returned his attention to Miyuki, who stared defiantly back.

'Your weapons and clothes in the bag are of ninja origin. What clan do you belong to?'

Miyuki stayed tight-lipped.

'No matter. A ninja is a ninja. All traitors.'

Seeing Miyuki rile at the insult to her honour, Jack had to restrain her. Her fiery temper would get them into even more serious trouble than they already were. And they each needed to keep a level head if they were to have any hope of escape.

Captain Kurogumo noted Jack's intervention.

'I'll deal with the ninja later,' he promised. 'But you, *gaijin*, are of real interest to me. Quite extraordinary – a *gaijin* samurai!'

He clicked his fingers and a young boy came running across the deck, carrying a pair of samurai swords. Their distinctive red handles marked them out as Jack's *daishō*. The boy, fresh-faced and eager, knelt before the captain and held the weapons out to him. Captain Kurogumo took up the *katana* and, unsheathing it, examined the blade.

'A Shizu sword!' he exclaimed in disbelief. 'Unless I'd witnessed it for myself, I'd have thought anyone a liar who told me you were a samurai . . . and I'd have cut out their tongue. But your fighting skills are undeniable. You put a number of my men to shame.'

Captain Kurogumo glanced up to where four pirates hung by their wrists from the yardarm. 'You can cut them down now,' he shouted to Skullface. 'Let's hope they've learnt their lesson and won't be beaten so easily by a *boy* next time.'

The pirate captain took a few practice swings with the *katana*. He smiled appreciatively at its perfect weight and balance. Then he struck out at the pirate boy. The blade sliced through the air, its tip stopping just short of his throat. The boy swallowed nervously as a single bead of blood welled up from where the steel point had pierced his skin.

Sheathing the blade with satisfaction, the captain asked Jack, 'Who gave you these swords?'

'A friend,' he replied.

'A very *special* friend indeed, to part with such fine blades.' With a wave of his hand, the captain ordered the pirate boy to return the swords to his quarters. 'I'm intrigued – how on earth did a *gaijin* become a samurai?'

'It wasn't by choice,' said Jack coldly. 'I was a rigging monkey on a trading ship before ninja pirates like *you* killed my father.'

'Now *that* is interesting,' said Captain Kurogumo, raising his eyebrows at the revelation. 'So, young warriors, the question is what to do with you. As samurai and ninja, you don't warrant mercy. But it's not in my nature to slaughter children . . . without good reason.'

He gave a flash of his shark teeth.

'Tatsumaki must decide your fate.'

# 16

# FUGU

Exposed on an open deck, the cage offered scant protection from the elements and Jack and his friends were forced to sit in the full glare of the sun. Although Captain Kurogumo had promised food and water, he still hadn't provided them with either. And Jack didn't hold out much hope he ever would. The pirates held little concern for the well-being of their captives.

Jack had to be grateful for small blessings, though. From their conversation with the captain, it seemed he was unaware of Jack's reputation or the bounty on his head.

'So who's Tatsumaki?' asked Jack, his mouth parched.

'Or what?' corrected Yori. 'The word means "tornado".'

'Perhaps the captain's going to set us adrift in the middle of a storm,' suggested Saburo, who looked faint from hunger. 'And let fate decide our lives.'

'Then we might have a chance,' said Jack. 'I've survived countless tempests at sea.'

The Korean slave was cackling again.

'Tatsumaki comes out of nowhere . . . creates havoc . . . then . . .' His gnarled fingers exploded outwards. '. . . disappears into nothingness.'

His wild eyes stared at the young warriors with amused pity. 'All that remains is chaos and desolation. For you to pin your hopes on Tatsumaki is like putting your head inside a hungry lion's mouth!'

The Korean slave laughed, then broke into a coughing fit. His skeletal body shuddered with the effort. Jack, along with the others, began to feel an overwhelming sense of despair at their situation. Glancing round at the despondent expressions of the other prisoners, it seemed inevitable that death would be their only way out.

The cage door opened and the pirate boy appeared with a jug of water.

'Compliments of the captain,' he said, setting it down next to Jack.

The boy retreated and the gate was closed.

Jack snatched up the water but, seeing Yori lick his dry lips in anticipation, offered the jug to his friend first.

'No, after you,' insisted Yori.

Jack lifted the brimming jug to his lips and took a huge welcome gulp. Almost at once, he gagged violently.

'It's seawater!' he rasped, spitting and hacking up bile.

The sound of hearty laughter reached their ears. Skullface and his gang were lounging beside the main mast, clapping each other on the back at their prank.

'How's the water, fishface?' jeered Snakehead, his tattoo of the two-headed serpent stretched out along his gangly legs upon the deck.

Jack vomited, expelling the last of the salt water. The pirate gang roared even louder.

'That trick never fails on new prisoners,' grinned Skullface.

Wiping the back of his hand across his mouth, Jack glared at the ninja pirate. 'Tastes better than you look!'

The other pirates stopped laughing and uttered an exaggerated cry of shock.

Skullface took the insult more seriously. Seizing a wooden club, he strode over to the cage. 'You need some respect beaten into you, *gaijin*.'

He raked the club over the bars, its studded tip clattering against the bamboo.

'You don't scare me, bonehead!' retorted Jack, trying to goad the ninja pirate.

Now Miyuki was having to restrain him. But Jack wanted to provoke Skullface into opening the gate and starting a fight. Then he could defeat the pirate, disarm him and the four of them could attempt an escape.

'You couldn't beat an egg!' taunted Jack.

Bristling at the slur, Skullface slammed his club into the bars. 'You'll regret that!'

He pushed aside the guard and went to open the gate. But at that moment a clanging filled the air. A squat cook stood at the rear cabin's doorway, thumping a large pot with a ladle.

Skullface snorted. 'Saved by the bell, *gaijin*,' he said, waving his club at Jack. 'But I'll return and beat you to a pulp.'

Skullface headed over to the disorderly queue of pirates and pushed his way to the front. The tantalizing smell of cooked rice and fish drifted towards them.

'What I'd do for some rice now,' moaned Saburo, his stomach growling.

'When we escape,' said Jack, 'you can have the biggest bowl of rice you've ever dreamed of.'

'Well, we won't be getting out of here fast if you keep picking fights, Jack,' said Miyuki. 'What were you thinking of?'

Jack explained his tactic. 'We need to make our move before we become too weak to fight back.'

'Agreed. Let me take out the guard with Fall Down Fist.'

Jack nodded his assent at the plan.

'Skullface is coming back,' whispered Yori urgently.

'OK, as soon as I step out to fight, Miyuki will jump the guard,' instructed Jack. 'Yori and Saburo, see those barrels by the port bow? Make a run for them, push a couple over the side and then we'll all jump ship together. We can use the barrels as life rafts.'

Nodding, the four friends readied themselves for their escape attempt.

But Skullface and his gang seemed to have forgotten about his promised threat. They sat themselves down by the cage, greedily stuffing their faces with food.

'Anyone hungry?' asked Skullface, wafting a plate piled high with steaming rice in front of the prisoners' noses.

Before he could help himself, Saburo replied, 'Yes! I am.'

Skullface's black hole smile reappeared.

'Of course you are,' he said, shovelling a thick slice of fresh fish into his own mouth and chewing appreciatively.

He finished his meal and stood up. 'Here's the deal. We'll feed four prisoners. No more. So who will it be?'

A Japanese sailor, skinny as a rake and with a desperate look in his eyes, threw himself to the ground. 'Me, please,' he begged.

Skullface nodded. 'Who else?'

The *Golden Tiger*'s last crewmember couldn't hold back and prostrated himself beside the sailor.

'Only two more places left for lunch,' said Skullface in a lighthearted tone.

Again, Jack noticed the Korean slave was keeping silent, despite appearing the most starved among them. None of the other prisoners were jumping at the opportunity for food either.

Skullface became impatient for volunteers. 'The plump one then,' he said, pointing to Saburo.

'And who's going to be the fourth?' asked Tiger, his eyes raking over the wretched prisoners.

'What about the *gaijin*?' the crucifix pirate suggested.

Skullface shook his head. 'No, Crux, he doesn't deserve food. Besides, I have other plans for him.' He looked round the cage. 'That miserable captain looks like he could do with cheering up.'

As the guard opened the cage to let the chosen diners out, Jack nodded to Miyuki. She made a move to rush the guard. But out of nowhere a spearhead blocked her path.

'Not so fast, my pretty one,' snarled Snakehead, keeping the spear's barb to her chest.

One by one, the four prisoners stepped out of the cage. Saburo, wary and reluctant to move, was forced out by spear tip. Skullface politely invited them all to sit in a circle facing one another.

He looked round the deck in irritation. 'Where's that new cabin boy got to?'

The young pirate appeared a moment later, carrying a large plate. Skullface snatched it from him before clipping the boy round the ear. 'Be quicker next time, or I'll invite you to lunch too.'

The pirate boy bowed apologetically, then hurried away.

With a flourish, Skullface presented the plate upon which lay four translucent slices of fish.

'*Fugu sashimi*!' he announced.

Miyuki gasped. Jack saw the look of horror on her face. 'What's the matter?'

'*Fugu* is highly toxic,' she replied. 'It's the most deadly poison a ninja can use. We put it on blowdarts. You *can* eat *fugu*, but it must be prepared properly. Otherwise you'll die.'

The four prisoners were clearly aware of the lethal nature of the dish before them. The captain of the *Golden Tiger* got to his feet.

'Thank you,' he blustered, 'but I'm not that hungry.'

The pirate Crux shoved the captain back down. 'Don't you know it's rude to leave the table before you've finished.'

Skullface leant over the prisoners and, with a twisted grin, announced, 'Only *one* slice of the *fugu* is poisonous. Enjoy your meal!'

# 17

# DYING

The four prisoners glanced at each other in wide-eyed panic. On the plate, death awaited one of them. But the four slices looked identical. No one wanted to make that first choice.

'Eat up!' encouraged Skullface, holding a knife to Saburo's throat. 'Or die . . .'

Faced with no alternative, Saburo extended a trembling hand. Undecided, it hovered over the plate of *fugu*.

'Don't do it, Saburo!' cried Jack, shaking the bars of his cage in impotent rage. He couldn't believe the pirates were gambling with his friend's life like this.

'Shut your trap!' snapped Skullface, savouring the futility of Jack's protests. 'He's got a one-in-four chance.'

Cajoled by the knife at his neck, Saburo selected the slice furthest from him. Taking a deep breath, he placed it tentatively on his tongue. Then, closing his eyes, he began to chew.

'Swallow it all,' insisted Skullface.

With a forced effort, Saburo consumed the potentially deadly fish. Once Skullface was satisfied that every bit was gone, he removed the knife and moved on to his next victim – the crewman.

In a frantic bid to escape the fatal meal, the crewman scrambled away. But Tiger seized him by the hair and dragged him back. Wrenching the man's head up, Tiger held his jaw open. Skullface, using the tip of his knife, delicately picked a *fugu* slice and dropped it into the man's throat before clamping his mouth shut. Choking, the crewman eventually swallowed the fish whole and Tiger let him go.

Resigned to his fate, the Japanese sailor took the slice nearest him and, in full knowledge that this could be his last meal, he savoured every bite.

With three slices gone, the captain tried to stall for time. He clearly hoped he would see some telltale symptoms in the other prisoners before he had to commit to eating the last piece of *fugu*.

'No point holding out,' said Skullface. 'The effects aren't immediate.'

With violent encouragement from Crux, the captain of the *Golden Tiger* ate the last remaining slice. The four prisoners stared at one another, grimly awaiting the signs that one of them was dying . . . meaning they would live. As this sick game progressed, the pirates started to bet on the outcome.

'I'll wager three pieces of silver that the fat one dies,' said Skullface.

'Four pieces on the captain,' said Crux, giving his charge an encouraging pat on the shoulder.

More stakes were placed as a crowd of pirates gathered round for the macabre spectacle. The four prisoners became pale with dread. Inside one of their stomachs a poison was slowly leaking into their bloodstream, all for the entertainment of the Wind Demons.

'My lips are tingling!' gasped Saburo, turning to Miyuki in terror.

The betting among the pirates reached fever pitch at this revelation.

'That's normal,' reassured Miyuki. 'It's the reason why people eat *fugu* in the first place.'

Saburo calmed a little, but Jack could see he was close to hysteria. And he couldn't blame his friend.

'No more bets,' announced Skullface, and the ninja pirates settled down to await the outcome.

Still none of the prisoners displayed any symptoms of poisoning. Jack began to hope that Skullface was simply playing a cruel joke on them. But the betting had been deadly serious and Jack realized his optimism was misplaced.

The Japanese sailor picked at his teeth to reveal bloody gums and this triggered a frenzy of excitement among the pirates. But Jack knew this was more likely the result of malnutrition than poison.

The tension grew as the time ticked by.

Jack clasped the bars of the cage and whispered, 'You'll be fine, Saburo. I'm sure you will.'

Saburo glanced at Jack, a resigned expression on his face. He attempted a brave smile. 'My mother always said my appetite would get the better of me one day.'

'Look! My one is winning,' Snakehead cried excitedly.

He pointed to a bright red rash that was blossoming over the skin of his chosen bet. The other pirates studied the unlucky *fugu* victim.

Realizing all eyes were on him, the crewman glanced down

at his erupting skin. He broke into a cold sweat and began to claw at his neck.

'*Water!*' he begged. '*My throat's burning.*'

The crewman tried to stand, but his legs gave way and he collapsed to the deck. His body started convulsing as he lost all coordination.

'Ple . . . eeease . . . help . . . me . . . breathe . . .'

The crewman's speech became incoherent. He floundered on the deck like a suffocating fish. As the crewman died before their eyes, there was a great shout of triumph.

'*Yes! It's not me!*' cried the captain, punching the air in joyous relief.

The crewman's movements gradually weakened until he lay still, an occasional blink being the only vital sign he was alive. Then he gave a last shuddering breath and his eyes became fixed in a dead stare.

Snakehead and several other pirates began celebrating their win, while the rest of the crowd cursed their bad luck and dispersed. Jack himself experienced a bitter twist of emotions – elation that Saburo had survived and immense sadness at the passing of the crewman. No man should have to suffer such a horrible and agonizing death.

With the show over, the three surviving prisoners were flung back into the cage. Saburo rejoined his friends, who welcomed him with open arms. The captain, still grinning at his fortune, slumped gratefully in his corner. But the Japanese sailor remained where he'd been thrown, a rash visible across his face, his body twitching erratically, barely breathing.

'Oh dear,' said Skullface with mock concern. 'It appears the cook didn't prepare *any* of the *fugu* properly.'

He began to laugh, a cruel cackle that rose in pitch as the captain and Saburo's expressions changed from relief to deep shock. Skullface strode away with his gang, leaving the three prisoners to their fate.

As the bleak realization sank in, the captain began to blubber. 'NO . . . no . . . not me . . . I don't want to die.'

The Japanese sailor was no longer breathing and his body lay still.

'I can't feel . . . my tongue,' said Saburo in alarm.

Without wasting a second, Miyuki grabbed the jug of seawater and brought it to Saburo's lips.

'Drink!'

Saburo stared at her in bewilderment, but she forced the jug into his mouth, making him take several gulps. Saburo immediately vomited at her feet.

'What are you doing?' exclaimed Jack, rushing to support his friend.

'More!' ordered Miyuki, tipping the jug up. 'If we can flush his stomach of the poison, there's a chance he may survive.'

Saburo heaved again, and this time small slivers of half-digested translucent fish splattered across the deck.

In the corner, the captain was sobbing loudly. 'I don't want . . . to die . . . don't want to . . .'

'Stick your fingers down your throat,' instructed Miyuki, but the captain was too absorbed in his own self-pity to follow her advice.

Saburo was becoming drowsy. Jack and Yori eased him to the floor. They lay their friend on his side along the rear of the cage, Yori rolling his pilgrim stole into a makeshift pillow. Miyuki hunted through the folds of her clothes, pulling out a small pouch that the Wind Demons hadn't discovered on her. She rifled inside it and took out a twist of paper containing a black tablet.

'Hold his head steady,' she told Jack and Yori.

Saburo's breathing was laboured and he felt like a dead weight in Jack's hands. All of a sudden, Saburo went into spasm.

'By the love of Buddha, stay with us,' pleaded Yori, tears running down his cheeks.

Saburo's convulsion eased and he turned weakly to Yori. 'Not . . . going . . . anywhere . . . my friend.'

'Eat this,' Miyuki ordered, shoving the black square into Saburo's mouth.

'It tastes . . . disgusting,' lisped Saburo.

'Of course it does, it's charcoal. It'll bind with the toxin inside you and prevent further absorption. Now swallow it, before your body can't even do that.'

Saburo crunched down on the tablet. On the other side of the cage, there was a heavy thump as the captain keeled over, clutching his chest.

Jack and Yori gently lay Saburo back on his pillow. His lips twitched into a sad smile.

'Wish . . . I was . . . seasick . . . now . . .' he wheezed.

Kneeling by his side, Yori put his hands together and began to murmur incantations.

Jack turned to Miyuki. 'Is there nothing *more* we can do for him? It's a ninja poison – don't you have an antidote?'

Miyuki gravely shook her head. 'There's no known antidote to *fugu*. But Saburo's strong. All we can do now is wait and pray.'

# 18

# PIRATE BOY

Saburo gazed up into Jack's face. He looked almost peaceful. But Jack knew that was the effect of the *fugu*. Miyuki had explained that the fish's toxin slowly paralysed the muscles, leaving the victim fully conscious until the lungs gave out and the person died from suffocation. That's what made it such an effective poison for ninja assassinations.

'Can you still breathe?' asked Jack.

Saburo blinked his eyes twice. *Yes*.

'Wriggle your toes.'

Jack glanced towards Saburo's feet, but nothing moved.

'That's good,' he lied, not wishing his friend to give up hope. 'Now, can you feel your hands?'

Saburo blinked once. *No*.

'Hang on in there,' urged Jack. 'Miyuki says if you can just survive the night, you'll make a full recovery.'

Two blinks.

Yori remained at Saburo's side, deep in prayer. Jack stood and joined Miyuki where she was tying his pilgrim jacket to the bars as a sunshade for Saburo. It was now mid-afternoon, the sun relentless as the pirate ship continued on its southern course. Jack helped her secure the last corner.

'So how many people have survived *fugu* poisoning?' asked Jack under his breath.

Miyuki thought for a moment. 'One.'

Jack stopped what he was doing and stared at her in disbelief.

'That I know of,' added Miyuki hurriedly. 'It was Soke. That's how I knew what to do to limit the poison.'

'So what happens if Saburo stops breathing?'

Miyuki chewed her lower lip, her expression uncertain. 'If it comes to that, I'll have to breathe for him.'

Jack furrowed his brow. 'What do you mean?'

'I'll blow air into his lungs – hopefully keeping him alive until the poison wears off and he can breathe on his own again.'

Jack had never heard of such a bizarre remedy, but he trusted Miyuki and the mystic healing abilities of the ninja, having benefited from their skills himself.

'Can't you also use *kuji-in*?' he suggested.

Miyuki considered this. 'Ninja magic won't have any effect on the poison . . . although *Sha* might keep his heart and organs strong. It's worth a try.'

Miyuki knelt close to Saburo. Clasping her hands together, she extended the index finger and thumb to make the hand sign for *Sha*. With eyes shut, she moved her hands in figure-of-eight patterns over his chest and chanted the healing mantra.

'*On haya baishiraman taya sowaka* . . .'

Saburo's laboured breathing seemed to calm almost at once. Sitting next to Miyuki as she performed the ritual, Jack used his pilgrim stole to waft cool air over Saburo's prone body while Yori continued to pray, each of them doing what they could to save their friend's life.

It was too late for the captain, however. Although his body still twitched occasionally, the poison had seeped into every limb and muscle. His eyes flickered around in despair, his life ebbing away with each feeble breath.

'He'll be fish food soon,' the Korean slave muttered. 'We're *all* fish food.'

The gate opened. The pirate boy hefted a large cooking pot, which he dumped in the middle of the cage. A thin gruel of rice water slopped over the sides. The prisoners leapt hungrily at it, feeding like a pack of wild dogs.

Jack was about to go over and see what he could scavenge for his friends, when the pirate boy hastily approached. From under his arm, he produced a jug and swapped it for the empty one. Then, reaching into the folds of his jacket, he removed a couple of cooked fish and presented them to Jack.

'More poison and salt water?' enquired Jack bitterly.

'No, it's fresh,' insisted the pirate boy. 'And these are mackerel.'

Jack eyed the boy distrustfully.

'Honest. Last time Skullface made me switch the water for a joke.'

'Well, *we're* not laughing,' said Jack.

The pirate boy looked shamefaced. 'Just take them before anyone notices,' he urged. 'I'm risking the whip for you.'

His stomach knotted with hunger, Jack grabbed the fish. He dipped a finger into the jug and tasted it. The water *was* fresh. Realizing the pirate boy was genuine, he bowed his head gratefully. 'Thank you. What's your name?'

'Cheng.'

'I'm Jack.'

Cheng grinned, the smile lighting up his whole face. The boy had delicate features, with high thin eyebrows, almond eyes and fine lips. His hair was tied into a short braid at the back and his body was lithe, yet deceptively strong. He didn't appear to be the typical ninja pirate . . . or Japanese, for that matter.

'Where are you from?' asked Jack.

'A village near Penglai, China.' Cheng studied Jack with fascination. 'I've never met anyone with golden hair before —'

'Oi, cabin boy! What's taking you so long?'

Skullface was standing at the bow with his gang, coiling ropes.

'Just spitting in their food,' Cheng shouted.

Skullface grunted appreciatively. 'We'll make a pirate of you yet!'

Cheng turned back to Jack, his eyes deep wells of sympathy. 'I hope your friend lives,' he whispered, before clambering out of the cage.

Jack's faith in human nature was restored a little. Watching Cheng cross the deck back to the ship's galley, he wondered how a Chinese boy like him had ever become involved with the Wind Demons.

He picked up the jug of fresh water and leant over Saburo. 'Can you still swallow?'

Saburo blinked twice. With Yori's help, Jack raised his friend's head and offered him a few sips. Some dribbled out of the side of his mouth, but the water appeared to revive him. Jack gave Saburo a little more before letting his friend rest.

Breaking apart the two fish with his fingers, he shared their precious meal.

'Can Saburo have any?' asked Jack.

Miyuki shook her head. 'He might choke. Besides, we want the poison to pass through his system first.'

As a matter of courtesy, they sat out of Saburo's sight while the three of them devoured the mouth-watering mackerel. Immediately Jack felt his strength return. But the vital meal was over all too quickly.

As they were licking their fingers clean and drinking their ration of water, Saburo went into spasms. They rushed to his side. His breathing was erratic and his eyes bulged.

'What's happening?' asked Yori.

'The poison must have reached his lungs,' replied Miyuki. She immediately resumed her *Sha* healing ritual. But this time it had little effect. Saburo continued to shudder in the *fugu's* death grip.

'I can't channel enough *ki*,' gasped Miyuki, a bead of sweat breaking out on her brow. 'We're losing him.'

Jack immediately took up position opposite her. Having been trained in *kuji-in*, Jack knew the hand sign and mantra for *Sha*. But he'd only ever practised it on himself. He just prayed that the combined power of their *ki* would be enough.

Saburo's convulsions reached a peak. Then, little by little, they diminished until his body was only trembling, and his breathing became more steady.

'Just a little longer,' urged Miyuki, 'and we can save him.'

'Hey, *gaijin*!' snarled an all-too-familiar voice. 'We've unfinished business to settle.'

'Later,' said Jack, trying to concentrate on the healing.

'Now,' insisted Skullface.

The tip of a spear was pressed against Jack's neck.

Jack refused to budge. His friend's life was at stake.

'Don't make me push any harder,' threatened Skullface, the spear's iron barb now on the verge of puncturing his skin.

Yori knelt next to Jack and whispered, 'I'll take over if I can.' They both knew that Yori had only studied Miyuki's healing techniques and had never performed them before on anyone.

With the greatest reluctance, Jack stopped. Saburo's condition worsened. As Yori took up the *Sha* chant and began circling his hands, Jack was pushed out of the cage. Unable to take his eyes off his immobile friend, he was manhandled by Skullface's gang into the middle of the deck. A crowd of pirates had gathered in a circle to watch the *gaijin* prisoner's punishment.

Spear in hand, Skullface confronted Jack. He advanced until they were nose to nose. 'You've not only disrespected me, *gaijin*. You've upset other members of the crew.'

Four pirates stood to Jack's right, glaring at him, their wrists ringed red with rope burns. They appeared to be itching for a fight.

Jack quickly assessed his opponents. They looked tough, but he'd defeated them on-board the *Golden Tiger*. And he could defeat them again. Skullface was another matter. His scar-ridden body was evidence that he was battle-hardened and no doubt a vicious fighter. Jack realized he must overcome Skullface first, while he remained strong enough, before dealing with the other pirates.

'Let's get this over with,' said Jack, slipping off his sandals for a better grip on the wooden deck.

'Oh, you're not fighting me . . . or them,' said Skullface, with a sly grin. 'You're fighting the ship's champion, Manzo.'

Stooping to clear the cabin doorway, a ninja pirate of Herculean proportions stepped out on to the deck. Three times the size of Jack, he had a bald head solid as a cannonball, a wiry beard and fists like hammers. Muscles rippled across his broad chest and his tree-trunk legs thudded with every step upon the wooden deck. Aside from the black spider tattoo, he had a screaming demon bursting from his brick-like stomach. To complete his terrifying presence, he had *kanji* symbols branded on to the backs of his hands. His right bore the character for 'thunder':

雷

His left bore the symbols for 'lightning':

稲妻

Manzo banged them together and, fists raised, thundered towards Jack.

# 19

# FIST FIGHT

Jack felt his heart stop at the sight of this colossus. Manzo was the stuff of nightmares – a hulking mass of muscle, bearing down on him like a charging bull. The pirate wasn't carrying any weapons. This was clearly to be a fist fight. Not that it mattered – Manzo's hands *were* his weapons and could demolish Jack in a single swipe.

Dressed only in his breeches, Jack was unencumbered and would be able to move fast. And he'd have to. He couldn't afford to let his guard down against such a dangerous opponent. Bouncing on the balls of his feet, he prepared to engage with the pirate.

As Manzo lumbered towards him, Jack recalled his *taijutsu* match in the *Taryu-Jiai* three years ago. During that inter-school martial arts contest, Jack had fought Raiden, a samurai student of similar proportions to Manzo. Jack had stood little chance of beating him then. But prior to the fight he'd had a vision of a red demon and a butterfly. The demon had tried to squash the butterfly with an iron bar, but the butterfly had survived by evading the attacks until the demon collapsed with exhaustion, subdued by its own efforts.

This ninja pirate boasted a tattoo of a screaming red demon. *The vision had spoken again!* If he could tire Manzo out first, then he might be able to defeat him.

A huge fist – Thunder – rocketed towards Jack's head. Jack ducked and skipped aside. Lightning now came at him, a devastating hook punch to the ribs. Jack sucked in his stomach and arched his body. The fist shot past, grazing his skin but doing no other damage. He backed away as Thunder returned for an uppercut. Then Lightning attempted a savage cross punch.

Jack continued to evade the brutal attacks, Manzo being strong, but slow.

'Hit him!' cried Tiger.

Becoming more and more frustrated, Manzo started throwing wilder punches. Jack ducked and weaved. He bobbed beneath Thunder; jumped away from Lightning. Not a single punch landed on target and the ninja pirates, who'd been baying for blood, now began to boo and jeer at the pathetic display.

'Stop running, you coward!' heckled Crux.

'Call yourself a samurai!' derided Skullface. He beckoned to the crowd. 'Move in!'

The circle of pirates tightened, restricting the fighting distance between Jack and Manzo. As Thunder and Lightning came at him in a series of chain punches, Jack had to retreat rapidly. Unknown to him, Snakehead stuck out a foot and he tripped over it, sprawling on to the deck.

Manzo seized his chance, raising his leg high to stamp-kick Jack in the chest. There was a horrible crunching sound as his foot connected. But Jack had rolled away at the last second and it was the deck that had taken the full force of the blow.

The wooden plank splintered and Manzo's foot shot through, his ankle becoming trapped.

Jack leapt up and went on the attack. With the devastating speed and power of a trained warrior, Jack launched a round-house kick at Manzo's back.

The pirate barely registered the blow. Undeterred, Jack fired off a blazing side-kick into the ribs. Manzo grunted, but didn't crumble. Jack stepped in and drove a spear elbow at his kidneys. The pirate simply batted Jack away as if he was no more than an irritating mosquito. The swipe of his forearm sent Jack careering across the deck. Stunned, Jack cautiously circled the snared pirate. Trying not to panic, he racked his brains for a martial arts technique that might have some effect on this impregnable rock of a man.

Manzo finally managed to free his foot and turned to face Jack once more. He blew across the tops of his fists as if clearing them of dust, then he banged them together and smiled, certain of victory.

But Jack smiled too. He had a secret weapon . . . one that Sensei Yamada had taught him at the *Niten Ichi Ryū*.

*Chō-geri*.

The Butterfly Kick – a highly advanced and indefensible manoeuvre that could cut a swathe through any attack. All the limbs were extended in a position similar to that of a butterfly's wings in flight.

As the ninja pirate advanced, Jack sprang into the air, his torso twisting, his arms swinging in a wide arc. Both his legs shot out, twirling before him. The first would smash Manzo's left guard aside, the second would hammer into his head, connecting with his jaw at the knockdown point.

As tough as Manzo was, he'd drop to the deck like a sack of sand.

But Jack was out of practice. He misjudged the distance and his legs got tangled up in the complex attack. He flew past Manzo, entirely missing his target. Trying to correct his mistake, he flapped his arms like a crazed bird, only to crash-land on his back.

For a moment, there was complete silence. Then an almighty booming laugh burst from Manzo. The rest of the pirates fell about too. Jack felt an utter fool. Not only had he failed to defeat his opponent, he'd made himself a laughing stock.

'What was *that*?' cried Skullface, wiping tears from his eyes. 'Lame Duck Leaping technique?'

Badly winded, Jack tried to suck in air and clamber to his feet. Before he'd reached all fours, Manzo seized his ankle. Jack was spun headlong through the air. He collided into the mast, pain rocketing through his shoulder.

Dazed and disorientated, Jack lay in a heap at its base. The next moment he was grabbed by the throat and wrenched upwards, until his feet were kicking helplessly above the deck. Spluttering, Jack tried to break the pirate's hold. But it was futile. Manzo's grip was like a vice.

Jack felt the blood pounding in his head and his lungs started to burn. He glanced over to the cage. Yori was still performing the *Sha* mantra. But Miyuki was now bent over Saburo, fingers clasping his nose, her mouth pressed to his. She lifted her head, took a deep lungful of air, then blew into his mouth. She repeated the process and Jack caught the look of sheer desperation on her face.

He realized both he and Saburo were fighting for their lives, neither able to breathe. Jack had to fight back. But, with his legs flailing off the ground and his breath fast running out, what could he do against a man as powerful as Manzo?

The pirate grinned triumphantly and brought up his right fist to end it all.

Black spots were dotting Jack's vision. None of the samurai techniques Sensei Kyuzo had taught him were having any effect. He was out of ideas . . .

He saw Miyuki look up in horror at his plight.

'*Eight Leaves Fist!*' she cried and the day Miyuki had shown him the Sixteen Secret Fists of the ninja flashed before his eyes. He might have exhausted all his samurai skills, but he still had a ninja trick or two . . .

Cupping his hands, Jack used the last of his strength to clap Manzo either side of the head on his ears. Manzo reeled from the unexpected ninja attack. His legs buckled and he lurched to one side, the strike causing complete loss of balance. Releasing Jack, Manzo staggered across the deck as if the ship was in a ferocious storm.

Jack dropped to the floor, gulping in lungfuls of air. He rose back to his feet, using the mast for support. Meanwhile, Manzo had recovered from the shock of the blow. Furious at being robbed of his victory, he pushed through the pirates and snatched up a grappling iron lying against the gunwale. The three spiked hooks attached to the end of the stout wooden pole were like a vicious bear claw. Used for gaining purchase on an enemy vessel, the *kumode* made a deadly weapon and would rip the guts out of anyone who stood in its way.

Manzo returned to finish off his opponent, but was dumbstruck to find Jack had disappeared.

'He's gone aloft!' shouted Crux.

But Eight Leaves Fist had temporarily deafened Manzo as well. The pirates had to point to where Jack was escaping to. Still unsteady on his feet, Manzo used the *kumode* to help him climb the mast after Jack.

Returning to familiar territory, Jack's skills as a rigging monkey flooded back. He shimmied to the top without effort. Spreading his arms for balance, he then walked out along the main spar.

Manzo clambered up to his level. At this height, the mast swayed like a pendulum. The pirate looked nervous and uncomfortable. His bulky physique was fine for pulling in ropes, but totally unsuited for rigging duties.

Clutching on to the mast, Manzo tentatively stepped on to the spar and slashed with the grappling iron. Jack shuffled backwards beyond the claw's reach. Leaning out, Manzo took another swipe at Jack. The bear claw passed a hair's breadth from his bare chest. But Jack had reached the end of the spar.

'Nowhere to go!' snarled Manzo.

'Come and get me then,' goaded Jack.

Lured by how close he was to winning, Manzo let go of the mast for a last attack. As he swung the *kumode*, the ship rocked to one side and he lost his footing. Arms flailing, Manzo tumbled through the air. He smashed into the deck below, buckling the wooden boards. The great man-mountain lay spread-eagled, groaning briefly before falling unconscious.

*The bigger they are, the harder they fall*, thought Jack.

The pirates were enraged at the defeat of their champion. 'Bring me bow and arrows!' demanded Skullface.

The next moment Skullface had an arrow trained on Jack.

Jack darted along the spar. He felt a brush of feathers and heard a soft *whoosh* as the arrow clipped his arm, drawing a thin line of blood.

Clinging to the mast, Jack saw more pirates run to fetch their bows. Skullface's furious response was now turned into a game. They nocked their arrows and took aim.

'First to hit the *gaijin* earns a jug of *saké*!' promised Skullface. 'Two jugs if you kill him!'

# 20

# SEA SAMURAI

Jack was a sitting target. It would only take a single arrow to dislodge him and he'd plummet to his death. His choices were limited. He could jump into the sea – yet even if he survived the fall, he'd be adrift in open water and where would that leave Saburo and his friends? Or he could make a leap for the rigging and slide to the deck. That would certainly be faster than descending the mast. But he'd still be faced with a gang of armed pirates.

An arrow skimmed past his nose. Another struck the mast by his hand.

Deciding he'd at least be able to fight back on deck, Jack prepared to jump for the rigging. With the ship swaying, it was a dangerous and daring move. He couldn't afford to misjudge the leap . . .

'*HOLD YOUR FIRE!*'

Captain Kurogumo had appeared on the stern's upper deck. Behind him stood Cheng, looking anxiously up at Jack. The crew lowered their weapons.

'What's all this about?' demanded the captain.

'The *gaijin* was trying to escape,' explained Skullface.

Noting the fallen Manzo, Captain Kurogumo glanced up. 'And *where* exactly is he escaping to?'

Skullface's mouth opened then closed. He struggled for a reply as the captain's jet-black eyes bored into him.

'H . . . he's a troublemaker.'

'He's a *gaijin*,' replied Captain Kurogumo. '*And* a samurai that shouldn't be underestimated. Now lock him back in the cage.'

Skullface and the other pirates bowed obediently. Turning to his gang, he ordered, 'You heard the captain. Bring him down, Snakehead.'

'Why me?' complained the ninja pirate.

'Because you're a rigger and –'

'*SUIGUN!*' cried the lookout on the foremast.

The pirates all froze.

'Where?' shouted Captain Kurogumo, baring his shark teeth in displeasure.

'Sea Samurai to starboard,' replied the lookout, pointing towards a nearby island.

From Jack's perch atop the main mast, he too spied a fleet charging out of a hidden bay. Its flagship was an immense *atake-bune* with a giant golden shell emblazoned upon its mainsail. The boat was flanked by three smaller *seki-bune* battleships and four open-decked *kobaya* galleys. This had to be the patrol from Imabari. Judging by their sudden appearance and the speed of their attack, they'd been lying in wait for the pirates.

'MAN YOUR STATIONS!' the captain commanded.

The ninja pirates instantly forgot about Jack as the ship erupted into furious activity. The Wind Demons raced to their positions, seizing weapons, donning breastplates and raising defences. Black brocade curtains were lined along the gunwales, fire buckets lit and set upon the deck, muskets primed. In a matter of moments the unruly pirates were transforming into a well-drilled fighting machine.

The Sea Samurai surged across the waves, powered by the thrust of their oars and the wind in their sails. The insistent beat of the boats' drums grew louder and more urgent. On the top decks, Jack saw rows of archers preparing to launch their first volley.

This was just the opportunity he and his friends had been praying for. Amid the chaos of battle they could make their escape. Jack threw himself for the rigging just as the opening salvo of arrows hailed down – some were on fire, aiming to set the sails ablaze. Jack caught hold of a rope, swinging in mid-air, before he wrapped his legs round and slid hand over hand down to the deck.

With all eyes on the attacking Sea Samurai, Jack picked his way through the pirates towards the cage. He spotted Manzo's *kumode* lying beside him and snatched it up. Taking the last few paces at speed, Jack rushed the guard and slammed the wooden end of the grappling iron into his jaw. Not expecting an attack from behind, the guard dropped like a felled tree.

As his body thumped to the deck, there was a bloodcurdling roar. Jack looked up, thinking his escape attempt had been discovered. But the three *seki-bune* had closed round the *Black Spider* and the Wind Demons were sounding their battle cry. The air was filled with the *crack* of muskets, the acrid reek of gunpowder and the *whoosh* of flaming arrows. A deep boom rolled like thunder as a cannon was fired. A moment later, a huge geyser of water foamed over the bow of the *Black Spider*.

Another deluge of arrows rained on to the deck. Three ninja pirates cried out as the steel tips found their target.

Several arrows clattered off the bamboo cage, one passing through and impaling a Korean prisoner in the arm. Inside, Miyuki and Yori huddled over Saburo's body. Jack noticed neither of them were performing *Sha* and Miyuki had given up breathing for him.

*He was too late!*

Jack rammed the bear claw of the *kumode* into the gate's bars. Throwing all his weight against it, he forced the lock apart and the gate sprang open. He darted over to his friends.

'Is Saburo . . . *dead*?' asked Jack, almost too afraid to utter the fatal word.

Miyuki turned to him, her face drawn and exhausted. 'No, I think he's over the worst of it . . . but we still need to keep an eye on him.'

Letting out a sigh of relief, Jack smiled at his incapacitated friend. Tugging his pilgrim jacket from the bars, he said, 'We have to escape right *now*. Do you understand?'

Saburo blinked twice.

Miyuki grabbed Jack's arm. 'Saburo can't swim. How do you expect to get him off the boat?'

'We tie him to a barrel and tow him.'

'It's too dangerous,' argued Miyuki. 'He's still paralysed. If he swallows just one mouthful of water, he could drown.'

'We've got no choice. There's an island nearby. We escape now . . . or die at the Wind Demons' will –' An explosion rocked the boat, wood splintering as a cannonball ripped through the deck. 'Or by the hands of the Sea Samurai!'

Arrows peppered the brocade curtains, shredding them and

setting others alight. In the background, the *atake-bune* loomed closer, turning its guns broadside.

'The decision is not for us to make,' said Yori.

The three of them looked to Saburo.

'Do *you* want to swim for it?' asked Jack.

Two blinks.

# REPEL BOARDERS

Lifting Saburo on to their shoulders, Jack and Miyuki staggered out of the cage. The other prisoners had already fled, all except the lice-ridden Korean slave.

'Get out of here while you can,' urged Jack.

But the Korean merely sat in the corner, picking at the scraps in the cooking pot and observing the battle. He sniggered each time a ninja pirate was wounded or killed.

'And miss *this*?' he cackled. 'Revenge never tasted so sweet.'

The *atake-bune* fired its cannon. The mid-section of the starboard gunwale exploded in a shower of splintering wood, bone and flesh. The Korean applauded the destruction.

Leaving the slave to relish the battle's bloody progress, Jack and the others stumbled away. Yori was out front, holding the *kumode* to fend off any ninja pirates. But the Wind Demons were all intent upon repelling the Sea Samurai. They were ditching the burning curtains and firing a barrage of arrows and musket shot at the enemy ships. Several of the pirates carried handheld cannon that they rested on the bulwark. Lighting the fuses, they bombarded an advancing *kobaya*, dismembering the samurai crew on-board and sinking the boat.

'Hurry!' urged Jack as one of the *seki-bune* came alongside the *Black Spider*. Its mainsail had been dropped and the mast lowered to form a bridge on to the pirate ship. But Saburo was a dead weight, his feet dragging behind as they struggled over to the barrels on the port side.

Grappling irons were thrown and the *Black Spider* held fast. A heavy iron ball bounced on to the deck before them, a short fuse burning fiercely.

'*TAKE COVER!*' screamed Miyuki, dropping Saburo beside a pile of coiled ropes and diving on top of him.

Jack and Yori threw themselves next to their friends just as the *horoku* bomb detonated. Iron shards tore in all directions, shredding canvas, timber and pirates alike. As the smoke cleared, screaming filled the air and a massive hole was blasted in the deck. Sea Samurai were clambering across the *seki-bune*'s bridging mast.

'REPEL BOARDERS!' cried Captain Kurogumo, who wielded a fearsome crossbow. He fired off a bolt. It struck the first samurai in the chest, passing straight through to kill the samurai behind as well. They both toppled into the sea between the two boats.

As the captain reloaded, another wave of samurai charged on to the *Black Spider* and the Wind Demons engaged them in brutal hand-to-hand combat. Jack raised his head above the cover of the ropes, which had been ripped to ribbons by the *horoku*'s devastating destruction. The Sea Samurai fought tooth-and-claw for supremacy of the *Black Spider* and, as the Wind Demons were pushed back, the route to the bow became blocked.

'We need our weapons,' said Miyuki.

Jack nodded, also aware that he couldn't jump ship without his father's *rutter*. He saw Cheng rush past with a bucket of sand to douse a fire taking hold near the mast. Jack ran over and grabbed the pirate boy.

'Where are our belongings?' he demanded.

Shocked to see Jack and his friends free, Cheng hesitated to reply.

'Our weapons!' urged Jack. 'We *just* want to escape.'

Looking round at the Wind Demons' desperate situation, Cheng came to a decision. 'In the captain's cabin. Follow me.'

'Stay there and protect Saburo,' Jack called to Miyuki and Yori as he raced after Cheng.

They sprinted towards the ship's stern, passing Manzo who sat rubbing his bald head, staring in utter disbelief at the battle raging around him. Skullface and his gang were embroiled in a bitter conflict with a unit of Sea Samurai. Although they were outnumbered, they fought like wild animals, hacking the invaders to pieces.

Reaching the cabin, Cheng slid open the door and led Jack down a corridor. Inside it was dark and cool, the sounds of fighting seeming distant as they ran to the far door.

The captain's cabin was simple and understated. There was a *tatami* straw bed in one corner, several seating cushions and a long, low wooden table. Light filtered in through bamboo slats and Jack could see his swords and Miyuki's utility belt laid out across the table's surface. Their canvas sack was beside it on the floor, along with their pilgrim bags. Jack quickly hunted through them for the *rutter*. But it wasn't there.

'What are you looking for?' asked Cheng.

'A logbook,' replied Jack, his panic rising.

'Is this it?'

Jack turned to Cheng, who stood beside the bed. There lay the *rutter*, its pages open. The captain had evidently been trying to decipher it, when he'd heard the commotion on deck earlier.

'Thank you,' said Jack, relieved, as Cheng handed him the logbook.

Wrapping it carefully in its waterproof oilskin, Jack placed the *rutter* inside the canvas bag along with all their other belongings. Jack slipped his swords through his belt and grabbed his straw hat. Even in the midst of the battle, he didn't want to stand out.

'If any of the crew stop us,' said Cheng, helping Jack pick up the bag, 'I'll say you forced me at knife point.'

Jack nodded and grinned. 'I was going to anyway!'

Above them, the sound of feet thundered across the upper deck.

'Enemy to the stern!' came a cry, followed by the clash of swords.

'We're running out of time,' said Jack, hurrying down the corridor.

He and Cheng emerged into the sunlight. The *Black Spider* was swarming with samurai. Yet still the Wind Demons fought on.

'Summon the dragon!' ordered Captain Kurogumo, firing off his last crossbow bolt before drawing his sword to behead an unfortunate samurai.

The lookout lit the fuse of a black cylinder attached to the foremast. It sparked, then a bright red flare shot up into the sky, blazing a trail of smoke that would be seen for miles. Not wanting to be around when the sea dragon made an appearance, Jack ran as fast as he could to Miyuki and the others. He handed Yori his *shakujō* and Miyuki her *ninjatō*.

'We can't fight *and* hold Saburo,' said Miyuki.

'I'll help carry him,' offered Cheng.

Putting Yori's staff under Saburo's arms, Yori and Cheng managed to lift his inert body off the ground. Jack and Miyuki drew their swords and began to fight their way through the confusion of combat. Pirate or samurai, they didn't care – just as long as they edged closer to the barrels.

They were almost to the bow, when a fresh unit of Sea Samurai boarded the *Black Spider*, forming an impenetrable barrier of swords and armour. The unit's commander confronted Jack, blocking his path with his *katana*.

'There's no escape . . . pirate boy.'

## 22

# A Pirate's Punishment

Jack stood, head bowed, on the deck of the *atake-bune* flagship. His friends were by his side, Saburo at his feet, immobile but breathing steadily. The surviving Wind Demons, bloody and beaten, were next to them – including Captain Kurogumo, with Skullface and his gang. They were *all* held in check by a contingent of samurai guards, armed with spears.

Their situation had gone from bad to worse. Not only had the Sea Samurai captured them but they believed Jack and his friends to be ninja pirates!

The guards parted to let through a samurai in blue ceremonial armour. The man's face was stern and his stare as cold as stone. His cheeks were pinched and he had a pencil-thin moustache that drooped either side of a downturned mouth. On his head, he wore an ornate helmet with a large golden shell-crest set upon its peak. And in his right hand, he held a short stick with a hard brass tip, storm-tossed waves decorating its surface.

'I'm Captain Arashi, commander of *daimyo* Mori's naval forces.'

At this news, there was a sharp intake of breath from several

124

of the pirates. Captain Arashi preened his moustache between finger and thumb, apparently satisfied with the response. 'I'm glad you've heard of me – or at least, my reputation. If you cooperate, it'll make your punishment far swifter . . . although no less painful.'

He planted the tip of his stick under the jaw of the nearest Wind Demon, Crux, forcing the pirate to look him in the eye.

'Where's your pirate base located?'

Crux remained tight-lipped. With crippling speed, Captain Arashi rammed the brass tip into Crux's throat. The ninja pirate staggered backwards, choking loudly and gasping for air.

'I only ever ask a question once,' stated Captain Arashi. 'And I *expect* a truthful answer.'

Crux glared at the samurai before spitting blood at the man's feet.

Captain Arashi shook his head with disappointment. He turned to two of the guards. 'Keel-haul this one.'

Crux's eyes widened in horror as he was seized and his hands bound behind his back. The two guards dragged him over to the starboard bulwark. They tied a stout line under his arms and around his chest. The line had been threaded through a block hung from the lower yardarm and passed under the ship. The end of the rope on the port side was fastened to Crux's ankles.

'Hoist him,' ordered the captain.

The two guards raised Crux off the deck and clear of the starboard bulwark. As he swung above the water, the other pirates looked grimly on.

'May this be a lesson to you all,' said Captain Arashi, indicating for the guards to let go of the line.

Screaming, Crux dropped out of view and plunged into the sea.

'Are they *drowning* him?' whispered Yori in alarm.

Jack, who'd heard of the punishment of keel-hauling from other sailors on-board the *Alexandria*, shook his head. 'No, it's far worse than that.'

The two guards pulled on the line until it went taut. Then, hand over hand, they hauled in the rope from the opposite bulwark. At one point, the line appeared to have stuck on the keel and they needed help to yank it free.

Crux eventually reappeared on the port side . . . or what was left of him.

Yori covered his eyes, nearly fainting from shock. Crux's body had been dragged across the barnacles on the hull. The rough shells had grated the skin and flesh from Crux's stomach, chest and face. The pirate was completely unrecognizable, his crucifix tattoo the only remaining clue to his identity. Blood poured from the open wounds.

'A fitting punishment for a pirate,' said Captain Arashi with satisfaction.

He let the tortured pirate hang there for all to witness the gruesome fate that awaited them. A spluttering of breath was heard from Crux's torn lips. Half-drowned, the ninja pirate wasn't dead yet.

'And again!' said the captain, indifferent to the man's suffering.

The Wind Demons stood in sickened silence as their fellow pirate was hauled under the ship once more. This time, all that emerged from the sea was a ragged carcass of lifeless flesh.

Captain Arashi approached the next Wind Demon in line.

'Where's your pirate base located?'

Despite the grisly threat hanging from the yardarm, the pirate didn't answer. It became apparent to Jack that the Wind Demons must have their own code of honour. Like *bushido* or *ninniku*, these men had made an unbreakable oath that bound them to silence, even in the face of torture and death.

'Cut off his hands,' ordered Captain Arashi, his patience at an end.

A samurai stepped forward, *katana* drawn. 'Hold out your arms.'

The pirate refused, so another guard forced his limbs into position. The *katana*'s steel blade flashed through the air; the punishment over in the blink of an eye. Two soft fleshy lumps thudded on to the deck. A second later, the pirate began shrieking in agony, clutching his bloody stumps to his chest.

'He's bleeding all over my ship,' complained the captain. 'Throw him to the sharks.'

Jack was starting to reel from the sadistic brutality of Captain Arashi. The Sea Samurai were proving as cruel and heartless as the Wind Demons. Jack held out little hope that the captain would show either him or his friends a single ounce of mercy.

A third pirate refusing to answer was pulled from the line and bound, shirtless, to the mast. A muscular samurai held a short rope of nine waxed cords, each with a small knot in the end.

'One hundred lashes,' commanded Captain Arashi.

Jack gasped. That number was a death sentence.

The samurai commenced the flogging and the pirate screamed as the knotted rope whipped across his bare back and tore into his skin. By the time four dozen lashes had been inflicted, the pirate's back resembled raw meat.

Yet still the punishment continued ... 49 ... 50 ... 51 ... 52 ...

The flesh became mangled and the pirate hung limp from his bindings.

... 74 ... 75 ... 76 ...

The pirate no longer screamed. Flogged to death.

Captain Arashi approached Yori, who stood trembling before him. 'I hope *you* won't need persuasion, little one.'

Yori looked up with fearful eyes. 'But we're *not* pirates. We're samurai!'

Captain Arashi raised an eyebrow in amusement. 'I haven't heard that one before.'

'It's the truth. We were held prisoners by the Wind Demons.'

'I only have *your* word for that. Why should I believe you? My commanding officer informs me that you were fighting his men.'

'We were only trying to escape from the pirates' ship.'

Captain Arashi backhanded Yori across the jaw. 'I despise people who lie.'

'We're not lying,' pleaded Yori, a thin stream of blood running from the corner of his mouth. 'We'd been on a pilgrimage to Shikoku Island when our boat was attacked ...'

Captain Arashi ignored him and glanced down at Saburo. 'What's the matter with him?'

'Poisoned by the pirates,' replied Miyuki.

The captain snorted. 'Quick answer, young girl, but don't think that will convince me of your innocence.' He kicked

Saburo's prone body and got no reaction. 'Throw this corpse overboard too.'

'NO! He's only paralysed!' protested Jack from beneath his hat.

Captain Arashi's eyes narrowed. He stepped over Saburo to confront the straw-hatted pirate boy. Putting his stick's brass tip to the brim, he pushed the hat clear of Jack's face.

'By all the storms in the sea, I never expected to lay eyes on *you*!'

# 23

# THE BILGE

'The Shogun will bestow great fortune upon us for capturing the *gaijin* samurai,' Captain Arashi declared to his crew. He reassessed the group of five before him. 'Take them below and put them under guard. Set sail for Imabari; I want us there by the morning.'

Jack and his friends were separated from the Wind Demons. Cheng was assumed to be one of them and the pirate boy didn't argue when a guard ordered him to help Miyuki carry Saburo. He preferred to take his chances as a wanted samurai rather than a condemned pirate.

A unit of guards escorted them below deck. The interior of the *atake-bune* was gloomy, lit only by a few oil lamps and the diamond-shaped shafts of sunlight that seeped through the loopholes and gun ports. The first and second decks were dedicated to battle. A number of cannon lined each side, although Jack observed that none matched the European artillery in terms of size or power. The Sea Samurai appeared to depend upon small-arms' fire – arrows, bows, muskets and ammunition were neatly stacked beside each loophole. The samurai themselves sat in groups, recovering from the exertions of combat, some nursing wounds. They looked up in curiosity as Jack and the others were marched down the steps.

The stale smell of sweat struck their nostrils on the next deck. Eighty bare-chested men stood beside two rows of *yuloh*-style oars. The large heavy sculls were pivoted on a pin and counterbalanced by a rope running from the underside of the handle to the wooden floor. At the far end a large round drum hung from the ceiling. The captain's command to set sail was given and a man started to pound out a heavy rhythm. The oarsmen grunted and groaned as they pushed and pulled on the massive roped oars, their muscles straining to propel the immense battleship through the water. From a standing start, the *atake-bune* slowly yet steadily picked up speed.

The deck beneath was given over to storage. Gunpowder, cannonballs, grappling irons, spears and other weaponry were stockpiled towards the stern. Spare ropes, sailcloth, wood and repair materials were stowed in the bow. In between, bales of rice, barrels of fresh water and other provisions were packed to the low rafters. Having to stoop as they passed through, Jack spotted their canvas bag and his red-handled swords among the pile of confiscated weapons from the pirates. He prayed the *rutter* was still safely hidden inside the bag.

'Keep moving!' said the guard, prodding Jack with his spear.

Ushered towards a set of rickety wooden steps, Jack descended with the others into the very bowels of the ship. Here in the dingy bilge – only a single oil lamp for light – a dank mildew smell filled the air. Their feet sloshed into knee-deep grimy water. As their eyes adjusted to the dark, Jack could make out a large wooden grille that separated the square-ended bow from the rest of the ship. One of the guards unlocked a small door.

'I hope you'll be comfortable during your stay!' he laughed.

The other guards grunted their amusement as they shoved Jack and his friends into the slimy confines of the ship's on-board prison. Miyuki and Cheng lost their footing on the slick deck and Saburo fell face first in the water. Jack rushed to pull his friend out before he drowned. Rolling him on his back, he dragged Saburo to the side, propped up his head and wiped the putrid water from his face.

'Are you all right?' asked Jack.

Saburo didn't blink.

Jack shook him. 'Saburo! Are you –'

'*Yesssss,*' came the faintest of replies, no more than a breath.

Jack smiled with relief and held his friend close.

Bedraggled and dripping wet, Miyuki and Cheng got back to their feet.

'No thanks to them,' spat Miyuki, glaring at the guards as they locked the door. Two remained behind to keep watch over their charges, sitting on the steps to avoid the noxious bilge-water.

Jack and his friends didn't have that luxury. They were forced to crouch in the darkness and sludge. Yori discovered a narrow ledge and they laid Saburo along it. He was still unable to move, yet the fact that he'd spoken gave them hope. But the cold dank prison was no place for him to recover. Jack took off his jacket, placing it over his friend in an attempt to keep him warm, while Miyuki quietly resumed her *Sha* healing.

From far off, a bloodcurdling scream was heard.

'Sounds like the captain's boiling that pirate alive!' laughed one of the guards.

Cheng winced at their cruel jibe. 'Not having arrived at the Yellow River, the heart is not dead,' he whispered to himself.

'What did you say?' asked Jack.

'It's a Chinese proverb,' explained Cheng, sitting on his haunches beside him. 'It means only when there is no road left should we feel despair. And, because of you, I've escaped the fate of my fellow pirates.'

'Don't thank me yet,' said Jack. 'Our road is almost running out too.'

He studied Cheng and noticed something odd. 'Why don't you have a spider tattoo like the other Wind Demons?'

Cheng self-consciously touched his neck and looked embarrassed. 'I haven't earned my right to one yet. Any Wind Demon must prove themselves on a raid first – either by killing, stealing or saving another pirate's life. I suppose now, I won't ever get my tattoo.'

'But why would you *want* to become a pirate?' asked Yori, appalled by the idea.

Cheng's brow furrowed. 'In my village, nothing ever happened – except for never having enough rice to eat. And the pirates always seemed to have food. Every time I visited Penglai port, I heard their tales of adventure, riches and foreign lands – it sounded so exciting!'

Cheng looked round at their dismal prison with its scurrying rats and foul stench. 'This is *not* how I imagined the life of a pirate.'

# 24

# HULLED

Jack guessed that night had fallen. There were no windows or portholes in the bilge. The only indication of their progress across the Seto Sea was the creaking of the ship, the splash of the oars and the grunts of the rowers. The tortured screams from the top deck had stopped some time back: either Captain Arashi had obtained his answer . . . or the Wind Demons were all dead.

Jack realized he and his friends were on course to meet the same fate. When the *atake-bune* docked at Imabari in the morning, they would be delivered into the hands of *daimyo* Mori. The ruthless sea lord would have the means to transport them direct to Edo where the Shogun resided. Once there, their lives would no doubt be brought to a swift end.

Yet only the day before, the four of them were sailing south to Nagasaki and freedom. Aside from a dishonest captain, little had stood in their way. Now all their hopes had been dashed by a combination of vicious ninja pirates and cruel Sea Samurai.

'Look! Saburo's wiggling his toes!' cried Yori in delight.

Jack saw them move too. Pleased as he was at the news, his

smile was tinged with sadness. His friend was coming back from the brink only to face a death sentence from the Shogun.

'Well done, Miyuki,' said Jack, laying a hand upon her shoulder. 'Only your ninja skills could have saved him.'

Completing her chant, Miyuki lay back against the hull, rubbing her temples. She was too exhausted to reply, the intense healing having taken its toll.

'*Water*,' Saburo wheezed through dry cracked lips.

Yori ran to the wooden grille and called to the guards. 'We need food and water.'

'Drink what's at your feet,' snarled one of the guards, barely bothering to look up.

Yori glanced in revulsion at the scum floating over the brackish water. He thought for a moment then worded his reply carefully. 'Your captain needs us alive for the Shogun. If you let one of us die, I'm sure he'll be most *displeased* with you. And we all know what punishments await those who displease the captain.'

The two guards exchanged an uncertain look. Huffing in irritation, the first guard got to his feet and disappeared up the steps. He returned with a jug and a bowl of cold rice. Opening a small hatch in the grille, he passed the vital supplies to Yori.

'That's your lot,' said the guard, slamming the hatch shut.

Handing Cheng the rice, Yori lifted the water jug to Saburo's lips while Jack supported his head. Saburo swallowed eagerly. He even managed a mouthful of rice. The combination was enough to return some colour to his cheeks.

'Thank you,' he said. His eyes flicked to Miyuki. 'I owe you my life.'

'That must be the first time a samurai has said *that* to a ninja!' she replied with a fatigued grin.

As the five of them shared their meagre meal, Jack contemplated how they could break out. But their predicament appeared even more hopeless than in the pirate cage. The wooden grille was solid, the iron lock unbreakable, and the guards too far away to subdue. And once in Imabari, surrounded by a garrison of samurai, escape would be all but impossible.

'I *should* have gone on alone,' said Jack, looking regretfully round at his friends. 'It's my fault you're in this mess.'

'It was our choice,' Miyuki reminded him. 'We knew the risks.'

'But you'd have been safe at home by now. Not trapped in this hell-hole.'

'It's better to be in chains with friends,' said Yori, 'than to be in a garden with strangers.'

Jack sighed. Yori always had an answer. 'How did I ever deserve such good friends as –'

'Listen!' interrupted Miyuki, suddenly alert.

Jack and the others fell silent.

'I thought I heard the sound of gunfire –'

The distinctive *crack* of a musket rang out, followed by panicked shouts and urgent commands. Above, the beat of the drum grew more insistent and Jack sensed a change in course.

'What's happening?' asked Yori.

Jack was about to reply when the outer hull imploded. Timber shattered apart and a dragon's face, twisted and scarred with hooked teeth and blood-red eyes, blasted into the bilge. The whole boat jarred under the impact. The two guards shrieked in terror as they were hurled from the steps. Jack and the others were thrown to the floor. By the time they found their feet, the dragon had disappeared and seawater gushed through the breach in the hull. The two guards scrambled up the steps as the bilge flooded.

'Don't leave us here!' cried Cheng, pulling futilely at the grille.

The water level rose around them, while above the thunder of cannon and musket fire filled the air. The *atake-bune* shuddered again, keeling to one side.

Jack front-kicked the prison door. His leg jarred against the unyielding grille.

'Let me try,' said Miyuki. She targeted the lock. But that held firm too. She bent to examine it. 'Maybe I could pick the lock. But I need something thin and pointed.'

They frantically began to search the prison for a loose nail or anything that would serve as a pick. But in the darkness of the bilge, they came up with nothing. The water level continued to rise. It flowed over the ridge where Saburo lay and Cheng quickly sat him up. Jack's pilgrim jacket floated away. Grabbing it, Jack felt Akiko's pearl under the lapel.

'Here!' said Jack, passing Miyuki the pearl with its golden pin fastening.

Miyuki waded through the water to the grille and began to jiggle the lock. All the time, the sea flooded in through the gaping hole.

Jack and Cheng had to stand Saburo on his feet.

'I can . . . move my fingers,' said Saburo, his lips managing a lopsided smile.

'Let's hope you can float too!' replied Jack, struggling to keep his friend upright.

The water was now chest high and rising. Yori was on his tiptoes. Still Miyuki struggled with the lock.

'The gold's too soft . . . it keeps bending . . .'

She ducked beneath the surface. Yori began to tread water. There was barely a head's height between the sea and the bilge ceiling. Saburo spluttered as he struggled to hold his chin up.

'We're all going to drown!' cried Cheng.

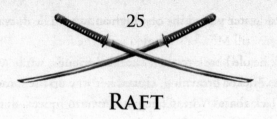

# 25

# RAFT

In the confines of the bilge, the water lapped at their mouths. Miyuki still hadn't surfaced and their air supply was fast running out. The *atake-bune* shook with another explosion.

'Yori . . . hold Saburo's head up,' gasped Jack. 'I'll find Miyuki.'

Struggling to stay afloat himself, Yori managed to get a footing on the narrow ledge and support their friend. Jack took several deep lungfuls of air, then dived. Peering through the murky waters, he spotted a dark shadow against the grille. Miyuki, her feet wedged against a beam, was pushing with all her might at the door. Joining her, Jack could see a piece of timber from the hull had wedged itself across the entrance. Miyuki signed to him that the grille was unlocked. Together they put their weight against it. The door stayed jammed shut. They tried once more. It gave a fraction. They kept pushing. Jack felt his lungs burn with the effort and he could only imagine Miyuki's desperate need for air.

Little by little, the door edged open . . . until there was enough space for Miyuki to slip through. Swimming to the other side, she pulled the obstruction away. The door swung clear.

Jack headed back to their stranded friends, while Miyuki, on the verge of drowning, clawed her way up the steps to the hold. Jack found Yori, Cheng and Saburo squeezed into the last pocket of air.

'Follow me!' he cried, and the four of them half-swam, half-crawled through the flooded bilge, Jack and Cheng dragging the semi-paralysed Saburo behind them. They scrambled up the steps and burst to the water's surface. Miyuki was there to greet them and heaved Saburo on to the hold's deck. He lay there, panting, like a beached whale. Jack and the others clambered out next to him.

'We *all* owe you our lives now, Miyuki,' said Jack.

Miyuki laughed. 'Perhaps you'll forgive me for this then?' She passed Jack the black pearl with its gold fastening, twisted and bent beyond repair.

'I'll forgive you anything if we escape this ship,' said Jack, pocketing the pearl.

From above, the clash of swords and the screams of dying men resounded throughout the vessel. The blast of cannon and musket fire assaulted their ears. But even through this barrage Jack noticed the oarsmen's drum was no longer beating, as if the very heart of the *atake-bune* had been ripped out.

'Sounds like we'll have to fight our way out,' said Jack, struggling to his feet on the listing deck.

He ran over to their canvas bag. Inside were their clothes, pilgrim bags and – to his great relief – the *rutter*. Jack seized his red-handled swords from the pile of confiscated pirate weapons. Miyuki found her *ninjatō* and utility belt, tying it round her waist. Cheng rifled through the weapons, selecting a vicious-looking knife and a short sword. Easily spotting his *shakujō*, Yori then searched for Saburo's swords. He put them inside the canvas bag before fastening it shut.

'We head straight for the top deck and jump ship,' instructed Jack.

'What about Saburo?' asked Yori.

'I noticed a rowing boat hanging near the stern. If it's still there, then we cut it loose and make for the nearest island.'

Nodding their agreement, Yori and Cheng once again carried Saburo between them. Miyuki drew her *ninjatō*, ready to beat a path through the Sea Samurai. Holding his *katana* in one hand, Jack grabbed the canvas bag with the other. 'Let's go!'

As they climbed the steps, the deck above exploded in a flash of fire and flaming debris. All five of them were blown off their feet and sent hurtling back into the hold. The ceiling caved in, extinguishing all light. Jack felt a sharp pain across his brow and the warm rush of blood as he fell to the floor.

Clamping a hand to his head to stem the bleeding, he shouted into the darkness, 'Yori? Miyuki? Is everyone all right?'

Dazed groans answered his call.

A flickering orange light returned to reveal a hold full of smoke and dust.

Yori, Cheng and Saburo were in a heap among the ropes and sailcloth. Miyuki had landed on the rice bales. It had just been Jack's bad luck that his head hit the wooden water barrels. The gash didn't feel too bad, but they were all scratched and bleeding from splinters of blasted timber.

'What now?' asked Cheng, looking in dismay at the destroyed steps.

Their way out was completely blocked by wreckage. Water swirled at their feet. The ship was sinking fast.

Jack glanced back at the hatch to the bilge. 'We swim through the hole in the hull.'

'But what about the dragon?' asked Yori in horror.

'We don't have any other option,' replied Jack, retrieving his *katana* as the light in the hold blazed brighter.

'I'd rather take my chances with a dragon than this ship,' said Miyuki. She pointed to the fire spreading through the wreckage towards the stocks of gunpowder in the bow.

Jack handed Yori the canvas bag, then pulled Saburo over to the hatch.

'Take several slow deep breaths,' he said, giving Saburo and Yori a crash course in ninja breathing techniques. 'Clear your lungs completely, then suck in a large gulp of air and hold it.'

Saburo nodded. As soon as he'd taken his last big breath, Jack dragged him into the swirling water, the others following close behind. The blaze of the fire lit up the bilge and Jack easily spotted the hull's gaping hole, black and jagged like the mouth of a shark.

Miyuki swam through first, Cheng right behind her. Yori was next. He briefly struggled with the canvas bag, which had air trapped inside and was acting like a float. As it cleared the hull, Yori shot up like a cork. Slowed by Saburo's bulk, Jack was last and had to kick hard. With his arms round his friend's chest, they made it through the hole. Then Saburo stopped with a jolt. Their eyes met in panic. Jack yanked on his friend, but to no avail.

Looking down, he saw Saburo's breeches had snagged on the serrated edge of the hole. Jack tugged again. After the third wrench, the cloth finally tore free. But the mistake had cost them precious time and energy. Jack pumped his legs, praying for the surface before they ran out of breath. The darkness of night meant he couldn't tell how much further there was to go. Then their heads cleared the water and Jack immediately wished they hadn't. They'd surfaced in the middle of a ferocious sea battle. Captain Arashi's fleet was being torn apart by a fire-breathing dragon, the flames from his burning ships flickering a hellish orange glow across the Seto Sea.

The dragon charged straight over a *kobaya* in its path, splitting the smaller boat in half and crushing its crew. One of the surviving *seki-bune* fired off a cannon. But the iron ball merely bounced off the spiked back of the beast. The dragon roared flame in retaliation, setting fire to the battleship's mainsail along with several of the crew. Screaming, the Sea Samurai threw themselves overboard, tumbling like human comets into the water.

As Jack fought to keep Saburo above the surface, dead and dismembered bodies of other Sea Samurai washed past.

'*Jack!*' cried Miyuki, swimming over with Yori and Cheng in tow.

Yori was hanging on to the canvas bag and his staff for dear life.

'We . . . need . . . a boat,' gasped Jack, Saburo's dead weight slowly slipping from his grasp.

'Look there!' cried Cheng, pointing to wreckage from the *kobaya*.

A section of deck drifted near and Miyuki grabbed hold.

Clambering on to the makeshift raft, she hauled Saburo to safety, then helped the others. They all collapsed with exhaustion. Unguided and unpowered, the raft was tossed on the waves.

Mercifully, they drifted away from the *atake-bune* just before it exploded, the Seto Sea swallowing the great battleship whole.

# 26

# ADRIFT

Jack felt the warmth of the morning sun on his face and heard the gentle lap of waves. Opening his eyes, he discovered his friends sprawled across the raft, fast asleep. Yori was curled round the canvas bag in the middle, with Saburo propped against him.

Sitting up, Jack inspected the splintered section of deck that had saved their lives. Rectangular with the main beams beneath, the raft was buoyant and large enough to hold them all. But their weight made it unstable and even the smallest waves threatened to capsize them.

Surveying the horizon, Jack's hopes rose . . . then fell. None of the devastation from the previous night was visible and no samurai or pirate ships pursued them. But now the Seto Sea stretched unbroken in all directions. With no land in sight, he guessed their raft had been caught in an outgoing tidal current – which meant they could be drifting into the vast and dangerous expanse of the Pacific Ocean. Glancing up at the sun, Jack tried to calculate the direction they were heading in. But, without any landmark to judge their progress by, it was impossible to tell. And since he wasn't familiar with these waters, even if he could establish a bearing, he wouldn't know whether their current course was a good or bad thing. He shook Cheng and the others awake.

'Where are we?' asked Saburo, groggily sitting up.

Jack stared in amazement at his friend.

'What?' said Saburo, blinking and wiping his eyes.

'You're better!'

Saburo gave a pained smile as he rubbed a stiff shoulder. 'I wouldn't say that. I feel like twenty sumo wrestlers have jumped on my bones. My muscles burn every time I move.'

'Those symptoms will fade in a few hours,' explained Miyuki, also glad to see their friend on the road to recovery. 'All you need now is water, food and rest.'

Saburo's eyes lit up at the mention of food. 'I'm famished! What do we have to eat?'

Jack laughed. 'You almost died from eating *fugu*! And the first thing you think about is *food*!'

'Well, I don't want to die of starvation,' said Saburo seriously.

'We should still have some rice,' said Yori, opening the canvas bag. His face dropped and he began to dig deeper. 'Oh, no . . . it's all gone.'

'*Everything?*' enquired Jack, fearing for the *rutter*.

'No, just our food. Someone must have taken it.'

'What about water?'

Yori held up a cracked empty gourd. 'Two are broken; the others are missing. We must have lost them during our escape.'

'Then we need to find land as soon as possible,' urged Jack, realizing their situation had become perilous. 'Now . . . Captain Arashi gave orders to head back to Imabari. Before that, the pirates caught us maybe half a day's sail south-west of Omishima Island and then the *Black Spider* took a southern tack for most of the day. Since the dragon attack, we've been adrift half the night . . . Cheng, do you have *any* idea where we might be?'

Cheng shook his head apologetically. 'I joined the Wind Demons barely a month ago. This is the first time I've sailed the Seto Sea.'

Jack bit his lip in frustration. They were well and truly lost. With no food, no water and no idea in which direction land lay, their chances of survival were very slim indeed. He tried not to despair.

'There are hundreds of islands in the Seto Sea,' said Yori hopefully. 'We're bound to come across one soon.'

Although Jack wasn't about to give up, he couldn't share Yori's optimism. Being at sea level, he knew they only needed to be a few miles offshore before the coastline disappeared below the horizon. They could be passing an island *and* salvation right now and never know about it.

'One of us needs to stand lookout at all times,' said Jack decisively. 'Without sail or oar, we're at the mercy of the currents, so if we spot land, we may have to swim for it.'

'I'll take first watch,' Cheng offered.

The raft rocked as the pirate boy gingerly got to his feet. Shading his eyes, he began to sweep the horizon for any islands.

'Keep an eye open for boats too,' advised Miyuki. 'Fishing ones preferably. We *don't* want to be saved by pirates or Sea Samurai!'

'And look out for drifting wood, stationary clouds or birds,' added Jack. 'They all indicate land. Especially birds. At dusk they tend to fly towards the shore. And if there's a roosting site near, we may even hear their cries.'

Cheng nodded and resumed his search.

'Dusk?' questioned Saburo, his expression troubled. 'But it's still only morning.'

Jack nodded gravely. 'It could be a while before we get lucky. So we need to be prepared for a long voyage. What else is left in the bag?'

Yori had a hunt through. 'Our samurai clothes, our packs, the pilgrim bags, your *rutter* and Saburo's swords.'

Jack looked down at the ragged remains of his pilgrim outfit. There was little point in changing clothes until they reached dry land, but they needed to protect themselves from the sun.

'Put our belongings in the packs, then tie them to the raft,' instructed Jack. 'We can make a shelter with the canvas bag. It may be spring, but that sun will soon burn out here on the water.'

Yori got to work, happy to be guided by Jack's seafaring expertise rather than think about their dire situation. Jack found a loose piece of wood from the raft's edge to act as a supporting strut and wedged it in between the planks. Driving the steel tip of her *ninjatō* into the deck, Miyuki used this as a second strut. Together, they erected the makeshift shelter and helped Saburo into its shade.

'We still have our weapons,' said Miyuki, pulling a straight-spiked *shuriken* from her utility belt. 'With Yori's staff, I could make a fishing spear.'

'Good idea,' said Jack. 'Then at least we might catch some food.'

'But what are we going to drink?' asked Yori. 'We can't use seawater.'

'The canvas is ready for when it rains. That'll be our only source.'

They looked up into the sky. It was crystal blue and cloudless.

'We might be waiting a long time,' said Saburo glumly.

The sun had reached its zenith and was beating down relentlessly upon the raft. The canvas bag did little to alleviate the scorching heat and the shade it offered was only large enough to accommodate two people. The others had to sit in the sun's full glare, their discomfort compounded as the salt water dried and cracked their skin. Already weak from their imprisonment, their exposure quickened the debilitating effects of thirst and hunger. As time went on, the five friends became more listless and a growing sense of desperation spread among them.

So far there had been no sight of land or any other ships. Jack worried that the raft had floated out of the tidal current and was no longer drifting in *any* particular direction. Or worse, they were in the Pacific Ocean and beyond saving.

Miyuki crouched at the edge of the deck, spear in hand. She hadn't moved for over an hour, waiting with dogged determination for a fish to swim by. A school of tiny blue ones flitted beneath the shadow of the raft, but none offered a realistic catch.

'Can't we make a sail from this canvas?' suggested Cheng.

'The raft is too unstable,' replied Jack. 'One wild gust and we'd capsize. We could cut paddles from the decking, but we have to be careful not to weaken the raft's structure –'

All of a sudden, Miyuki lunged. There was a splash followed by a shimmer of silver in the air.

'Got one!' she cried in delight.

Miyuki pinned her catch to the deck, where it flapped and struggled. She gave another twist to the spear and the fish fell still. Prising it from the *shuriken* spike, she offered her catch to the others. 'Who's hungry then?'

Saburo automatically reached out, then stopped himself. 'Do you think it's poisonous?'

Cheng shook his head. 'No, it's a yellowtail. Very tasty. We can also drink the fish.'

They all looked at the pirate boy dubiously.

'Let me show you,' he said, taking the yellowtail from Miyuki's hands.

Putting his lips to the fish's eyeball, he sucked hard. They heard a squelching pop as it burst and then saw Cheng swallow.

'That's disgusting!' exclaimed Saburo, his appetite suddenly gone.

'You can also drink the fluid along the spine,' said Cheng, before offering the other eye to Jack.

Driven by thirst, Jack clamped his mouth over the slimy eye and sucked.

# 27
# ALBATROSS

Over the course of the afternoon, Miyuki managed to spear another two yellowtails. Using his knife, Cheng cut the three fish carefully in half before presenting them to Yori, Saburo and Miyuki to drink from their spines. The fluid would ensure everyone's survival that day, but wasn't enough to quench their thirst. The soft pink flesh of the fish, though, more than satisfied their hunger.

With their bellies full, their spirits rose a little and Yori eagerly took up position as lookout, determined to spot an island. But the promise of land remained as elusive as ever, their raft bobbing over the water and seemingly going nowhere.

With Cheng's knife, Jack crafted a crude pair of thin-bladed paddles from a piece of broken decking. But, until they knew for certain which direction to head in, the paddles wouldn't be of much use.

'I think I saw something!' Yori cried, pointing to a patch of sea off their stern. But his voice was one of panic, not relief.

'What was it?' asked Jack.

'I . . . don't know,' he replied. 'It was big and black . . . like a dragon . . .'

All eyes now watched the waters surrounding them. Their sense of vulnerability became starkly apparent – a tiny defenceless raft stuck in the middle of the sea, with nothing between them and the monsters of the deep. Danger lurked in every wave, fear in every ripple.

'Over there!' shouted Miyuki.

A dark mass, twenty times the size of their raft, breached the surface off their starboard side. A fountain of seawater spouted into the air, accompanied by a large snort. And a single black eye regarded them with keen interest.

Miyuki wielded her fishing spear to fend off the beast. Yori clung to Jack in terror.

'Don't worry,' said Jack. 'It's just a humpback whale. It won't attack us.'

'I've never seen an animal so *huge*,' Saburo breathed in awe.

The humpback circled the raft, but didn't approach any closer.

'It seems to be . . . studying us,' said Yori, his fear giving way to curiosity and admiration.

The whale slapped the water with a pectoral fin, sending a shower of spray over the raft. Jack and the others were drenched. Sheltered beneath the canvas bag, Saburo escaped the soaking and laughed. 'Or else it's looking for a water fight!'

Then with slow grace the whale arched its back and dived, its fluked tail rising into the air as if waving farewell before slipping beneath the surface. For a moment no one said anything, stunned by their encounter with this benign creature.

Their silence was disturbed by the screech of a seabird. Jack looked up. A white-feathered albatross glided effortlessly overhead. Such birds were believed to be the souls of lost sailors and to kill one was bad luck. But its sighting now was a stroke of fortune. The albatross was taking a westerly course. Jack and the others immediately began to scan the horizon.

'Birds mean land,' said Yori excitedly, shading his eyes against the bright glare of the sun. 'So where is it?'

The shimmering sea yielded up nothing but a distant haze. Jack knew the albatross was a long-distance forager and could fly many miles out from land. But it was late afternoon, so the sighting offered hope. And in a situation as desperate as theirs, hope might be the only thing that carried them through their ordeal.

'It must be just beyond the horizon,' said Jack, picking up the makeshift paddles and handing one to Cheng. 'There's only one way to find out.'

Kneeling either side of the raft, they began paddling westward while Miyuki and Yori maintained a lookout.

The albatross flew on ahead until it was no more than a speck in the sky.

They rowed after it, swapping with the others when they became tired or their hands too raw. Without any landmarks, it was impossible to tell if they were making headway or just fighting against the tide. But the act of paddling made them all feel as if they were taking charge of their own destiny.

The sun dropped lower in the sky, its rays turning the water golden until it glimmered like silk. But still the sea stretched on. If they didn't spot land before sundown, they'd be faced with trying to survive the night. Not only would they have to cope with the chilling cold and their mounting thirst but in the dark they might pass by their only salvation.

Jack dug his paddle in, focusing on his rhythm. His shoulders ached and his palms were blistered. On the other side, Saburo grunted as he fought the pain searing through his muscles. They'd tried to dissuade him from rowing, but he was determined to help. Yori sat in the shade of the canvas, nauseous and dizzy from overexposure to the sun. Jack had a blinding headache, but did his best to ignore it. They had to row on. It was all they could do.

Cheng laid a hand upon his shoulder. 'Let me take over,' he said, seeing Jack sway with exhaustion.

Jack shook his head, knowing the pirate boy was equally tired. 'I can keep going a little longer –'

'Land!' cried Miyuki, her voice cracked and parched.

Jack stood. He couldn't see anything, but Miyuki's sharp eyes glimpsed the rise of an island on the horizon. With a renewed burst of energy, Jack and Saburo started paddling again.

'I can see it too!' shouted Cheng.

Gradually the dark outline of a peak grew against the sky. Several seabirds circled above, calling out as if beckoning them towards the safety of shore. With every pull of their paddles, the raft floated nearer to land. But Jack became aware that they were approaching far faster than was possible simply by rowing. The raft was caught in another current.

This was good news . . . until Jack realized that it was sweeping them *beyond* the island. At this speed, however hard they paddled, they wouldn't be able to break away from its drag.

'We're going to miss the shore!' he exclaimed in alarm. 'Miyuki! Cheng! We have to swim for it.'

The three of them jumped into the water, leaving Yori and

Saburo to keep paddling. Holding on to the raft's stern, they began kicking as hard as they could.

The combined power of feet and paddle drove them across the tugging current. To their immense relief, the island drew steadily closer, with their raft on a direct course for a sandy cove.

'Not far now!' encouraged Yori, paddling for all he was worth.

They were going to make it . . . then Jack spotted the distinctive shape of a grey dorsal fin rising out of the water.

# 28

# WHITE DEATH

'SHARK!' cried Jack, kicking harder for the shore.

Miyuki and Cheng pumped their legs too. Yori and Saburo paddled frantically. But they were still far from the safety of the cove. The fin cut through the water towards them. There was little hope of out-swimming the shark. Yet if they stopped now, the raft would drift past the island and back out into open sea.

'FASTER!' urged Miyuki, glancing over her shoulder at the approaching fin.

Then the shark disappeared.

'It's gone,' said Saburo with relief.

'But *where's* it gone?' Cheng panted, looking round in panic.

'Get out of the water!' cried Yori, ditching his oar and putting out his hand to pull them on-board.

The three of them scrambled on to the raft. As Jack lifted himself out, the plank beneath him snapped and he felt his heart lurch as he fell back into the sea. His head went under. The swirl of water filled his ears. He sensed the malicious shark coursing straight for him. Bursting to the surface, he flailed for the edge of the raft. Yori and Miyuki seized his outstretched arms and yanked him on to the deck.

'Stop paddling,' spluttered Jack to Saburo.

'But the island –'

'The shark's attracted to the splashing.'

Saburo immediately stopped.

The five of them huddled in the middle of the flimsy raft, the waves lapping around its sides. A foreboding silence descended. No one dared breathe, their eyes fixed on the rippling surface of the sea. A slate-grey shape with a pointed snout slid beneath them. Jack shuddered at the sight, feeling his blood run cold. The shark was at least double the raft's length.

They waited for the inevitable attack, all the time their raft slowly drifting further from the cove.

'Let's make a swim for it,' said Miyuki. 'Before it's too late.'

Jack shook his head. 'If we do, one or more of us will surely die.'

'Maybe that's the sacrifice we have to make to save ourselves,' said Saburo.

Jack looked at his loyal friend. The resigned yet valiant expression on his face told him that Saburo thought he'd be the slowest and most likely victim, his belief in the code of *bushido* giving him the courage to make such a suggestion.

'No, we *all* survive,' said Jack, unsheathing his *katana*. 'We didn't come this far to be beaten by a shark.'

He gripped its red handle tightly with both hands, steeling himself to fight off the fearsome predator. His eyes hunted the surrounding waters. But no fin re-emerged.

After a while, Miyuki asked, 'Do you think it's actually gone?'

Risking a closer look, Jack peered over the sides of their

raft. The sea dropped away into inky blackness, but there was no sign of the shark.

'Shall we start paddling again?' suggested Cheng, glancing towards the receding shoreline.

Jack shook his head. 'Not just yet –'

'Jack . . .' interrupted Yori, pointing to his forehead. 'Your cut's reopened.'

They all watched in horror as several beads of blood dripped from the wound into the sea. They spread across the water like a blossoming rose.

For several moments, no one spoke or dared move. There was just the lap of the waves against the raft as they drifted further and further from the salvation of the island.

'It *must* have swum on,' said Cheng, picking up Yori's paddle. 'Let's go before it comes back.'

But, as he plunged the paddle into the sea, a shadow rocketed upwards from the depths. Jack and the others flung themselves to the other end of the raft as a huge mouth bristling with serrated teeth burst from the water. Its jaws snapped through the wooden beams, the timber cracking like brittle bones. As the monstrous beast shot clear of the sea, its long white underbelly was revealed. A stink of rotting fish filled the air before the shark slammed back into the water, sending a small tidal wave across the remains of the raft. Jack and his friends clung to each other, desperate not to be washed overboard.

The shark, robbed of its prey, dived back down to unseen depths.

'White Death!' exclaimed Cheng in between hysterical gasps. 'The Wind Demons . . . told tales . . . of such a shark . . . that eats men whole!'

Jack had never seen a great white shark before. But he too had heard stories of how this bloodthirsty creature split boats in half and devoured entire crews. Now that he had stared directly into its malevolent black eyes, Jack believed the gruesome legends. This was the most feared shark of the seven seas. Cruel, vicious and cunning, the great white was an unstoppable force of nature. Gripped by an almost overwhelming terror, it took all Jack's willpower not to lose his nerve entirely. Panic would only get them killed quicker.

'Grab any weapon you can find,' he instructed. 'And form a circle.'

Miyuki eased her *ninjatō* from the crumbling deck. Cheng shakily held his knife, Yori his *shuriken*-tipped staff and Saburo the paddle. His samurai swords were bound to their packs, still secured to the raft, but he couldn't risk reaching for them. While the raft wasn't yet sinking, any sudden movement could tip them all into the sea.

They raised their weapons as the great white made a pass. Rolling slightly so that its snout and saw-like teeth emerged, the shark's cold fathomless eye regarded them with menace. Then the beast sank beneath the waves without a trace.

Jack knelt beside the others on the fragile raft. His heart thumped in his chest, the blood rushed through his veins. He tried to calm his breathing, but the thought of that ravenous shark circling them petrified him to his very core.

The sea erupted behind him. The great white clamped its jaws on to the corner of the raft and furiously shook its head from side to side. In a matter of moments, the deck was being torn apart. Saburo smashed his paddle on to the shark's snout. Still the beast ripped into the raft, getting closer with every bite. Saburo struck at it again as Miyuki went for its gills. The double attack convinced the shark to release its grip and the monster swam off.

'The raft won't survive another attack like that,' panted Saburo, wiping the salt water from his eyes with the back of his arm.

'Maybe it won't have to,' said Yori hopefully, pointing to the retreating shark. 'You've scared it off.'

Cheng shook his head. 'I don't think so. We just made it angrier.'

With a flick of the tail, the shark turned and came back at them. The fin scythed through the waves, picking up tremendous speed.

'Brace yourselves!' cried Jack, grabbing hold of Yori and Miyuki.

The great white rammed the raft. The deck buckled, broke and was tossed into the air. Together Jack, Miyuki and Yori were flung from the raft and splashed down into the sea, the breath knocked from them. Gulping in salt water, Jack spluttered as he broke the surface. He heard a cry. Saburo and Cheng somehow had managed to cling to the remains of the raft, now little more than a few planks of wood held together by their sodden packs.

'It's coming for you!' cried Saburo in alarm.

Jack whipped his head round. A grey dorsal fin sliced through a wave. But it wasn't headed in his direction.

'Yori, watch out!'

Turning to face the shark, Yori held out his *shakujō*. Yet it was obvious that the great white would chomp through it like a toothpick. Jack thrashed his way towards his friend, desperate to protect him with his sword. But he was no match for the frightening speed of the shark.

The great white broke the surface and opened its jaws wide to devour Yori in a single bite.

# 29

# STAY OF EXECUTION

As the great white closed in for the kill, there was a deafening bang like a thunderclap overhead. Flesh, bone, teeth and blubber splattered across the water and the raft. Yori floated, unmoving, among the bloody remains.

Wiping seared shark meat from his face, Jack couldn't believe his eyes. The *Black Spider* was sailing up right behind them, Captain Kurogumo at the helm. Leering over the side was Skullface and his surviving gang members. Tiger was clutching a smoking handheld cannon.

'Look, it's our floating treasure chest!' exclaimed Snakehead, laughing in delight. He threw them a line. 'I'd hurry if I were you,' he said, pointing to three grey fins cutting through the water. One was already ripping into the bloody carcass of the great white.

Jack grabbed Yori, still in shock from his near-death experience. Together with Miyuki, they swam for the rope. Saburo and Cheng paddled for all they were worth, the raft slowly sinking beneath them. Clambering on-board, they were immediately relieved of their packs and weapons.

'We thought we'd never find you,' said Skullface cheerfully.

'You came looking for *us*?' said Jack, astounded.

Skullface gave a black-toothed grin. 'Of course, you're far too valuable for shark bait.'

The pirate gang escorted them across the deck towards the stern. The *Black Spider* was battered and broken from its battle with the Sea Samurai. Arrows still peppered the planks and blood stained the wood. They had to skirt the large hole blasted into the deck by the *horoku* bomb, and a group of pirates were working hard to fix the shattered starboard gunwale. Manzo was among them, holding a new beam in place. He glared at Jack as they passed. The giant pirate had a bandage round his head and a large cut across his upper arm. In fact, few of the pirates had escaped the sea battle unharmed. Jack guessed at least half of the crew had been decimated in the attack or tortured to death by Captain Arashi.

Climbing the steps to the upper deck, Jack and his friends were met by Captain Kurogumo. Still clad in his green and black dragon-scale armour, he appeared unscathed and in surprisingly good humour.

'Welcome back!' he said, opening his arms wide as if greeting old friends. 'Why the sour faces? I've just rescued you from certain death.'

'Only to face an *uncertain* death with you,' retorted Miyuki.

Captain Kurogumo smiled, revealing his set of pointed teeth. The resemblance to the great white shark was unsettling. 'True, I'm not in the habit of rescuing samurai or ninja.' He approached Jack and laid a hand on his shoulder. 'But when *you* are prized so highly and coveted by the Shogun no less, then I can't resist doing good.'

Jack shrugged the captain off. 'So you're turning us over to the Shogun's samurai?'

'Why would I want to do that?' replied the captain, putting on an offended air.

'Then what do you have planned for us?' Miyuki demanded.

Captain Kurogumo eyed her with contempt. 'You'll know *your* fate once you meet Tatsumaki.' He turned to Skullface. 'Lock them away.'

'What about your cabin boy?' enquired Skullface, seizing Cheng by the scruff of his neck.

Captain Kurogumo scrutinized Cheng, who visibly shrank under his stony gaze. 'Traitors of the *Black Spider* are punished with death by hanging.'

'But I forced him to help us,' protested Jack.

'Is that so?' said the captain, unconvinced by Jack's ready defence.

'At knife point,' added Cheng hurriedly.

Captain Kurogumo grunted his displeasure at such weakness. Nonetheless he relented. 'I suppose we are lacking in crew numbers; and, Cheng, you were showing real promise as a pirate. I'll stay your execution for the time being. But you need to prove your worth . . . or it's the noose!'

Cheng bowed gratefully for his reprieve. 'By the word of the Wind Demon, I vow my life to you.'

'I'll hold you to that,' said the captain menacingly. 'Skull-face, have your men take the others away.'

Tiger seized Jack by the arms, wrenching them behind his back.

'Be more careful with them this time,' cautioned the captain. 'Remember, they're our esteemed guests.'

Tiger eased his grip and Skullface imitated a formal bow to their captives. 'This way, if you please.'

With little alternative, Jack and his friends followed. But Yori stopped at the steps and turned back to the captain.

'I have a question. How did you survive the dragon?'

Captain Kurogumo raised his eyebrows. 'You really want to know our *secret*?'

Yori nodded.

The captain leant in close to Yori and, with a conspiratorial whisper, revealed, 'We feed it little juicy samurai!'

The startled expression on Yori's face caused Captain Kurogumo to laugh out loud.

They could still hear him laughing when Skullface imprisoned them in the cage on the main deck.

'I'll be watching you like a hawk,' he warned Jack. This time, he left two guards at the gate before stalking off with his gang.

'Ah! The fish food returns!' croaked a familiar voice. In the corner, the Korean slave rocked on his haunches, observing Jack and the others with crazed amusement.

Saburo slumped to the deck, his head in his hands. 'After all we've been through, we're back where we started! I almost wish we *had* been eaten by that shark.'

'I don't,' said Yori quickly, shuddering at the memory. 'We should be grateful for small blessings – at least we're alive!'

Jack looked up at the sun, which hovered over the starboard bow of the *Black Spider*. 'And we're heading in the right direction this time.'

'How can you be so upbeat?' said Saburo. 'Even as we speak, the pirates are likely devising some evil way to torture us.'

'No, we're valuable to the Wind Demons now – that means they won't harm us.'

'*You* are,' corrected Miyuki darkly. 'I doubt that we're so privileged.'

With regret, Jack realized she was probably right. 'Well, we escaped before,' he said, eyeing the cage's weakened lock. 'We just need to find the right moment to do it again. And remember Cheng is on our side.'

'Is he?' questioned Miyuki, glancing towards the upper deck where Captain Kurogumo was talking intently with the pirate boy, who appeared to be nodding obediently.

As the evening stretched on, Jack bided his time. Yet not even the slightest opportunity to escape presented itself. The guards remained vigilant and the pirate ship sailed on across the Seto Sea, unopposed. Jack tried to keep his friends' spirits up, but they were so exhausted that he worried they wouldn't have the strength to make a run for it, when an opportunity did present itself.

Just before sundown, Cheng appeared with a jug and two large bowls of rice. The guards opened the gate and allowed him in.

'Food and water by orders of the captain,' he explained.

'Is it safe?' asked Saburo warily.

Cheng nodded. 'I prepared it myself . . . since the cook's dead.'

Ravenous and parched from their ordeal on the raft, the four friends tucked into the simple feast. The jug of water disappeared in a few shared gulps, the food going down almost as quickly.

Cheng waited by the cage as they ate.

'Can you help us escape?' Jack asked quietly in between mouthfuls.

'I'd like to, but I can't,' replied Cheng under his breath. 'They're watching my every move. If you escape, the captain says he'll flay me alive.'

Jack nodded his understanding. 'Where are we being taken?'

'Pirate Island – the Wind Demons' lair.'

'Is that where Tatsumaki is?'

Cheng nodded.

'Have you met this Tatsumaki?' asked Miyuki.

Cheng shook his head. 'I have never been to the Pirate Island before. Its location is a closely guarded secret.' He looked at them all with a grave expression. 'But I've heard that no one sees Tatsumaki and lives.'

# KAMIKAZE

Dawn broke like a bleeding wound, the distant scudding clouds turned crimson by the sun's fiery rays. The southerly breeze was insistent, but the Seto Sea remained unnaturally calm.

*Red sky in the morning, sailor's warning*, thought Jack absently as he rubbed the stiffness from his aching muscles.

The night had been cold and uncomfortable on the rough wooden deck. He and his friends had huddled together, with one of them always on watch in case there was a chance of escape . . . or the pirates tried to surprise them.

Standing up to stretch, Jack was greeted by a breathtaking sight. A magnificent fire-red *torii* floated in the middle of the sea. So large was the structure, the *Black Spider* could have passed through, if its masts were lowered. With four supporting pillars and a curving green-tiled roof, the towering gateway marked the entrance to the harbour of a small forested island. Within the natural shelter of the bay, a large temple also floated on the waters. Daubed in the same fire-red colour, the main hall faced out to sea, its walkways and windows open to the elements, its roofline reflected in the rippling waves. Beyond the temple, a forested mountain rose into the sky, its peak wreathed in a ring of mist like a gateway to the heavens.

'Is *that* Pirate Island?' Saburo gasped, clambering to his feet.

Wiping the sleep from his eyes, Yori shook his head. 'No, this has to be Miyajima – the legendary Shrine Island.'

'It's so serene,' breathed Miyuki in awe.

'Why is the temple on the sea?' asked Jack.

'The island is sacred,' Yori explained in a reverential tone. 'Commoners must not set foot on Miyajima. So the shrine was built as a pier above the water. By separating it from the land, the shrine exists in a limbo between the pure spirit world and our impure world.'

'But why is the gate so far out?'

'The shrine is dedicated to the three daughters of Susano-o, the Shinto deity of seas and storms. Anyone wishing to pay their respects must steer their boat through the *torii* in order to cleanse themselves before approaching the sacred island.'

Jack hoped the Wind Demons were devout worshippers of Susano-o. With land so close, this could be the opportunity they'd been waiting for.

Captain Kurogumo emerged from his quarters and climbed to the upper deck. Cheng followed close behind, bearing a tray with a china cup, a pot of steaming tea and a small jug of *saké*. He was evidently working hard to impress. Ignoring the tea, the captain went straight for the *saké* and knocked it back in one go. He coughed and banged his chest appreciatively, the potent rice wine invigorating him for the day. With a quick glance in the direction of the island, he talked with the helmsman. After some deliberation, Captain Kurogumo gave the order to sail on.

Rousing themselves, the pirates went about their duties.

Skullface replaced the cage guards with fresh men before barking out orders to the other pirates. A skeleton crew was assigned to sail the *Black Spider*, while the majority worked on repairing the damage to the ship.

Powerless to alter their course, Jack despondently watched the great *torii* recede into the distance, until only the peak of Shrine Island was visible above the horizon. Once again, the Seto Sea widened into an open and unending expanse of water.

It wasn't until mid-morning that Cheng managed to bring more water and rice to their cage.

'Why didn't we stop at the shrine?' asked Jack after he'd taken a long draught from the jug.

'Sea Samurai patrol these waters,' Cheng explained, in a hushed voice so as not to let the guards hear him. 'The captain can't risk another confrontation with only half the crew and his ship in such a poor condition.'

'Do you know if we'll pass land again?'

'They don't tell me anything,' said Cheng, shaking his head. 'But I overheard the captain say that he intends approaching Pirate Island at night – so no one can follow us and *you* won't know how to get back.'

Jack sighed. Captain Kurogumo was sly and shrewd. He wasn't taking any chances with them this time.

With an apologetic smile, Cheng left the cage and resumed his cabin-boy duties. Jack and the others finished their meal in silence. They all appreciated just how dire their situation had become.

As the day drew on, the wind picked up and the sea turned rough. The *Black Spider* started to pitch and roll over the rising waves.

'Looks like we're in for a rough ride,' observed Jack, glancing up at the darkening sky.

They all looked south towards a mass of ominous black thunderclouds. Captain Kurogumo gave orders to reef the mainsail, stow loose cargo and tie down any unsecured loads. As Skullface and his gang went to work, it became apparent that these instructions didn't include the occupants of the cage. The prisoners were left helpless and exposed on the open deck.

With no land in sight offering a safe harbour, the *Black Spider* continued on its course. Jack realized the captain's plan was to run before the storm. But the wind grew stronger, building rapidly into a gale. The sea heaped up, white foam blowing in streaks from the crests of the waves. The sky overhead lit up with forked lightning. A second later, a deep roll of thunder roared and shook the heavens.

The storm was almost on top of them.

Racing before it, the *Black Spider* heeled and listed wildly. The pirates hung on as best they could while making frantic adjustments to the sails.

Saburo threw up over the deck. 'You said –' as he wiped a hand over his mouth – 'I wouldn't be seasick after three days.'

'There's no cure for a storm,' Jack replied grimly. Even he was struggling to find his sea legs in such a ferocious tempest.

The *Black Spider* surged in fits and bursts across the tumultuous sea, but the damaged ship groaned in protest, threatening to split apart with each and every battering. As the storm bore down on them, they were plunged into a hellish darkness. The sea was whipped into a cauldron of spray and gargantuan waves.

Jack and his friends desperately clung to one another,

shivering from cold and terror at the sheer power of the storm. A monstrous wave broke over the ship and pummelled the cage, half-drowning those inside.

'*KAMIKAZE!*' yelled the Korean slave and raised his fists in a salute to the black boiling sky.

'What did he say?' cried Jack, thinking the slave had gone truly mad.

'Wind of the Gods,' Yori shouted above the crash of waves and the crack of thunder. 'The pirates should've paid their respects . . . Susano-o is very angry.'

# SEA ANCHOR

The typhoon hit the *Black Spider* with full force, the wind shrieking and howling like a banshee, deafening the crew and blinding them with spray. The Seto Sea churned and seethed as if wrestling with the storm-clad sky. Lightning bolts flashed and thunder boomed. Waves the size of mountains tossed the pirate ship like a piece of driftwood and Jack truly feared for their lives.

Captain Kurogumo, who'd lashed himself to the tiller, remained fixed to his course, running before the wild wind. The reefed sails were stretched to breaking point, the masts threatening to snap, and the deck warped and shuddered dangerously as the *Black Spider* rose up over the perilous peaks before plunging into the deep troughs. All of a sudden there was a ripping noise and the foresail was rent in two, the canvas now flapping half-useless in the gale.

*Wind can be light . . . or tear a house apart*, thought Jack, remembering the teachings of the Five Rings from the Grandmaster. The storm's terrible power seemed intent on destroying the *Black Spider* and sending them all to the bottom of the sea.

A foaming wave surged across the main deck, and Jack and the others were thrown against the bars of their cage. Submerged in freezing water, they spluttered and choked for air. For a moment, Jack thought the ship had capsized altogether, then their heads broke the surface. The receding wave clawed at them, but they were saved by their bamboo prison. The two guards weren't so fortunate. They were swept off their feet and borne away, screaming and flailing, into the dark swirling sea.

Jack spotted Cheng clinging to the main mast.

'CHENG!' he cried.

The pirate boy glanced over, his face pale and terror-stricken. Then, as the *Black Spider* rose up the next swell, the deck cleared and he threw himself towards the cage.

'Open the gate!' demanded Jack.

'The captain will kill me,' replied Cheng, keeping a firm grip on the bars as the wind and rain lashed at them.

'This storm will kill us all if you don't let us out!'

Cheng wavered as Yori pleaded with him.

'You owe it to us,' Miyuki reminded him, seizing the pirate boy by the arm. 'We've saved your life *twice*!'

Cheng pulled the knife from his belt and Miyuki immediately backed away.

With a quick glance to check no other pirates were watching, Cheng wedged the blade into the gap between the lock and cage and sprang the gate open.

'Stay here!' Jack instructed his friends, much to their confusion.

'But we can escape now!' said Miyuki.

Jack shook his head. 'Our only hope is if I can save this ship first. You're far safer in the cage.'

He grabbed Cheng and they weaved across the heeling deck. Clambering up the steps to the helm, Jack grabbed a safety line and staggered over to Captain Kurogumo, who was fighting to keep control of the tiller with his helmsman. Running before the wind was usually a good strategy in a storm. But, when the waves grew too large or the helmsman too tired, the ship became vulnerable to broaching or, worse, pitchpoling.

The captain stared at Jack in shock before turning furiously on Cheng. 'I'll hang you for this!'

'*But I can save the ship!*' shouted Jack above the noise of the storm.

Captain Kurogumo laughed bitterly. 'Only the gods can save us now!'

'Not if we make a sea anchor and heave-to.'

'Are all *gaijin* such dumb sailors?' snarled Captain Kurogumo contemptuously. 'We'd be pulled under the water. Knocked down by the waves. Besides, the sea's too deep to drop anchor.'

'A *sea* anchor,' corrected Jack, struggling to keep his feet as the ship suddenly lurched. 'It anchors itself to the water, not the seabed.'

'I've never heard of such a thing,' snapped the captain, rapidly losing patience. 'And we certainly don't have one.'

'I can make one,' persisted Jack. 'It'll act as a brake . . . turn the bow into the waves . . . stabilize the ship against the wind. We'd go straight through the heart of the storm . . . but it'll be over quicker.'

A wave broke over the stern and they were deluged in seawater. The safety line slipped through Jack's fingers, but Cheng held firm and caught him behind. When the wave had passed, only the captain remained at the tiller.

'If you keep running downwind, the *Black Spider* will pitch-pole!' cried Jack. 'The bow will bury itself in a wave! We'll be thrown end over end! Your ship will be smashed to match-wood!'

Captain Kurogumo scowled at Jack. 'Who do you think you are, *gaijin*? I'm the captain of this ship! I know what needs to be done – and we *run* from a storm this big.' He called down to Tiger. 'Throw them *both* in the cage.'

Ascending the steps, Tiger seized Jack and Cheng and began to drag them away. But at that moment the *Black Spider* crested a huge wave and hurtled down the other side. The ship nose-dived into the bottom of the trough, the impact shattering the newly repaired starboard gunwale. The *Black Spider* spun towards the wind and heeled violently, on the verge of broaching. Jack, Cheng and Tiger were thrown against the stern's bulwark. But miraculously, at the last second, the ship righted itself. Even so, Jack caught the grim expression on Captain Kurogumo's face. They both recognized the *Black Spider* had reached its limit.

With their survival in the balance, Captain Kurogumo yelled to Jack, 'Make the anchor!' His eyes narrowed. 'But don't you *dare* trick me.'

Ordering Tiger to help the *gaijin* in whatever way he could, Captain Kurogumo focused all his strength on stopping the *Black Spider* from broaching again.

'I need sail, rope and wood,' Jack told Tiger.

'In the hold,' he replied gruffly.

Scrambling down to the main deck, Jack beckoned Miyuki and the others to follow them into the hold. Water poured in through the hatch and the floor was awash with displaced cargo.

Tiger pointed out the spare sailcloth. 'And how much rope do you need?'

'Ten times the ship's length,' replied Jack.

Tiger's eyes widened in disbelief. 'That'll be *all* of it then.'

Jack handed out marlinspikes to Miyuki, Yori, Saburo and Cheng, then instructed them on how to splice the ropes together. They hurriedly set to work on forming a single length of line.

'Making an escape, hey?' Skullface dropped into the hold, sword drawn. He brought the blade to Jack's throat.

'No, I'm trying to save us all,' protested Jack. 'Even you.'

Tiger stepped from the gloom of the hold. 'Captain's orders are to help him.'

Skullface stared incredulously at his gangmember.

'We need Manzo,' said Jack, pushing away Skullface's sword. 'Bring him down here.'

Skullface looked incensed, but he stomped up the steps nonetheless. Manzo appeared a moment later. Jack ordered him and Tiger to carry the sailcloth, while his friends hauled up the massive length of rope. Back on the main deck, the storm continued to batter the *Black Spider*.

'I need the side of the cage,' Jack shouted to Manzo.

Unmoved by the wind and waves, the giant pirate strode over and wrenched off the front wall, leaving the cage in a state of half-collapse. Laying the bamboo frame upon the deck, Jack directed his friends to fasten the sailcloth to it. The task proved almost impossible as waves and spray washed across the deck, but eventually the job was done – resulting in a large kite-like structure. Jack fixed the long length of rope to the frame and handed the other end to Manzo. 'Tie this to the anchor chain in the bow. And bring back the anchor itself.'

Manzo did as he was told and Jack lashed the *Black Spider*'s anchor to a corner of the frame.

With the sea anchor complete, Jack yelled to Captain Kurogumo, 'LOWER THE SAILS!'

Against his better judgement, the captain gave the order. Without sail power, though, the *Black Spider* lost much of its steerage and they were in serious danger of broaching.

'LAUNCH THE SEA ANCHOR!' Jack ordered Manzo.

With a grunt, Manzo tossed the heavy canvas frame over the side. They watched as the sea anchor slowly sank beneath the surface, the rope trailing out behind them.

'HOLD FAST!' warned Jack.

As the line reached its end, the chain was yanked taut. The *Black Spider* jolted and spun on its axis. Its bow turned to face the howling wind and cresting waves. A mountain of foam and sea charged towards them, threatening to engulf them all.

'This is sheer madness!' Tiger exclaimed, diving for a safety line.

'Curse you, *gaijin*,' bawled Captain Kurogumo from the helm.

Skullface stood nose to nose with Jack, his sword still drawn. 'I'll meet you in hell, *gaijin*.'

# 32

# PIRATE ISLAND

Like a ghost ship, the *Black Spider* drifted aimlessly on a sea smooth as glass. Not a puff of wind. Not a cloud in the sky. The mainsail hung limp, the foresail in tatters, the rudder all but useless. Bodies lay strewn across the deck, drying out like dead fish for market in the early morning sun. Captain Kurogumo dangled, unmoving, from the tiller arm. Several pirates were draped over the gunwales. Jack was wrapped round the remains of the cage, his friends caught like crabs within its bars. Nothing and no one stirred.

High above, a great albatross circled the lifeless vessel.

The seabird sounded a mournful shriek.

Jack's eyes blinked open. His bones ached, his skin was rubbed raw, and his throat as dry as parchment. He could scarcely believe he was alive. Indeed, he had no right to be.

The *Black Spider* had passed directly through the eye of the storm, the typhoon being the most violent he'd ever witnessed. They had battled the entire night, riding wave upon mountainous wave, until exhaustion finally took them all. It was a miracle that the ship was still intact. But the sea anchor had kept their prow to the wind, avoiding a broach and preventing the ship from pitchpoling. And, with their progress slowed, the storm had blown over and mercifully left the *Black Spider* behind and intact.

Jack scanned the main deck. Most of the Wind Demons had survived, although several had been unavoidably lost to the sea. The Korean slave was also missing, taken at the height of the *kamikaze*. Easing himself to his feet, Jack quietly roused his friends, putting a finger to their lips. He woke Cheng too and signed for him to follow. Tiptoeing through the maze of pirate bodies, the five of them descended into the hold. Jack pulled out a cask of fresh water.

'Drink your fill,' he whispered, opening the wooden lid with a marlinspike.

They began to scoop as much water into their mouths as they could. Meanwhile, Jack found a knife, a wooden spar, two paddles and a square of sailcloth, then filled a crate with provisions. He quickly gulped down some fresh water himself, before pulling out a second cask and explaining, 'We'll take as many supplies as we can and all swim out to the sea anchor.'

'But what then? I couldn't see any land,' questioned Miyuki.

'I'll dive down and cut the *Black Spider*'s anchor. The bamboo frame will float like a raft. We'll make a sail and escape under our own wind.'

'You had this planned all along,' said Saburo in admiration.

Jack half nodded. 'It was more a prayer than a plan.'

'But what about sharks?' asked Yori.

'That's the risk we have to take,' he replied, laying a sympathetic hand on his friend's shoulder. 'But the storm should have frightened them off. First we need to retrieve our packs from the captain's cabin. We must be quick, though.'

Gathering their supplies, they hurried up the steps out of the hold. As they emerged from the hatch, a circle of steel blades greeted them.

'Leaving so soon?' asked Captain Kurogumo, baring his pointed teeth in a hideous grin.

With no cage to hold them in, Jack and his friends were put to work on repairing the ship with the rest of the pirates. The rudder needed fixing, the torn sail mending, the sea anchor retrieving, and the starboard gunwale had to be shored up a second time.

Despite their status as prisoners, Jack noticed that he and his friends had gained much respect among the Wind Demons. Their actions had saved the ship and most of the crew. Such a debt of life was not easily forgotten or ignored. Even Captain Kurogumo paid due regard, acknowledging Jack's service to the *Black Spider* by pardoning Cheng for his treachery. Over the course of the day, they shared equally in the pirates' meals and many of the crew spoke to Jack, intrigued by his seafaring experience and knowledge.

It took until sundown before the *Black Spider* was shipshape enough to sail again. By then, a light sea breeze had picked up and the captain gave orders to set a course for Pirate Island.

Jack and his friends were escorted to an empty cabin, where more food and water awaited them. But the pirates' gratitude and trust only went so far and two guards were posted at the door.

'I'd get your heads down if I were you,' snarled Skullface. 'You may have won favour on this ship, but you still have Tatsumaki to answer to.'

As soon as the pirate had left, Miyuki began searching the room.

'What are you looking for?' asked Saburo.

'A way out,' she replied, but it quickly became apparent that escape wasn't an option. The cabin's narrow window was barred and the walls were made from solid stems of bamboo.

Exhausted by both storm and ship work, Jack realized they had no choice but to take Skullface's advice. 'We should rest. We'll need our strength for whatever tomorrow might bring.'

Settling down, the five of them soon fell into a deep sleep. The *Black Spider* sailed on through the night, following its secret course across the Seto Sea.

'We're here!' announced Cheng, with a mixture of excitement and trepidation.

Jack woke to see the pirate boy peering through the bars of their window, the golden light of dawn reflected in his face. Despite his lithe strength, Cheng still seemed too delicate to be a pirate – as if he were a butterfly pretending to be a spider.

The door slid open. Skullface and his gang stepped inside.

'Rise and shine, young samurai!' he said, prodding the still-sleeping Saburo with the tip of his sword.

They led Jack and the others on to the upper deck. Captain Kurogumo greeted them with a brief nod of the head. Both hands gripped the tiller, his eyes fixed upon two islands off the starboard bow. They lay side by side, separated by a narrow strait. The first and larger of the islands had sheer cliffs on all sides, giving it the appearance of a giant's fortress. Its smaller sister was little more than a wide thrust of rock, with a crown of trees and sun-bleached scrub dotting its flanks. There was no sign of a settlement, let alone a harbour.

Captain Kurogumo steered the *Black Spider* towards the narrow channel.

'Only pirate ships dare approach these islands,' boasted the captain. 'A fierce tidal race rips through the strait. Any other boat to try has been wrecked upon the rocks. *Unless* you know how and when to sail these treacherous waters, you're done for.'

Caught by the current, the *Black Spider* picked up speed. Commanding his men to lower the mainsail, Captain Kurogumo leant upon the tiller and guided his ship into the confines of the strait. The Wind Demons fell silent as their captain wove a tricky course between cliff boulders and submerged rocks. As they sailed through the channel, Jack noticed two things almost at once. First, there was a hidden wooden fort on top of the smaller island, its battlements bristling with cannon and heavily armed pirates. The second was the craggy gap in the larger island's cliff face – undetectable from the open sea.

Captain Kurogumo nosed the *Black Spider* towards the opening.

'Welcome to our humble lair,' said the captain.

Jack and his friends gasped in wonderment. On the other side lay a huge blue lagoon encircled by sheer walls. Sheltered from wind and storm, it made the ideal secret harbour. At least thirty pirate ships were docked at the floating jetty that skirted the base of the northern cliff. Jack's attention was caught by a crew of Wind Demons unloading goods from a ship bearing the crest of a sea serpent. They were hauling their spoils up the rock face on a system of pulleys, winches and wooden elevators. As his gaze rose, he couldn't believe what he was seeing. Overlooking the lagoon, a pirate settlement clung to the sides of the precipice. A network of walkways and ladders connected hanging cabins, houses and storerooms to create a vertical town. Ninja pirates swarmed like ants up and down the levels. At the very summit, a citadel dominated the cliff top. The wooden structure resembled a dragon's head, with a fortified balcony protruding like a thrusting jaw over the lagoon.

A dark figure stood fearlessly at its end, observing the *Black Spider*'s approach.

# TATSUMAKI

'Pirate Island is a collapsed volcano, its crater flooded by the sea,' explained Captain Kurogumo, steering the *Black Spider* towards an empty mooring. 'As a secret sealed in blood, no Wind Demon will ever reveal its location. And nor will you,' he added ominously.

Jack looked gravely at his friends. They all shared the same condemned expression and he too wondered if this hidden lagoon would be their final resting place. Despite all their efforts and hardships, he now realized his quest to reach Nagasaki and return home to his sister, Jess, had been little more than a pipe dream, a mountain that would forever remain insurmountable.

The crew of the *Black Spider* threw dock lines to the awaiting pirates on the jetty, and the ship was secured and the gangway lowered.

'Now we mustn't keep Tatsumaki waiting,' said Captain Kurogumo, ordering Skullface and his gang to escort the prisoners.

The sharp end of Skullface's sword ensured that Jack and his friends didn't dawdle. They were forced down the gangway and on to the jetty. As they headed for a winched lift, they heard a scream from above. Looking up, they saw a body flailing through the air. Having fallen from the balcony, the man dropped like a stone. He hit the water with a bone-cracking smack, the impact instantly killing him.

The Wind Demons barely paid the dead man any attention as he sank into the lagoon without a trace. The dark figure at the end of the balcony remained.

'Tatsumaki must be in a *bad* mood today,' observed Captain Kurogumo with a sorry shake of his head.

Stepping on to a bamboo-framed platform, the captain indicated for Jack, Yori and Skullface to join him. Miyuki, Saburo and Cheng stayed behind, guarded by Tiger and Snakehead, as four men worked a winch to draw the lift upwards. The rickety construction ascended steadily. Jack was glad he had a head for heights, but Yori looked far less at ease, clutching on to the frame with white knuckles. As each level passed, Jack noted there was an obvious hierarchy – the further up the cliff face they went, the more prevalent the share of ill-gotten gains became, with the dwellings increasingly spacious and well-appointed. By the time they neared the top, some houses were as opulent as royal palaces.

The lift finally reached the citadel level. The four of them stepped off on to a suspended walkway and the lift descended to collect the others. As they stood outside a barred gate waiting for its return, Jack feared what the leader of the Wind Demons might have in store for him and his friends. To toss a man from such a perilous height was the act of a cruel and callous pirate. By all counts, Tatsumaki seemed to be even more sadistic and ruthless than the Sea Samurai Captain Arashi.

But Jack had faced such brutal men before and overcome them: the ninja-hater *daimyo* Akechi, the bandit leader Akuma and, of course, his long-dead nemesis Dragon Eye. Whatever fate awaited him and his friends within the citadel, Jack was determined to fight for their lives with every ounce of strength he possessed.

The lift reappeared and Miyuki, Saburo and Cheng, along with their armed escort, joined them on the walkway. Captain Kurogumo rang a large brass bell hanging beside the entrance. A moment later, the gates parted to reveal a sumptuous hallway inside. Silk curtains lined the walls and windows, ornate lanterns hung from the beams and off to the sides were numerous soft *tatami*-matted rooms, filled with exquisite paintings and ornamental weaponry. They were led down the hall and out on to the balcony.

The heady view took Jack's breath away. The entire ring of the crater was visible: a tree-lined ridge with a panorama of the rippling Seto Sea beyond. The sun rose directly in line with the balcony. Below, like an enormous eye, the crystal-blue lagoon stared back up at them, the pirate ships now little bigger than children's toys.

A figure leant upon the balcony rail, admiring the magnificent vista.

'You must be *very* relieved you've found them, Captain?' said the figure, turning round.

Jack was momentarily stunned. He'd presumed they were meeting the pirate leader, so this wasn't what he expected . . . not at all.

A striking svelte woman with a white painted face, red lips and a swathe of black powder across her eyes stood before them. She wore a Chinese-style blouse and flowing skirt of the finest black silk with crimson thread embroidered like swirling smoke. Her hair was long, dark and cut through with a bold streak of red on one side. The impression was one of heart-rending beauty and terrible power.

Captain Kurogumo bowed his head low. 'I promised – on my life – that I would find them.'

'I'm glad,' said the woman lightly. 'I wouldn't have wanted to throw my favourite captain overboard!'

She gave him a teasing smile. Alluring as it was, Jack noted it was as hard as ice and the captain wasn't eased by her barbed compliment.

The woman turned her gaze upon Jack and bowed her head respectfully.

'I've been so looking forward to meeting you,' she said, her voice smooth as velvet. 'I'm Tatsumaki, the Pirate Queen.'

# 34

# SARU

Jack had never imagined that the notorious Tatsumaki would be a woman. But this was no less reason to fear her. She held sway over the fiercest of pirates and her reputation preceded her.

Not wishing to rouse the Pirate Queen's anger, Jack bowed in acknowledgement of her greeting. 'I'm Jack Fletcher –'

'I know who you are,' she interrupted, strolling over to him. 'The *gaijin* samurai wanted by the Shogun no less. Worth ten *koban* alive or . . . dead.' She ran her fingers through his blond hair. 'That's a great deal of gold for a golden-haired boy,' she mused.

Jack shuddered, as much from the knowledge of the increased bounty on his head, as from her chilling touch.

Yori stepped forward and bowed low. 'With the greatest respect, your majesty,' he began. 'While I appreciate such a reward has its temptations for a pirate, may I remind you that the enemy of your enemy is your friend – this makes Jack your ally. By letting us go, you'll be defying the Shogun. And that would be a *true* piratical act.'

Tatsumaki eyed Yori with admiration and amusement. 'You

certainly have a gift with words, young monk. But, as you've just hinted, Jack's true value goes beyond riches. It's about having influence over the powers that be.'

At that moment, the sun's rays fell on the balcony, bringing with it the full warmth of the day.

'Saru!' called Tatsumaki.

A small red face peeked through the silk curtains of a window.

'*Tessen*,' she ordered.

The face disappeared then reappeared, clutching a slim iron fan. The monkey, with grey-brown fur and a short tail, scampered along the balcony rail. A key jangled round its neck. Approaching the Pirate Queen, the monkey bobbed its head in an imitation of a human bow, then handed over the *tessen*.

'Thank you, Saru,' said Tatsumaki. With a sharp flick of her wrist, the fan's metal spine snapped open to reveal a red painted dragon on a black lacquered surface. The Pirate Queen began gently wafting herself.

The bell rang and the gates to the opulent citadel were opened. Manzo appeared, bearing their packs and weapons. He laid them before Tatsumaki like spoils of war.

'These are all their possessions,' said Captain Kurogumo. He held up Jack's red-handled swords for the Pirate Queen to inspect. 'These belong to the *gaijin*.'

'Impressive weaponry,' she observed, noting the Shizu signature on the blade. 'I trust that your fighting skill lives up to this sword's reputation. I'm intrigued. Who would teach a foreigner such martial arts?'

Jack was about to answer, when the monkey leapt from the balcony rail and landed on his shoulder.

Tatsumaki laughed as the monkey began grooming his hair. 'Saru's taken a liking to you!'

'Must be his ugly foreign face,' snorted Skullface. 'Saru thinks he's a monkey too.'

Jack tried to extricate himself from the nimble beast, but Saru simply scrambled behind his back. Suddenly appearing from beneath his right arm, she reached a paw inside his jacket and snatched out the hidden black pearl. Before Jack could stop her, Saru leapt away, screeching in delight and brandishing her prize.

'Give that back!' cried Jack, going after the monkey.

But Skullface stopped him mid-stride with the edge of his sword. 'Leave your new girlfriend be,' he sneered.

Saru leapt into Tatsumaki's arms. The Pirate Queen offered the monkey a nut in exchange for the pearl. Saru took it, apparently satisfied with the deal, and perched on the balcony rail to nibble at her treat.

Tatsumaki admired the jet-black pearl, its gleam radiant in the morning sun. 'Captain, I thought you said you had taken *all* their possessions.'

'Yes, I . . .' blustered Captain Kurogumo, '. . . just wanted to test Saru's skill.'

Tatsumaki smiled knowingly. 'Well, as my Saru found this rare and valuable pearl, I say finders keepers. I think you'll agree that's fair.'

'Very fair,' replied Captain Kurogumo through gritted teeth, while glaring at the interfering monkey.

The Pirate Queen pocketed the pearl.

'You keep strange company, Jack Fletcher,' she remarked, for the first time paying the others attention. 'A monk, a samurai, a pirate and . . . a ninja.'

Tatsumaki regarded Miyuki with contempt. 'Throw the traitorous ninja over the side.'

Snakehead seized Miyuki by the hair and dragged her towards the end of the balcony. She kicked and fought, but Tiger grabbed her legs and they carried her the rest of the way to the edge.

'NO!' protested Jack, struggling against Skullface, who'd seized him round the throat.

Both Yori and Saburo were imprisoned within Manzo's iron-like grip.

'Such compassion for a ninja,' Tatsumaki remarked in surprise. 'I was led to believe a ninja killed your father.'

'Yes, but not her,' corrected Jack. 'Now *please* let her live!'

'Give me one good reason why. Her kind tried to wipe out the *Fuma*.'

'But Miyuki had nothing to do with that battle. She's innocent.'

'An *innocent* ninja!' laughed Tatsumaki. 'That's an interesting concept. But nothing comes for free in this life. She must pay the debt of her ancestors.'

'You've my pearl for payment,' persisted Jack. 'Take my swords as well.'

'They're mine already,' said Tatsumaki, indifferent to Miyuki's fate.

Snakehead and Tiger swung Miyuki over the balcony rail and awaited the Pirate Queen's final command to drop her. Jack felt his heart wrench at seeing Miyuki on the verge of plunging to her death. Only now did he realize just how much she meant to him. He turned to Tatsumaki in desperation and offered the most valuable thing he possessed. 'I'll reveal the secrets of the *rutter*.'

'*Rutter*?' queried Tatsumaki, intrigued.

'He must mean this,' said Captain Kurogumo, retrieving the oilskinned book from Jack's pack. 'It's a navigational logbook, but I haven't been able to make head or tail of it.'

'It's encoded and in my language,' Jack explained hurriedly. 'But I can decipher it for you – *if* you let Miyuki live.'

'And why would such a logbook be of interest to me?' asked Tatsumaki. 'Explain quickly – my men are losing their grip on your friend.'

'You want influence and power,' said Jack hurriedly. 'Then the *rutter* can give you dominion over the seas. The knowledge inside this logbook ensures safe passage across the world's oceans. With it, you could control the trade routes between nations to your advantage.'

Tatsumaki's interest was piqued. 'So *this* is the reason why the Shogun is so determined to catch you.'

She held up her hand to Snakehead and Tiger, as Miyuki dangled precariously over the lagoon far below. The Pirate Queen looked to Captain Kurogumo, who was grinning from ear to ear.

'We could pirate *all* the ships we wanted,' he enthused. 'Demand protection tolls. The Wind Demons would command the world's riches!'

Miyuki's life hung in the balance as Tatsumaki considered Jack's offer.

'Spare the ninja,' she ordered, much to Snakehead and Tiger's disappointment.

The two pirates pulled Miyuki back from the brink and dumped her on the balcony deck.

Tatsumaki smiled warmly at Jack. 'Give me your hand.'

Jack warily held it out. The Pirate Queen flicked the top of her fan across his open palm. He winced as its hidden razor edge cut a line into his skin. Blood oozed forth. Then she did the same to herself and pressed their palms together.

'It's a blood oath. If this *rutter* is as powerful as you say, I'll let you and all your friends go free. Trick me or attempt to escape, and you'll *all* be thrown overboard into the lagoon. Understand?'

Jack nodded.

'I'm not certain *everybody* does,' said Tatsumaki, looking directly at Cheng. 'Some are still deceiving me.'

# 35

# DECEPTION

'Do you think Cheng's been thrown into the lagoon?' asked Yori, trying to get a view of the balcony through their barred window. All he could see was the sheer drop into the crater.

Jack and his friends had been escorted into a luxurious, yet secure, room within the citadel. Painted scrolls of dragons and tigers adorned the bamboo walls and silk cushions were spread out across the *tatami*-matted floor. A low table was laid with several bowls of cooked rice, exquisitely sliced fish and fresh water. They were now the esteemed guests of the Pirate Queen. But the two armed guards outside their solid bamboo door were a clear reminder that in truth they remained prisoners.

Cheng, detained by Tatsumaki for further questioning, had yet to reappear. The pirate boy's fate was uncertain after Captain Kurogumo had listed his acts of treachery. But, whatever deception he was practising, Cheng had remained tight-lipped.

'We haven't heard anybody scream,' said Saburo optimistically, tucking into the feast while he had the chance. 'At least . . . not yet.'

Jack sat with Miyuki, who'd been quiet ever since her last-minute reprieve of execution.

'Tatsumaki won't harm you. You're safe now,' Jack comforted her.

Miyuki gave him a half-hearted nod. 'But for how long? She's using the influence of our friendship to control you. Once you've given that woman what she wants, we'll no longer be considered useful. And we'll *all* end up in that lagoon – you too.'

'Tatsumaki's made a blood oath with me,' Jack reminded her, holding up his healing hand.

'And you trust a *pirate* to keep their word?'

Jack had no answer to that. 'Then I'll take my time decrypting and explaining the *rutter*. There's bound to be an opportunity for escape before I complete it.'

Miyuki turned on Jack. 'I don't understand you. You're giving away the *one thing* that guarantees your safe return home. Worse, you're breaking your vow to your father. I thought you promised not to reveal the *rutter's* secrets – never to let the logbook fall into the wrong hands. A true ninja would never betray their clan by divulging such information, especially to the likes of Tatsumaki. That Pirate Queen's the *last* person on earth you should be handing this knowledge to.'

The words stung Jack. He realized he'd made a pact with a devil and the consequences weighed heavily upon him. 'But I *couldn't* let her kill you.'

Miyuki's midnight-black eyes met his. 'Jack, don't you know that I'd die for you –'

The door slid open. Skullface dumped clean clothes on the floor beside them.

'There's an *ofuro* next door. You'll take turns to bathe. Under guard.' The tattooed pirate seemed irritated at having to act like their servant. He glared at Jack. 'Be ready by sundown. Tatsumaki expects your company.'

Skullface turned to leave.

'Where's Cheng?' demanded Jack. 'Is he all right?'

Skullface grinned maliciously. 'Oh, you won't be seeing *him* ever again. I can assure you of that.'

The afternoon passed slowly in mournful silence. Although Cheng had never truly been a part of their group, his kindness and courageous interventions had saved their lives on a number of occasions and they each grieved over his loss. Jack had become used to the pirate boy's gentle presence and would deeply miss him.

'Not having arrived at the Yellow River, the heart is not dead,' murmured Yori. 'I must remember to tell Sensei Yamada that. It's a good life lesson . . .'

'And one we should heed now,' said Jack. 'Our journey isn't over. Remember, where there are friends, there's hope.'

Yori managed a brave smile at their shared saying. But it immediately faded as a brutish guard opened the door.

'Next,' he grunted, shoving a scrubbed and cleaned Saburo back into the room.

Having eaten, bathed and changed into a fresh kimono, Jack felt revived and was ready to face the challenges ahead. Between them, they'd agreed a plan to bide their time and observe the Wind Demons in their lair. They would study the pirates' defences for weaknesses, use stealth to acquire weapons and provisions for the necessary sea voyage, and keep an eye out for a suitable boat to steal. Having travelled to Pirate Island in the dark of night, they also needed to discover their approximate location in the Seto Sea. Only then could they hope to make a realistic escape from the isolated isle.

The door opened. 'Follow me, *gaijin*,' ordered the guard gruffly.

Leaving his friends in the room, Jack was led on to the balcony. With the sun setting behind the citadel, the crater below had fallen into shadow. Torches were lit along the walkways, their flames looking like burning lava against the cliff walls. But it was the lagoon itself that bizarrely gave off the greatest light. The waters sparkled luminescent blue, swirling in dotted fans of light as if an entire galaxy of stars had dropped into the sea. The vision was truly magical and for a moment Jack could only stare in wonder.

'Sea fireflies,' said a voice from behind.

Jack turned to see a girl with short black hair, almond eyes and thin delicate lips. She wore a silk Chinese blouse of jade green, with a matching skirt embroidered with silver clouds.

'That's what Tatsumaki told me.'

Jack did a double take. 'Is that *you*, Cheng?'

The girl nodded, then bowed. 'Li Ling is my real name.'

'We thought . . . you were dead . . .' he said, flustered. 'And a boy!'

Li Ling smiled apologetically. 'I'm sorry to have deceived you, but I couldn't risk telling anyone. Tatsumaki, though, saw straight through my disguise.'

'But why pretend in the first place?' asked Jack, getting over his initial shock.

'I got the idea from Hua Mulan,' Li Ling explained. When she saw that Jack had no idea whom she was talking about, she continued, 'Mulan was eighteen when she joined the army disguised as a man. She fought for the Emperor for over ten years to become the greatest female warrior in China. We still sing of her exploits in the *Ballad of Mulan*. I wanted to be just like her – but as a pirate. And the Wind Demons would never have let me join their crew if they knew I was a girl.'

'How wrong you were,' said Tatsumaki, appearing from behind a billowing curtain. The Pirate Queen was robed in an ankle-length dress of red silk brocade, a golden Chinese dragon shimmering from the lower hem to the tip of her mandarin collar. 'Now you know that girls make the greatest pirates of all.'

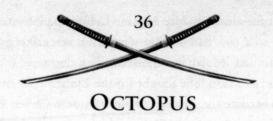

# 36

# OCTOPUS

'Boasting as always!' bellowed a voice thick as tar. A large barrel-chested pirate with heavy jowls and bloodshot eyes limped towards them from the direction of the citadel gate. He carried a vicious-looking trident, which doubled as a walking stick, its wooden end thunking loudly on the deck with each step.

'Captain Kujira, I'm so glad you could join us,' said Tatsumaki. 'This here is Li Ling, a promising new recruit; and Jack Fletcher, the *gaijin* samurai, who needs no further introduction.'

The pirate captain offered Jack a stiff bow, while studying Li Ling out of the corner of his eye.

'Another girl determined to follow in your footsteps,' he smirked, directing his comment at Tatsumaki. 'I hope she knows what she's letting herself in for.'

'Feeling threatened, are we?' interjected another female voice.

A pirate woman of Amazonian build strode over. Dressed in a long flowing robe of deep-blue velvet decorated with white curls of cresting waves, she seemed to part the very air as she walked. Beneath her robe Jack glimpsed a bodysuit of black leather armour, and crossed in her belt were a pair of *sai* – dagger-shaped shafts of steel with two curved prongs projecting menacingly from their handles. The woman's dark hair was tied back by a pure white bandanna with the red emblem of a shark's fin stamped at its centre. Several bands of gleaming gold encircled her muscular biceps. But most distinctive about the pirate woman's appearance were her black-painted fingernails, which had been sharpened into points, making her fingers look like talons.

'I'm Captain Wanizame of the pirate ship *Great White*,' she declared.

Jack found himself compelled to bow. What the captain lacked in natural beauty compared to Tatsumaki, she more than made up for by her domineering presence.

'Me, feel threatened? Never,' snapped Captain Kujira, making himself stand a little taller. 'Always delighted to have more female company.'

At that moment, Captain Kurogumo made an appearance. He entered with a tall man of yellow complexion. Armed with a slim blade in an emerald-green *saya*, the man wore a simple olive-coloured kimono of glistening silk. He had a narrow, elongated skull and a thin nose that was little more than a pair of nostrils. Having paid his respects to Tatsumaki and the other pirate captains, he turned to Jack and introduced himself.

'Captain Hebi of the *Jade Serpent*,' he said, his voice slick and sibilant like a snake sliding through grass. The unnerving impression sent a cold shudder down Jack's spine. 'So you're our guide to the treasure of the world's oceans?' he continued, his tongue flickering along his lips. 'I'm fascinated about what lies on the far side of these seas.'

Mesmerized by the pirate's dark piercing eyes, Jack felt his mouth go dry and his limbs grow heavy.

'Captain Hebi, you'll have more than enough time to question Jack later,' interrupted Tatsumaki. 'Let's attend to more civilized matters first.'

The Pirate Queen clapped her hands and two servants parted curtains to reveal a long, low table set for dinner. Lanterns lit the open-air room and incense burned to keep the mosquitoes at bay. Bowls of steaming white rice were interspersed with plates of exotic fish, their flesh forming a rainbow of colours – white, yellow, pink, red and black.

Tatsumaki invited them all to sit. Jack took his place between the hefty Captain Kujira and his captor Captain Kurogumo. As they settled down on their cushions, the servants poured out fresh water and cups of hot *saké*.

'*Itadakimasu*,' proclaimed the Pirate Queen, raising her cup. 'We thank the Seto Sea for all she provides . . . and the trading ships for all she doesn't!'

'*Itadakimasu*!' the captains responded heartily, lifting their cups too.

Picking up their *hashi*, they began to feast upon the banquet before them. They were not long into the meal when there came a screeching from behind. Saru's red face bobbed out from a window and she scampered over to leap on to Jack's shoulder. The monkey started cooing gently in his ear and grooming his hair again. The pirate captains laughed at the touching display of affection.

'I've never seen Saru so fond of a stranger,' said Captain Kujira, popping a red slice of tuna in his mouth.

'Ow!' cried Jack as Saru tugged at a lock of his hair. He

tried to push the troublesome creature away. 'Will you leave me alone?'

'Think yourself lucky,' remarked Captain Wanizame. 'She usually claws prisoners' eyes out.'

Jack immediately stopped grappling with the monkey, fearful of such a vicious reprisal, and surrendered to her hair pulling. But every time he brought a lump of fish or rice to his mouth Saru went wild and flailed her skinny arms.

'She's hungry. Give her this,' said Tatsumaki, passing Jack a small plum.

Saru took the fruit from Jack and examined it carefully. She then dunked it in Jack's cup before popping it in her mouth. Jack was astonished.

'Snow monkeys are highly intelligent,' Tatsumaki informed him. 'Not only does Saru clean her food before eating but she loves to bathe in hot springs, just like us.'

'I didn't know there were springs on this island,' remarked Captain Kujira.

'No, there aren't. That's why Saru uses the *ofuro* next to Jack's room.'

Jack almost choked on his rice at the thought of having shared a bathtub with the monkey. He caught the sly grin on Tatsumaki's face and wondered if it was her idea of a joke. But somehow he didn't think so.

'Captain Kurogumo, I was worried for you yesterday,' expressed Captain Wanizame. 'That storm was a hull-breaker.'

'The *Black Spider*'s a tough ship,' replied Captain Kurogumo.

'I heard the *gaijin* saved you and your crew,' said Captain Hebi.

Captain Kurogumo grunted. He clearly had no wish to

disclose his inability to ride out a typhoon before the Pirate Queen.

'A sea anchor, I believe,' continued Captain Hebi. 'Ingenious. I must have one made for my ship.'

Tatsumaki raised her right eyebrow in interest. 'Captain Kurogumo, you never mentioned this.'

'The boy's a fine mariner,' he admitted. 'And, by all accounts, a talented navigator too. He gave us quite a chase when we first pursued the cargo ship he was on. But we caught him.'

'Only because of the dragon!' said Jack, his pride pricked by the captain's suggestion that he'd been captured through the pirate's more skilful seamanship.

The Pirate Queen and her captains shared an amused look.

'Jack, your value is increasing all the time,' said Tatsumaki. 'I'm even more intrigued. Where does all this knowledge come from?'

'My father,' Jack replied proudly.

'He was evidently a great man.'

'He certainly was,' said Jack. 'Until Dragon Eye murdered him. But now my enemy's dead, all I want is to go home.'

The table fell silent at the mention of the infamous ninja's name. All the Wind Demons appeared unsettled, as if someone had walked across their graves.

In an attempt to break the tension, Li Ling asked, 'Where's home?'

'London, England,' replied Jack. 'That's why we're headed to Nagasaki. To find a trading ship to take me back.'

'Why Nagasaki?' asked Captain Kujira. 'Osaka has plenty of vessels you could use.'

'Japanese ships couldn't handle the open ocean. They sit too low and don't carry enough sail,' explained Jack. 'Only a European galleon can sail that far.'

'How far is far?' enquired Captain Hebi.

'Two years' sailing. Mostly out of sight of land.'

Captain Kujira whistled through his teeth.

'I can see now why you value this *rutter* so highly,' said Tatsumaki.

Jack nodded. 'It's my father's life work.'

Captain Kujira looked to the Pirate Queen. 'It's all well and good possessing such knowledge. But it seems an unnecessarily long and hazardous voyage simply to pirate foreign lands, when we already have a supply of rich pickings on our own shores.'

'I agree,' said Captain Wanizame. 'Any venture would be highly dangerous without the appropriate ships.'

'We could build some with the *gaijin*'s help,' Captain Hebi suggested.

'He may be a sailor,' snorted Captain Kurogumo, 'but I doubt he's a shipbuilder.'

The Wind Demons continued to debate the prospects and pitfalls of pirating the greater oceans. As the discussion progressed, Jack sensed his value to the pirates rapidly dropping — along with his and his friends' chances of survival.

'There are riches beyond your wildest desires,' interrupted Jack. 'In the South Americas alone, you'll find cities of gold, streets of silver, rivers of jewels. If you pirated the Spanish and Portuguese galleons sailing in those waters, you could fill this *entire* crater with treasure in less than a year.'

The Wind Demons gazed with avaricious eyes over the

expanse of the lagoon. The image of it piled high with gold and jewels whet their piratical appetites.

'Such a prize is very tempting, if not irresistible,' said Tatsumaki. 'Don't you agree?'

The pirate captains nodded vigorously and Jack was relieved to have bought himself some more time.

'Ahh, the main dish,' announced Tatsumaki with delight as four servants brought in a tray and placed it before the Pirate Queen.

A large gelatinous blob sat in the middle of a huge plate. Tentacles spiralled out from the body, rows of suction cups pearly white and glistening in the lamplight.

The dish writhed and reeled over the tray.

'Live octopus! My favourite!' said Captain Kujira, licking his lips.

Jack stared at the quivering mass, unable to hide his disgust as each of the captains hacked off an arm.

'Live octopus builds strength and stamina,' pronounced Captain Wanizame, shoving the thrashing limb into her mouth and chewing appreciatively.

Captain Hebi dangled his in the air and, like a fish gobbling a wriggling worm, let it slide down his throat. Captain Kujira bit into his fleshy tentacle, its powerful suckers sticking to his chin so that he had to prise them off before swallowing each piece.

Tatsumaki caught the horrified expression on Jack's face.

'Before going into a sea battle, it's customary to eat octopus,' she explained, dipping her tentacle in soy sauce. 'With its eight arms, the creature protects us against enemies from all directions.'

'You're going into battle then?' asked Jack, struggling to keep the contents of his stomach down.

Nodding, Tatsumaki ripped off a quivering octopus leg and handed it to Jack. The tentacle continued to writhe in his grip.

'All of us are – so eat up!'

# 37

# THE LIFE OF A PIRATE

It took every ounce of Jack's willpower not to gag. The actual taste of the tentacle wasn't a problem – the flavour was mildly pleasant. But, as he chewed the rubbery flesh, the octopus's suckers stuck to his teeth, tongue and roof of his mouth, making it almost impossible to swallow. With continual grinding, however, he managed to take most of it down.

Li Ling wasn't so successful. She started choking on her tentacle, a piece of octopus determinedly clinging to the back of her throat. Her face went blue as she gasped for air. Only a heavy-handed slap between the shoulder blades from Captain Wanizame saved her from suffocation.

'I thought you said she was a *promising* recruit,' sneered Captain Kujira to Tatsumaki.

Upon hearing this jibe, Li Ling snatched the last leg of the octopus and stuffed it in her mouth whole. She chewed manically, her cheeks and eyes bulging, before swallowing hard. The tentacle disappeared in a single gulp.

'Li Ling has the makings of a great Wind Demon,' laughed Tatsumaki with some pride.

More *saké* was poured and the Pirate Queen raised her cup for a toast:

'Bound by sea and storm, we the Wind Demons pledge to plunder; to destroy all samurai with lightning and thunder.'

The pirate captains clamoured their approval and downed their drinks. Encouraged by Tatsumaki, Li Ling did the same, coughing hard as the fiery alcohol burnt her throat. But Jack refused to join in their ritual.

'Don't you wish to be a Wind Demon too?' said Tatsumaki.

'No,' replied Jack. 'My father said pirates are the plague of the oceans.'

The genial atmosphere at the table died. The pirate captains glared fiercely at him, Captain Wanizame drumming her sharpened fingernails on the tabletop as if wanting to rip the skin from his body.

Tatsumaki, tutting at the remark, held up her hand to calm her captains. 'Jack merely needs educating in what it truly means to be a pirate.'

Fixing him with her startling brown eyes, she declared, 'The existence of the sea means the existence of pirates. The lands surrounding the Seto Sea are among the poorest in all Japan. Much is barren or too steep to cultivate. The communities around its shores and on its islands are constantly in threat of starvation. So the people depend upon the seas for survival. But, when drought or typhoons hit, what can good men and women like us turn to in order to survive? *Daimyo* Mori and his samurai won't help. So we must help ourselves.'

'By raiding, stealing and killing others!' exclaimed Jack.

'And how is that any different to what the Sea Samurai do?' challenged the Pirate Queen.

'The samurai protect these communities from pirates like you.'

Tatsumaki laughed. 'The samurai are bigger thieves than any pirate. They do nothing, yet they tax the poor to fill their own stomachs, even when the farmers and fishermen have barely enough to feed their own families. At the slightest sign of resistance, they raze villages to the ground, destroy their fishing nets and sink their boats. Make no mistake: *daimyo* Mori rules with an iron fist. He shows no charity to his people.'

Having heard the tales of *daimyo* Mori's cruelty and witnessed with his own eyes the brutality of his navy commander Captain Arashi, Jack was compelled to believe Tatsumaki. He'd also encountered similar stories of samurai persecution and indifference when he'd fought for the farmers of Tamagashi village. Resistant as he was, Jack found himself being swayed by the Pirate Queen's argument.

'The Wind Demons don't pillage such communities or steal from struggling fishermen,' she asserted. 'We only target the Sea Samurai and rich traders – cargo boats, grain ships and vessels carrying rice tax. Then we redistribute our gains to those less fortunate.'

'Like us pirates!' said Captain Kujira, sharing a laugh with the other captains.

'*And* local fishing villages,' stressed Tatsumaki, remaining deadly serious. 'We offer them protection from the Sea Samurai too. So, Jack, that is the true life of a pirate.'

Despite her argument, Jack still couldn't believe that a pirate was more saintly than a samurai, especially considering the opulence of her citadel and the riches on display all over Pirate Island. 'You expect me to have sympathy for Wind Demons?'

'No, just your understanding,' replied Tatsumaki. 'Why not judge for yourself when you come on the raid tomorrow? See exactly the sort of riches the samurai keep from their subjects.'

'I'm no pirate,' stated Jack.

'We're intercepting a ship destined for the new capital Edo. It's a *shuinsen*, one of the Red Seal ships of the Shogun himself. We've been planning this raid for months. The boat will be well guarded and armed with cannon. And with Captain Kurogumo having lost so many men, we need a skilled warrior like yourself on-board.'

Jack shook his head. 'I refuse to go.'

'Don't you want to strike a blow against the Shogun?' persisted Tatsumaki.

'I'd rather escape his clutches, not run towards them.'

'But the ship will be carrying rice tax that we can give back to the villages.'

'You don't need me to do that. And don't you want me to translate the *rutter*?'

'That can wait a day or so. This treasure ship is here and now. Besides, it's the perfect opportunity for me to see you in action for myself. I *insist* you go with us . . . otherwise I can't promise the continued safety of your friends.'

From her veiled threat, it was clear that the Pirate Queen wouldn't take no for an answer. And Jack had to admit that the chance to help local farmers, as well as put a thorn in the Shogun's side, was appealing. But more importantly such a raid presented other opportunities.

'I'll only agree if my friends come too,' said Jack.

Tatsumaki grinned at him. 'Not on your life. They remain here as insurance that you'll obey my commands.'

Realizing Tatsumaki held all the cards, Jack asked, 'How will I know you'll keep your word?'

'You don't. It's a matter of trust,' Tatsumaki replied. 'But he who is afraid to shake the dice will never throw a six.'

# 38

# CUTTING OUT

'There's our prize,' said Tatsumaki, pointing to the *shuinsen* anchored in Hikari Harbour two nights later.

Under the faint light of a crescent moon, Jack could just make out an impressive three-masted ship of over five hundred tons with a double keel. The design was a strange combination of Chinese junk and Spanish galleon – the oriental-style batten sails and red bamboo framework on the gunwales contrasted with the European beaked prow, aft-mounted rudder and distinctive quarter gallery. The *shuinsen* was the first Japanese vessel Jack had seen capable of ocean-going voyages. Built as a cargo carrier, it was armed with just six cannon for a last defence. Tatsumaki warned her pirates that its escort of two *atake-bune* and four *seki-bune* were the real firepower.

'We're outnumbered and outgunned,' observed Jack.

The Wind Demons had brought only three ships – the *Great White*, the *Jade Serpent* and Captain Kujira's *Killer Whale*. With the *Black Spider* under repair, Captain Kurogumo and his crew had joined the *Great White*, along with Jack, Li Ling and Tatsumaki.

'Our plan isn't to attack the flotilla,' replied the Pirate Queen. 'We'll use stealth to "cut out" the *shuinsen*.'

The Wind Demons were all dressed in black *shinobi shozoku* in readiness for the assault. So too was Jack. He'd been allowed Miyuki's *ninjatō* for the raid and the sword was strapped to his back. Tatsumaki explained that Captain Kurogumo's crew, with his help, were to steal the Red Seal ship and sail the vessel back to Pirate Island. Meanwhile, the pirates under Captain Hebi and Captain Kujira's command would disable and distract the *shuinsen*'s armed escort. Captain Wanizame and her crew would deal with the small castle that overlooked the harbour.

Li Ling stood trembling beside Jack as the Pirate Queen disclosed her plan.

'Don't worry,' he whispered, patting the sword on his back. 'I'll protect you.'

'I'm not scared,' Li Ling shot back. 'I'm excited. This is my first chance to earn my spider!'

Tatsumaki gave the command to lower the rowing boats and the Wind Demons clambered over the sides. Jack found himself in a boat with Li Ling, Skullface and the surviving members of his gang. No one talked, but Skullface's eyes never left Jack the entire way. The Wind Demons' ships had been anchored just round the headland, out of sight of any samurai lookouts, and the little armada of rowing boats took their time to reach the harbour entrance. Painted black, they were almost undetectable against the sea.

Jack still couldn't believe that he was taking part in a pirate raid. Nor had Miyuki, Yori and Saburo been able to comprehend his decision. But once he'd explained his plan to discover Pirate Island's position in the Seto Sea and so plot their escape route, they understood. Unfortunately, Tatsumaki had other ideas and when the Wind Demons had set sail early that morning, Jack had been kept below deck until Pirate Island was far beyond the horizon.

The raiding party silently entered the harbour. Captain Wanizame's unit broke off and headed for the castle. As Jack's boat glided past the first of the *atake-bune*, a group of Captain Hebi's Wind Demons slipped into the water and dived beneath the surface. Another boat came to rest behind the shelter of a *seki-bune*'s rudder and the crew immediately set to work dismantling it.

Captain Kurogumo's five boats pulled alongside the *shuin-sen*, while the remaining Wind Demon force glided past to the other Sea Samurai vessels. Skullface was in charge of Jack's unit. With a gloved hand, he signalled for them to scale the Red Seal ship's hull. Bringing their rowing boat as close as they dared, they reached up and grabbed hold of the planking. Each of them wore *shuko*, the steel claws digging easily into the wood. Jack's sailing experience enabled him to climb the sides without fear. But the surface was slimy and he had to take great care with his footing. Slowly and soundlessly, the ninja pirates crawled up to the top of the gunwales.

Peering over the lip, Jack caught sight of several samurai guards patrolling the main deck. One was directly in front, his back turned to him. More were stationed on the stern-castle's upper deck, where black shadows clung just below handrails, waiting for the signal to pounce.

Jack had a horrific sense of déjà vu. Once again he was back on the *Alexandria*, the night of the fateful attack by Dragon Eye. Except this time, *he* was one of the ninja pirates preparing to slaughter an innocent crew. But what choice did he have? If he didn't obey Tatsumaki's orders, she would kill his friends. Besides, the Wind Demons would be stealing the ship, with or without him. All he could do was avoid unnecessary bloodshed.

A cricket chirped in the night, the samurai guards paying it no attention. On its second call, the Wind Demons attacked. Blades, sharp and silent, went ruthlessly to work. One by one, the samurai slumped to the deck. Jack leapt over the handrail to confront his guard. Not wanting to kill him, he hit the guard with Fall Down Fist. The blow caught the man across his neck and he dropped like a sack of rice.

Another samurai emerged from a cabin door. His eyes widened in panic upon registering the ninja ambush. As he went to raise the alarm, Jack targeted him with a knifehand strike to the throat. The samurai spluttered, no longer able to cry out. But he still managed to launch a counter-attack, slamming Jack into the handrail. They wrestled for supremacy. Jack's *shuko* claws bit into the man's flesh. The samurai reached for his *tantō*. Jack, crossing his forearms, grabbed the lapels of the guard's kimono and fought to put him in a blackout choke. But the samurai was strong. The man drew his knife from its sheath, ready to plunge the blade into Jack's heart. His eyes bulged, then a second later he collapsed on top of Jack.

Skullface heaved the body off.

'You *should* have just killed him,' he hissed angrily, his blade wet and glistening in the moonlight as he pulled it from the samurai's back.

Skullface signalled for his unit to check the hold. Jack and Li Ling followed. They entered the main cabin and headed down the steps. Sounds of muffled struggles could be heard throughout the ship. They crept down a corridor. To their right, three samurai were asleep. Tiger, Snakehead and Manzo entered the room and ensured the three men never woke again.

To Jack's relief, they didn't encounter any further guards as they entered the hold. Li Ling was ahead of him and she gasped in amazement. As Jack's eyes adjusted to the dimly lit interior, he too saw the countless chests of gold and silver stacked one on top of the other. Bundles of the finest Chinese silk were piled high in crates. And between them were examples of exquisitely lacquered furniture – tables, trays and cabinets. There was only one treasure missing.

'Where's the rice?' asked Jack.

Skullface snorted. 'Rice? There's no rice. This is a Red Seal ship!'

From above deck came the furious clanging of a bell.

# 39

# SITTING DUCKS

Jack and the others burst from the main cabin just as the ring-ing gave out. Hunting for the source of the alarm, Jack spotted Captain Kurogumo standing beside the ship's bell, sword held high and dripping with blood. But he hadn't been the one to sound the bell. A head bounced down the steps and came to rest at Jack's feet. He recognized the face — it was the samurai he'd knocked unconscious with Fall Down Fist.

Torches began to blaze throughout the harbour as the samurai garrison was called to arms, having been alerted by the bell ringing. On-board the *atake-bune* and *seki-bune* ships, the crews rallied to battle stations.

'Raise the sails!' ordered Captain Kurogumo to his men.

A gunshot rang out and the captain was blasted off his feet.

Jack, Li Ling and Skullface scrambled up the steps to the helm. Captain Kurogumo lay on his back, clasping his side and groaning weakly. The deck was slick with blood. But, in the darkness, they couldn't tell whether it came from the captain or the headless corpse. Li Ling immediately applied pressure to the wound, the captain cursing her in pain.

'Give me that *obi*,' she said, pointing to the dead samurai.

Skullface tore off the man's belt and handed it to her. She bound it round the captain's chest in an attempt to stem the bleeding. As she pulled the bandage tight, Captain Kurogumo cried out and writhed in agony, before his eyes rolled back in their sockets and he fell still.

'Is he dead?' asked Jack.

Li Ling shook her head. 'He's breathing . . . just.'

With their captain down, Skullface took charge.

'Cut the dock lines!' he called to his gang as more musket shots were fired.

Tiger and Snakehead rushed off with the others and began hacking at the ropes. Arrows whisked through the air and a Wind Demon fell screaming overboard.

'*Get the mainsail up!*' Skullface barked, noticing the canvas was only half unfurled.

A Wind Demon shouted, 'It's jammed.'

'Put Manzo on to it.'

'He already is.'

The colossal ninja pirate was at the front, yanking on the main halyard, but to no avail.

In frustration, Skullface slammed his sword into the wooden handrail, splinters flying. 'We're sitting ducks!'

A unit of samurai thundered up the gangway. With all the Wind Demons occupied, there was no one to stop them. The soldiers were halfway across before Manzo spotted the threat. He let go of the halyard and charged over. Using his great strength, he lifted the gangway – samurai and all – and tossed the end over the side. The samurai tumbled into the water, shrieking as the heavy gangway crashed on top of them.

'The foresail's up,' announced another ninja pirate.

'That's not good enough!' snapped Skullface. 'We won't harness enough wind to make an escape. We *need* the mainsail.'

'I'll fix it,' offered Jack.

Skullface eyed him doubtfully.

'I was a rigging monkey. I know what I'm doing,' he insisted.

Skullface nodded and Jack ran off, leaving Li Ling to tend to the unconscious captain. Jack launched himself at the nearest shroud supporting the main mast. Hand over hand, he scaled the rigging with practised ease. Skullface gave the order to trim the foresail and took hold of the tiller; the canvas caught the night breeze and the *shuinsen* pulled away from the jetty. Below, Jack could hear the angry shouts of samurai and the blast of muskets. He prayed none of them looked up – he'd make easy pickings for a sharpshooter.

Jack reached the masthead. Although the Chinese junk sail worked in reverse to the square-rigged *Alexandria* – the canvas being raised rather than lowered – he immediately spotted the problem. The halyard block was damaged, its sheave cracked. In the Wind Demons' rush to raise the mainsail, the halyard had slipped off the broken sheave and jammed.

'Give me some slack,' Jack called down, securing the rope on a cleat to hold the sail in place. With great difficulty, he worked the halyard free and realigned it. Releasing the cleat, he then instructed the Wind Demons to unfurl the sail slowly. Inch by inch, the sail's yard spar rose up the mast. At the same time, the Sea Samurai on the other vessels were raising their sails and dropping their oars, determined to give chase.

From his vantage point, Jack could see across the entire harbour. The first *seki-bune* had left the jetty to block their escape.

But, with its rudder sabotaged, the ship had no steerage and it ploughed straight into the harbour wall. As they passed one of the immense *atake-bune*, it made no attempt to pursue them. The holes drilled in its hull by Captain Hebi's men had done their job and the ship was sinking fast. But, instead of abandoning ship, the quick-thinking samurai captain ordered his men to open fire. Cannon and musket shot strafed the *shuinsen*'s deck. Wind Demons dived for cover as the red bamboo guardrails and bulwarks exploded in a shower of splinters and iron shot. Even Jack had to shelter behind the mast as a number of arrows and bullets whistled past his head. Below, the screams of wounded ninja pirates pierced the night. But Skullface ordered no retaliating fire. Faced with an entire garrison, as well as the Sea Samurai force, their only hope lay in escaping the confines of the harbour. They were ahead of the surviving Sea Samurai ships, but they still had to sail past the castle and its formidable bank of cannon.

'Back to your stations!' commanded Skullface. 'They won't dare sink a Red Seal ship.'

But Skullface was wrong.

Lanterns burnt inside the castle, and through the loopholes Jack could make out silhouettes working furiously to load the cannon. It would be touch-and-go if the *shuinsen* made it through in one piece.

As they reached the harbour entrance, a loud boom thundered from the castle's direction. This first explosion was followed by the blast of several more cannon. Jack instinctively ducked, vainly shielding himself from the approaching iron shot.

But nothing hit the ship. Jack looked up to see the castle half in ruins where all the cannon had backfired.

'WANIZAME!' roared Skullface, brandishing his sword in triumph. The rest of the crew cheered in salute of their fellow ninja pirates, who'd accomplished their mission with devastating effect.

The *shuinsen* entered open water without further resistance. By now, the mainsail had been fully raised and trimmed towards the wind. The ship immediately picked up speed and pulled away from Hikari Harbour.

Behind, Jack could hear the heavy beat of drums as the samurai crews rowed after them. Powered by oar and sail, they were quickly gaining on them. One of the *seki-bune* was forging ahead of the others when it came to a juddering halt, its bow suddenly veering off to one side. There was a wrenching of wood and half the jetty was dragged into the sea – the *seki-bune*'s anchor having been tied to the harbour structure.

But that still left two *seki-bune* and a fearsome *atake-bune* in pursuit. These appeared to have escaped the Wind Demons' sabotage tactics. As they raced after the *shuinsen*, the armed samurai on-board shot arrow and musket at the ninja pirates fleeing in their rowing boats. The Wind Demons paddled hard for the safety of their own ships, but they were being picked off one by one . . . until Captain Kujira's *Killer Whale* rounded the headland and lay down a barrage of suppressive cannon fire.

Glancing back towards the harbour, Jack spotted a blaze coming from the top tower of the castle. For a moment, he thought this was the work of Captain Wanizame's crew . . . then he realized it was a distress beacon, its rising flames visible for miles.

# 40

# SEA FOG

Jack scanned the dark skies from atop the main mast and located the pole star. The *shuinsen* had struck a course dead south. Behind, a lone *seki-bune* pursued them. The other two Sea Samurai ships had been intercepted by the Wind Demon vessels and they were now engaged in a full-scale sea battle. The thundering blast of cannons rolled across the water and the muzzle flash of guns lit the sky like a distant storm.

The *seki-bune* kept coming, relying upon its oarsmen for speed, its main mast having been crippled in the firefight. But the wind-powered *shuinsen*, weighed down by its precious cargo, was considerably slower. Only its head start on the *seki-bune* was preventing their immediate capture. Skullface gave orders for every inch of sailcloth to be raised, planning to maintain their advantage for as long as possible in the hope that the samurai crew would eventually tire.

As the chase went on, they soon lost sight of their fellow Wind Demons and their fate in the battle remained unknown. But the castle beacon continued to burn brightly on the horizon – sending its distress call into the night sky.

Jack stayed aloft, keeping an eye on the stars and committing their course to memory. If he and his friends did manage to escape from Tatsumaki's clutches, then he needed to know their way back to land from Pirate Island. But such a prospect was becoming more and more unlikely as the heavy beat of the oarsmen's drum increased and the *seki-bune* gained on them.

'Load the stern cannon!' ordered Skullface.

Tiger and Snakehead went below, just as a hail of steel-tipped arrows peppered the deck. The *seki-bune* had drawn into firing range and the Wind Demons were forced to take cover. Jack had a bird's-eye view of the Sea Samurai priming muskets and preparing to launch a second volley of arrows. Then a heavy boom resounded from within the *shuinsen*. It was followed by the splinter and crack of wood and the cries of injured men. But no Sea Samurai on the upper deck were hurt. Tiger and Snakehead's aim had been purposefully low, the shot destroying the oars along the enemy's port side. Disabled, the *seki-bune* rapidly fell behind.

The Wind Demons gave an almighty roar of defiance. Nothing could stop them now. They'd stolen the Shogun's Red Seal ship! Then Jack caught a flicker of a sail on the horizon. He looked harder and five more sails emerged from behind the shadow of an island, the pale moonlight reflecting off a golden shell on their white canvas.

'*SUIGUN* TO THE SOUTH!' cried Jack, realizing the beacon's call had been answered.

Dawn broke and the Sea Samurai patrol were closer than ever. Following Jack's warning, Skullface had grabbed the tiller and immediately altered course west. But a short while later, across the waters, came a deep resonating tone like the call of a prim-eval bird. Jack, who'd been ordered down from the rigging, shuddered at the unnerving noise.

'It's a *horagai*, a conch-shell trumpet,' Li Ling had explained, still nursing the unconscious Captain Kurogumo. 'The *seki-bune* must be signalling our position to the patrol.'

With the benefit of both sail and oar, it hadn't taken long for the Sea Samurai to find them.

'We'll never escape now,' growled Tiger, eyeing their relentless pursuers.

The day not yet begun, a chill rose up from the cold sea, but the wind blew warm and moist. Jack had experienced such conditions countless times before and began to search for further signs. He smiled to himself when he spotted the haze on the horizon.

'Head north,' said Jack to Skullface.

'That way lies land,' replied Skullface, ignoring his sugges-tion.

'And sea fog.'

Skullface laughed mockingly. 'I thought you knew how to navigate, *gaijin*. We won't be able to see a thing!'

'Exactly,' replied Jack. 'And nor will the Sea Samurai.'

Skullface instantly understood, but didn't like the idea one bit. 'We could run aground or hull ourselves on rocks.'

'There must be charts in the captain's cabin,' said Jack. 'If you can pinpoint where we are, I can pilot you safely through the fog.'

Skullface glanced back at the ever-advancing samurai fleet and cursed. He turned to Tiger. 'Get the *gaijin* what he needs.'

The ninja pirate returned with both chart and compass. Having calculated their position and studied the chart, Jack instructed Skullface to take a bearing north-north-west.

The Sea Samurai fleet altered their course accordingly and the race was on.

The bank of sea fog seemed impossibly far away, its presence too indistinct to judge their distance from it. But the closing gap between the *shuinsen* and Sea Samurai was all too easy to gauge. The drums beat faster, the oars dug deeper, and distance grew shorter as the Sea Samurai realized the Wind Demons' intention and tried to stop them.

'We're not going to make it,' said Snakehead.

The Sea Samurai bore down on the *shuinsen* in a final burst of power.

Then a sudden gust of wind wafted a billowing cloud of fog towards the Wind Demons and they were enveloped within its whiteness. The bewildering fog was so thick that the ninja pirates could not see from bow to stern.

'Head east,' said Jack, holding the compass before Skullface's eyes.

Skullface leant upon the tiller and the Wind Demons trimmed the sails. Unable to see the white canvas, they pulled on the sheets until they could no longer hear the luffing of the sails. Jack counted time in his head. When he thought the *shuinsen* had gone far enough, he instructed, 'Lower the sails, drop anchor and silence your men.'

'What?' said Skullface, incredulous.

'Just do it!' hissed Jack.

Grudgingly, Skullface gave the order. The sails were furled and the *shuinsen* came to a halt. Blinded by the fog, the Wind

Demons had only their ears to rely upon to warn them of the Sea Samurai's approach.

At first, all that could be heard was the lapping of the waves. Then, in the foggy distance, there came the creak of a ship and the splash of oars. The drums had been silenced, no doubt so that the samurai captains could detect the *shuinsen*. Other ships could be heard further off, but this one was close enough to hear the hushed voices of the samurai on deck.

'We were right on their tail!' rasped a voice in annoyance.

Jack held his breath, terrified of making even the slightest sound as the Sea Samurai ship rowed directly towards them. Skullface glowered at Jack, convinced that he'd doomed them to die.

The faintest of silhouettes passed perpendicular to their stern, then disappeared again in the fog. The sound of paddling receded into the distance. The Wind Demon crew gave a collective sigh of relief.

'Raise the foresail only,' whispered Jack. 'Continue on an easterly course, but slowly.'

'But we're behind the enemy, why not just head south?' said Tiger.

'We can't leave the fog bank yet. They're bound to have left one or two lookout ships to attack us as we emerge. We have to put some distance between us and them first.'

On Skullface's command, the crew quietly went about raising the anchor and sail. The *shuinsen* crept through the fog, playing a fraught cat-and-mouse game with the Sea Samurai. When they heard a ship ahead, Jack had to alter course. He studied the chart, but for the most part had to navigate by instinct, guessing their progress and praying he was right. The *shuinsen* wove between hidden islands and rocky outcrops, the deadly obstacles looming out of the fog like monsters of the deep before diving back into the white swirling mist.

Muffled by fog and distance, they heard the crunch of wood, followed by shouts of anger.

Skullface grinned. 'That's one less ship to worry about.'

Jack scrutinized the chart again. 'If I'm right, we should be far enough away from any lookout ship now and can use this island as cover, before heading south.'

Leaning on the tiller, Skullface let the *shuinsen*'s bow turn until the compass point hit its mark. Gradually, like a veil of smoke, the fog lifted and they left the Sea Samurai patrol behind to continue its futile search.

# 41

# A PIRATE'S SHARE

'The Sea Samurai were so close I could have spat on them!' boasted Skullface as he described their miraculous escape to Tatsumaki. The other pirate captains rolled their eyes at his bragging, but nonetheless were delighted to see their prize intact.

The *shuinsen* was safely docked within the lagoon after sailing a circuitous route back to Pirate Island. The surviving crewmembers of the *Great White*, the *Jade Serpent* and the *Killer Whale* crowded on to the jetty, noisily celebrating its unexpected arrival. Having won the battle against the Hikari Sea Samurai, they had returned a day earlier and believed the Red Seal ship lost.

Tatsumaki regarded Skullface sternly. 'And what made you decide to enter the fog? That was reckless . . .'

'The *gaijin*'s to blame,' said Skullface, quick to avoid criticism.

'. . . and brilliant,' she added, much to the ninja pirate's dismay.

Tatsumaki turned to Jack, a smile curling the corner of her lips. 'Another trick you learnt from your father?'

'No,' Jack admitted. 'I got the idea from the Ring of Wind – evasion is far better than engagement,' he explained, remembering his Five Rings lesson with the Grandmaster. 'I was taught that the best move is simply not to be there.'

Tatsumaki studied him intently, her dark eyes seeming to search his soul. 'You certainly didn't learn *that* as a samurai. That's ninja thinking!'

The Pirate Queen stopped two pirates, who were unloading one of the treasure chests, and summoned them over. For a moment, Jack thought that she was going to have him thrown overboard. Then she opened the lid of the chest and took out a generous handful of silver coin.

'In recognition of saving the ship and Captain Kurogumo's crew, I declare you an official Wind Demon,' said Tatsumaki with due ceremony. 'And as a *real* pirate on your first raid, you've earned your share.'

The Pirate Queen filled Jack's hands with the treasure. Skullface scowled at seeing Jack get the reward. But Jack let the coins fall through his fingers and tumble to the deck.

'I don't want your blood money. I just want freedom for me and my friends.'

Tatsumaki gave a laugh like a peal of bells. 'Of course,' she said agreeably, leaving the coins where they lay. 'Just as soon as you've deciphered the *rutter*.'

'Why should I believe you ever will?' said Jack. 'You lied to me about the rice.'

Tatsumaki looked offended. 'Are you telling me there *wasn't* any?'

She turned to her pirate captains for confirmation. They all shook their heads in an act of unified regret.

'I'm sorry I misled you, Jack,' said Tatsumaki, her tone seemingly earnest. 'But I promise, on my honour, some of the Shogun's coin will go to the local villages – including your share, if that's your wish.'

Jack was totally disarmed by the Pirate Queen's apparent sincerity. Although he guessed she used her charm to manipulate people, he found it hard to resist and nodded his appreciation that his share would be given away.

'Now on to more important matters,' said Tatsumaki. 'How was Captain Kurogumo injured?'

Upon their return to Pirate Island the captain had regained consciousness, but was still too weak to give an account himself.

'One of the samurai guards wasn't dead and sounded the alarm,' explained Skullface gravely. 'Captain Kurogumo dealt with him but was shot in the process.'

'You left a guard alive!' exclaimed Captain Hebi. 'That would never have occurred with my men.'

'Nor Captain Kurogumo's,' asserted Skullface. 'Usually.' He glared at Jack, his suspicions left unspoken.

Jack averted his gaze to the deck, knowing that it had been his fault the alarm was raised.

'One thing's for certain,' remarked Captain Kujira, noticing the exchange, but misreading Skullface's angry look. 'Without Jack's intervention and expert seamanship, we would never have got our prize.'

Skullface opened his mouth in silent outrage at Captain Kujira's praise of Jack.

'We need more pirates like this boy!' agreed Captain Wanizame, clapping a hand on Jack's shoulder.

'Perhaps we can persuade Jack to stay?' said Tatsumaki, turning to him. 'It's obvious you're more than welcome.'

Jack was led away, albeit reluctantly, by the Pirate Queen and her captains to celebrate their victory, leaving a seething and embittered Skullface to carry on unloading the *shuinsen*.

'We thought you'd been thrown overboard,' said Yori, when Jack was finally returned to their guarded room in the citadel.

Jack smiled reassuringly at his friends. 'You know I'd never leave you like this.'

'What happened to you?' asked Saburo, his expression a mixture of concern and relief.

Jack recounted the pirates' raid on Hikari Harbour and their narrow escape from the Sea Samurai patrol. When he'd finished, Miyuki exclaimed in disbelief, 'You've been made a *Wind Demon*!'

Jack nodded sheepishly. 'But it does have its advantages,' he said, pulling a roll of paper from the trouser leg of his *shinobi shozoku*.

'A sea chart!' she gasped, her eyes widening in amazement.

'I used it to navigate the *shuinsen* out of the fog. Once clear, Skullface forced me to go below deck so I wouldn't see the final approach to Pirate Island. But he forgot that I had the chart. Although I might not know *exactly* where we are, I've a good enough idea which direction we need to sail in to reach landfall.'

'Is it far?' asked Miyuki.

'In a small boat, perhaps two or three days' sailing.'

'We've been saving food for the voyage,' said Yori eagerly.

He picked up a silk cushion from the corner of the room. Inside, the stuffing had been replaced with small balls of rice. 'I realize there's not much, but at least it's a start.'

'What about water?' asked Jack.

Saburo shook his head. 'We haven't been allowed to keep any water jugs,' he explained. 'But I thought we could use the bucket from the *ofuro* and . . . fill it with the bathwater.'

Jack couldn't stop himself grimacing at the idea. Then he remembered that he'd sucked fish eyes. Surely Saburo's bath-water couldn't be any worse than that!

'Our main problem is escaping from this room,' said Miyuki. 'The guards check on us regularly and rotate every few hours to stay sharp. We're not even given *hashi* to eat with, in case we use them as weapons.'

'There must be another way out of here,' said Jack.

'Without a knife, the bamboo is simply too tough to break through,' she explained. 'I did manage to loosen a floorboard, though. But that's no help.'

'Why not?'

'See for yourself.'

Miyuki pulled back one of the *tatami* mats and lifted the floorboard. Through the narrow gap, Jack had a giddy view of the lagoon far below.

'There's nothing to hold on to,' said Miyuki. 'We'd plunge straight to our deaths.'

# 42

# TARGET PRACTICE

'There's no land *whatsoever*?' questioned Tatsumaki, as she studied the blank hand-drawn map of the Pacific Ocean.

The *rutter* was laid out on a table in one of the citadel's antechambers. In response to the Pirate Queen's question, Jack pointed a finger to a couple of specks in the middle of the page. 'My father discovered fertile islands *here*, directly east by south of Japan. He's written down the course we took. Any ship would need to use them as a stepping-stone to the Americas.'

Captains Hebi, Wanizame and Kujira knelt opposite, scrutinizing the information Jack had given them so far. It was enough to whet their appetites, but not so they could act effectively upon their newfound knowledge – Jack had been careful to leave out crucial facts every so often.

'If we set up a pirate base on these islands,' mused Captain Hebi, his eyes narrowing deviously, 'we'd have a stranglehold on trade passing through the Pacific.'

Captain Wanizame and Captain Kujira nodded their agreement.

'Excellent work, Jack,' said Tatsumaki, closing the logbook and caressing its leather cover. 'Keep this up and you and your friends will be on your way in no time at all.' The Pirate Queen stood, beckoning for an attendant to collect the *rutter* for her. 'We'll meet again tomorrow.'

The pirate captains and Jack bowed her farewell as she strode out of the room, the attendant following in her wake. Saru, who'd been perched on Jack's shoulder like a faithful parrot, leapt down and raced after her mistress. Jack's eyes followed the three of them through the open door into the citadel's inner sanctum. He hoped to discover where the *rutter* was kept, but the *shoji* slid shut before he could find out.

'Come with me, Jack,' said Captain Kujira, walking stiffly with the help of his trident in the direction of the main gate.

Jack looked over in surprise. He was usually shepherded straight back to the guarded room after the *rutter* meetings, or else forced to translate more of his father's notes to a scribe. Watched like a hawk at all times, he'd been unable to acquire a knife, or any other tool as yet, to help facilitate their breakout. Trapped in a prison within a prison, he and his friends were frustrated by the lack of progress in their escape plans. Miyuki now paced the floor like a caged tiger and even Saburo was going off his food. Only Yori remained patient at their prolonged confinement, continuing to methodically stockpile rice.

'Where are we going?' Jack asked.

'On-board my ship, the *Killer Whale*,' replied the captain. 'Tatsumaki wants you to observe its firepower first-hand.'

They entered the bamboo lift and descended to the lagoon. While Jack had taken every opportunity to memorize the citadel's layout, this was his first chance to explore the jetty. The lagoon was bustling with pirates repairing ships, loading supplies and unloading booty. Fish of all kinds were being bartered for stolen goods and raucous shouts burst from dark dens stinking of stale sweat and spilt *saké*. Those pirates not at work were involved in gambling, arm wrestling, or else groggily recovering from the previous night's hangover. The atmosphere along the jetty was one of a tinderbox waiting to explode.

Captain Kujira led the way through the chaotic rabble, his trident thudding on the wooden dock with each step, its sound parting the pirates. As they headed towards the *Killer Whale*, they passed the Shogun's stolen Red Seal ship. Jack was amazed to see that it had been stripped of all its sails, rigging and any other useful items, and now appeared as empty as a beggar's purse.

'A *shuinsen*'s of no use to us,' explained Captain Kujira, upon noticing Jack's surprise. 'It's too easily recognizable. We need everyday cargo boats or, even better, Sea Samurai ships.'

Jack was momentarily taken aback to see a *seki-bune* moored at the jetty. The ship was in a poor state, its mast and rigging destroyed, but the hull appeared intact.

'I captured it during the battle,' said Captain Kujira proudly. 'A ship like this will allow us to pass samurai checkpoints unopposed – no one would ever suspect pirates to be on-board!'

Jack now saw that the *shuinsen*'s main mast was being transferred to the *seki-bune*, along with other spare parts, to restore the ship to seaworthiness.

'Jack, Jack!' cried Li Ling, running over to them. 'Look what *I*'ve got.'

She turned round and lifted her dark hair to reveal a small black spider freshly tattooed on the nape of her neck.

'Was that for saving Captain Kurogumo's life?' Jack asked.

Li Ling nodded enthusiastically. 'And Tatsumaki's asked me to join *her* crew. Can you believe it?'

'Well . . . congratulations,' said Jack, trying to sound pleased for her.

'*And* I get to wear the black and crimson uniform of her ship!' she added, showing off her new jacket.

'Girl pirates!' Captain Kujira grunted at her exuberance, before impatiently limping on.

The *Killer Whale* was moored at the far end of the jetty. Docked alongside was the *Black Spider*. The ship's repairs were almost complete and the vessel had regained much of its former glory and menace. As they passed by, Skullface and his gang appeared at the gunwales. Jack felt their glare upon him as he and Li Ling ascended the gangway to the *Killer Whale*'s main deck.

'Cast off!' ordered Captain Kujira.

The *Killer Whale* left the dock and sailed out through the gap in the crater wall. As they entered the straits, Jack noticed a single-sail skiff had cast off too. It carried five ninja pirates and was loaded with fresh supplies. The boat was headed for the dock below the hidden fort atop the sister island. Jack tried to contain his excitement as he eyed the skiff longingly.

'Are we going on another raid?' he asked Captain Kujira, wondering when the *Killer Whale* intended to return.

'No,' replied Captain Kujira, laughing. He pointed to a small raft upon which three samurai were frantically paddling away. 'It's time for target practice.'

# 43

# HEAVEN AND EARTH

Captain Kujira guided Jack and Li Ling down to the *Killer Whale*'s gun deck. The wooden beams were blackened with soot and the tang of burnt gunpowder hung permanently in the air. An impressive array of cannon lined both sides of the ship, their muzzles protruding into the bars of sunlight that flooded in through the open portholes. The pirate crew, with their muscular torsos bare and grime-streaked, obediently awaited the captain's order to commence firing.

'Heaven and Earth won us the battle against the Sea Samurai,' Captain Kujira said smugly, patting the first two cannon of the starboard row.

Jack gave him a quizzical look.

'This here is Earth,' he explained, admiring the long iron barrel of the first cannon with a bore the size of a man's fist. 'And this is Heaven.' Roughly a third longer with a calibre twice as large, the second gun looked as formidable and destructive as any European 24-pounder culverin. The two types of artillery repeated themselves in pairs down the length of the ship.

'But this one's my pride and joy,' announced Captain

Kujira, approaching a mammoth gun facing out of the bow. 'Crouching Tiger. This beast will hull anything, even an *atake-bune*!'

Jack and Li Ling were awed by the sheer dimensions of the weapon. Mounted upon a reinforced carriage, its barrel was broad and stout as a temple column and dominated the gun deck. Piled beside it was iron shot the size of small boulders and Jack had little doubt that a direct hit at the waterline from one of these would sink any vessel.

'We captured these weapons from a Korean battleship,' Captain Kujira went on. 'Such firepower gives us an advantage over the Sea Samurai. You see, they still fight as if they're on land. Their standard tactics are to launch a salvo of arrows, then approach close enough to board and battle hand-to-hand. But we favour bombardment, keeping our enemy at bay until they're too damaged and weak to fight back. Such long-distance artillery skills, however, require practice.'

He peered out through a porthole.

'Good, our target's gone far enough. Starboard battery to your stations!'

The pirates broke into well-drilled activity. The barrels were cleaned with a dry rammer, then charged with gunpowder. Once packed down, a second round of powder was put into the chamber. Then a wad of paper was inserted and rammed home. The barrel was swabbed out before a cannonball was gently rolled into place. But not all the guns were loaded with round shot. The pirate crew nearest Jack lifted a heavy iron-tipped arrow with thick leather flights into the muzzle of their cannon.

'Those are *daejon*,' explained the captain over the noise of the carriages being wheeled into their firing positions. 'They're far more accurate than shot, having a longer range yet packing no less of a punch. On impact they smash apart, sending deadly shards into the enemy. And for a truly devastating attack, the arrows can even be set on fire!'

The captain licked his lips at the very thought.

'Mark your target,' he commanded his crew.

The pirates gauged their guns' trajectory and adjusted the carriages appropriately.

'Starboard battery – FIRE!'

The deck resounded to the blast of cannon, each one as loud as a thunderclap. The carriages recoiled, bucking away from the portholes like wild horses, the muzzles discharging clouds of smoke into the ship. Jack's ears rang, his eyes stung and he hacked at the acrid stench of gunsmoke.

The haze cleared just as the barrage of cannonballs and iron-tipped arrows reached their target. The sea surrounding the raft exploded in plumes of boiling spray. For a moment, the samurai were tossed upon the waves before disappearing beneath the churning water. Then they bobbed back up, bedraggled but alive. Still clutching their paddles, they rowed desperately in a bid to get out of range.

'I think your crew need more practice,' remarked Jack, with great relief for the poor samurai.

Captain Kujira shook his head. 'You always aim short on your first shot. Otherwise if it goes beyond, you can't gauge how far over.'

The pirate crew began rapidly adjusting the angle of their cannon. Then the guns were reloaded with furious efficiency.

'FIRE!' ordered Captain Kujira.

Another round of explosions shook the *Killer Whale*. Jack felt the concussions deep in his gut. This time the raft was capsized by the violent waves. But still none of the cannonshot hit their mark. The samurai clambered back on-board the raft and resumed their frantic paddling.

Final adjustments were made by the pirates. When the cannon were primed once more, Captain Kujira personally checked the trajectory of each gun and instructed his crew on improving their technique. The last gunner, bowing to his captain's superior knowledge, offered his burning match. Accepting the honourable gesture, Captain Kujira touched the flame to the gun's vent. The Heaven cannon blasted out its *daejon*. Whizzing like a mighty firework, the flaming iron-tipped arrow arced across the sky towards the panicking samurai.

The raft exploded in a fountain of foaming sea spray and fiery splinters. When the water settled once more, the three samurai were nowhere to be seen.

The ninja pirates applauded their captain's consummate skill. Despite joining in the cheers, Li Ling noticeably blanched at the men's cruel deaths. Heartened to see this, Jack wondered if she really had the stomach to be a true pirate – he hoped not.

'Those men were defenceless,' he protested to Captain Kujira.

The captain gave Jack a dismissive look. 'They had a chance to get away. That's more than the Sea Samurai would ever allow us!' he snorted. 'Besides, *no one* escapes Pirate Island alive.'

He eyed Jack meaningfully. Only now did Jack realize

why Tatsumaki had wanted him to witness this atrocity
. . . to convince him how futile any escape attempt would
be.

# 44

# PIRATE TOWN

Unwilling to be deterred by the Pirate Queen's veiled threat, Jack announced that evening to his friends, 'I've found our boat!'

Miyuki, Saburo and Yori could barely contain their excitement at the news.

'So we leave tonight!' insisted Miyuki.

Jack shook his head. He told them about Captain Kujira's cruel display of target practice. 'We'd be spotted immediately by the lookouts on the other island – then blown to smithereens.' His friends' elation slumped into despondency.

'But what other option do we have?'

'None really,' replied Jack. 'Our only chance is to escape under cover of the next black moon.'

'But that's *two* weeks away,' despaired Saburo.

'I know, but we need that time to figure out how to break free from this room *and* get down to the jetty without being spotted,' explained Jack. 'Besides, I still don't know where the skiff is moored. And we don't want to be hunting for it in the dark.'

'Perhaps Tatsumaki will let us go before then?' Yori suggested optimistically.

'I wouldn't count on it,' said Miyuki.

'But Jack said she was pleased with the information he'd given her.'

'The Pirate Queen is just dangling our freedom as a carrot to keep Jack talking.'

Despite harbouring the hope that Tatsumaki would keep her word, Jack knew Miyuki was probably right. He was proving too valuable to the Pirate Queen for her to ever let him go. And Tatsumaki was astute enough to realize that the *rutter* was only as good as the pilot who interpreted it. She would need his first-hand experience to achieve the logbook's full potential. They would never be allowed to leave Pirate Island, blood oath or not.

Another week passed. The daily sessions with the *rutter* grew more in-depth and Tatsumaki's interrogation became more searching. Jack continued to skip crucial bits of information, but Captain Hebi seemed to sense when he wasn't revealing all the facts and had the unsettling knack of getting him to divulge more than he wanted. The longer he spent explaining the secrets of the logbook, the more the pieces of the puzzle fell into place for the pirates. Jack realized that he and his friends *had* to escape at the next black moon, before the Wind Demons acquired enough knowledge to use the *rutter* for their own ends, with or without him as pilot.

Fortunately, during the sessions, he'd gained more of the Pirate Queen's trust and was given greater freedom to roam her citadel, unaccompanied. But Tatsumaki still didn't take any chances, having instructed the guards to search him thoroughly before allowing him back in the room. This made it impossible to smuggle anything to his friends. So Jack spent his free time pacing out various escape routes and memorizing where sentries were posted. He even succeeded in gaining access to the balcony and began looking for safe ways down the cliff face to the lagoon. But apart from the bamboo winch lifts, operated by a four-man crew below, the only other option appeared to be through the vertical pirate town itself.

'Enjoying the view?' enquired Tatsumaki.

Jack looked up guiltily, feeling as if he'd been caught in the act of escape. 'I was admiring the town's remarkable construction,' he replied.

Tatsumaki placed both hands upon the rail and gazed over her domain. 'It's taken ten years of my life to build this. All under the nose of *daimyo* Mori. That's why he'll never defeat the Wind Demons – he has no idea where we are and never will. Would you like to take a closer look at the town?'

'You'd let me explore it . . . alone?' asked Jack, surprised at her suggestion.

Tatsumaki laughed. 'Not if you value your life. Pirate Town can be a bit unruly at times. You'll need a guide. And I'm confident you won't try to escape – I know how loyal you are to your friends. Besides there being nowhere for you to go.'

The next day Li Ling was waiting for him by the citadel gate.

'Tatsumaki's appointed me to be your guide,' she announced.

Jack was pleased to see her, but wondered whether he could fully trust Li Ling now that she was an initiated Wind Demon. It would be just Tatsumaki's style to make their pirate friend a spy.

'How's life as a pirate?' asked Jack.

'It's hard work,' she replied, showing him the blisters on her hands. 'But as one of her crew, I get a share of the treasure.'

Li Ling fished out a silver coin from the pouch on her belt. She polished it proudly and held it up to the sunlight.

*If that single coin is her reward*, thought Jack, glancing back at the resplendent rooms in the citadel, *it's obvious who's taken the lion's share*.

'Shall we go?' suggested Li Ling, leading him towards a narrow rope walkway sloping down the cliff face.

'We're not taking the lift?' asked Jack.

Li Ling shook her head. 'Only captains ride for free,' she replied.

'You have to *pay*?'

Li Ling nodded. 'Everything has its price in Pirate Town.'

They descended the walkway, a slim bamboo rail the only barrier between safety and a fatal plummet to the lagoon basin. Looking over the rail at the precipitous drop, Jack saw countless roofs projecting from the rock face. Smoke curled up from cooking fires and pirates thronged the gangways and ladders. Jack had a clear view of the ships docked at the jetty, but he was still too high up to spot the skiff.

'This top level is for captains only,' explained Li Ling as they passed by grand bamboo houses with balconies overlooking the lagoon. 'This one belongs to Captain Kurogumo.'

Jack glanced in. There appeared to be four rooms, each matted out with the finest *tatami* and separated by silk *shoji* decorated with painted battle scenes. A large treasure chest sat in one corner, surrounded by an impressive hoard of samurai armour, exquisite swords and other prize weapons. Jack's eyes widened — among the armoury were his red-handled Shizu swords.

'The captain's not there,' said Li Ling, thinking Jack was looking for him. 'Now he's well enough, he's inspecting the repairs to the *Black Spider*.'

Jack spotted movement on the balcony. A woman with long black hair, a white face and black teeth appeared. Dressed in a shimmering purple kimono, the *geisha* looked harmless enough until he spotted the *tantō* knife in her *obi*. Her dark eyes regarded him with suspicion. Reluctantly moving on and leaving his swords behind, Jack followed Li Ling down a rickety ladder to the next level.

More houses perched on the cliff face. These were smaller two-room abodes, but no less sumptuous.

'The quartermaster, pilots and ships' carpenters live here,' explained Li Ling. 'The lower levels are for the rest of the crews.'

'Based on rank order?' asked Jack.

Li Ling shook her head. 'Length of service, strength of arm and riches determine your position.'

'So where are your quarters?'

Li Ling forced a smile. 'At the very bottom . . .' Her eyes then hardened with resolve. '. . . For the time being.'

As they descended, Jack noticed the buildings became less elaborate. They still relied upon bamboo frames for strength, but the solid bamboo walls were replaced with pieces of spare decking, canvas sheets and even driftwood. It gave the vertical town a ramshackle look and the appearance that it could collapse at any moment. Only the sturdy storehouses maintained any sense of solid structure.

'This is the main street,' announced Li Ling.

The walkway was the busiest and the widest so far, allowing men to pass three abreast. It skirted the outside edge of a series of buildings with open shop fronts. But these shops didn't offer the typical wares. Many were bars selling cheap *saké*, or gambling dens where pirates could lose their riches on the toss of a dice. A tattooist had set up business in one cabin and was etching a black sea dragon on to the burly arm of a Wind Demon. In the store next to them, a woman and man haggled angrily over a vicious-looking battleaxe – the owner, clearly not getting the price she wanted, was threatening to show her potential customer how sharp the blade *really* was.

As Jack walked along the suspended street with Li Ling, he felt the eyes of many pirates following him. But they weren't the usual looks of astonishment at his blond hair and blue eyes. They were hungry, greedy stares.

Li Ling noticed the attention too and whispered, 'There are rumours that you're worth one hundred *koban* to the Shogun, alive or dead!'

Jack didn't know whether to laugh or be seriously afraid. But, whatever the actual bounty was now, he was a walking treasure chest to these pirates. He could only hope that Tatsumaki's influence was great enough to protect him from such lawless men.

'BELOW!' came a cry.

Li Ling pulled Jack into the cover of the nearest shop front. A splatter of brown-stained water dropped from above into the lagoon.

'I promise, you don't want *that* sort of rain to land on your head,' she smirked.

As Jack glanced over the rail, his eyes happened upon the skiff. The little boat was moored in the shadow of Captain Wanizame's *Great White*.

The promise of freedom was tantalizingly close.

# 45

# WIND WITCH

'Why don't you have your fortune told?' suggested Li Ling, pointing to a dark smoky cabin with dead snakes, dried lizards and bat wings hanging from the beams. 'It's customary for every pirate to visit the Wind Witch.'

'Have *you* visited her?' Jack asked, wrenching his eyes away from the skiff and giving the macabre shop a dubious look.

Li Ling nodded, her face beaming. 'The Wind Witch knows all. She told me that I would make a great pirate one day, and would command the South China Sea.' She gestured for Jack to go inside. He was about to protest, but Li Ling urged him forward. 'It'll be worth it,' she promised. 'I'll wait for you.'

Reluctantly, Jack found himself entering the Wind Witch's den. He had to stoop to pass through the many shrouds that hung from the ceiling like ancient cobwebs. The room stank of sulphur and charred hair. A couple of candles flickered in the gloom and a stone hearth smouldered red with the remains of a fire. Dried herbs, wrapped in bundles, were scattered on the floor. From tiny wooden cages, stacked along the rear wall, Jack heard scurrying and high-pitched squeaks and saw black shapes twitching in the darkness. In the centre of the room was a rough wooden table upon which a bowl, a small pile of animal bones and a dagger lay. But there was no sign of the Wind Witch.

Jack hesitated, wondering if he should call out. In truth, being wary of such magical practices, he was glad to have missed the witch. But, as he turned to leave, a heap of rags burst into life.

'Do not fear going forward; fear only to stand still,' croaked the old crone's voice.

'I think . . . I've changed my mind,' excused Jack, backing out of the doorway.

'To come so far and turn at the last step is a journey wasted,' said the Wind Witch. 'If you want to know the road ahead, Jack-*kun*, you must ask those coming back.'

Hearing his name, Jack faltered mid-stride. He had assumed that this Wind Witch simply weaved fortunes that people wanted to hear. Yet this old crone seemed to promise much more than that.

'Sit!' she demanded, beckoning him impatiently with a bony finger.

Jack warily took his place opposite the Wind Witch. He couldn't make out her features beneath the cowl of rags, but could smell her fetid breath and see the glint of her devil-black eyes.

'Fortune favours the fair,' said the witch, studying his features.

Jack's skin crawled as her eyes raked over his face. 'I don't have the means to pay you,' he admitted.

The Wind Witch clicked her tongue in annoyance. Then her hand shot out and seized him by the hair. Before he could pull away, she'd hacked off several locks with the dagger.

'The mane of a golden child will be payment enough,' she said, rubbing the locks between her skeletal fingers and sniffing them appreciatively.

Pocketing the hair in the sleeve of her raggedy clothes, she kept a few strands back and placed them on the table. Then the witch snapped some twigs into the bowl and, using the embers of the fire, set the tinder alight. She ground down herbs and sprinkled them over the flames, sending potent wafts of smoke into the air. With the dagger, she shaved off several pieces of bone into the bowl, then spat on the mix, her spittle sizzling in the fire.

'Your hand,' she instructed, without looking up.

Jack hesitantly held out his arm. The Wind Witch took hold and with the tip of her dagger blade pricked his thumb. Jack grimaced as she squeezed out three drops of blood. Next she grabbed one of the wooden cages, opened it and shook out a large black spider. Before the creature scuttled away, she dropped it into the flames where it writhed and died. Jack covered his mouth and nose as his nostrils filled with the stench of burning flesh. Finally, the witch added a few strands of his hair and the flames turned bright green.

Leaning over her burning concoction, the Wind Witch breathed in a lungful of the fumes, then settled back. When she spoke next, her voice was deep, hoarse and seemingly disembodied.

'*To gain freedom, one must wake from death and return to life . . .*' Her body shuddered within its trance. '*Pain will nourish your courage when the dragon returns . . .*' Curls of smoke spiralled out from her hooded face. '*Your journey's end has only just begun. The greatest sacrifice is yet to come —*'

Suddenly the Wind Witch gave a piercing shriek and knocked the bowl to the floor, extinguishing the flames.

'What's wrong?' asked Jack, alarmed at her erratic behaviour.

The Wind Witch shook her head, as if petrified out of her wits. 'Some things are not meant to be seen.'

She dismissed him with a wave of her hand. 'Leave. Now!'

'What did you see?' Jack insisted.

But the Wind Witch collapsed senseless among her heap of rags.

Jack jumped up, his heart racing. *What had she meant by her fortune-telling? And what could have been so terrifying to scare a witch?*

Hurriedly emerging from the den, he blinked against the bright sunshine. Shaken as he was by the experience, in the cold light of day, his encounter now seemed little more than a bad dream. He tried to persuade himself that the woman had been playing a trick on him, perhaps for not having the money to pay. Still, it was a frightfully convincing performance . . .

Jack looked for Li Ling amid the throng of pirates, but couldn't see her. Out of nowhere, Skullface stepped into his path.

'Li Ling's been summoned by Captain Kurogumo,' he explained. 'I'll escort you from here on.'

There was something in the pirate's manner that put Jack on his guard. He cautiously backed away.

'Where do you think you're going, *gaijin*?' asked Skullface, his grin a little too wide.

'To the citadel,' replied Jack.

'Then follow me,' invited the pirate, gesturing innocently towards a rickety side ladder.

'But that's not the way,' said Jack, turning to run.

Tiger and Snakehead suddenly appeared, blocking his path. Without warning, Manzo jumped out from a nearby cabin and bundled him inside. Caught in his bear-like grip, Jack was powerless to fight back. Within seconds, he was enveloped by a sack and bound tightly with rope, his wrists and ankles expertly hogtied behind him. Struggling against his bonds, Jack cried out for help.

'Shut him up!' hissed Skullface.

The last thing Jack felt was a heavy blow to the back of his head.

# 46

# KIDNAPPED

The floor pitched and rolled. For a moment, still bound within the sack, Jack thought his sickly disorientation came from the strike to his head. Then he registered the creak of wood, the splash of waves and the flap of canvas. He was at sea.

Apart from the dull throb at the base of his skull, Jack didn't think he was otherwise injured. He tried to move, but the ropes held him fast. His throat was dry from the dust within the sack. He considered shouting for help, but it was unlikely anyone would come running to his aid. It was better to remain silent and learn what he could before revealing to his captors that he'd regained consciousness.

He had no idea how long he'd been out for. No light seeped through the coarse sacking, so Jack guessed that he was either in the hold of a ship or else night had fallen.

He heard voices: only four and he recognized all of them – Skullface, Snakehead, Tiger and Manzo. If that was the case, he was probably on a small boat, otherwise there'd need to be more crew.

What had Skullface and his gang planned for him? His sudden abduction didn't bode well. It would certainly be against the wishes of Tatsumaki. And he'd witnessed the cruel games of torture that these pirates enjoyed playing with their prisoners. *Was this the danger the Wind Witch had foreseen?* If so, surely she could have given him better warning!

Jack listened as Skullface issued the command to lower the sail. A moment later, the boat bumped against a rock and the deck lurched as someone leapt ashore.

'Manzo, bring the *gaijin*,' said Skullface.

Jack was manhandled off the boat and tossed over the pirate's shoulder. Manzo's sandalled feet crunched on loose stones as they trekked away from the shoreline. No one spoke for a while. Then Jack was dumped unceremoniously on the ground. He couldn't help letting out a cry as he landed upon a jagged outcrop.

'The *gaijin*'s awake,' growled Manzo.

The sacking was roughly pulled off him and Jack was greeted by Skullface's leering tattooed features.

'Pleasant journey?' he mocked.

Jack coughed up the dust from his lungs and looked around. They were atop a barren island, little more than a lump of craggy rock with a single windswept tree clinging to its peak. A waning crescent moon hung in the night sky, lending a pale, ghostly sheen to the surrounding waters. There appeared to be no other islands in sight.

Jack's assumption regarding the number of kidnappers had been correct. The skiff, in which he'd placed so much hope for an escape, lay bobbing at the water's edge . . . empty.

'What do you want with me?' said Jack.

'You're an ill omen, *gaijin*,' spat Skullface. 'Ever since we picked you up, the *Black Spider*'s been cursed – captured by Sea

Samurai, caught in a *kamikaze* storm, the captain shot. You even took *my* credit for bringing home the Shogun's Red Seal ship.'

He kicked Jack viciously in the stomach. Jack doubled up with pain, rolling on the ground as he gasped for breath.

'That was my one chance to become a CAPTAIN!' snarled Skullface in outrage. 'So it's time to get rid of you for good, *gaijin*.'

Recovering from the blow, Jack wheezed, 'You're going to . . . maroon me?'

Skullface chuckled. 'No, that would be merciful.'

A cold inevitability struck Jack. 'Torture and kill me?'

'Tempting,' admitted Skullface, 'but we'll leave that to the Sea Samurai. You're worth more alive.'

'Look, their ship's here already,' said Snakehead, glancing out to sea.

Skullface grinned. 'Told you they wouldn't miss an opportunity like this to please their Shogun.'

The pirates' plan was now clear to Jack. They were going to exchange him for the bounty on his head. Following his instinct that the four pirates were acting on their own, he said, 'But Tatsumaki's sure to find out you kidnapped me. And when she does, she'll punish you all.'

Skullface laughed. 'Not likely. We'll say you escaped . . . and blame it on Li Ling. That pretty little pirate will lose her head before the sun's up.'

Jack felt all hope drain from him. Not only was he being sent to his death but Li Ling would suffer too. And what would happen to Yori, Saburo and Miyuki? Without him, his friends would hold no value to Tatsumaki. They'd be thrown to their deaths in the lagoon, fish food just like all her other victims.

Jack writhed against his bonds, determined to free himself.

'No use struggling, *gaijin*,' spat Tiger. 'They're on their way up.'

Jack became desperate. 'But I'm of great value to your Pirate Queen. I still have to translate the *rutter*.'

'You're of great value to *us*,' replied Skullface. 'We've negotiated ten *koban* each and a pardon in return for your head.'

Jack racked his brains for some samurai or ninja technique to save him from his predicament. But he was as powerless as a turtle on its back.

A figure strode up the rise to the crest of the peak. Dressed in a black *shinobi shozoku*, the man became silhouetted against the starry sky like a black ghost. He stopped before them, the moonlight reflecting in his eye . . . his single green eye.

# 47

# A GHOST FROM THE PAST

Jack's heart froze in his chest. The air suddenly seemed starved of oxygen, his mind unable to comprehend the chilling presence before him. It was simply not possible. He'd seen Dragon Eye plunge to his death. The ninja was dead, gone forever.

Yet here his nemesis stood – a ghost from the past sent to haunt him.

Jack might have thought himself going crazy, if he'd been the only one to see this phantom. The four pirates had swiftly drawn their swords to keep the ninja at bay.

'Who are you? Where's Captain Arashi?' demanded Skullface, his voice tight and edgy.

The ninja remained indifferent to the threat of blades.

'Dokugan Ryu,' he replied, with a curt bow of his head.

The mere mention of his name caused Tiger and Snakehead to exchange uneasy glances.

'I represent the interests of the Shogun himself,' Dragon Eye continued as a unit of Sea Samurai marched up behind him. 'Now hand over the *gaijin*.'

'The reward first,' Skullface insisted, trying to maintain control of the situation.

Dragon Eye nodded grudgingly to one of the samurai, who stepped forward and placed a small wooden chest on the ground. He opened it up to reveal a stack of forty oval-shaped coins.

*So that's the value of my life*, thought Jack, resigning himself to his fate. *Less than three koban a year!*

Skullface's eyes lit up at the hoard of shimmering gold. 'And our pardons from *daimyo* Mori.'

Dragon Eye produced a scroll of parchment sealed with a red wax stamp. Skullface examined the *daimyo*'s official seal in the moonlight.

'It *appears* genuine,' he said, giving Tiger the nod.

'You'd be wise not to doubt me,' said Dragon Eye. 'You have the reward. Now what about the *rutter*?'

Skullface looked confused. 'The *rutter*? We don't have it.'

Dragon Eye glared at the pirate. 'So where is it?'

'That wasn't part of the deal,' argued Skullface.

'Just answer the question,' snapped Dragon Eye, noting Tiger was about to claim the treasure chest.

A glint of steel flashed through the air. It was so quick that it might have been mistaken for a shooting star. Tiger collapsed backwards, his head parting from his shoulders and bouncing down the hillside.

Dragon Eye flicked the pirate's blood from his *ninjatō*, the tip of the blade stopping inches from Jack's face. In that moment Jack recognized the swirling *hamon* pattern along the steel and the swordmaker's name – Kunitome – etched by the hilt. This was the final proof that the dreaded ninja was no ghost. The sword was *Kuro Gumo* – Black Cloud – Dragon Eye's infamous blade.

'Don't make me ask you again,' said Dragon Eye, turning his attention back to Skullface.

Incensed at seeing his fellow Wind Demon slaughtered, Manzo launched himself at Dragon Eye. The ninja merely stepped aside, letting the pirate fly past before driving the *ninjatō* into his back. Manzo gave a great guttural groan, then toppled over the rocky crag.

Skullface now rushed Dragon Eye, slicing his sword across the ninja's chest. But Dragon Eye deflected the attack and countered at such speed that Skullface didn't realize he'd lost . . . until his sword dropped to the ground, his right hand still attached to the hilt.

Clasping his bleeding stump to his chest, Skullface crumpled to his knees, his mouth open in a silent scream, the pain yet to register.

Dragon Eye stood over him. 'Last chance. Who has the *rutter*?'

'Go . . . burn in hell!' spluttered Skullface.

Unmoved by the pirate's insult, Dragon Eye formed his fingers into Snakehead Fist. With a sharp sudden jab, he plucked out the pirate's right eye. Skullface now howled in agony, blood streaming down his cheek.

'Tatsumaki has it . . .' he wailed.

'And where is this Tatsumaki?'

'. . . on Pirate Island.'

'Where's Pirate Island?'

Despite his horrendous suffering, Skullface now held his tongue. Dragon Eye didn't hesitate. He tore out the pirate's other eye. Skullface's tortured screams filled the night sky. Jack could no longer bear to watch; nor could any of the samurai. Without his eyes, Skullface's tattooed head now became truly skull-like.

The shrieks faded into agonized sobs, but still Skullface refused to answer.

Jack heard a sickening crunch of steel on bone, then a body slump lifeless to the ground. As much as he'd loathed the pirate, Jack had to admit Skullface remained a loyal Wind Demon to the bitter end.

Dragon Eye now set his sights on Snakehead, who'd been too shocked by the sudden turn of events to react. The pirate immediately threw down his sword and surrendered. Offering the man no mercy, Dragon Eye struck a rapid combination of pressure points across Snakehead's body.

Jack instantly recognized the lethal ninja technique of *Dim Mak*.

Snakehead went rigid, paralysed to the spot by the ninja's Death Touch. Jack knew from his own bitter experience at the hands of Dragon Eye that a firestorm of pain would be spreading throughout the pirate's body, eventually crippling and crushing his heart.

'Where is it?' demanded Dragon Eye.

The terror in Snakehead's eyes was palpable, but he didn't respond.

Dragon Eye drove a thumb into a nerve point in the pirate's neck. Snakehead let out a scream. But uttered no words.

With the unit of samurai distracted once again by the gruesome torture, Jack broke the paralysis that had held him ever since laying eyes upon his old enemy. Determined to escape, he felt behind him until his fingers came across a particularly sharp piece of rock protruding from the ground. Then he began furiously rubbing its jagged edge against the rope binding his wrists. On several occasions, he had to bite down on his tongue as the rock cut into his skin.

Snakehead shrieked again, but weaker this time as Dragon Eye targeted a nerve point beneath his jaw. Jack realized time was fast running out. The rope became slick with his own blood, but he kept cutting away.

Without even a glance in his direction, Dragon Eye suddenly said, 'Cease your pathetic escape attempt, *gaijin*, or I'll cut your hands off too.'

Jack was given no choice but to comply as one of the samurai now held the edge of a *wakizashi* to his throat.

Dragon Eye resumed his systematic torture. Snakehead was now moaning and whimpering like a wounded dog. Eventually, his resistance was broken. In between feeble breaths, Snakehead revealed all – the location of Pirate Island, the strength of the Wind Demons' forces and even the danger of entering the tidal straits – before begging for the torture to end.

'With pleasure,' said Dragon Eye, severing the pirate's head from his body.

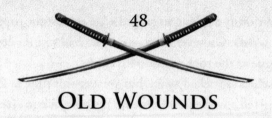

# 48

# OLD WOUNDS

Jack was bound to the main mast of the Sea Samurai's ship and surrounded by six armed guards. Dragon Eye was taking no chances with him.

The ninja stood upon the upper deck, a wraithlike figure against the star-studded sky, the samurai crew keeping a wary distance. He gave the order to cast off and the ship headed due north.

The bodies of the four Wind Demons had been left to rot on the barren island, the skiff at the shoreline their only grave marker. Even though Jack held little sympathy for the deceased pirates, he wouldn't have wished such torturous deaths on any of them. Their harrowing ends merely proved that Dragon Eye remained as ruthless as ever.

Jack felt the ninja's glare upon him. Even from across the deck, Dragon Eye's malice reached out like tendrils of ice. For a moment he found it hard to breathe, seized as he was by a suffocating combination of terror, despair and disbelief. His mind still couldn't grasp the ninja's miraculous resurrection. Was Dragon Eye somehow *immortal*? The idea sent a shudder through him. There was no way any normal man could have survived the drop from Osaka Castle's top tower, eight storeys down to the stone courtyard below. Besides, he'd witnessed Dragon Eye die with his own eyes . . . then again . . . thinking back to that war-torn night, he'd only seen the ninja *fall*.

He'd not actually seen him land . . . or had any real proof of his death.

Perhaps Dragon Eye had landed upon a lower roof? Or used a grappling rope to halt his descent? Maybe a *sakura* tree had broken his fall? Whatever had happened, there was no denying the fact that his nemesis was back and very much alive.

As Jack returned the ninja's cold pitiless stare, he felt the old wounds open up again. His heart bled with sorrows he'd once thought healed, or at least subdued. Grief for his dead father flooded through him in a fresh wave of loss. Visions of Dragon Eye thrusting the blade into his father's chest flashed before his eyes and he began to sob. All his struggles to overcome the ninja had been in vain. Justice had never been carried out. His father was dead, he and his sister orphaned, while his murderer *still* lived. Yamato, his friend and brother-in-arms, had sacrificed himself to save Jack and Akiko. Now it appeared Yamato had died for nothing . . .

Jack was struck by a startling revelation. *If Dragon Eye had survived, then so too might Yamato!*

A burst of unimaginable hope filled his heart. Even now, Yamato could be reunited with his father Masamoto, or roaming Japan searching for him. Jack tried to calm himself and temper his expectations. He knew the odds were stacked against such a possibility – otherwise Akiko, Yori or Saburo would surely have got word of their friend's survival. But there was still a slim chance and Jack wasn't willing to give up on his newfound hope. He used it to ignite a renewed determination to survive.

Jack had no idea how he could escape. Tied to a mast, guarded by samurai and watched by Dragon Eye, the situation was hopeless. He couldn't depend upon his friends to save him this time; they were relying upon *him* to free them. Still, he had no intention of letting them down.

A realization slowly dawned on Jack. He'd been warned of Dragon Eye's return – not once but twice.

First, the warrior spirit of Taira Masamori, the Great Pirate Queller – or whoever the man was – had given him a lesson in the Ring of Wind *'for when an old enemy returns anew'*. Jack recalled the unyielding oak on the cliff top that had lost its fight against the wind, and the flexible feather that had survived.

And, second, the Wind Witch had foreseen: *'Pain will nourish your courage when the dragon returns . . .'*

It was so obvious now. Both had tried to prepare him for this encounter with Dragon Eye.

Jack decided to follow their advice. He would *'go where the wind blows'*, letting the memory of his father burn like a fire within him.

# 49

# FLYING FAN

The Sea Samurai ship was still in sight of the barren island when there was a commotion on deck.

'What's the problem?' demanded Dragon Eye.

'One of my lookouts saw something,' replied the ship's captain, peering astern into the darkness.

'What *exactly*?' said Dragon Eye, impatient for details.

'I don't know. It looks like –' Suddenly a blinding blast of hellfire lit up the night sky. '– A SEA DRAGON!' screamed the captain as he dived to the deck.

The ball of flame rocketed towards the ship. Dragon Eye took cover just as the stern bulwark exploded into lethal shards of blazing timber. A samurai too close to the rail was engulfed. Screaming and flailing his arms, the burning man toppled over the side.

Held captive, Jack could only watch as the fire-breathing monster surged closer. It spat out another flaming ball. This time the rudder was hit. The ship lurched. The captain desperately tried to regain control, but there was little he could do. All steerage was lost.

'Port side, fire your cannon!' ordered Dragon Eye as the

creature charged headlong at the disabled ship.

From below came the hurried sounds of priming. A loaded cannon was hauled into firing position and a few moments later an almighty boom rocked the deck. The shot whizzed through the air and, more by luck than fine judgement, struck the dragon first time. But the cannonball just bounced off the armoured back of the beast.

Unharmed and undeterred, the dragon continued to hurtle towards them at terrifying speed.

'BRACE YOURSELVES!' snarled Dragon Eye, a second before the beast rammed into the port side. The bone-shattering impact sent samurai flying across the deck. Dragon Eye alone, as surefooted as a cat, kept his feet – as did Jack, but only because he was tied to the mast.

Jack now found himself staring into the jaws of death: tendrils of smoke rose from the dragon's throat, the gaping mouth of the beast large enough to swallow him whole. Two rows of jagged teeth threatened to rip the flesh from his body.

But the dragon held off, its fiery eyes staring unblinking at him. Then Jack watched in astonishment as Wind Demons, clad in black, clambered across the armoured back of the beast and swarmed on to the samurai ship's deck.

The crew, stunned by the dragon's surprise attack, were slow to react to this new threat, and some were slaughtered where they stood.

'THEY'RE JUST PIRATES!' bawled Dragon Eye, his *ninjatō* already at work.

The Sea Samurai snapped out of their shock and began to fight off the invaders. Weapons flashed through the night and the two sides clashed in a ferocious battle.

Leading the Wind Demons, a whirling dervish in black and red robes cut a path through the samurai crew. True to her name, Tatsumaki was a tornado of destruction as she wielded a formidable *naginata*. The curving blade atop the long pole sliced in arcs, felling Sea Samurai left, right and centre.

Jack was awed by the ferocious skill of the Pirate Queen as she spearheaded an attack towards the main mast.

Realizing her intention, Dragon Eye yelled, 'KILL the *gaijin*!'

A samurai broke off and headed for Jack. Struggling against his bonds, Jack tried to free an arm to fight back. But he was bound tighter than a hangman's noose. The samurai grinned as he raised his sword to hack the head off his defenceless victim. Jack writhed in desperation to avoid the lethal blade, knowing Tatsumaki could never reach him in time.

The Pirate Queen, realizing this too, pulled her *tessen* from her *obi*. With a flick of her wrist, the iron fan opened and she threw it in Jack's direction. The *tessen* spun through the air like a single-winged hunting bird. It skimmed in front of the samurai, causing him to falter in his attack. Then the man's eyes widened in shock. He dropped his sword and clasped his neck. Blood poured through his fingers, the fan's razor-sharp edge having sliced his throat wide open. Spluttering a final breath, the samurai collapsed at Jack's feet.

Moments later, he was surrounded by a protective cordon of Wind Demons.

'Secure the ship!' commanded Tatsumaki as her pirates laid waste to the remaining Sea Samurai.

A Wind Demon rushed to Jack's side.

'I thought you were as good as dead,' said Li Ling, pulling off her hood.

In a single swipe of her *naginata*, Tatsumaki sliced through the ropes binding Jack.

'Thanks for coming to my rescue,' he said, rubbing the circulation back into his arms.

Tatsumaki flashed him a triumphant smile as she retrieved her deadly fan. 'You're too precious to let *anyone* take you.'

Jack looked around at the slain samurai. 'Where's Dragon Eye?' he asked.

'Dokugan Ryu? But you said he was dead,' replied Tatsumaki, bemused.

Jack gave a despondent shake of his head. 'I was wrong.'

'That ninja must have more lives than a cat!'

The Pirate Queen ordered an immediate sweep of the ship. The Wind Demons turned over dead bodies, searched the cabins and hunted below deck. But it was as if Dragon Eye had never existed.

# 50

# THE KOKETSU

Jack stood before the sea dragon and laughed at how easily people had been fooled. In the moonlight, the beast had an unsettling lifelike quality. But close up, no longer distracted by the chaos of battle, he saw the creature for what it was – a strange and formidable battleship.

The design was unlike anything he'd ever seen, or could possibly have imagined. Protruding from the bow was the dragon itself, an immense figurehead large enough to contain a gun crew and a Heaven cannon that fired flaming shot. The armoured back of the beast was a curved roof of iron plates with vicious spikes thrusting up. Not only did this 'dragon skin' deflect cannonballs but it prevented the enemy from boarding the ship – grappling hooks couldn't gain purchase and any boarder foolish enough to try would find their feet pierced by the spikes. This iron-clad roof completely enclosed the ship's overhanging top deck and shielded the crew within. From a defensive point of view, the Wind Demons' battleship appeared unassailable.

But it was also an attack vessel. On all sides there were gun ports, three to the bow and stern and ten down either side.

The dragon's twenty legs were powerful *yuloh*-style oars, projecting down from the overhanging deck, giving the ship not only speed but manoeuvrability. Its long tail turned out to be the main mast, which had been lowered to protect it during the assault. At the waterline was another carved face, one that Jack recognized. A twisted and scarred protrusion with hooked teeth and blood-red eyes, it was the battering ram that had hulled Captain Arashi's *atake-bune*.

'She's named the *Koketsu*,' remarked Tatsumaki proudly. 'It means "Jaws of Death".'

Jack thought it an apt name for such a fearsome vessel.

'We captured her from the Korean navy,' the Pirate Queen continued. 'Only a handful have ever been built, so the Sea Samurai have never seen one before. That's why they believe in sea dragons!'

She gave a throaty laugh and climbed on to the ship's roof.

'Welcome aboard,' she said, offering her hand. 'Let's talk, while my men finish unloading the samurai ship of its weapons and supplies.'

Stepping up a gangplank, Jack followed the Pirate Queen along a narrow walkway between the rows of iron spikes to a wooden hatch. Clambering inside the belly of the beast, Jack found himself on the main deck. Unusually for a battleship, the deck was shared by both oarsmen and gunners. The twenty Heaven and Earth cannon were divided by twenty teams of hulking oarsmen, each so powerfully built they could have crushed a man's skull with their bare hands.

'These men are the pumping heart of the *Koketsu*,' proclaimed Tatsumaki as her muscular crew bowed their respects. She indicated the two rows of cannon. 'And these its teeth.'

As they headed for her cabin, Jack was surprised at how orderly and neat everything appeared. The Pirate Queen evidently maintained a disciplined ship. When she opened the door to her quarters, there came a screech of delight and a flash of fur landed on Jack's shoulder.

'Saru!' exclaimed Jack, for once glad to see the little monkey. Saru chattered back in answer, happily preening his hair.

Tatsumaki's cabin was in stark contrast to the opulence of her citadel. Functional and uncluttered, it housed a lacquered cabinet in one corner, a low table in the centre and a weapons rack down one wall – upon which Tatsumaki now laid her *naginata*. Drawing up a red silk cushion, she sat upon the polished wooden floor behind the table and invited Jack to join her. Jack took his place opposite, Saru still perched on his shoulder, contentedly chewing on a piece of fruit.

'How did you find me?' asked Jack.

'Li Ling raised the alarm, when she discovered you hadn't returned to the citadel,' explained Tatsumaki, cleaning the edge of her lethal *tessen* before fanning herself with it. 'At first, we thought you'd escaped. The skiff was missing. But you were last spotted with Skullface and his gang. And they were missing too. Then it was just a combination of guesswork and luck that we found you. That barren island is the closest to our base. But, if we'd arrived any later, you and that samurai ship would have been long gone.'

There was a knock at the door and Li Ling entered with another female pirate, hefting a small wooden chest.

'This was the only treasure we found on-board,' Li Ling informed Tatsumaki.

She placed it on the table and opened it to reveal the stack of gleaming *koban*.

'That was the reward for my head,' explained Jack.

'And now it's payment for your rescue,' said Tatsumaki, closing the lid and taking possession of the gold. 'Though *you* still owe me for saving your life.'

Jack realized it was a debt that would be hard to repay.

'I also found this,' said Li Ling, handing Tatsumaki the scroll with the *daimyo*'s wax seal. 'It looks important.'

Tatsumaki broke the seal and read the contents. She scowled. 'Where's that traitor Skullface and his gang now?'

'Dragon Eye tortured them to death,' replied Jack gravely, recalling the gruesome scene.

'Good.' Tatsumaki crushed the pardon in her hands. 'Saves me the trouble. We can now return to Pirate Island without further delay.'

Jack wondered whether he should tell Tatsumaki about Snakehead's confession. If Dragon Eye had got away, then the Sea Samurai would probably launch an assault on the island. The Pirate Queen would be grateful for the warning. She might even trust him more; maybe release him and his friends as promised. Then again, a surprise attack could be just the opportunity they needed – in the confusion of battle, they might be able to slip away unnoticed. But it would be a risky strategy, since they could be caught or killed by either side. And Dragon Eye would be hunting him down too.

'Something on your mind, Jack?' asked Tatsumaki.

Jack realized that his best chance of survival lay with Tatsumaki and the Wind Demons. He took a deep breath before replying. 'Snakehead revealed the location of Pirate Island.'

For a moment, Tatsumaki's face appeared to turn to stone. 'To whom?'

'Dragon Eye and his samurai escort.'

The Pirate Queen's expression relaxed slightly. 'Then we have nothing to worry about. They're all dead.'

'Not Dragon Eye, though,' reminded Jack.

'I don't see how that ninja can elude death a second time. If he's no longer on the ship, he must have drowned.'

'You should never underestimate Dragon Eye,' said Jack.

'But we're in the middle of the Seto Sea,' contended Tatsumaki. 'Even if he managed to swim back to the island, it's barren and he'd be marooned.'

'Not if he found Skullface's boat.'

Tatsumaki snapped her fan shut with such force that it sounded like a bone breaking. A second later, she was on her feet, ordering her pirates to stop plundering the samurai ship and set sail at once for the barren island. The *Koketsu* surged across the sea. But, when it rounded the headland, the skiff was gone.

# 51

# NIHON MARU

'WIND DEMONS! Will you *RUN* before the Sea Samurai?' challenged Tatsumaki. The Pirate Queen stood atop the *Koketsu*'s dragonhead, her *naginata* in hand, her mane of black hair with its angry red streak billowing out behind her.

'NO! NEVER!' responded the Wind Demons, who crowded the walkways and jetty of Pirate Island, hungry for a fight.

'Will you *BOW* before their pirate-murdering lord?'

'NO! NEVER!' they yelled, clashing their weapons furiously.

'Will you *SURRENDER* your hard-fought riches?'

'NO! NEVER!'

'This island is *your* castle,' pronounced the Pirate Queen. 'Defend it with your lives. *Destroy all samurai with lightning and thunder!*'

She raised her *naginata* in a salute and the Wind Demons howled a battle cry so loud that it echoed round the lagoon walls and shook the vertical town as if the crater were erupting once more.

Jack stood with Li Ling on the jetty in front of the *Koketsu*. He glanced up to the citadel high above. Miyuki, Yori and

Saburo would no doubt be looking down, wondering what all the shouting was about. Although he'd managed to get a message to them that he was alive and well, he hadn't seen them since his return three days ago and they were probably thinking the worst. But, following his kidnapping, Tatsumaki was unwilling to let him out of her sight.

As soon as they'd docked at Pirate Island, Tatsumaki had summoned every pirate captain to a council of war. A few of the captains suggested relocating to a new island before their sworn enemy attacked. But the majority felt that *daimyo* Mori's personal war against the Wind Demons had gone on long enough.

'We've never been stronger!' argued Captain Kurogumo, once again fighting fit.

In the end, they voted unanimously to stay the course and conquer the Sea Samurai, once and for all.

The ensuing days had been a blur of preparation. Weapons were sharpened; cannon were inspected and cleaned; iron shot and *daejon* fire arrows loaded aboard; *horoku* hand bombs assembled and primed; extra casks of gunpowder stowed below decks; defensive brocade curtains hung along the gunwales; and every ship made ready to sail at a moment's notice.

A bell tolled three times.

'TO YOUR SHIPS!' cried Tatsumaki, knowing the Sea Samurai had been sighted.

The Wind Demons thundered along gangplanks, raised sails and took up oars.

Li Ling turned to Jack. 'Being a pirate certainly isn't dull,' she said, forcing a smile.

'A ship is safe in harbour, but that's not what ships are for,' replied Jack, recalling the words of his father. 'I suppose it's the same for pirates. If you want to be one, you have to go out and fight.'

'For riches or for worse!' she said, patting her sword and clambering aboard the *Koketsu* to take up her post. Jack, however, had other plans now that all the Wind Demons were distracted. He turned to head the other way back to the citadel. Then he felt a hand on his shoulder.

'Stay with me, Jack,' said Tatsumaki pointedly. 'The safest place for you is in the belly of the dragon.'

Fifty pirate ships in all left the lagoon and entered the straits. The *Koketsu* was at the head of the fleet. No longer a secret weapon, it was now the flagship of the Wind Demons in a battle that would ultimately decide who ruled the Seto Sea.

Jack looked out of the front porthole with Tatsumaki and Li Ling. He gasped at what he saw. It seemed as if the pirates' fate was already sealed. Stretching from east to west was a formidable armada of over a hundred warships. A deadly combination of swift *kobaya*, warrior-bearing *seki-bune* and heavily gunned *atake-bune* were closing in on Pirate Island. The Wind Demons' ships were outnumbered two to one. But if the Pirate Queen was unnerved by the samurai's display of force, then she didn't show it.

'We know these waters,' she said. 'We have the advantage.'

'I must be seeing things,' said Li Ling, pointing to a structure in the middle of the Sea Samurai fleet. 'That looks like a . . . castle?'

'That's the *Nihon Maru*,' replied Tatsumaki darkly. '*Daimyo* Mori's command ship.'

Jack stared with Li Ling in disbelief at the massive floating fortress. Dwarfing even the biggest *atake-bune*, the immense vessel looked like a replica of *daimyo* Mori's *Mizujiro* castle that stood watch over the Kurushima Straits. Its wooden sides were raised into defensive battlements and there were two open fighting towers, one in the bow and one in the stern. An entire army appeared to line the ramparts and cannon thrust out of every porthole. It even boasted a three-storey keep in the centre, complete with whitewashed walls and graceful curved roofs of green tile, on top of which sat a large golden shell. With its three massive sails dominating the skyline, the command ship was like a leviathan of the deep: colossal, terrifying and invincible.

'How will we ever defeat *that*?' whispered Li Ling to Jack.

Jack had no idea. He just prayed Tatsumaki did. Otherwise they were all destined for a watery grave.

# 52

# FIRE SHIPS

The stretch of water between the two opposing fleets glistened brightly in the morning sun. A lone albatross dived into a wave and snatched a fish from the sea. In the distance, the low resonating tone of a *horagai* trumpet sounded. A moment later, the water exploded in a plume of white foam, the idyllic scene shattered by the concussion of cannon fire from the *Nihon Maru* and its fleet. Then trails of smoke scorched the sky as *daejon* fire arrows rained down in retaliation.

Jack steadied himself against a beam as the *Koketsu* was rocked by a blast landing off their port bow. Sea spray shot through the open portholes, drenching and chilling the gun crews.

'They missed!' cried Li Ling in delight.

'First one's always short, remember?' said Jack, and Li Ling's grin vanished.

Tatsumaki shouted commands and the oarsmen strained to the fevered beat of the drummer. The *Koketsu* spun on its axis, its broadside pivoting towards the approaching enemy ships.

'FIRE!' she yelled.

The deck shook with cannon bursts, ten in quick succession.

Gun carriages recoiled and the crews immediately set to work reloading. As the sulphurous smoke cleared, Jack saw the iron shot and *daejon* arrows bombard the samurai fleet. Many fell short into the sea, but a few struck their targets first time. The starboard side of a *seki-bune* was ripped asunder by a *daejon* fire arrow, while a *kobaya* of samurai troops was holed and rapidly sank beneath the waves.

The Wind Demons cheered, then Jack's ears rang again as they unleashed a second round of shots. A retaliating barrage from the Sea Samurai followed and there was a deafening *thunk* as a cannonball bounced off the armoured roof.

'That must have left some dent!' cried Li Ling, who'd clapped her hands to her ears against the noise.

Grateful to be shielded within the *Koketsu*, Jack saw that the other pirate ships didn't benefit from such protection. A pirate galley had been caught by a vicious strafing of grapeshot and had lost half its oarsmen. Another ship was fast taking on water, having been hulled by a cannonball. Captain Wani-zame's *Great White* had suffered a direct hit to its main mast and the sail now burnt fiercely. Her crew was fighting to hurl the flaming canvas overboard before it engulfed the entire ship.

If the Wind Demons continued to suffer losses at this rate, Jack realized they wouldn't survive long. *Daimyo* Mori was going to tear their ships apart.

Tatsumaki read his thoughts. 'The Sea Samurai's cannon are no match for our Korean guns,' she declared. 'Just watch what we can do to them.'

She pointed in the direction of Captain Kujira's *Killer Whale*. An enemy boat strayed into the ship's line of fire and moments later disintegrated like matchwood as Captain Kujira targeted it with devastating accuracy. The *Killer Whale* boomed repeatedly with its Heaven and Earth cannon and another samurai ship was crippled. Every so often the pounding blasts were punctuated by the thunderous detonation of Captain Kujira's 'pride and joy'. Each time Jack heard Crouching Tiger roar, a samurai ship would heel to one side, mortally wounded by the mammoth gun.

Yet the Sea Samurai continued to bear down on the Wind Demons, *daimyo* Mori's command ship, at the heart of the armada, invulnerable to the pirates' relentless barrage. Archers on-board the samurai boats unleashed volley after volley of arrows that flew through the air like swarms of deadly bees. It was as if the sky was raining death. Pirates screamed as steel tips pierced their bodies and they dropped to the deck, writhing in agony.

'Send in the fire ships!' snarled Tatsumaki. 'Before these samurai get close enough to board us.'

Li Ling raced off to raise the signal flag that would relay Tatsumaki's command to the other pirate captains. Shortly after, six small boats piled high with rice straw and gunpowder charges pulled ahead of the Wind Demons' ships. Jack was stunned to see a skeleton crew on-board each boat – their mission being suicidal.

The Sea Samurai bombarded the boats as they approached. But the targets were too small for accurate cannon fire and the crews were shielded from arrows and musket shot by the straw bales. The pirates rowed ever closer to the samurai fleet, then at the last possible moment they ignited the straw, set their boats on a collision course and leapt over the sides.

Havoc reigned among the Sea Samurai ships as they sought

to avoid the floating bombs. The fleet had to break formation, the ships opening themselves up to the lethal cannon attacks of the Wind Demons. Most of the *kobaya* and *seki-bune* vessels proved manoeuvrable enough, but the *atake-bune* were slower and more cumbersome. One found itself too close as the first fire ship exploded. A whole section of its starboard side was set ablaze. Flames fanned out, spreading over oars, up rigging and across sails until the whole ship was an inferno.

The Wind Demons gave a mighty cheer at the initial devastating success of Tatsumaki's tactic. The next fire ship detonated, taking out a *kobaya* lost in the smoke and confusion. But the three following bombs were too far from their targets to cause any serious damage. The last fire ship, however, was on a direct course for the *Nihon Maru*.

Jack and the Wind Demons watched with bated breath as the burning boat edged ever nearer the *daimyo*'s command ship.

Then, at the last moment, a *kobaya* surged out of nowhere, its crew rowing furiously. They collided with the fire ship, knocking it off course. They continued to propel the blazing explosives away from the *Nihon Maru*. Just as they reached a safe distance, a ball of flame engulfed the *kobaya* and its crew.

This time, no one on-board the *Koketsu* cheered; the Wind Demons honourable enough to recognize the samurai crew's extraordinary courage and sacrifice to save their lord.

Then the pounding of the cannon resumed. By the time the Sea Samurai had managed to regroup into their attack formations, at least ten of their ships had been crippled or sunk.

But their advance was ultimately unstoppable and the Sea Samurai fleet ploughed into the Wind Demons like a tidal wave.

# 53

# SMOKE BOMBS

Jack braced himself as the *Koketsu* rammed an *atake-bune*. The impact was like a charging bull hitting a brick wall. There was a horrendous crunch of wood and the *Koketsu* shuddered to a bone-jarring halt. Jack had barely found his feet, when Tatsumaki gave the order to 'retreat and turn'. The oarsmen, well versed in hit-and-run assaults, leant upon their oars and wrenched the *Koketsu*'s battering ram free.

Watching the seawater rush into the *atake-bune*'s hull, Jack recalled the terrifying escape he and his friends had been forced to make from Captain Arashi's bilge prison. He now wondered how they'd ever survived.

As the *Koketsu* withdrew, the Sea Samurai blasted away with muskets, the shot clattering like hail upon the armoured roof, but otherwise doing little damage. As soon as they were in position, the Wind Demon gunners unleashed a broadside volley of cannonballs. The already weakened hull of the *atake-bune* crumbled under the blistering barrage. The ship heeled violently before sinking beneath the waves.

'Three down!' declared the head gunner, marking the wooden carriage of his cannon with a knife. The carriage's surface was covered in such score lines, too many to count. Jack didn't dare contemplate the number of souls lost according to that gunner's tally. But, as the sea battle raged on, he had no doubt that the number would be equalled by the end of the day.

All around the *Koketsu*, Sea Samurai and Wind Demons fought for supremacy. The long-distance bombardment had turned to brutal close-quarter fighting. Ships drew alongside one another, exchanging cannon, arrow and musket fire, before grappling hooks were slung across and the decks became floating battlefields. Swords, axes, knives and spears were all put to deadly use.

As samurai and pirates slaughtered one another, it was as if Pirate Island had been plunged into the depths of hell. The Seto Sea ran red with blood. Sharks circled, taking advantage of the bloodbath, so that even survivors found themselves fighting for their lives. Clouds of black smoke from burning ships obscured the blue sky and the morning sun was transformed into a fierce weeping eye.

The *Koketsu* alone weaved in and out of the battling ships. Capable of sudden bursts of speed, and highly manoeuvrable due to its U-shaped hull, it evaded boarding attempts and wreaked havoc upon the samurai fleet. It charged straight over a *kobaya* of samurai troops, splitting the vessel in two. When Captain Hebi's *Jade Serpent* was trapped in the crossfire of two *atake-bune*, the *Koketsu* rushed to her aid, sinking one and leaving the other crippled and at the mercy of Captain Hebi's cannon.

As Tatsumaki and her crew sought out their next victim, a *seki-bune* drifted towards them, its crew dead upon the deck.

'Looks like someone got there before us,' observed Li Ling.

'Shall we sink it?' the head gunner asked Tatsumaki, his knife already primed to add another score mark.

The Pirate Queen shook her head, smiling. 'Not unless you need more target practice!'

But, as the *Koketsu* passed the dead ship, Jack noticed something odd. The tiller had been tied fast, keeping the ship on course. He was about to point this out, when the *seki-bune*'s oars suddenly sprang to life and the ship surged towards them. Its main mast dropped with an almighty crash on to the roof of the *Koketsu*.

'IT'S A TRICK!' shouted Tatsumaki, giving orders to pull away.

But it was too late. The supposedly dead crew leapt to their feet, weapons drawn, and charged over the makeshift gangplank. A round iron projectile flew through one of the *Koketsu*'s open portholes. The hand bomb rolled across the deck, its fuse burning fiercely. On instinct, Jack pushed Li Ling behind a pile of cannonballs, then dived at Tatsumaki, knocking her to the ground. A moment later, the bomb exploded, iron shards flying in all directions to maim gunners and oarsmen alike.

Protected behind the carriage of a Heaven cannon, Jack and Tatsumaki escaped the worst of it.

'I guess that makes us even,' Tatsumaki admitted to Jack, before pulling herself to her feet.

Jack nodded, glad to no longer owe the Pirate Queen a life debt. But they were far from safe as more hand bombs landed on the gun deck. This time the explosives were soft-cased, their contents wrapped in wicker cartons. Jack instantly recognized them as *endan* – ninja smoke bombs. Having been shown how

286

to make one by Kajiya, the ninja blacksmith, he knew they could also contain lethal fragments of iron or broken pottery.

'TAKE COVER!' he warned Li Ling, who'd thought the danger was over. Jack ducked back behind the cannon with Tatsumaki.

A moment later, the *endan* detonated and clouds of smoke billowed out. So did shards of pottery – they whizzed through the air, embedding themselves in the ship's wooden beams as well as Wind Demons unable to find cover. Within seconds, the gun deck was plunged into an eye-watering fog. An explosion mid-ship was rapidly followed by a fierce battle cry. The *Koketsu* had been breached.

'REPEL BOARDERS!' cried Tatsumaki, rallying her crew.

Jack heard the pirates draw their weapons and rush to meet the invading Sea Samurai.

'Stay here!' Tatsumaki ordered Jack, unsheathing her sword and disappearing into the smoke.

Jack listened as steel clashed against steel and the cries of wounded men and women filled the air. Although this wasn't his battle, his survival depended on Tatsumaki and her crew prevailing. But there was no guarantee of victory, and in order to protect himself he needed a weapon.

Leaving the cover of the gun carriage, Jack headed for the Pirate Queen's cabin. He crouched low, where the smoke was thinner, but it was still disorientating and he had to use all his ninja skill to keep his bearings. Suddenly two men burst out of the fog, hands at each other's throats. Jack dodged aside as they fought tooth-and-claw to kill one another. Then the smoke enveloped them again, the outcome of their struggle unknown.

Hurrying on, Jack kept his hands out before him, ready to fend off any attackers. His fingers touched a wooden panel and he fumbled along until he found a door. A man screamed close by and Jack caught a glimpse of a bloody *katana*. Sliding the door open, he dived inside and shut it before anyone could follow.

He was pounced upon from behind, hands clawing at his face.

'It's me, Saru!' reassured Jack, having almost jumped out of his skin.

The terrified monkey stopped screeching and leapt back on to her cage, her fingers anxiously pawing the key round her neck, while her eyes remained fixed on the door for more intruders.

*She's one effective guard!* thought Jack as he made his way over to the weapons rack.

A *katana* rested on the lower shelf. He snatched it up and secured it to his *obi* just as he heard a girl scream. Disregarding his own safety, Jack flung open the cabin door.

'LI LING?' he shouted above the noise of the battle and the groans of the dying.

'Jack, HELP ME!'

Heading in the direction of her voice, he found her trapped between two cannon. A cruel cut across her arm had forced her to drop her weapon. A samurai twice her size closed in for the kill. He lunged at her with his sword. Li Ling ducked behind a barrel, the steel blade glancing off the iron muzzle. The samurai struck again, but this time Jack intervened. Blocking the thrust with his *katana*, Jack side-kicked the man over an Earth cannon. The samurai tumbled head over heels and was knocked out cold by a pile of cannonballs.

'This way!' said Jack, grabbing Li Ling's hand and pulling her towards Tatsumaki's cabin.

But no sooner had they taken two steps than a shrouded face materialized out of the smoke.

Dragon Eye.

# 54

# SPIKE

The ghostly apparition caused Jack to halt in his tracks. Frozen with shock, his limbs simply refused to respond as the ninja advanced, the blade of Black Cloud dripping red with blood.

Only when he sensed the tug from Li Ling as she dragged him away did the spell break. They fled blindly through the fog, colliding into beams, cannon and bloody brawls. In the confusion of smoke and battle, it was hard to tell who was friend and who was foe. Shadows fought through the swirls, every figure threatening to be Dragon Eye.

Jack stumbled over a dead body and lost his grip on Li Ling. A pirate woman grappling with a samurai bowled into him. The three of them staggered across the deck, Li Ling vanishing into the smoke. A knife flashed past Jack's eyes before burying itself in the samurai's throat. The pirate woman, seized by bloodlust, turned on Jack to do the same to him. But a flicker of recognition stayed her hand at the last moment.

Then her eyes bulged and she collapsed to the deck, sliced clean through from shoulder to hip. The glistening blade of Black Cloud preceded the ominous silhouette of a *shinobi shozoku*.

Jack dived away, hoping to lose Dragon Eye amid the

smoke. But, everywhere he turned, the ninja seemed to loom towards him. Ducking and weaving between the cannon, Jack made a sudden switch for the other side of the ship. The smoke cleared briefly and he spotted daylight. Above him, an exploded hatch offered a way out. Scrambling up the steps, he emerged on to the *Koketsu*'s roof.

Coughing and eyes watering, Jack barely had time to register the mayhem of the sea battle before a samurai rushed at him with a sword. The blade cut down to his left. Jack blocked the attack with his *katana*. The samurai struck again. This time, Jack executed an Autumn Leaf strike. The technique was rushed, but it was enough to disarm his attacker and the sword clattered to the iron deck.

In desperation, the weaponless samurai threw himself at Jack. They both crashed backwards. The impact knocked the breath out of Jack and his *katana* slipped from his grasp. Pinned beneath the samurai, Jack felt the man's fingers wrap round his throat. Wrestling to free himself, Jack used his forearm to attack the inside of the samurai's left elbow, while simultaneously palm-striking him in the jaw. The double-assault broke the samurai's balance and he collapsed sideways. Jack fought his way on top.

But the samurai offered no resistance. He'd gone limp in Jack's grip.

It wasn't until the blood ran in rivulets down the curving iron roof that Jack realized why. He'd been fortunate enough to land on the walkway, while the samurai had rolled on to the spikes. With great care, Jack got to his feet and stepped away from the impaled samurai, whose face was fixed in a contortion of agony.

Jack retrieved his *katana* and was considering his next move, when Dragon Eye rose out of the hatch.

'Don't make me kill you, *gaijin*. Surrender!'

Jack raised his sword in reply.

'So be it,' hissed the ninja, flicking the blood from Black Cloud's blade.

Tightening his grip on the *katana*, Jack braced himself for a fight to the death. Their last encounter had been an epic struggle. It had taken all his courage, every ounce of strength and mastery of the Two Heavens just to survive. Even then, he'd needed his friends Akiko and Yamato to ultimately defeat Dragon Eye. Yet *still* they had not been able to kill the ninja.

This time, Jack had only a single sword. And he was alone.

Jack tried to push his doubts aside. They would just get him killed. His swordmaster Sensei Hosokawa had taught him that he must *'stare death in the face and react without hesitation. No fear. No confusion. No doubt.'* He repeated the mantra in his head, clearing his mind into a warrior's state of *mushin*: *'Expect nothing. Be ready for anything.'*

Dragon Eye advanced, squatting low like a crab to counter the pitch and roll of the ship. He held Black Cloud aloft in his right hand, the blade poised like the stinger of a scorpion.

Jack mirrored his stance, but gripped his *katana* in two hands above his head, the blade's tip pointed directly at the ninja's face.

Almost too fast for the eye to see, Dragon Eye flicked his wrist and a *shuriken* spun towards Jack's throat. With his mind open to any attack, Jack reacted without hesitation. He cut down with his sword, meeting the throwing star halfway. The *shuriken* ricocheted off the blade into the turbulent sea. Jack had scarcely recovered from this opening strike, when Black Cloud swooped down from the sky. His arm jarred as their blades clashed. Dragon Eye pressed forward, forcing Jack to retreat.

'Careful where you step, *gaijin*,' taunted Dragon Eye, slicing for Jack's legs.

Jack leapt over the blade. For a moment, he was suspended above the armoured roof. A moment of panic gripped him as he sought for safe gaps. But, with the agility of a trained ninja, Jack replanted his feet between the spikes.

Dragon Eye cursed and cut for his midriff this time. Jack stepped back out of range, his foot narrowly missing a vicious spike. He thrust with his *katana* in retaliation, but Dragon Eye deflected the attack and once again slashed for his legs. Jack jumped away. This time his foot scraped down a spike, ripping the skin from his ankle. Crying out in pain, he stumbled to recover his balance. Dragon Eye immediately cut for his head. Jack ducked, only to be kicked in the chest. The force of the blow lifted him off his feet and sent him flying.

As he arched through the air, the image of the impaled samurai flashed before his eyes . . . but the face of the dead warrior was *his own*.

In a final bid to save himself, Jack twisted and flung out his limbs as if he were performing a horizontal Butterfly Kick. He landed upon all fours like a cat and, by the skin of his teeth, managed to hold his body above the deadly spikes.

But his fortune was short-lived. Dragon Eye rushed over, seized him by the hair and forced his head towards the deck. A sharpened point thrust directly in line with Jack's right eye.

'I'm going to present your head to the Shogun on a spike!' snarled Dragon Eye.

# 55

# WEAK SPOT

Jack's muscles trembled as he strained to keep his head up, the spike now a fraction away from piercing his eyeball. Dragon Eye pushed harder and points of pain erupted along Jack's chest where the sharpened tips of other spikes were about to puncture his ribs. His arms were close to giving out. Jack gritted his teeth, calling upon all his reserves of strength.

But Dragon Eye was too strong. Jack had nothing left.

Then the pressure was gone, Dragon Eye's hands no longer gripping him. He heard high-pitched screeching and angry shouts. Scrambling to his feet, Jack turned to see Saru tearing into the ninja's face and remaining eye. Dragon Eye howled, wrestling to rid himself of the beast. He managed to seize Saru's tail and fling her off. The monkey twirled helplessly through the air, bouncing once on the roof, before disappearing over the side.

'No one harms Saru and lives!' shrieked Tatsumaki, her expression one of thunderous fury as she charged towards the ninja, flanked by four Wind Demons.

Dragon Eye took one look at the fearsome Pirate Queen and leapt from the *Koketsu*'s roof on to the *seki-bune*'s deck.

He pointed Black Cloud at Jack. 'I'll be back for you, *gaijin*,' he promised.

Then before any of them could give chase, he jumped on to a piece of passing wreckage. Jack watched the ninja float away and disappear among the carnage of battling ships.

'And *I'll* be after you,' vowed Tatsumaki, a tear streaking the black powder around her eyes.

Jack felt a lump in his throat as he tried to console the Pirate Queen. 'Saru was a brave monkey. She saved my life.'

'Just be sure you kill the ninja next time!' she replied, staring wretchedly in the direction Saru had been tossed.

Then a small red face bobbed up from the roof edge. Having checked the coast was clear, Saru scampered between the spikes and leapt into Tatsumaki's arms.

'Saru! My little Wind Demon!' exclaimed the Pirate Queen, rubbing her head affectionately. 'I knew you were tougher than any ninja.'

Relieved Saru was alive, Jack glanced towards the other Wind Demons, who were all bloody and bruised.

'Is Li Ling OK?' asked Jack.

One of the pirates nodded. 'She's helping clear the deck of samurai scum.'

'So you've beaten them?'

'Not yet,' replied Tatsumaki, gravely scanning the floating battlefield. 'There's plenty more where they came from.'

The Seto Sea was awash with burning boats and sinking ships. Bodies, dead or dying, floated past like shoals of fish. Vessels still seaworthy locked horns, their crews firing point-blank at one another before boarding and fighting hand-to-hand. Despite their superior cannon, the Wind

Demons were being decimated by *daimyo* Mori's larger and more organized force. Sea Samurai swarmed over the pirate ships, slaughtering the crews and seizing the vessels. Jack reckoned that the pirates must have lost nearly half their fleet.

Amid the devastation the *Nihon Maru* pressed forward, laying down suppressive fire, protected behind a defensive ring of *seki-bune*. Signal flags and the blare of *horagai* issued from its keep, directing the Sea Samurai's formations and attack manoeuvres. Any weaknesses in the Wind Demons' defences were quickly spotted and exploited. The tide of battle was rapidly turning against the pirates.

But Tatsumaki remained defiant and undaunted. 'Ten sailors wisely led will beat a hundred without a head,' she declared. 'We must sink their command ship.'

The *Koketsu* shook, its beams almost rattled loose by the impact. Oarsmen clung on determinedly to their oars. Gunners fought to stay standing as their cannon almost broke free from their chains. Li Ling went flying but Jack somehow kept his feet.

'RETREAT AND TURN!' bellowed Tatsumaki above the cacophony of musket shots raining down upon the iron roof and the blasts of cannon from the defending *seki-bune* ships.

The *Koketsu* was rocked by a direct hit to its port side. The crack and crunch of wood as a cannonball ploughed through the deck was followed by the screams of injured pirates.

'Put that fire out!' cried a gunner to his men, as flames licked the inner walls of the gun deck and spread towards their explosive charges.

Jack wondered just how much more damage the *Koketsu*

could sustain. The wooden gunwales were being blown to smithereens, the roof pounded to scrap metal by close-range cannon each time they charged the *Nihon Maru*. And so many oars had been blasted to splintered stumps that they'd already lost two rowing units. Soon the ship would be no more than a floating coffin.

Through a gaping hole in the *Koketsu*'s side Jack could see Captain Kurogumo's *Black Spider* and Captain Wanizame's *Great White* embroiled in a furious battle with the Sea Samurai. Their mission was to keep the defending *seki-bune* at bay, while the *Koketsu* and Captain Kujira's *Killer Whale* attempted to sink the *Nihon Maru*.

Tatsumaki had rallied their best remaining ships for the task. But they'd been met with overwhelming resistance. Trapped within the heart of *daimyo* Mori's armada, enemy fire came from all directions. The Wind Demons had so far lost three of their ships in the attack and more were on the brink of defeat. The pirates were simply being obliterated . . . and all for nothing.

The *Nihon Maru* remained stubbornly afloat, its hull immune to the pirates' bombardment. Even Captain Kujira's Crouching Tiger had failed to make an impact.

'FIRE!' ordered Tatsumaki with an almost desperate cry.

The *Koketsu* rang to the thunder of Heaven and Earth cannon. When the gunsmoke cleared, the Wind Demons gave a despairing groan. Their fourth attempt had achieved little more than the splintering of a few boards.

'It's hopeless!' cursed the head gunner, plunging his knife into the wooden gun carriage. 'That hull must be reinforced with iron.'

'We *cannot* give up,' said Tatsumaki.

'What else can we do? We've thrown everything we've got at this monster.'

'Try AGAIN on the starboard side,' she ordered furiously. 'There has to be a weak spot. A chink in its armour somewhere.'

The weary oarsmen propelled the *Koketsu* down the seemingly endless length of the *Nihon Maru*. All the time musket shot, arrows and cannon battered the crumbling pirate ship. Jack took shelter with Li Ling behind a pile of ropes as shards of wood and lethal projectiles tore through the air. Jack realized their chances of survival were almost nil. The *Nihon Maru* was proving indestructible and another ramming raid would surely see the *Koketsu* blasted out of the water. If by some miracle they managed to retreat to the protection of Pirate Island, the Sea Samurai would simply surround them. *Daimyo* Mori would show no quarter to the Wind Demons – he had a personal vendetta to wipe the pirate clans out forever.

With their downfall assured, Jack thought of Yori, Miyuki and Saburo imprisoned in the citadel. Would they be shown any mercy by the Sea Samurai? It seemed unlikely. His friends would either be killed in the fighting or recognized as his accomplices and put to death for treason. Jack cursed himself for letting them ever come on this journey in the first place. He should have *insisted* that they left him in Tomo Harbour. Now he was powerless to save his loyal friends.

As the *Koketsu* rounded the *Nihon Maru*'s bow and took up position for a fifth and no doubt final run, Jack glanced up at the insurmountable sides of the command ship. Hundreds of armed soldiers lined its battlements, primed to launch a devastating salvo at them. Jack noticed that the *Nihon Maru* was now listing heavily to starboard. For a moment, he thought that she had been holed. But it was just the weight of the soldiers causing her to tilt, *daimyo* Mori having mustered the majority of his men to one side for maximum firepower.

Seeing this, Jack smiled to himself. He had found the weak spot.

# 56

# TUG-OF-WAR

'FIRE!' ordered Jack to the gunmen.

The *Koketsu* roared with cannon blasts. Jack watched the *daejon* arrows arc into the smoke-filled sky.

'For all our sakes, your plan had better work,' said Tatsumaki.

Jack could only pray that it would. The Pirate Queen had taken some persuasion to stop her ramming raid, but once he'd pointed out the *Nihon Maru*'s weak spot she'd understood. Hurried adjustments to every cannon followed, the gunners toiling hard as they shifted their weapons into the steepest possible trajectory. Ropes were lashed together and fed out of the portholes before being secured to the *Koketsu*'s stern. Every Wind Demon, except the gunnery crews, was assigned to the oars. But the most difficult part of the plan was to ensure the *daejon* arrows hit their target first time.

There would be no second chance.

When the head gunner had been assured of their accuracy, Tatsumaki gave Jack the privilege of issuing the firing order. For a brief moment, Jack had hesitated. He'd questioned himself about aiding the Wind Demons. But with his survival and the fate of his imprisoned friends at stake, he'd realized there was no other option. Between the Sea Samurai and the Wind Demons, the Pirate Queen was the lesser of two evils.

The *daejon* arrows shot upwards, their tethers trailing out behind them. The Sea Samurai on the battlements ducked as the ten projectiles soared past. They entirely missed the *Nihon Maru*'s battlements. Jack could just imagine the relief on the samurai's faces . . . and the utter shock and bewilderment as the iron-tipped arrows struck the *Nihon Maru*'s keep. They embedded themselves in the whitewashed walls up to their flights. A unit of samurai rushed to rescue their lord from the keep's upper tower. But Jack's plan wasn't to kill the *daimyo*.

'ROW LIKE THE WIND!' he shouted and threw his weight behind the nearest oar with six other men as the drummer took up the rhythm.

The *Koketsu* surged away from the *Nihon Maru*, gaining speed with every oar stroke. Then the ship suddenly jarred to a halt as the ten ropes tied to its stern snapped taut.

'Keep rowing!' grunted Jack.

The oarsmen pushed and pulled on the *yuloh* oars, their muscles bulging, sweat pouring down their backs, as the *Koketsu*'s timbers creaked and groaned with the strain.

Jack glanced through the stern porthole. The *Koketsu* appeared dead in the water, all forward momentum lost.

'ROW HARDER!' he cried above the drummer's insistent beat.

Like a tug-of-war between David and Goliath, the *Koketsu* fought against the monumental bulk of the *Nihon Maru*. But the command ship was immovable.

'It's *not* working!' said Tatsumaki, glaring at Jack.

'It will,' he replied. 'Just give it a chance!'

But doubts were being raised in his own mind too. However hard the Wind Demons rowed, they were simply not powerful enough to overcome the mighty *Nihon Maru*. The pirates plunged their oars in again and again. The ropes stretched to their limit. Then two of them snapped. Jack's plan was fast unravelling.

'COME ON!' he roared. 'FOR YOUR QUEEN!'

A tremendous burst of effort came from the Wind Demons and the *Koketsu* edged over a wave. Three more ropes broke. Oars dived into the water, propelling the *Koketsu* onward. Jack stared in desperate hope at the command ship. With its keep being dragged sideways, the deck was now heeling dangerously. The Sea Samurai, finally understanding what was happening, rushed to the port side to counter the perilous slant of the deck. But the *Nihon Maru* had reached tipping point.

*The bigger they are, the harder they fall*, thought Jack.

Strong and immense as the *Nihon Maru* was, he'd realized its design was top-heavy and unstable. The command ship's superstructure was its Achilles heel. Like a harpooned whale, the *Nihon Maru* keeled over. A final pull from the *Koketsu*'s oarsmen sent it crashing into the Seto Sea.

With their command ship down and sinking slowly beneath the waves, the remaining Sea Samurai ships floundered in confusion and panic. Their fighting spirit crushed by their *daimyo*'s defeat, they turned tail and fled.

The Wind Demons on the *Koketsu* gave a triumphant battle cry. Their call was echoed by cheers from the *Black Spider* and the other surviving pirate ships. The battle for Pirate Island had been won.

# 57

# SECOND WAVE

'The Wind Demons are forever in your debt, Jack,' declared Tatsumaki. 'And so am I.'

They stood upon the armoured roof, the Wind Demons hailing their victory as the *Koketsu* docked at the lagoon jetty. More pirate ships limped in, their crews battleworn but jubilant.

Jack bowed respectfully to the Pirate Queen. 'You can easily repay that debt.'

Tatsumaki raised an eyebrow. 'Really?'

'Release me and my friends.'

She pursed her lips, apparently reluctant.

'Do you think I should, Saru?' she asked, turning to the monkey upon her shoulder. Saru bobbed her head enthusiastically and Tatsumaki smiled at Jack. 'Your request is granted.'

'Also, hand back my swords and our weapons.'

'That's acceptable to me,' replied Tatsumaki, nodding amiably, 'though it might be harder to persuade Captain Kurogumo to part with those Shizu swords of yours.'

'And return my father's *rutter*.'

Tatsumaki laughed at his audacity. 'Next you'll be asking for a boat!'

'That had crossed my mind,' replied Jack.

The Pirate Queen studied him. 'Are you certain you don't want to stay here as a Wind Demon? We can protect you from the Shogun. And you've proved yourself a fine pirate. I'd even make you captain of your own ship.'

It was Jack who laughed out loud this time. His father would turn in his grave at the thought of his son becoming a pirate. He shook his head. 'I have to get to Nagasaki. I must return home to my sister.'

Tatsumaki nodded. 'I suppose we all seek different treasures in life,' she replied wistfully. 'I'll arrange a boat for you.'

'And the *rutter*?' pressed Jack.

The Pirate Queen's expression became hard as a diamond. 'I'm afraid that belongs to me.'

'But we made a blood oath!' exclaimed Jack, holding up his scarred hand.

'I only promised to set you free,' replied Tatsumaki coolly. 'And that's exactly what I've agreed to do. Think yourself fortunate that you and your friends are escaping with your lives.'

Jack felt cheated and angry. Without his father's *rutter*, his whole future and that of his sister Jess were at stake. But, surrounded by armed Wind Demons, he was in no position to argue. And why should he be so surprised by Tatsumaki's mercenary decision? She was a pirate, after all!

'Don't look so resentful, Jack,' said Tatsumaki with a conciliatory smile. 'I'd be happy for you to remain with us as our pilot to the South Americas. Together we could rule the seven seas . . . even sail to England . . .'

She let the suggestion hang in the air.

Jack didn't say anything, realizing that she was simply trying to appease him with the possibility. But their ultimate destinations were totally opposed. He wanted to sail home. Tatsumaki wanted to plunder the oceans. He'd never reach England that way. And even if they eventually did, they'd be blown out of the water for being pirates by the British Navy! Besides, Jack still held key information to the *rutter* and he had no intention of *ever* revealing those secrets to Tatsumaki and her Wind Demons.

'I'll make my own way home,' he said eventually. 'With my friends.'

Tatsumaki sighed in disappointment at his decision. 'Then you're free to go.'

'Look!' cried Li Ling, emerging from the hatch. 'It's Captain Kurogumo.'

There was a great roar as the *Black Spider* came alongside, Captain Kurogumo and his crew punching the air in salute to the *Koketsu*. Upon the main deck was the golden-shell figurehead from the *Nihon Maru*.

'It's *solid* gold!' yelled Captain Kurogumo, baring his sharpened teeth in avaricious delight.

'We should melt it down and make you a throne, Tatsumaki, now that you're Queen of the Seto Sea!' pronounced Captain Hebi as he approached the *Koketsu* and performed a ceremonial bow.

The Wind Demons gave an almighty cheer at this new title for their leader.

Gazing upon her exultant followers, Tatsumaki said, 'It won't be long before we have enough gold to make thrones for *all* of us!'

Another cheer erupted from the Wind Demons.

Captain Hebi was joined on the jetty by Captain Kurogumo and the other surviving captains. Jack noted there were pitifully few left.

'Where's Captain Wanizame?' asked Tatsumaki, searching among the grime-streaked faces for the Amazonian pirate.

Captain Kurogumo spat in anger. 'Those cold-blooded samurai slaughtered her and every soul on the *Great White*.'

'What about Captain Kujira? He was on the final assault with us,' said Tatsumaki in growing disbelief at their losses.

But the *Killer Whale* wasn't to be seen anywhere among the battered fleet.

Captain Hebi's expression darkened and he shook his head regretfully. 'We've paid a heavy price for this victory.'

'We may have lost many souls . . . *but* we've won so much more,' Tatsumaki proclaimed, trying to rally their spirits. 'Tonight we celebrate our conquest and honour those who died this day. Tomorrow, we commence a reign of piracy on a scale never before witnessed. We shall rule this sea by LIGHTNING and THUNDER!'

The captains roared their approval and the Wind Demons went wild, stamping their feet on the decks and clashing their weapons. Standing among the baying pirates, Jack wondered at the terror that was about to be unleashed upon the Seto Sea. Then, cutting through the noise, he heard a bell toll three times.

Tatsumaki and the pirate captains heard it too, exchanging uneasy looks as a rowing boat powered across the lagoon from the sister island.

'SEA SAMURAI . . . sighted on the northern horizon!' panted the lookout as he reached the *Koketsu*.

'But they're *defeated*,' exclaimed Captain Kurogumo.

The lookout shook his head. 'It's a second wave!'

Dismay and alarm spread among the Wind Demons. They looked to their Pirate Queen for guidance.

'We've beaten them once,' said Tatsumaki, undaunted by the new threat. 'We can do it again.'

'Tatsumaki, we don't have the strength to fight another battle,' argued Captain Hebi.

'Are you suggesting that we *run* before the Sea Samurai?'

'What other choice do we have? We might not be beaten but we're certainly broken. Just look around you.'

Tatsumaki eyed their war-torn ships and wounded pirates. Livid at their weakened state, she nonetheless agreed with his assessment. 'Come hell or high water, we'll have our revenge on these Sea Samurai. This war is *not* over!'

'But what about our hoards of riches?' challenged Captain Kurogumo. 'Are we simply to surrender them to the samurai?'

'Certainly not,' replied Tatsumaki, her resolve hardening. 'Grab what treasure you can, then make for Demon Island in the Sea of Japan.'

Not needing to be told twice, the pirate captains and their crews disbanded. They surged up Pirate Town's walkways in a frenzied rush to recover their stashed riches before the Sea Samurai fleet arrived.

Tatsumaki gathered her more disciplined crew together. She sent the gunners to restock their ammunition store, the other Wind Demons to load essential provisions for the voyage ahead, and the oarsmen, chosen for their strength, were ordered to accompany her to the citadel to retrieve the best of her treasure.

Jack was forgotten amid the whirlwind of activity. He was left behind on the jetty as Tatsumaki and her oarsmen headed for the bamboo lift. Pushing his way through the unruly mob of pirates, Jack hurried after her but was stopped by the strong arm of an oarsman.

'Sorry. No room for passengers,' said Tatsumaki, closing the gate behind her.

'What about the boat you promised?' asked Jack, realizing he and his friends would be stranded without one.

Tatsumaki gave a half-apologetic smile as the lift rose into the air. 'It's everyone for themselves now, Jack. Remember, we're pirates . . . not samurai!'

# 58

# CURSED

*So much for the Wind Demons being forever in my debt!* thought Jack as his eyes scanned the lagoon for an escape boat.

But the only ones docked at the jetty were those that had survived the battle – and they were far too large for a four-man crew to handle, and were already taken. The lookout's rowing boat was also gone, having returned to the hidden fort with news of the Wind Demons' immediate withdrawal. Jack just had to hope that, following the conflict, he'd find a suitable vessel washed up on the island's rocky shores. Otherwise, he'd be asking Tatsumaki for passage on-board the *Koketsu* – and that no doubt would come at a price.

But Jack realized his first priority was to free Miyuki, Yori and Saburo. Turning to run up the gangway into Pirate Town, he bumped straight into Li Ling coming the other way.

'Sorry, Jack!' she gasped, dropping the sack of rice that she'd been lugging. 'I didn't see you. Where are you going anyway?'

'The citadel. I have to release my friends, then somehow find a boat off this island.'

'Aren't you coming with us?'

Jack shook his head. 'No, a pirate's life isn't for me.'

Li Ling looked saddened by the news.

'You could join us,' suggested Jack, not wishing his Chinese friend to die at the hands of the Sea Samurai . . . or become a bloodthirsty pirate.

'And miss all this excitement?' she replied, glancing round at the chaos. 'This is what I dreamed of, Jack. I'm a Wind Demon now and always will be.'

'Then take care,' he said, realizing that her fate was her own choosing and it wasn't for him to change her mind. 'But don't ever lose that kind heart of yours.'

Helping to lift the rice sack on to Li Ling's shoulder, he turned to go. He'd only taken a few steps when she suddenly said, 'I know where there's a boat.'

She pointed to a small iron gate beyond the jetty at the base of the cliff.

'I shouldn't be telling you this, but that passage leads to a hidden sea cave. Tatsumaki has a boat stowed there for emergencies.'

'You're a life saver, Li Ling. What sort of boat?'

'A skiff. Tatsumaki asked me to check its supplies before we went into battle with the Sea Samurai. But you'll need the key for the gate.'

'No, we won't,' replied Jack confidently. 'Miyuki can pick locks.'

'Not this one. It's a Chinese double lock.'

'So where's the key?' asked Jack.

'That's the other problem,' she replied, biting her lip awkwardly. 'It's attached to Saru's collar.'

'It's lucky that Saru likes me,' said Jack, although he had

no idea how he would take it without the Pirate Queen noticing. He'd figure that out once he was reunited with his friends.

'Good luck!' cried Li Ling as Jack sprinted up the gangway into Pirate Town.

The main street was crammed with marauding pirates, elbowing one another out of the way as they seized their precious loot. Some were raiding the shops and stores. Others were ransacking the cabins of their recently dead friends, scuffles breaking out each time a highly valuable item was discovered.

Jack rushed past, dodging between the Wind Demons and their fights. He clambered up ladders and along the suspended bamboo walkways. The citadel seemed impossibly high up and he was aware that with every passing second the Sea Samurai were sailing closer and closer.

Finally, with his heart pounding and his lungs burning, Jack reached the top level. As he staggered past the door to Captain Kurogumo's house, he remembered his Shizu swords were inside. Sliding open the *shoji*, he hurried into the main room and over to the corner where he'd seen the treasure chest and weapons. He spotted his *daishō* immediately. His hand was almost upon the red hilt of his *katana*, when he felt the sharp tip of a knife in his back.

Behind him, silent and still as a statue, stood the white-faced *geisha*.

'Just claiming what's mine,' explained Jack calmly.

The *geisha* said nothing. She merely pressed the blade harder into him. Jack hastily moved his hand away from the *katana*'s hilt and the pressure eased a touch.

'Stealing from a pirate?' tutted Captain Kurogumo, stepping out from the balcony.

'Samurai aren't thieves,' replied Jack. 'You know they belong to me.'

'*Once* belonged to you,' corrected Captain Kurogumo.

'Tatsumaki said I could have them back, for defeating the *Nihon Maru* and saving the Wind Demons.'

'*Did* you save us?' challenged Captain Kurogumo, baring his shark-like teeth in a flash of anger. 'We're fleeing from the Sea Samurai. Our fleet is decimated. Pirate Island is lost to us forever. Skullface was right about you. You've cursed the Wind Demons!'

A great cheer echoed up from below – the *Killer Whale* had entered the lagoon.

'Captain Kujira survived after all,' remarked the pirate captain with a twisted smile. 'Unlike you, *gaijin*,' he added, drawing his sword.

With the *geisha*'s *tantō* close at his back, Jack dared not move. Before he could even reach for his *katana*, Captain Kurogumo's *kissaki* would pierce his heart in a split second and he'd drop to the floor, stone-cold dead.

*So this is to be my end*, thought Jack. *Run through by a dishonourable pirate. No chance to free my friends or see Jess ever again.*

Then the *Killer Whale* opened fire, its cannon booming as if the volcano itself was exploding. The cliff walls shuddered under the impact of heavy iron shot.

'What in the name of –' cried Captain Kurogumo, losing his footing as the balcony rocked wildly.

Another salvo blasted Pirate Town. A cannonball struck the supports of Captain Kurogumo's house and the building started to sheer away from the cliff face. In the chaos of the moment, Jack spun round, knocking the *tantō* from the *geisha*'s grasp with his elbow. Then using a palm-strike to her chest he sent her crashing into the balcony rail.

As the bamboo house pitched violently, Jack snatched up his swords and dived for the door. He managed to grab hold of the walkway's supporting post, just as the building completely broke away. He hung suspended in the air, watching Captain Kurogumo and the *geisha* flailing among the falling wreckage of their house, the pirate's precious weapons cascading out like lethal jewels into the lagoon far below.

As their screams spiralled away, Jack thought that perhaps he really *had* cursed the Wind Demons – or at least Captain Kurogumo – for capturing him and his friends in the first place.

# 59

# COLLAPSE

The *Killer Whale* continued its bombardment of Pirate Town. Jack could only presume that the Sea Samurai had taken over the ship, cunningly using it to masquerade as Wind Demons and fool the lookouts. Cannonballs tore into the town's lower levels and ripped through the main street. *Daejon* fire arrows embedded themselves in the walls, setting the bamboo buildings ablaze. Pirates, screaming and on fire, plunged to their deaths. Many fled in blind panic. Some managed to reach the jetty and their ships, but others, trapped by the fires, had to leap into the lagoon for their lives.

Jack tossed his swords on to the walkway, then hauled himself up. Without a moment to lose, he sprinted for the citadel. The gates were wide open and he charged straight in. Two oarsmen were dragging a treasure chest brimming with silver and gold towards the lift. They ignored him as he flew past and headed down the corridor to where his friends were imprisoned.

A blast rocked the citadel and Jack was knocked off his feet. Lanterns clattered to the floor. Scrambling back up, he staggered round a corner and dashed towards the room. The guards were gone, but the door was still barred. He heard frantic hammering on the other side.

'Yori! Miyuki! Saburo!' cried Jack, yanking the bolt free. He flung the door open and was greeted by the familiar faces of his friends. He felt as if he hadn't seen them for months. As they exited, he embraced each of them in turn.

'Good to see you too,' said Saburo, smiling at Jack's unreserved emotion.

Yori was too overcome to say anything, tears of relief welling up in his eyes.

Returning Jack's embrace, Miyuki whispered in his ear, 'I *really* thought I'd lost you forever.' Then she stepped away, Japanese formality taking over once more, and focused on their situation. 'Let's get out of here. I've had enough of this Pirate Queen's hospitality.'

'Do you still have the sea chart?' asked Jack.

Miyuki nodded and held up the roll of paper.

'Excellent. There's a boat through a gated tunnel beside the jetty, but first we have to get the key,' Jack explained. 'And if we're lucky, find your weapons and the *rutter* too.'

They turned to go when Yori remembered: 'The rice!'

He ran back into the room just as a tremendous explosion shook the building. The floor beneath Yori collapsed.

'NOOOO!' yelled Jack as his friend disappeared.

He rushed to the door, where a huge gaping hole now exposed the perilous plunge to the lagoon. Fragments of wood and *tatami* mats twirled through the air, vanishing into the distance. A gunpowder store on the level below burned fiercely, having been hit by a *daejon* arrow.

'YORI!' cried Jack, his eyes searching for his fallen friend.

'Down here!' replied a tiny terrified voice.

A section of floor hung precariously from a few broken beams. Yori clung to the edge, his legs dangling in mid-air.

Dropping on to his stomach, Jack reached for him. 'Grab my hand!'

Yori shook his head. 'I can't. It's too far.'

The floor gave a little as a beam split further. Yori cried out in panic.

'Take my ankles,' Jack instructed Miyuki and Saburo.

Using the door frame as a brace, they lowered him over the abyss. Jack stretched out his arms to his friend. He could hear the terrible sound of splintering wood and snatched in desperation for Yori's hand . . . and missed.

He tried again. 'Now!'

Yori let go with one hand – the floor broke away and tumbled down the cliff face – and he just managed to clasp Jack's fingers. Jack held on to Yori with all his might, his friend swinging helplessly over the lagoon. Miyuki and Saburo wrestled to pull them both in.

'Hurry!' urged Jack, feeling Yori's fingers slipping through his grasp.

As Jack was dragged back over the threshold, he lost grip of Yori . . . but Saburo made a grab for his jacket and pulled their friend to safety. They collapsed in a heap on the corridor floor, panting from exhaustion and shock.

'Sorry . . .' gasped Yori. 'I dropped . . . the rice.'

Jack burst into laughter at his unnecessary apology. 'As long as I didn't drop *you*, nothing else matters.'

Another explosion shook the building.

'This citadel's becoming a death trap,' said Saburo, scrambling to his feet. 'Let's go!'

'We need to get the key first,' reminded Jack.

He led them down a corridor towards Tatsumaki's quarters. They hurried past open *shoji* on every side. Discarded loot and treasure were scattered across the floors, only the best having been taken by Tatsumaki's oarsmen.

'Our packs!' exclaimed Saburo as they passed by one of the ransacked rooms.

Darting inside, they grabbed their belongings. They were relieved to discover their weapons stacked in a corner. Miyuki secured her *ninjatō* to her back and her utility belt round her waist. Saburo thrust his *katana* and *wakizashi* into his *obi*, while Yori was thrilled to be reunited with his trusty *shakujō*.

They heard the Pirate Queen shouting from a nearby room. 'Hurry up!' she ordered. 'The Sea Samurai fleet are almost upon us.'

Creeping down the corridor, Jack and his friends peeked round a door into the citadel's main hall. Tatsumaki stood with her back to them, directing the loading of her last remaining treasure chests. Saru sat upon an open chest, nibbling a piece of her favourite fruit.

'There's the key,' whispered Jack, spying the glint of metal hanging from her collar.

'How can we get it?' said Saburo. 'You can't just walk up to Tatsumaki and politely ask.'

'I have an idea,' said Miyuki.

Reaching into her pack, she pulled out a blowpipe.

# 60

# THE KEY

'Are you going to kill the Pirate Queen?' asked Yori as Miyuki inserted a tiny dart into the pipe.

Miyuki took careful aim and blew. The dart whisked through the air towards its target.

'Ow!' cried the Wind Demon, swatting at his neck and dropping the treasure chest he was carrying. 'Pesky mosquitoes!'

'No, just distract her,' Miyuki replied with an impish grin, as the chest crashed to the floor and hundreds of silver coins spilled out.

'You clumsy idiot!' exclaimed the Pirate Queen, rushing to save her precious treasure.

While Tatsumaki and the oarsman were busy gathering up the silver, Jack seized the opportunity to sneak over to Saru. The monkey caught sight of him and bobbed up and down, chattering excitedly as he approached. Jack put a finger to his lips in a desperate attempt to calm the monkey. Saru seemed to understand and settled as soon as he stroked her head. With great care, Jack removed the key from her collar.

The Wind Demon continued shovelling handfuls of silver

back into the treasure chest, while the Pirate Queen looked on, chastising him for his stupidity with the sharp edge of her *tessen*. Having pocketed the key, Jack's eyes fell upon the distinctive black oilskin covering of the *rutter*. The logbook had been stowed in Saru's open chest. Reaching in, Jack's hands clasped round the oilskin, its cool touch reassuringly familiar. Hastily, he slipped the *rutter* into his pack. All the time Saru was watching him, quietly nibbling on her fruit.

Jack was about to return to the others, when he noticed an object gleaming beneath where Saru was perched. The black pearl with its twisted gold pin was here too. He couldn't leave his sole connection to Akiko behind. But, as soon as he picked it up, Saru screeched loudly and snatched the pearl from his hand. She clasped it possessively to her chest and screeched again.

Tatsumaki spun round. 'Jack!' she exclaimed, taken by surprise. 'Have you changed your mind? Are you joining us?' But, looking at Saru and then at the chest, she realized what he was up to. 'You're welcome to the key you've stolen, but if you value your life, put the *rutter* back now.'

Jack shook his head. 'It's everyone for themselves, Tatsumaki. Remember, you're a pirate . . . and I'm a samurai!'

He ran for the door. Tatsumaki flicked her wrist in his direction. The iron *tessen* snapped open and spun across the room.

'Watch out!' cried Miyuki as the razor-sharp fan swooped for Jack's head.

At the last second, Jack dodged aside and the *tessen* embedded itself in the door frame.

'After him!' cried Tatsumaki furiously. 'That *gaijin*'s stealing our future!'

Four Wind Demons chased after Jack into the corridor. But he and his friends were faster than the hulking oarsmen and had already turned the corner and were out of sight.

'This way!' said Jack, leading them through the citadel's many chambers towards the main gate, where he prayed the lift would still be working.

Jack burst through a large set of double doors on to the main balcony and ran straight into Dragon Eye.

'I'll have that,' said the ninja, holding out his hand for the *rutter* as if having expected its arrival.

In contrast, Jack was completely unprepared for the appearance of his resurrected enemy. He faltered mid-stride and didn't know whether to turn and flee or charge right through him.

'He's still *alive*?' gasped Saburo, already backing away.

Yori could only stare in wide-eyed horror at Dragon Eye, the metal rings on his *shakujō* trembling in his grasp. Even Miyuki was momentarily frozen to the spot, intimidated by the ninja's chilling presence.

Behind them, Jack could hear the pounding of the Wind Demons' feet getting closer. They were trapped.

'The *rutter*,' demanded Dragon Eye. 'Don't make me ask you again.'

Jack caught a glint of steel and the image of Tiger's head bouncing down the hillside flashed before his eyes. With lightning reactions, Jack unsheathed his *katana*, the Shizu blade moving like quicksilver through the air. There was a clash of steel upon steel and the blade of Black Cloud was stopped a hair's breadth from Saburo's neck. Saburo managed a nervous gulp at the lethal stand-off.

'You don't get away with that trick twice,' said Jack, launching a fearsome front kick at Dragon Eye's chest.

The ninja staggered backwards under the blow.

'And you'll *never* harm any of my friends again,' he vowed, his *katana* slicing down for the ninja's head.

But Dragon Eye was quick to recover. He deflected Jack's attack and threw out his hand.

'Watch out!' cried Yori.

A cloud of *metsubishi* powder shot towards Jack's face. Jack spun away and the blinding dust dispersed harmlessly into the air.

'You'll have to do better than that,' goaded Jack.

'There they are!' shouted a Wind Demon, thundering down the corridor.

Recovering her wits, Miyuki drew her *ninjatō* and turned to face the pirates. 'Jack, this is no time for settling old scores. We *have* to leave. NOW!'

But Dragon Eye blocked their escape route.

'You go,' urged Jack, tossing Yori the key. 'I'll hold off Dragon Eye.'

*Pain will nourish your courage when the dragon returns . . .*

Recalling the Wind Witch's words, Jack thought of his father, of Yamato and all that he'd lost as a result of this ruthless ninja. Immediately, he felt the flames of courage ignite in his veins.

'I'm no longer scared of you!' declared Jack and charged at his sworn enemy.

'You should be,' snarled Dragon Eye, deflecting Jack's *katana* and countering with a vicious slice upward with his own sword.

Black Cloud almost carved Jack in half, but he leapt away, somersaulting to land deftly on the balcony rail.

'It's *you* who should be fearing me, now I've the skills of a samurai *and* a ninja.'

Covertly reaching into his pack, Jack flung a *shuriken* at Dragon Eye. The throwing star whirled through the air. Dragon Eye twisted away, but was a fraction too slow. The star cut his upper arm and he let out a surprised grunt of pain. Before Dragon Eye could recover, Jack leapt off the rail, unsheathing his *wakizashi*, and launched a blistering Two Heavens attack. His swords were a whirl of fury as he drove the ninja down the balcony, clearing the way for his friends to escape.

'This time I'll defeat you for good,' promised Jack.

Blocking each and every sword blow, the ninja laughed, 'Dragon Eye can *never* die!'

Below in the lagoon, the *Killer Whale* let loose another devastating round of cannon fire, turning Pirate Town into a ruin of blazing buildings and crumbling walkways. Crouching Tiger's distinctive roar resounded off the crater walls and a boulder-sized cannonball obliterated a storehouse and all its surrounding buildings. The damage was so widespread that a whole section of Pirate Town caved in on itself. The citadel's foundations shook as if in the grip of an earthquake and the idyllic lagoon became awash with flaming wreckage and dead bodies.

'Come on, Jack!' cried Miyuki, running for the gate with the others. 'The balcony's collapsing.'

But it was too late. Locked in mortal combat, he and Dragon Eye tumbled down the sloping floor. They fought in each other's grip before crashing heavily into the balcony rail. Jack lost his swords, seeing them spiral on to a roof far below. The balcony now hung loose like a lolling tongue over the carnage and threatened to break away entirely.

Defenceless against Dragon Eye and on the brink of plunging to his death, Jack scrambled up the bars of the balcony rail towards Miyuki and his friends. But Dragon Eye, scuttling along like a black spider, pounced on to his back and pulled him down to the bottom again. They wrestled with each other against the rail. The ninja was no longer in possession of Black Cloud, but his hands were just as deadly. He drove a spearhand fist into the soft flesh of Jack's gut. Jack gasped as a shockwave of pain rocketed through his body, the agony too great for him to even scream. Somehow he managed to land a powerful elbow strike to the ninja's temple and Dragon Eye reeled backwards. Keeping up the attack, he threw a blistering upper-cut. The fist connected with Dragon Eye's jaw and he collapsed against the slanting balcony rail. Jack leapt on top of him and jammed a thumb into a nerve point between the ninja's ribs. Dragon Eye screamed.

'You're not the only one to know such techniques,' said Jack, driving his Finger Sword Fist in deeper.

The balcony shuddered, giving warning of its precarious state. But, with Dragon Eye dazed and numb with pain, Jack realized this might be his only chance.

'Did Yamato survive as well as you?' he demanded.

'Who's . . . Yamato?' groaned Dragon Eye.

'The young samurai you fell off Osaka Castle with.'

Despite the pain, Dragon Eye managed a pitiless laugh. 'So that's who the boy was –'

'You *knew* he was Masamoto's son!' Jack shouted. Angered by the ninja's contempt, he slammed him against the balcony rail. 'Just tell me, is Yamato alive or not?'

# 61

# FREEFALL

Dragon Eye didn't reply. Instead he raked the centre of Jack's chest with Extended Knuckle Fist. The searing pain forced Jack to let go. But, before Dragon Eye could follow up his attack, the balcony rail split apart and the two of them dropped like stones.

Jack tumbled over and over, panic seizing him as the cliff face rushed past. But, cutting through the terror, he heard a voice in his head saying: *The feather doesn't resist. It simply goes where the wind blows . . . bear this in mind, young samurai, for when an old enemy returns anew.*

Trusting in the Ring of Wind and the wisdom of the warrior spirit, Jack imagined himself as light as a feather. As he plummeted through the air, he didn't fight it any more. He let the updraught carry him away from the cliff face. Dragon Eye, arms flailing and venting his rage, flipped head over heels the opposite way. Jack realized this was how it must have been for Yamato when he let go from Osaka Castle's top tower — freefalling out of control towards certain death with his sworn enemy.

But Jack felt strangely at peace. Like Yamato, he would die

with honour, sacrificing himself for his friends. He had the *rutter* and its secrets would perish with him. And there was no way on earth that Dragon Eye could survive this time.

The wind whistled past his ears, almost as if heaven was calling to him. Jack felt like a bird soaring through the sky. For one heady moment, he thought he might fly all the way to England.

Then the rippling surface of the lagoon came rocketing towards him.

The warrior spirit's words came to mind once more: *Follow the way of the water and do nothing to oppose it . . .*

Rather than tensing for impact, Jack made himself relax. He recalled how the albatross dived into the sea to hunt for fish, spearing through the waves at tremendous speed.

*Its nature becomes my nature . . .*

Jack pointed his arms down, making himself straight as an arrow.

He hit the surface. The sudden chilling shock of the lagoon knocked all breath from his lungs. The rush of wind became the roar of water. His body was pounded and crushed on all sides as he plunged deeper and deeper. The concussion of cannonfire turned to muffled rumbles. The ethereal bars of light that played near the surface faded into oblivion.

Jack touched bottom, his fingers raking through sand as fine as silk. His lungs were now burning from lack of oxygen and he was on the verge of blacking out. Sparkles of light flickered before his eyes and a serene stillness enveloped him.

He drifted through this watery hidden world . . . then he burst to the surface, noise and light rushing back to him. Shouts, screams, cannonfire and waves surrounded him.

Wreckage, ropes and broken beams floated past. He gulped in several desperate lungfuls of air. He was alive – battered, bruised and aching, but definitely alive.

He swam for the crater's rocky shore.

Above, Pirate Town was burning but the citadel, like its Pirate Queen, defied the destruction, resolutely clinging to the cliff walls. Those pirates still remaining on the crumbling levels clambered down what ladders, walkways and foundations were still fixed to the crater face.

As Jack approached the shore, he spotted a black shape spread-eagled upon a rock. He headed towards it. He had to be *certain* this time: confirm the ninja's demise with his own eyes.

# 62

# IMPOSTER

Jack clambered on to the rock and stood over the lifeless body of Dragon Eye. A large pool of blood was trickling into the lagoon. His nightmare was over.

Then a single bloodshot eye flickered open and Jack's heart froze.

'This *isn't* possible. No man can be immortal!'

The ninja began to laugh. Dropping to his knees, Jack grabbed Dragon Eye by the lapels of his jacket and shook him furiously.

'Why won't you just *die*?' he cried, all his pain and frustration welling up.

The ninja flopped limp as a rag doll in his grip. He spluttered and choked, unable to breathe, let alone reply to his question. Jack now saw that Dragon Eye was, in truth, a broken and dying man. He lay him back down and stared in utter disbelief.

His shaking had partly dislodged the ninja's hood to reveal a *second* eye.

Whipping the hood completely off, Jack was met by a stranger's face. During the Battle of Osaka Castle, he'd discovered

Dragon Eye's real identity to be the exiled samurai lord Hattori Tatsuo. But this ninja *definitely* wasn't him. Along with possessing two eyes, there was no facial scarring from the childhood pox. And this man was some ten years younger than the Dragon Eye he knew and feared. Only his build, jawline and green-tinted eyes were similar.

'*WHO* are you?' demanded Jack.

'Dokugan . . . Ryu,' replied the ninja weakly.

Jack shook his head. 'No, you're not. I've seen Hattori Tatsuo's face with my own eyes. You're an imposter.'

The man grunted, accepting defeat. 'I'm a *kagemusha* . . . his Shadow Warrior . . . that's why, *gaijin* . . . Dragon Eye can *never* die!'

'But my guardian Masamoto killed Hattori's double in the Battle of Nakasendo.'

'The perfect deception!' wheezed the ninja. 'And now another of our clan will take over the mantle from me . . .' The ninja gloated at the shock on Jack's face. 'Black Cloud will have a new master . . . and Dragon Eye's legend will live on!'

For the first time Jack understood the warrior spirit's *true* meaning of 'an old enemy returns *anew*'.

All of a sudden he was seized by the throat, the ninja's fingers cutting off his air supply. He writhed in the iron-like grip as the man rose up before him.

Squeezing the life from Jack, the *kagemusha* spat into his face, 'I'll haunt you . . . to your grave, *gaijin*!'

Then the man slumped back down and fell still, his two eyes staring soulless at the smoking sky.

Recovering his breath, Jack bowed his head and began to sob.

'Jack!' called Miyuki, running along the shoreline. 'Are you all right?'

Yori and Saburo dropped down beside him, astonished to see Dragon Eye unmasked and their friend in one piece.

'Why are you crying?' asked Saburo. 'Dragon Eye's really dead this time.'

Jack shook his head. A small flame of hope in his heart had just been extinguished. 'Because . . . because it means Yamato is dead too.' He grieved once more for his loyal friend and brother, the pain of loss as raw as the first time.

Yori rested a hand upon Jack's shoulder. 'Yamato lives on through you, Jack. In everything *samurai* that you do. His spirit is your spirit. *Forever bound to one another*.'

Jack wiped his eyes, comforted by Yori's wise words.

Miyuki knelt beside him. 'I can't bring your friend back, but I did manage to recover these.' She handed him his Shizu swords. 'I realize you can't be a samurai without them.'

Smiling gratefully, Jack stood and sheathed the blades into their *sayas*. He felt strengthened by their presence, but even more so by the support of his friends at his side.

'Let's go,' he said, turning in the direction of the gated tunnel. 'We've got a boat to catch.'

# 63

# A FAVOURABLE WIND

Leaving the dead ninja behind, Jack and the others headed towards the gate. But, as they approached, they heard a low rumble and felt the ground start to tremble.

'RUN!' screamed Miyuki, realizing what was happening.

The four of them charged along the lagoon's shore. But it didn't look as if they were going to make it. Pirate Town was collapsing like a deck of cards. Roofs cascaded on to one another, walkways crumbled and buildings toppled. An avalanche of flaming wood, broken beams and loose rocks poured down the crater walls.

As they sprinted for their lives, Jack caught a glimpse of Li Ling urging the last surviving Wind Demons on-board the *Koketsu*, before giving the order to cast off. He couldn't see Tatsumaki among them, though. But, when he glanced up to check the state of the landslide, he spotted a lone figure standing on the lip of the citadel's broken balcony.

*Like a true captain*, thought Jack. *She's going down with her ship.*

The citadel, finally surrendering to the inevitable, began to tumble piece by piece into the lagoon.

'FASTER!' urged Jack as the first of Pirate Town's wreckage and rubble splashed into the lagoon. A huge boulder ploughed into the *Jade Serpent*, taking all on-board with it.

Saburo stumbled and Jack dragged him to his feet. They threw themselves the last few paces to the iron gate.

Yori fumbled for the key.

'Come on!' begged Miyuki as more rocks and debris rained down on them.

In his haste, Yori dropped the key. Groping on the ground, he snatched it up and rammed it into the lock. He turned the key and pushed.

'It's stuck!' he cried.

Saburo drove his shoulder into it and the gate burst open. They all dived inside just as Pirate Town engulfed the lagoon. The roar of rock and wreckage resounded down the tunnel like the bellow of a dragon. Then all went silent and they were plunged into darkness.

Coughing and spluttering from the dust, Jack called out, 'Everyone OK?'

Three voices answered, hoarse but relieved. Gingerly getting to his feet, Jack took the lead and they blindly followed the tunnel wall.

'Are you certain we're going the right way?' asked Saburo after a while.

In the pitch-black, Jack had no idea if the tunnel split off at any point.

'I think so,' he said, trying to be reassuring. Then relief swept over him. 'I can hear water lapping.'

They kept edging through the darkness, the sound of waves growing louder with every step.

'I can see light!' exclaimed Yori.

Up ahead, the faintest of gleams was wavering over the moist surface of the rock wall. Turning a corner, they emerged into a small cave, sunlight dimly reflecting from the sea outside and illuminating the space. A skiff was tied to a metal ring in the wall, its mast lowered so that it could enter and exit the low cave entrance.

'Li Ling's done us proud,' said Jack, inspecting the boat and finding it fully stocked with provisions and two casks of fresh water.

They clambered on-board and stowed their packs and weapons. Jack gave the *rutter* a reassuring pat as he tucked it beneath the gunwales. With the demise of Tatsumaki and her captains, and the logbook back in his possession, his father's precious knowledge was safe once more. Jack knew he'd been reckless to reveal so many of its secrets to a band of ruthless pirates. But he believed his father would have understood his bonds of friendship to Miyuki, Yori and Saburo. All of them had been willing to sacrifice their lives for him. And in return, he would lay down his life, and whatever else it took, to save them.

Saburo picked up one of the oars and pushed off. Carefully navigating between submerged rocks, they rowed out of the sea cave and into bright sunlight. The cave was located on the southern side of the island, so they were safely out of sight of the approaching Sea Samurai fleet. As soon as they were clear of the shoreline, Jack raised the mast and hoisted the sail.

'Keep rowing,' Jack instructed Saburo and Yori. 'We need to get as much distance between us and this island as possible.'

As they pulled away, the rim of the crater came into view.

333

Black smoke and flaming ash rose up from the caldera, the extinct volcano now looking dangerously active as Pirate Town burned. On its western side, a few Wind Demon ships had made it out of the lagoon and were fleeing into the distance. Jack spotted the distinctive armoured roof and dragonhead of the *Koketsu*. He just hoped that Li Ling would be able to outrun the Sea Samurai.

'Which way are we heading?' asked Miyuki, pulling out the sea chart.

Jack studied the map. He plotted a course that would take them across the wide expanse of the Seto Sea, through the Kanmon Straits and on to their final destination, Nagasaki. Having got his bearings, he pointed over the starboard bow.

'West,' he said, striking a course towards the setting sun.

Feeling the fresh sea breeze on his face, Jack smiled at his friends. 'And we're in luck for once. The wind's in our favour!'

# NOTES ON THE SOURCES

The following quotes are referenced within *Young Samurai: The Ring of Wind* (with the page numbers in square brackets below) and their sources are acknowledged here:

1.  [Page 277] 'A ship is safe in harbour, but that's not what ships are for.' By William Shedd, theologian (1820–1894).
2.  [Page 296] 'Ten soldiers wisely led will beat a hundred without a head.' By Euripides, Greek playwright (484–406 BC).

# NINJA PIRATE SHIP COMPETITION

A *Young Samurai* competition was held in the Young Times section of *The Times* newspaper to name the Ninja Pirate Ship that would feature in *The Ring of Wind*.

The winner was:

**Jonathan Harper**

for his suggestion of the ***Koketsu***, which means Jaws of Death (or Tiger's Den, or dangerous place).

Out of the countless excellent entries, this one stood out immediately. It fitted the image of my ninja pirate ship perfectly, since the vessel has a dragon-shaped battering ram on its prow to sink other ships.

Congratulations, Jonathan!

PS Remember to look out for more competitions and prizes on *www.youngsamurai.com*

# JAPANESE GLOSSARY

**Bushido**

*Bushido*, meaning the 'Way of the Warrior', is a Japanese code of conduct similar to the concept of chivalry. Samurai warriors were meant to adhere to the seven moral principles in their martial arts training and in their day-to-day lives.

Virtue 1: *Gi* – Rectitude
*Gi* is the ability to make the right decision with moral confidence and to be fair and equal towards all people no matter what colour, race, gender or age.

Virtue 2: *Yu* – Courage
*Yu* is the ability to handle any situation with valour and confidence.

仁

礼

真

名誉

忠義

Virtue 3: *Jin* – Benevolence
*Jin* is a combination of compassion and generosity. This virtue works together with *Gi* and discourages samurai from using their skills arrogantly or for domination.

Virtue 4: *Rei* – Respect
*Rei* is a matter of courtesy and proper behaviour towards others. This virtue means to have respect for all.

Virtue 5: *Makoto* – Honesty
*Makoto* is about being honest to oneself as much as to others. It means acting in ways that are morally right and always doing things to the best of your ability.

Virtue 6: *Meiyo* – Honour
*Meiyo* is sought with a positive attitude in mind, but will only follow with correct behaviour. Success is an honourable goal to strive for.

Virtue 7: *Chungi* – Loyalty
*Chungi* is the foundation of all the virtues; without dedication and loyalty to the task at hand and to one another, one cannot hope to achieve the desired outcome.

# A Short Guide to Pronouncing Japanese Words

Vowels are pronounced in the following way:
'a' as the 'a' in 'at'
'e' as the 'e' in 'bet'
'i' as the 'i' in 'police'
'o' as the 'o' in 'dot'
'u' as the 'u' in 'put'
'ai' as in 'eye'
'ii' as in 'week'
'ō' as in 'go'
'ū' as in 'blue'

Consonants are pronounced in the same way as English:
'g' is hard as in 'get'
'j' is soft as in 'jelly'
'ch' as in 'church'
'z' as in 'zoo'
'ts' as in 'itself'

Each syllable is pronounced separately:
A-ki-ko
Ya-ma-to
Ma-sa-mo-to
Ka-zu-ki

| | |
|---|---|
| *arigatō gozaimasu* | thank you very much |
| *atake-bune* | large Japanese naval warship |
| *bō* | wooden fighting staff |
| *bonnō* | the 108 worldly desires that Buddhists believe all humans are afflicted with |

| | |
|---|---|
| *bushido* | the Way of the Warrior – the samurai code |
| *chō-geri* | butterfly kick |
| *daejon* | (*Korean*) large rocket-like arrows tipped with iron and leather flights |
| *daimyo* | feudal lord |
| *daishō* | the pair of swords, *wakizashi* and *katana*, that are traditional weapons of the samurai |
| Dim Mak | Death Touch |
| *doku* | poison |
| *dōshin* | Edo-period police officers of samurai origin (low rank) |
| *endan* | ninja smoke bombs |
| *fugu* | blowfish or puffer fish |
| *Fuma* | Wind Demons |
| *gaijin* | foreigner, outsider (derogatory term) |
| *geisha* | a Japanese girl trained to entertain men with conversation, dance and song |
| *haiku* | Japanese short poem |
| *hamon* | artistic pattern created on a samurai sword blade during tempering process |
| *hashi* | chopsticks |
| *horagai* | conch-shell trumpet |
| *horoku* | a spherical bomb thrown by hand using a short rope |
| *itadakimasu* | let's eat! |
| *kagemusha* | a Shadow Warrior |
| *kamikaze* | lit. 'divine wind', or 'Wind of the Gods' |
| *kanji* | Chinese characters that are used also by the Japanese |
| *katana* | long sword |
| *ki* | energy flow or life force (Chinese: *chi*) |
| *kiai* | literally 'concentrated spirit' – used in |

| | |
|---|---|
| | martial arts as a shout for focusing energy when executing a technique |
| *kimono* | traditional Japanese clothing |
| *kissaki* | tip of sword |
| *koban* | Japanese oval gold coin |
| *kobaya* | small Japanese naval boat |
| *Koketsu* | Jaws of Death (or Tiger's Den, or dangerous place) |
| *komusō* | Monk of Emptiness |
| *kuji-in* | nine syllable seals – a specialized form of Buddhist and ninja meditation |
| *kumode* | spiked 'bear paw' on a stout pole used as a grappling iron and weapon |
| *metsubishi* | blinding powder, a ninja weapon |
| *metsuke* | technique of 'looking at a faraway mountain' |
| *Mizujiro* | 'castle in the sea' |
| *mochi* | rice cake |
| *mon* | family crest |
| *mushin* | a warrior's state of 'no mind' |
| *naginata* | a long pole weapon with a curved blade on the end |
| *Namu Daishi Henjo Kongo* | This is the mantra of Kobo Daishi, which translates as 'Homage to the Saviour Daishi, the Illuminating and Imperishable One!' |
| *nenju* | Buddhist rosary beads |
| *Nihon Maru* | Japanese naval flagship |
| *ninja* | Japanese assassin |
| *ninjatō* | ninja sword |
| *ninjutsu* | the Art of Stealth |
| *ninniku* | the philosophy of the ninja, 'cultivating a pure and compassionate heart' |

| | |
|---|---|
| *Niten Ichi Ryū* | the 'One School of Two Heavens' |
| *nōkyōchō* | temple stamp book |
| *obi* | belt |
| *ofuro* | bath |
| *omamori* | Buddhist amulet to grant protection |
| *osame-fuda* | paper prayer slips |
| *o-settai* | the action of giving of food and money to pilgrims |
| *ronin* | masterless samurai |
| *sai* | a pointed, dagger-shaped metal truncheon, with two curved prongs called *yoku* projecting from the handle |
| *saké* | rice wine |
| *sakura* | cherry-blossom tree |
| *Samsara* | the Buddhist concept of a 'world of suffering' |
| *samurai* | Japanese warrior |
| *sashimi* | raw fish |
| *saya* | scabbard |
| *seki-bune* | medium-sized Japanese naval warship |
| *sensei* | teacher |
| *Sha* | ninja hand sign, interpreted as healing for *ninjutsu* purposes |
| *shachihoko* | an animal in Japanese folklore with the head of a dragon and the body of a carp |
| *shakujō* | Buddhist ringed staff used primarily in prayer, and as a weapon |
| *Shichi Hō De* | 'the seven ways of going', the art of disguise and impersonation |
| *shinobi shozoku* | the clothing of a ninja |
| *Shogun* | the military dictator of Japan |
| *shoji* | Japanese sliding door |
| *shuinsen* | Red Seal ship |

| | |
|---|---|
| *shuko* | climbing claws |
| *shuriken* | metal throwing stars |
| *sohei* | warrior monks |
| *suigun* | 'water army' |
| *sumimasen* | excuse me; my apologies |
| *sūtra* | a Buddhist scripture |
| *taijutsu* | the Art of the Body (hand-to-hand combat) |
| *tantō* | short knife |
| *Taryu-Jiai* | interschool martial arts competition |
| *tatami* | floor matting |
| *tessen* | iron fan |
| *torii* | a distinctive Japanese gate found at the entrance to Shinto shrines |
| *wagesa* | a stole, a strip of cloth worn by monks and priests |
| *wakizashi* | side-arm short sword |
| *wako* | Japanese pirates |
| *yuloh* | a large, heavy sculling oar used in the Far East |

**Japanese names** usually consist of a family name (surname) followed by a given name, unlike in the Western world where the given name comes before the surname. In feudal Japan, names reflected a person's social status and spiritual beliefs. Also, when addressing someone, *san* is added to that person's surname (or given names in less formal situations) as a sign of courtesy, in the same way that we use Mr or Mrs in English, and for higher-status people *sama* is used. In Japan, *sensei* is usually added after a person's name if they are a teacher, although in the Young Samurai books a traditional English order has been retained. Boys and girls are usually addressed using *kun* and *chan*, respectively.

# ACKNOWLEDGEMENTS

This seventh book in the Young Samurai series was a true voyage of discovery, terror and excitement. For one thing, I didn't know if I would ever reach my destination – a book is like an open ocean: formidable, unpredictable and awe-inspiring. Luckily, I was accompanied on my voyage by my ever-faithful crew.

Thank you and love to my family: my gorgeous and understanding wife, Sarah, my hardworking Mum and Dad, my supportive in-laws, Sue and Simon, my loyal Steve and Sam, and Karen, Rob and Thomas (*who are family in my heart*). And, of course, with the birth of my son, Zach, I had an extra passenger on-board while writing! Although you stopped me doing my duty as 'captain' of the story for the first few months, you quickly turned into an indispensable member of my closest crew – giving me smiles when I needed them most, laughs when I was at my lowest, and love at all times of the day. I couldn't have written this book without everyone's wonderful support.

A huge thanks must also go to the engine of this 'ship': Charlie Viney, my agent and friend; Shannon Park, my editor;

the Puffin team – Wendy Shakespeare, Julia Teece, Jayde Lynch, Vanessa Godden, Sara Flavell and Paul Young; and Franca Bernatavicius and Nicki Kennedy, my overseas agents.

Well done to Toby Cronshaw who won the *Young Samurai* website competition to suggest the name for the fearsome pirate leader who would be Jack's adversary in this book. Your suggestion of Tatsumaki, which means 'tornado' and is also a respected Japanese name, was perfect. My pirate queen needed to be just like a tornado – to be able to appear out of nowhere, cause havoc and then disappear again into nothingness having taken what she needs, only leaving a legacy of confusion and emptiness.

Noah Benoit, long-time fan of the series, needs to be thanked for suggesting that Jack should have a *female* enemy character at some point. I hope Tatsumaki lived up to your expectations!

I'd also like to give credit to Jennifer Bell of Foyles bookshop, London, for suggesting the idea of having a monkey in the story. I hope you like Saru, because you breathed life into the little creature who became vital to Jack's survival.

Finally, a true bow of respect goes to Tiwa Ethan Adelaja, Luneth Pangya and Sharuk Rahman for their fantastic Young Samurai Duelling Card entries! Anyone who wishes to download these brilliant Duelling Cards can find them at *www.youngsamurai.com*

*Arigatō gozaimasu* to all my faithful readers, librarians, teachers and booksellers!

Chris

Any fans can keep in touch with me and the progress of the Young Samurai series via the website *www.youngsamurai.com*

# CAN'T WAIT FOR THE NEXT JACK FLETCHER BLOCKBUSTER?

# YOUNG SAMURAI

## THE RING OF SKY

Here's a **sneak preview** . . .

# 1

# FOOTPRINTS

**Japan, summer 1615**

Spluttering and choking, Jack hacked up a lungful of salt water. His fingers gripped the wet sand as another wave broke over him, threatening to drag him back into the chill sea. The constant roll of breakers was like the restless breathing of a great dragon that, having had its fill, spat him out on to the shore. The only other sound was the plaintive cry of a seagull circling overhead.

With the last of his strength, Jack clawed his way up the beach. Once clear of the waves, he rolled on to his back, gasping from the effort, and opened his eyes. The sky was a wide expanse of crystal blue, not a cloud in sight, no trace of the storm that had raged the previous night. The early-morning sun shone down in warming golden rays from the east, hinting at the fine summer day to come.

Jack had no idea how long he lay there recovering, but when he opened his eyes again the salt water had cracked his lips and his kimono was bone dry. His mind whirled like the churning ocean and his entire body felt sore and bruised, having been pummelled by waves, rocks and the reef in his desperate swim towards land. So far as he could tell no bones were broken, although every muscle ached and there was a painful throb in his left side. But, to his relief, he realized this was just the hilt of his sword jammed against his ribs.

With great care, he groggily sat up. By some miracle, he still possessed both his *katana* and the shorter *wakizashi*. A samurai warrior's sword was considered to be his soul. And Jack – trained in the ways of the samurai *and* the ninja – was thankful not to have lost his. For in a country that now deemed foreigners and Christians to be the enemy of the state these weapons were his lifeline.

His pack was also tied round his waist. Bedraggled and misshapen, its contents looked to be in a sorry condition. He emptied it on to the sand. A cracked gourd fell out, along with a couple of crushed rice balls and three slim iron *shuriken*. The ninja throwing stars were followed by the heavy thump of a book – his father's *rutter*, a priceless navigational logbook that offered the only means of safely crossing the world's oceans. Jack was reassured to find the *rutter* still protected within its waterproof oilskin cover. But the sight of the broken gourd *was* cause for concern. Having spent much of the night battling for his life, Jack was weakened by hunger and thirst. Snatching up the gourd with a trembling hand, he poured the last dregs of fresh water into his parched mouth. Then, without bothering to brush the sand off, he consumed the cold rice balls in a few ravenous bites. Meagre and salty as they were, the rice revived him enough to clear his head and take stock of his situation.

Glancing round, Jack discovered he'd washed up in a sheltered bay. The beach was bounded by craggy headlands to the north and south while, behind, a small cliff rose westwards to a scrub-lined ridge. On first inspection the bay appeared to be deserted. Then Jack spied a piece of wreckage bobbing at the shoreline. With a sinking heart, he recognized it instantly. Sprawled out like a huge drowned moth was the broken mast of the skiff, its tattered sail rippling in the waves.

Only now did the realization hit Jack that his friends were missing.

Scrambling to his feet, he ran down to the shore and frantically searched for any sign of them. Finding no bodies on the beach or in the shallows, he scanned the bay and horizon for their boat. But the little skiff was nowhere to be seen. With a growing sense of despair, Jack feared Yori, Saburo and Miyuki were lost at sea, gone forever.

Then Jack spotted two sets of footprints in the sand and a spark of hope was rekindled. Dropping to one knee, he inspected the prints and applied his ninja tracking skills. Grandmaster Soke had taught him how to identify tracks by their size, shape, depth and pattern. Immediately – and with dismay – Jack could tell these didn't belong to any of his friends. They were too large. Made by an adult and facing opposite directions, it was evident that the two sets belonged to the same individual. Both prints possessed a similar uneven pattern, indicating the person had either a limp or an odd gait. Jack also noted the approach had been hurried, but the departure *urgent*; the sand was more heavily displaced and the prints wider apart, signalling a change of pace into a run.

Whoever it was, their presence was unlikely to be favourable for Jack.

He caught the sound of distant voices to the north. Hastily gathering up his belongings, Jack fled the opposite way. He ran along the beach towards the southern headland, all the time keeping his eye out for the slightest proof his friends had survived. Approaching the rocky outcrop, he noticed the opening to a cave and made directly for it. Just as he entered its cool darkness, he heard a shout from behind.

'The *gaijin*'s over here!'

Jack glanced back to see an old fisherman with bandy legs leading a patrol of armed samurai on to the beach. Hiding inside the cave's entrance, Jack observed the fisherman totter over to where the mast lay.

'Where is he then?' demanded the leader of the patrol, a sour-faced man with a topknot of black hair and a thick moustache.

'I promise you,' protested the fisherman, pointing a gnarly finger at the marks in the sand, 'I saw him with my own eyes. A foreigner washed up on this beach *and* he had samurai swords.'

The leader bent down to examine the evidence. His eyes followed Jack's tracks along the beach.

'He can't have got far,' snarled the leader, drawing his *katana*. 'We'll hunt this *gaijin* samurai down like a dog!'

Home is within reach, but the
Shogun's samurai are closing in . . .

**Can Jack make it back to
England alive?**

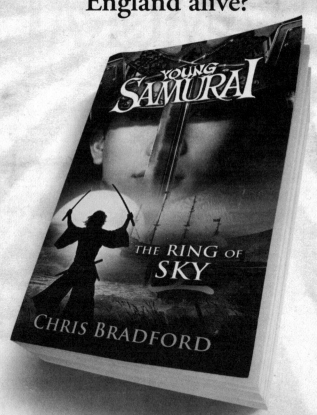